Debbie waited in the nursery until she heard the front door and was sure that Max had gone. Then she checked on the sleeping baby and went downstairs to find Anna.

'Anna?' she said gently. 'Anna, Max has gone.' Anna sat huddled against the kitchen wall, her face buried in her hands. She made no move.

'Anna, can I get you some tea or something?'

Anna lifted her head. She rubbed her hands over a face that was swollen from weeping, and stood up. Her legs felt weak and she had to hold onto the wall for support.

'Thanks,' she said. 'Tea please, with sugar.' She pulled a chair out and slumped down onto it. 'I'm sorry that you had to witness that.' She was cold and reached for a cardigan that hung over the back of the kitchen chair. 'Life can be so ugly sometimes.'

Debbie busied herself with the tea and made no reply. She didn't feel guilty – Max had asked for it – but she did feel sorry for Anna, a casualty of war.

'Is Maya all right?' Anna asked.

'She's fine. Asleep.'

'Good. I'll have my tea and then I'd better get back to my work.'

Debbie stirred the pot and poured out a cup. Anna took the mug and warmed her icy fingers round it. 'I'll be in my study,' she said. 'Give me a shout, would you, when Maya wakes up?'

'Yes, OK.' Debbie watched Anna go. She would do no such thing of course, she would wait until *she* was ready to hand the baby over. She smiled. Things were beginning to work out even better than she could have imagined.

Also by Maria Barrett:

ELLE
DANGEROUS OBSESSION
DECEIVED
DISHONOURED
INTIMATE LIES
BREACH OF PROMISE
INDECENT ACT
THE DREAM CATCHER

DAMAGED LIVES

Maria Barrett

WARNER BOOKS

A *Warner* Book

First published in Great Britain in 2000
by Little, Brown and Company
This edition published by Warner Books in 2001

Copyright © Maria Barrett 2000

The moral right of the author has been asserted.

*All characters in this publication are fictitious and any
resemblance to real persons, living or dead, is purely coincidental.*

A CIP catalogue record for this book
is available from the British Library.

ISBN 0 7515 2479 4

Typeset by Palimpsest Book Production Limited,
Polmont, Stirlingshire
Printed and bound in Great Britain by
Clays Ltd, St Ives plc

Warner Books
A Division of
Little, Brown and Company (UK)
Brettenham House
Lancaster Place
London WC2E 7EN

www.littlebrown.co.uk

For JB
With love

ACKNOWLEDGEMENTS

It is only now, in the final stages of completing this novel, that I realise just how hard the year of writing it has been. Superwoman I am not, and the fact that this book is here at all owes a great deal to one person, who not only helped with the nitty gritty and the drudge, the hand holding and emotional support, but who also inspired me to go that bit further and achieve as much as I possibly could. He knows who he is and the next pint of Stella is on me.

I am also extremely grateful to the three people who supported me in the background; Susan Quinn, Edwina Ball and Laura Hale. They made a very big difference to the year.

Warm thanks must go to the people I work with, most especially to Helen Anderson (who is a master of plot), Mic Cheetham, Barbara Boote and all at LB. My thanks to all the people who helped with my research, most importantly; Dr Mike Shillingford, Kirsten Barber and DS Del Cuff.

And finally thank you the team; Wils, Lily and Edward. You keep things in perspective.

Chapter One

The social worker unlocked the door of the ground-floor flat and shoved it hard to open it, wedging a pile of post behind it. The place smelt stale and the air inside it was cold and damp. She stepped in to the hall, switched on a light, and the bare bulb lit up.

'The electricity's on,' she said over her shoulder. 'If we can get these storage heaters working it should warm up quite quickly.' The young woman behind her nodded. She had two bags with her, one of which she had clutched tightly all the way from the bed and breakfast. 'Come on in and have a look round,' the social worker called. 'It's not at all bad and they've done a good job cleaning it up.'

The young woman came in. She closed the door behind her, out of habit more than anything else – where she had come from no doors were ever left open – and followed the social worker into the front room. She shivered and the other woman looked up from where she was fiddling with a heater. 'You couldn't go into the kitchen and look through the drawers for a screwdriver could you? They might have left you one.' The young woman disappeared and the social worker heard her rummaging around in the kitchen drawers. She stood straight and went through. 'Any luck?'

'No. Why d'you need one?'

'The dial's jammed.'

'Will a knife do? There's some cutlery in this drawer here.' The young woman took out a knife, appropriately blunt, and held it up.

'Let's have a go and see.' The social worker took the knife and went back to the front room. 'No,' she called. 'It's no good. The damn thing's jammed. I'll just check the bedroom heater.'

A minute or so later she reappeared in the kitchen. 'I'm afraid that none of the heaters seem to be working. Typical isn't it? It's bloody freezing and there's no heat. Look, why don't you unpack and I'll go back to the office and organise an electrician. I'll see if I can get someone over right away.'

The young woman nodded.

'I'm sorry about this, I really am. It's crummy, not having things working.'

'It's OK. It's hardly your fault.'

'No.' The social worker looked across at the young woman and made a mental note. It read: *Deals well in difficult situations, shows no signs of stress at the unexpected.* 'Will you be OK here on your own for a while?'

The young woman shrugged. 'Of course.' But that was a lie. She wasn't OK on her own, not here or anywhere. She was afraid; fear was something she lived with from day to day. 'When will you be back?' she asked.

'I'll call round again this afternoon with your social security book and we can go down to the post office together. I expect you'd like to get some shopping.'

Again the young woman shrugged.

'Well, whatever.' The social worker went out into the hall for her bag, picked it up and slung it over her shoulder. She held out a slip of paper. 'I've written my mobile number down here. You can ring me on this if you're worried about anything, OK?'

'Yes, thanks.' The young woman took the slip of paper and tucked it into the pocket of her jeans. The social worker opened the front door. 'See you later,' she said, 'hopefully with an electrician.'

The young woman remained in the kitchen doorway. 'Yes,' she answered. 'Hopefully.'

The social worker went out and shut the door firmly behind her. She made her way down the cold grey corridor and made another mental note. This one read: *Communicates well, has no difficulty in understanding instructions and arrangements*. She filed it away with the other one to be typed up in the office later on. Then she took out her Dictaphone and switched it on. She used it constantly in an effort to keep track of her ever mounting pile of tasks at work. 'Note one to myself,' she said into it. 'As soon as you get in, ring the director of the housing association for the Harbridge estate and ask him if there's any particular heating service they use. Note two; type up observations on the community care patient. Note three; compose a letter of complaint to the director of the housing association, re. the above matter. How am I supposed to settle someone like this into the community when they haven't even got a basic living tool like heating? Note four; get some lunch.' She stopped the tape, reached her car parked in a side alley, dropped the Dictaphone in her bag and dug for her keys. As she pulled them out and put them into the lock she glanced round, suddenly aware of just how deserted and empty this place was. She was blocked in by concrete – the side, windowless wall of the flats on her right and the back of some garaging on her left. It struck her that it was a foolish place to park in an area like this and she hurried to unlock the car.

She never managed it.

A cudgel blow came from behind and smashed in the right side of her head. Her legs buckled under her and she hit the floor. Another blow came, this one more violent, then another, but she knew nothing about them. She had died instantly on that first impact. Her body was removed quickly into a waiting car and her keys were left in the lock of her Nissan Micra, the life expectancy of which, on an estate like Harbridge, was approximately six hours.

At the same time, in the Harringey Department of Social Services, the central computer system went down. A virus spread through it, deleting files and destroying information in a matter of minutes. All the screens went blank, the whole system crashed and any record of the community-care patient on the Harbridge estate was irretrievably lost.

Chapter Two

It was Friday afternoon, three o'clock, and Anna picked up her briefcase, stuffed several documents into it, zipped her laptop into its carry case and took her jacket off the back of the chair. Her secretary came in with the last few letters to sign and said, 'You look done in, if you don't mind me saying so.'

Anna tried to smile, but it hit her face as a sort of grimace. She scribbled her signature, then tried a joke. 'I am done in, haven't you noticed?' She rubbed her stomach and her secretary's face changed, in the way that some women's do when babies are mentioned.

'You should get home and put your feet up,' she went on. 'Get Max to cook dinner.' Again Anna tried to smile, but it didn't sit right on her face at all today.

'If Max cooks dinner,' she remarked, 'the shock of it'll bring the baby on!' This time the joke did work and her secretary laughed.

'Oh God, get a take-away then!' she said. 'Andrew'll have a fit if the baby comes before they've had their vote tonight.'

Anna pulled on her jacket. 'Ah yes, the vote.' She had developed an almost dismissive air to cover what had become strangling nerves. She felt continually sick, her mouth and hands dried up at the very mention of her selection for associate partner and yet all she said now was, 'May the best lawyer win, Pam.'

'That'll be you then, won't it?'

Anna patted Pam on the arm as she went past. 'Thanks for the support, I appreciate it.' She heaved her handbag onto her shoulder and picked up her two cases.

'Here, let me . . .'

'No, really, it's fine. I'm pregnant, not infirm.'

Pam took the cases. 'Give them here! No one said you were infirm, but you really shouldn't be shifting those bloody great things around at this stage of the game.' She carried them out of the office and along the corridor to the lifts.

Anna pressed the call button.

'Shall I bring them down for you?'

'No, honestly, it's fine. I've got a cab waiting. I've got to lug them up to the client anyway, at the other end.' The lift came and Anna stepped inside.

Pam handed the cases in and said, 'Good luck, Anna, for tonight.'

'Thanks.' Anna held up crossed fingers and the lift doors closed. As she travelled down to the ground floor, she leant back against the mirrored interior of the lift and stared at her worn-out reflection.

It was after seven by the time the cab pulled up outside Anna's house, opposite the common. The driver leant into the back and said, 'Need a hand with the bags, love?'

'No, no thanks, I can manage.' It was a matter of principle; Anna had always managed, that's how she'd got so far. She climbed ungracefully out of the taxi, paid her fare and waited for her receipt. The lights were on in the house which meant that Max was home.

Walking up the path, she wondered if he might have remembered to pick anything up for dinner, then dismissed the idea as ludicrous. The only dinner Max could organise was on the telephone. Still, he might have ordered a take-away, she thought, placing her key in the lock, although whether she could face eating it was uncertain. She dumped her briefcase and laptop by the door and wandered into the sitting room, still in her coat.

'Oh, hi!' Max was on the sofa with his feet up, drinking a glass of wine. He jumped up and came across, helping Anna off with her coat. 'Tonight's the night then?' he said.

Anna nodded. Why was he stating the obvious?

'Nervous?'

She shrugged, then said, 'Churning actually.'

'What are the odds at the office?'

'Oh for God's sake, Max!' Anna snapped. 'It isn't the bloody three-twenty at Kempton!' She stopped, looked at his face and felt immediately contrite. He was only trying to make light of the situation, to ease the tension, and she couldn't blame him for that.

'Sorry, you're right. Insensitive of me.' He went across to the table and poured Anna a glass of wine.

'No, I'm sorry, I shouldn't have snapped. It's just nerves.'

'Of course it is. You look tired,' he said. 'What's for supper? Is there anything I can do to help?'

'There isn't any supper, I forgot to get something, so no, there's nothing you can do to help.' She meant it to be funny, but it came out wrong and simply sounded crabby. She slumped onto the sofa and he came to sit down next to her.

'What's the exact form then? The partners go to the Savoy, take a vote on who to offer partnership to, have dinner, then announce the vote afterwards, is that right?'

She nodded.

'And Andrew McKie will ring you when it's announced, yes? One way or another?'

'Yes, they call all the candidates.'

'So that'll be about ten o'clock I'd have thought.'

'Probably.'

'Right, well let's go and get a pizza then.' Suddenly enthused, Max glanced at his watch. 'There's a group from work drinking in the Wine Gallery, let's whiz up to Chelsea, grab a drink with them and then go for a pizza. We can get back in time for the call.'

'Max, I can't leave the house. What if Andrew rings earlier and I'm not in? Anyway, I'm too tired to go out, I've had enough hustle and bustle for one day.'

Max turned away. When had everything for Anna become such a chore, he wondered, at what moment had life ceased to be fun? He didn't remember her like this, he had always known she wasn't frivolous, that was part of the initial attraction – a serious girl – but why did everything now have to be such hard work? He drank his wine in silence for a few moments and Anna watched his back. He was pulling one of his faces, she could just sense it, one of his 'disappointed, life isn't fair' faces. God, he was such a child!

'Max, if it really means that much to you, why don't you go on your own? Go and have a few drinks in Chelsea, I'm really not bothered.'

Max turned back and Anna could see the barely concealed relief on his face. 'Are you sure? I mean I hate leaving you on your own.'

'Don't be silly. I'm quite happy staying here. I'll have a long soak in the bath, a drink and something on toast. Go on, go. I'm hardly in the mood for conversation anyway.'

'Actually I think I will. I'll be back for ten, I promise. I'll just have a couple of drinks and get back.'

Anna shrugged; they both knew Max was never punctual. 'Whatever,' she murmured. She had given him the opportunity and yet she seethed that he took it with such alacrity. Why the hell, just for once, couldn't he refuse the idea of a good time? Was staying in really so boring? Was she so dull that a night on their own was unimaginable? Anna harboured these thoughts, but would never admit to them, she was far too proud, and besides, the extent of their communication had become far too limited.

By the time she looked up, Max had his coat on. 'I'll get a cab from the common,' he said, bending forward to kiss her cheek. 'You sure you'll be all right?'

It wasn't a question, or certainly not one that wanted an honest answer. Anna nodded.

'See you later then.' He headed for the door, checked he had his keys and phone with him, opened it and walked out, without so much as a backward glance. Anna sat in the silence for several minutes, then heaved herself up out of the sofa and went to run a bath.

In the Wine Gallery, Chrissy Forbes heard her phone ring and bent to pick up her bag. It was lizard skin, claret red and immaculate; it matched her nails. She moved away from the little group she had been chatting to and took out her phone. She answered it. There was a brief conversation, after which she smiled.

'Good news?' asked a colleague, as she rejoined the group.

'I think so,' she answered, giving no more away.

'Business?'

She laughed, lightly touching the colleague's arm with her perfectly manicured hand. 'No it wasn't business, it was personal,' she said.

'I wish I was,' said the colleague, glancing down at those long, sharp nails and feeling the pleasure of a covert erection.

Chrissy laughed again. It was a tart, rather hard sound but it served only to thrill even more.

Andrew McKie walked into the lobby of the Savoy and relished the clear air and few moments' peace after the noise and smoke of the function room. His face was flushed and he had a thud in the pit of his stomach. He was fond of Anna, perhaps a little too fond. He admired her nerve, her sheer determination, and the fact that she was attractive didn't go amiss either. McKie my old son, he told himself, fishing his mobile out of his jacket pocket, you are too old for such excitement. He dialled Anna's number and sat down to wait for her to answer.

Anna was in her nightdress, towelling dressing gown and slippers, sitting in the study with a pile of photo albums scattered around her, when the phone rang at nine fifteen. She loved her photographs, had hundreds of them, all dated and neatly put into albums. It was her passion – happy memories captured on film. It was something her mother had always done, something she had never paid much attention to until her mother died and then she realised just how much it meant to be able to see, every now and then, how happy she had once been.

She placed the album she had open on the floor, face up, so that several photographs of her and Max on holiday in Cyprus stared up at her as she went into the hall to answer the phone. She knew it was Andrew; it couldn't be anyone else, not on a Friday night at this time. She took a breath before picking up the hand set and said, 'Hello Andrew.'

Anna was someone who people thought of as self-contained and confident, always reasoned, always in control, but there were many times, like now, when she felt very small and insignificant and when she wondered if she would manage to hold it all together long enough not to let the cracks show.

There was a momentary pause on the other end of the line after she had spoken – Andrew McKie wasn't expecting her to sound quite so composed – and Anna held her breath. A pause meant bad news and she had the most desperate sinking feeling that threatened to engulf her.

'Anna,' Andrew said, 'congratulations my dear. You are invited to join the partnership.'

Anna sat down on the bottom stair. Her hand was wet with sweat and, without any warning, she began to cry. Tears streamed down her face, she was unable to speak and on the other end of the line, Andrew, unaware of her silent weeping and knowing the extent of her self-containment, wondered if she was going to show any sort of reaction at all. He let a small silence pass, then said, 'We will courier the accounts and partnership trust deed across to you tomorrow morning. If you would like to look through it over the weekend, Anna, then we can meet first thing in my office on Monday morning and you can tell me whether you wish to accept the offer.' He waited. 'Anna?'

Anna swallowed. 'Yes, erm . . .' She still couldn't speak and for the first time since he had known her in almost six years, Andrew realised that Anna very probably wasn't nearly as tough as she made out to be.

'I am thrilled for you, Anna,' he said quietly. 'You deserve this and will go on to achieve much, much more, I'm sure of it.'

Anna fumbled in her dressing-gown pocket for a tissue, blew her nose, a loud noise which amused Andrew, and finally managed to say, 'Thank you, Andrew, for all your support.'

'Think nothing of it. Now go and celebrate, get Max to open some decent champagne and have a glass. It'll do you and that baby the power of good.'

'Thanks, Andrew, I will.'

'Goodnight, Anna, God bless and well done.' Andrew pressed the end call button on his phone and sat for a few moments staring into space. If he'd been asked five minutes ago what he thought Anna's reaction would be, he'd have said quiet celebration, a confident win. Never, never in a million years would he have thought she would burst into uncontrollable tears. He smiled, not because he was pleased that she had wept, but because at last it seemed that Anna Jacob had let a small piece of her true self come through. And that was definitely worth smiling about.

Max sat in the passenger seat of Chrissy's BMW convertible and pressed his window down. 'Do you have to smoke in the car?' he asked. She blew her smoke out of the window on her side and placed a hand on his thigh.

'Yes,' Chrissy replied, 'I do.' The hand moved up a few inches towards his groin but he stopped it, covering it with his own. 'Especially when my offer to come home for coffee is refused. It relieves the tension.'

Max shrugged. 'Sorry,' he said, 'you know the score.'

Chrissy rolled her eyes. 'Married man!' She sighed artificially. Max looked out of the window and Chrissy stared at his profile for a few moments. She liked it, strong and clean shaven, too masculine to be handsome, but then she liked that too, loads of testosterone. She was pleased she had got this far so quickly, even if it wasn't much to speak of. Rekindling an old affair with a now married man wasn't easy, particularly not a man like Max, who, despite his obvious unhappiness, was loyal to the core. But then that was half the challenge, that and the fact that Max was a very desirable man, in more ways than one, and if there was one thing that Chrissy loved in life it was a challenge. Her mother called it perverse, always wanting the unreachable, but then her mother was in a small semi in Bognor and Chrissy had – she stroked the pale beige leather interior of her car – all this. Finishing her cigarette, she dropped it out of the window and Max turned to her.

'I must go,' he said.

'Can I drop you home at least?'

He glanced at his watch. 'Thanks, but I'll get a cab. It's out of your way.'

'OK,' Chrissy said. 'I'm glad you came tonight, Max. It gave us a chance to get to know one another again.'

'Although not in the same way of course,' Max added.

Chrissy laughed. 'Certainly not in the same way. I don't

know that I'd be up to the sort of sexual athletics now that we used to practise, Max!'

Max glanced at her breasts; he couldn't help himself. She wore a white silk shirt under her jacket with no bra and it excited him. 'I'm sure you'd manage,' he said, dragging his eyes away. 'Somehow.'

'I'm sure I would.'

Max reached forward and opened the door. 'I really must go,' he said. 'Anna will be waiting up for me.'

'Ah, the wife.'

'Yes, the wife,' he said. He climbed out and leant in to say goodbye.

'Thanks for walking me to my car,' Chrissy said. 'I felt much safer in deepest, darkest Chelsea with you by my side.'

Max smiled. He felt safe to flirt from this distance. 'All right, so it was an excuse,' he said. 'You've seen through me.'

Chrissy started the engine and slipped a CD into the player. 'Max,' she said, flicking on the lights, 'I always did.'

Max stood straight and slammed the door shut. He stepped back onto the pavement and watched as she revved the engine, indicated and pulled out. He held up his hand to wave, turned to look at the oncoming traffic for a free cab and realised he had an erection. It was the first one he had had for months.

Anna was in bed when Max got in. She was pretending to read but she couldn't concentrate; she was too upset. She had put a bottle of champagne in the fridge earlier, but it was almost eleven and she didn't fancy it at all now. She heard the front door go, climbed out of bed and came to the top of the stairs. Max looked up at her from the hallway. He was late and she was angry, but she didn't want to spoil things with a row, not now, not tonight.

'Sorry, I couldn't get a taxi.'

She shrugged. She didn't want to shrug, she wanted to rant and rave and tell him what a useless, insensitive bastard he was, but she didn't have the energy. Besides, what was the point? Where would it get them?

He came up a few steps and looked at her. 'So?'

Anna nodded.

'You got it?'

'Yes, Max, I got it.'

'But Anna that's marvellous! Bloody marvellous!' He came up and took her in his arms. 'Partner at just thirty. You clever thing.'

'Phew! You stink of smoke.' She pulled away and sat down on the stairs.

'Oh God, do I? That's the bloody wine bar. Everyone in those places seems to smoke. Sorry.' He stepped back and sniffed his jacket. 'God, I do, don't I?' He took it off. 'I'll have a shower in a minute. But first, tell me all about it. What did Andrew say?'

'Oh, you know, the usual.'

'No, I don't know. I've never been married to someone who made associate partner before.' Max grinned. 'Anna, that really is bloody fantastic you know. You must be delighted.'

'Yes, yes I am. Sort of.'

'Sort of?' Max shook his head, still grinning. 'Typical bloody Anna, queen of the understatement! What the hell does sort of mean?'

'I don't know exactly, I suppose that I'm not as used to success as you.' Max's reputation as a free thinking account man was revered in the industry. He had made main board director three years ago at just thirty-three, and had a shelf full of DNAD awards.

'I think I feel a bit daunted,' Anna said.

Max sat down next to her and took her hands. 'Well don't. You'll do it, Anna, you always have.' Anna was strong, stronger than him, he knew that, and full of sense and reason. She was so strong that sometimes her capability overwhelmed him. 'Look, don't spoil tonight by worrying about the future.' This was Max's philosophy on life, he always said it and virtually always lived it. 'Just enjoy the moment.'

Anna smiled. 'Live for today, not quite the father image I'd been hoping for.'

Max didn't return her smile. 'Oh really? And what had you been hoping for, Anna? Pipe and slippers?'

'No! I . . .' Anna broke off. She had caught his swift change of mood and didn't know how to handle it. She never did. Any discussion about the baby always ended this way and Anna had long since given up expending the energy on trying to find out why. But she hadn't given up being upset by it. Every new exchange cut her to the quick. How could she want something so much and Max be hardly bothered by it? And she did want this baby; she could have lived without partnerships and high incomes, the house, the car, indeed most things she had worked for, but she couldn't have lived without a baby. It was in her, a basic need, running through the weave of her existence, and yet Max simply didn't care. Or if he did, he didn't show it.

She lumbered to her feet, pulling herself up on the stair rail, and went back to bed. Max sat where he was for a few minutes. It wasn't Anna's fault, he knew that, but it didn't stop him getting at her for his own inadequacies. It had been a joint decision; they had got the house, their careers established, the lifestyle and the income, and all they were missing was the baby. He had been just as keen as she had, in the beginning. He saw himself in a four-wheel drive with a car seat in the back, saw Anna successfully combining a glossy legal career with a clutch of blond, wholesome children. He saw the country house, Sunday lunches with friends, dogs and children tramping across open land. But none of it was real, not like the hideous largeness of Anna, or her complete exhaustion, not like the desperate need to have a good time and to celebrate every last drop of his vitality and youth. What had gone wrong? Why hadn't he been able to grow up and face this responsibility? It wasn't as if he didn't love Anna.

He stood up and, sighing, went into the bedroom after her. 'Sorry,' he said.

Anna glanced up from her book and stared at him.

'Beginner's nerves. I've not done this parent thing before. I guess I'm pretty tense about it.'

Anna knew she had a choice here; she could argue the point, make it known how she felt, that she was just as inexperienced as he was and that she was scared shitless to top it all, but she decided not to. It was late, they had been on this merry-go-round before and it got them nowhere. So, like the fact that he was late, the fact that he wouldn't talk about the baby went uncommented on.

'Me too,' she said, and the subject was closed.

'Shouldn't we celebrate your win?' Max asked, trying to inject some excitement into the air. 'Is there any champagne in the fridge? Shall we crack open a bottle?'

Anna shrugged. 'It's a bit late,' she said.

'Right, of course.' It wasn't meant as a criticism, but

Max's guilty conscience took it as one. 'How about a nice cup of fennel tea for your indigestion?' he suggested.

Anna turned away. 'No thanks. I'm exhausted. I think I'll turn off the light and get some sleep, if you don't mind.'

'No, I don't mind.' He came across and bent to kiss the top of her head. 'Goodnight, Anna. And well done.'

'Thanks.'

'I'll shower in the guest bathroom, so as not to disturb you,' he said, walking towards the door. 'I'm going to do a bit of work and maybe watch a vid.' He blew a kiss. '*Bonne nuit,*' then closed the door after him and went downstairs. Anna reached over and turned off the light.

For a long time she lay in the dark, half-upright on the mound of pillows to ease her heartburn, listening to the faint sounds of Max downstairs. She should have been jubilant, triumphant even, but all she felt was flat. Flat and naggingly depressed. So this was it? The pinnacle of her career had been marked with a cup of tea, alone, waiting for Max to come home. Perhaps tomorrow would be better; they at least had a party to go to. Perhaps tomorrow she would feel like a partner, because tonight, she felt very much on her own.

Down in the kitchen, Max took something out of the freezer that looked remotely edible and put it in the microwave. He programmed the oven and pressed start. As he took a tray and some cutlery out of the drawer, he remembered the dinners they used to have, the food they used to eat. There was an air of excess, of heady indulgence about Anna's cooking that had turned him on beyond belief. God, had it really been that easy, to get an erection about a clam sauce? Perhaps it had been the idea of this sharp, achieving woman at the stove for him, preparing for him, feeding him. But it hadn't been only that, had it?

Max stood and thought for some time, then he went to the fridge and took out a bottle of Becks. He opened it and drank straight from the bottle. No, he realised, it had been more, much more. Anna had been real. God, she had been so real, after a decade of flaky women with breast implants and pierced belly buttons, that he had been senseless with desire for her. She was strong and honest and clever. She could wrap him up mentally and seal him with brown tape and that turned him on more than he could ever have imagined. When they made love, she never watched herself in the mirror, she looked at him, at his body, she felt him; every minute move he made inside her she felt and cried out at.

There was a small, intrusive ping, and Max glanced behind him at the microwave. Tonight's offering was ready. He finished his beer and dropped the bottle in the bin. Anna liked to recycle, but frankly he couldn't be assed. He went to the small white plastic-coated oven on the sideboard and took out his ready meal. He looked at it and for a moment he remembered the first dinner he had shared with Anna. He felt immeasurably sad. Placing the meal on the side, he walked out of the kitchen into the sitting room and left the vague vegetable pasta exactly where it was.

Chapter Three

It was 3.00 am and Anna woke with a start. She rolled over in bed and was so wide awake that she thought for a moment it must be morning. But, glancing at the luminous dial on her alarm clock, she saw it was ten past three and sighed, heaving herself up and out of bed to go to the toilet. That done, she left the bathroom light on and climbed back into bed, picking up a book from the bedside table and opening it. There was just enough light to see and she read the first paragraph, but her mind wasn't focused and she found that she had to read it three times before she took in the words. So she put the book down and turned to look at Max in the half-light, asleep and gently snoring beside her.

Max. The clever, charming, amusing and different Max. Different from all the men she had ever met, quirky and funny, able to banish all serious thought and intention in one suggestion, like eating fruit salad off her tummy or going to Legoland on their day off. Max had driven a smart car when she'd met him, had worn bespoke suits and hand-made shoes. He was a member of the RAC in St James's and had an account at Justerini and Brooks, where he kept his wine in cellerage. But on their first date she had found a tape of Disney classics in his car stereo and they had driven down the King's Road singing along to 'Cruella De Vil' and 'King of the Swingers'. He loved musicals and *James and the Giant Peach*, he had a passion for ice cream and ate her cooking with such intense enjoyment that it had been an almost erotic experience to cook for him.

She had fallen in love with Max so easily; he had come into her grey life and opened up a world of vibrant colour for her. How could she not have fallen in love with him, at a time when she was so desperate for affection? It was just after her mother had died and she had failed to make a relationship with a father who had ignored her pretty much from the day she was born. She was lonely and sad, and far too serious for her own good. Max changed all that and she loved him for it.

She loved him still. She loved him deeply, loved his loyalty and his humour, only now something had shifted, gone adrift in the balance of things between them, and she didn't know what it was. She had somehow, in the last year of hard work and pressure for the partnership, lost the knack of being happy. She had thought a baby would change it, but it had only made it worse. Anna reached out and touched the smooth skin on Max's shoulder. What should have brought them closer together was breaking them apart and she didn't know how to stop it. Max stirred and she jerked her finger away, not wanting to wake him. Setting her feet down on the floor, she stood and reached for her dressing gown.

'Anna?'

She glanced back. 'Sorry, I didn't mean to wake you.'

Max blinked several times, then rolled over onto his side to look at her. 'Are you OK? Nothing to do with the baby?'

Anna hesitated. It was everything to do with the baby. 'I'm fine,' she said. 'I just feel a bit, I don't know, a bit low sometimes.'

Max opened the covers. 'Come back to bed,' he said. 'Come on, you're cold.'

Anna sat down and the whole bed sagged with her weight. She eased her large, swollen body in next to Max and rolled onto her side so that he could wrap his arms round her and tuck his body in behind her. 'Better? Less sad?' he whispered. She nodded and stroked his bare arms, suddenly aware of a long neglected desire for him. Max felt her relax and gently eased away, kissing the back of her head. 'You must get some sleep,' he murmured, moving apart, 'or you'll be exhausted in the morning. Shall I turn the bathroom light off?'

'Yes.' Anna closed her eyes. What was the point in desire that was constantly denied? He climbed out of bed, walked across the room to the bathroom and turned off the light. Then he felt his way back to her in the dark and slipped under the covers, reaching for her hand. 'All right now?'

Anna didn't answer him. What could she honestly say?

The young woman sat up in bed with the overhead light on, her knees tucked up under her and her body huddled over them in an attempt to keep warm. She was inside a sleeping bag and had two worn blankets left by the housing association over her shoulders, yet still she shivered. She had very little body fat to insulate her and the cold bit through to her bones. But it wasn't the cold that made her shiver, it was fear. She had heard him, outside, when darkness fell and smothered everything, she had heard his footsteps and his voice, whispering menaces behind the door.

The young woman laid her head down on her knees but was unable to close her eyes. She longed to sleep, but didn't dare. Where was the person who had brought her here? Why hadn't she come back? The young woman went over her conversation again and again, searching for some verbal clue as to why the social worker had not returned. There weren't any. 'I'll call round again this afternoon,' she had said. It was definite. 'See you later,' she had said. That was as certain as it could be.

The young woman tucked numb hands down inside the sleeping bag, aware that her fingers were now icy cold. She stared blankly at the faded wall and began again to count the Blu-Tack marks on the wall that had held up the previous occupant's poster collection. It was the only thing that kept her sane.

Chapter Four

The ward doctor was just finishing his tea in the nurses' office when the nurse came in.

'There's a patient on the gynie ward, routine termination, who wants to be discharged.'

'How long's she been in recovery?'

'A couple of hours. She's had a cup of tea but she doesn't want to eat anything.'

'Micturition?'

'Normal.'

'Right, let's send her on her way then.' He took a last gulp of tea and moved off.

'Here,' the nurse said, handing across the young woman's notes as they walked down to the ward. 'She's anxious to get away and she doesn't want any counselling.'

The doctor glanced at the file. 'No routine counselling before either I see. Does she seem all right?'

'A bit withdrawn, but yes, fine more or less.'

'Anyone to meet her?'

'I don't know.'

'Well, it's her right of course. If she wants to go, then let's discharge her.' He stopped. 'You're not happy?'

'I'm not unhappy, it was a perfectly routine TOP at ten weeks. She's recovered well, the drip's down, it's just that she doesn't seem right. She's got a nasty bruise under her right eye, it looks as if someone's given her an almighty thump and she's just, well, I can't really put my finger on it, just not right.'

'What's right? God knows what personal baggage she's carrying around with her.' He shrugged. He wanted to specialise in obstetrics and no matter how hard he tried to quell his feelings, he had to admit that he found this end of it all pretty tough to take. 'Look, I'll have a word, shall I?'

'Thanks.'

They went into the side room where a young woman sat on the edge of the bed, fully dressed, an overnight bag by her feet and a small soft toy in her hands. She glanced up.

'Debbie?' She nodded and the doctor came across to the bed. He sat down next to her. 'You want to go home, is that right?'

Again she nodded.

'Normally we'd say it's a bit early, we like patients to recover for at least three to four hours after a general anaesthetic, but you feel all right do you?'

'Yes.'

'You've had something to drink? Been to the toilet?'

'Yes.'

'And you don't feel at all woozy, dizzy in any way?'

'No.'

'Good, well I don't see any reason to keep you in. Is someone meeting you?'

She bit her lip. 'Yes, my friend is waiting in a taxi.'

'Fine.' He glanced up at the nurse. 'I notice that you didn't want any counselling at all, Debbie. Are you quite happy about that?'

'Yes.'

'Well if you want to change your mind, you can always phone the hospital and they'll put you in touch with the right person.'

'Right, erm, thanks.'

'OK, that's it then.' He stood up. 'Painkillers?' He glanced across at the nurse.

'She's got Co-proxymol.'

'Good. Well, I'll let you get on your way then. The nurse will see you off the ward. Goodbye Debbie.'

The young woman bent and picked up her bag, then stood. She felt the steady flow of blood into her maternity pad as she did so and was suddenly overwhelmed with a mixture of loss and relief. She thought she might weep. 'Thanks,' she managed to say, though what she was thanking him for she had no idea. 'Goodbye.'

Minutes later she was in the lift on her way down to the ground floor. She had disposed of her baby, she'd had it sucked out of her and flushed into the hospital waste system. She had killed the beginning of a new life and still, despite the terrible haemorrhaging grief, still she felt relieved.

Anna was sitting on the bed, looking through the file that had arrived from the nanny agency, and Max was in the shower. They were due out at the party in half an hour but Anna was nowhere near ready; she couldn't be bothered to tart herself up, she had nothing to wear anyway.

'There's about three here that I think are possibles,' she said, as Max came into the bedroom wrapped in a towel. 'I'll ring on Monday and arrange interviews. Perhaps you could give me an idea of your diary next week and we could see them together?'

Max stopped combing his hair and looked at her. 'Anna, I've already said that I don't want to get involved, OK? This whole nanny thing is your responsibility, not mine. I don't want to be mean, but I really can't see that I'll have much to do with the nanny.'

'Well you are being mean,' Anna said, snatching the file up and walking out of the bedroom. 'I don't exactly want the casting couch,' she called from the airing cupboard. 'All I want is a second opinion.'

Max was being unfair and he knew it. He came to the door and said, 'OK, put like that, you've got it. Why don't you interview first, then I'll see your final choice or choices. OK?'

Anna glanced up surprised. This was at least halfway. 'OK, thanks!' Coming back into the bedroom, she dropped a clean towel onto the bed and went to her wardrobe to search for something to wear. She took out a pair of velour leggings and a long black tunic, dumping them on the bed next to the towel.

'Anna!'

She stopped and looked at Max.

'Is that what you're wearing?'

'Yes.' She glanced at the clothes. 'What's wrong with it?'

'Well it's hardly stylish, is it? It's, well, it's pretty mumsy! This is quite a big agency bash and—'

'And you don't want to be let down by the large dumpy woman in the leggings, right?'

Max smiled. 'I wouldn't have put it quite like that, but how about the black cashmere dress I bought you, with a pair of sheer stockings and some high heels?'

Anna sighed wearily. 'Max, it may have escaped your notice, but I am thirty-nine weeks' pregnant and I don't somehow think that La Perla do a big line in maternity suspender belts.'

'OK, perhaps not the stockings . . .'

'No, not perhaps, definitely not the stockings.' She untied her dressing gown and glanced up, catching the look on his face. 'Look, I'll see if I can find some jumbo tights and wear the dress, OK?' She left the leggings where they were and took out the dress, kneeling down on the floor to get her shoes out because she could no longer bend. She dumped them both on the bed and said, 'I can't say I have even the slightest bit of enthusiasm for this party, Max. Would anyone notice if I didn't turn up d'you think?'

Max stopped buttoning his shirt. 'I would,' he said.

Anna looked at him. She wanted to labour the point, to ask would you? Would you really, Max, or are you just saying that? She wanted him to assert his love for her, but they were running late so there wasn't the time, and besides, he might not say the things she wanted to hear.

'Well, I'd better have a bath then,' she said.

'Aren't you going to wash your hair?'

She wasn't, but she caught a glimpse of herself in the mirror. She looked faded, a draft copy, with tired hair and loose limp clothes. 'Yes, of course,' she said, 'but I'll do it in the bath, it's more comfortable.'

Max nodded and caught her hand as she went past him. He kissed it briefly – which was the extent of their physical relationship – and then let it go. Anna went on into the bathroom. She closed the door behind her and sank down on to the edge of the bath. She had the oddest feeling that Max was slipping away from her, and the terrible sadness was that she didn't know how to stop him.

*   *   *

Debbie sat in an armchair in front of the gas fire and drank a cup of hot Ribena; there was something very comforting about hot Ribena and she was desperate for some comfort, however small. She had a rug over her knees and an unopened plastic wallet of photographs on her lap. She stared blankly at the wall, her mind in a nowhere state, the thoughts bleeding out of her like the remains of her dead baby. She longed for him, but the longing was laced with a sick fear and the dull, dark ache of disappointment. She opened the plastic wallet and looked down at the first photograph. Debbie and Darren, it said underneath, in her neat, sloping handwriting, November 1997. She traced the outline of his face with her finger, his clean, smooth features, his regulation inch-short hair, then she pressed the photograph against her breast and closed her eyes. She remembered every moment, every tiny, breath-taking moment of it all.

It had started on a night out with the girls, although why he had picked her she still didn't know to this day. She was hardly much to look at – not in his league anyway – but he'd asked her if she wanted a drink and she'd said yes, egged on by the others. It wasn't something she normally did, accept drinks from anyone. But they got chatting and . . . Debbie opened her eyes and flipped a few pages over in the photo holder. They hit it off, just like that, just the way they say you can in women's magazines. And he was so handsome, yes, that's a good word for him, handsome, so fit and clean cut and nicely dressed. Then he had asked to come back for coffee and she had said yes; well, she couldn't say no really, she was too overwhelmed by it all. So he came back and before she knew it they were in the bedroom and then it all happened, quicker than she'd thought it would and not bad at all really, for a first time. And afterwards he was very loving and he cuddled her all night.

Debbie flipped the pages over again. She looked down at an image of herself and Darren. January 1998, her handwriting said, Rob and Jane's engagement party. She was all dolled up, had had her hair done especially, and he was wearing a tie. They had been 'going out', as he called it, for about six weeks and she knew then – she knew he was the one for her. She knew then as well that she was pregnant.

'What the fuck do you mean you're pregnant?' he had shouted. Debbie dropped the photos onto the floor and pulled the blanket up tight around her. She could hear his voice echoing around the empty room. 'What the fuck do you think you're playing at? You can't be pregnant, you can't be!' He was drunk, of course. 'You're trying to trap me, aren't you? You think you can get one over on me, tell me you're pregnant and I'll marry you. That's it, isn't it, you're trying to trap me.' Debbie had stood there, shocked and tearful, unable to speak. As he put his hands up to his face, she tried to touch him to comfort him and herself. 'Get off me!' he had cried. 'You can't do this to me, you can't. For fuck's sake, I'm only twenty-one. I can't get married and have a baby. Jesus! I don't even love you.' He took her by the shoulders and shook her. 'I know about women like you!' he shouted. 'You can't do this to me, you can't fucking trick me like this, you bitch, you slut, you . . .' Then he hit her. The blow was so hard and so unexpected that she flew across the room into the opposite wall. She crumpled on impact and fell to the floor. He stood for a few moments looking at her. She thought he was crying but she wasn't sure, she couldn't focus properly. Then he ran into the bedroom, cleared his stuff out and left. She lay there, numb and in pain. For six hours she had lain there, unable to move, until finally, at seven in the morning, she had somehow managed to crawl into bed.

With the blanket up near her face, Debbie closed her eyes. Counselling, they said, often helps. What's to counsel? she thought, rubbing the silky edge of the blanket between her thumb and forefinger. What on earth can they tell me that I don't already know? I had a baby inside me, he didn't want it and nor did I, so I got rid of it. She put her hand up to her face. Simple as that. And despite the fact that her hand was wet, she didn't even register that she was crying.

'So who was the dolly in the little black dress then?' Anna said, in the car on the way home. She was driving; she always drove. 'She looked a bit overdressed for secretarial.'

Max stared straight ahead. 'Nice dig. Chrissy Forbes. She's the new account director for pet foods.'

'Ah, hence the likeness to an old dog! Does she have to taste any of it?'

Max suddenly laughed. 'She's hardly an old dog, Anna! I take it you didn't like her then?'

'She was all right. Condescending until she heard what I did, then she ignored me. She is what my mother used to call a man's woman.'

'Meaning?'

'She made a bit of a bee-line for you.' Anna smiled and glanced sidelong at Max.

'Did she? Oh, well it's probably because I used to work with her at Davis Scanton, years ago. We worked on a deodorant account together, in my very unmemorable early days. I was probably the only person she really knew there.'

'Is she married?' Anna was fishing for information but trying to keep the intense curiosity she felt out of her voice.

'I don't know. I don't think so, but I've never asked.'

She stopped at the lights and turned to look at Max. He was staring out of the window and she couldn't see his face. He was a lousy liar so it was probably just as well. 'So you don't have much to do with her then?'

Max turned. 'For goodness' sake, Anna, what is this? The Spanish Inquisition? I work with Chrissy, all right? That's all there is to it.'

The lights changed and Anna shifted gear. She couldn't see his expression, but she sensed that she had spoilt the mood of the evening – again. She pulled away and pressed a cassette into the stereo, turning the volume up before she had a chance to hear what it was. The aching voice of Billie Holiday filled the car, singing of love and deceit and the wrongness of her man. Bad choice, she thought, but she didn't have the nerve to acknowledge that by turning it off again.

Chapter Five

On Monday evening, having finished work late, yet again, Anna arrived home in a cab. 'It's just here, on the right,' she said. The driver slowed and pulled into the kerb. She looked at her house, then at her watch. 'Oh thank goodness she's still here!'

'Sorry love?'

'Nothing. Just muttering darkly under my breath.' Anna climbed out. 'Could you hang on a minute, there's someone to see me, I'll be back in a sec.' She slammed the door and ran up the garden path towards her front door.

'Hello? Debbie Pritchard, is it?'

A young woman turned and smiled nervously at Anna. 'Yes, hello.'

'Hi! Anna Jacob. Sorry to have kept you waiting, I got held up in a meeting and I've been hoping all the way home that you'd hang on for me. Have you been here long?'

'No, about ten minutes.'

'Oh God, sorry! It's good of you to wait.' Anna opened the front door, darted in and turned off the alarm. She switched on the hall lights and said, 'Go on in, Debbie, I'll just get my bags from the cab.'

Debbie dropped her briefcase just inside the front door. 'I'll give you a hand,' she said, 'with your stuff.'

'Oh, thanks!' Anna didn't usually accept help, but tonight she just didn't have the energy to argue. She probably would have let Debbie carry *her* in from the cab if she'd offered. She paid the driver while Debbie took her case and laptop into the house, then followed, relieved to be unburdened.

'Thanks. That was a great help. I can't tell you how much I've come to dread lugging all that stuff into the house at the end of the day. Thank God for taxis, if I had to go on the tube to work I think I might have re-signed.'

'I'm not surprised,' Debbie said. 'How many weeks are you?'

'Thirty-nine. I should be on maternity leave, but I've got a deal on and I'm needed.' Anna shrugged. 'So, I have to work. I haven't got anything ready yet and I'm really anxious about it to be honest with you. I thought I'd be swanning around the house getting the nursery organised by now, you know, popping to Peter Jones to buy babygros and pretty cot mobiles.' Anna walked on into the house, switching on lamps and checking the radiators. 'I've just been made partner and the buck stops with me.' She turned. 'Would you like some tea, Debbie? Or a coffee?'

'I'd love a coffee, thanks.' Debbie followed Anna into the kitchen and said, 'Can I make it? You look as if you need to sit down and rest for a few minutes.'

Anna sighed. 'Would you mind? The teas and coffee are all in the cupboard above the kettle and milk's in the fridge.'

'Right.'

Anna sat down at the kitchen table and reached for another chair to put her feet up. Her ankles were slightly puffy and she felt completely exhausted.

'What would you like, Mrs Jacob?'

'It's Ms Jacob, at work, and Mrs Slater everywhere else, but definitely Anna to you, please! I'd love a cup of blackcurrant tea, Debbie, if you wouldn't mind, it's up there in the Twinings box.'

'OK, right.' Debbie filled the kettle, switched it on and prepared the cups. That done, she went into the hall and brought back her briefcase. 'I've got a copy of my references here, along with my exam certificates and some course reports.' She handed them over to Anna. 'Have you seen my CV?'

'Yes, thanks, the agency faxed me a copy.' Anna looked down at the red folder on her lap and skimmed through the letters of reference in each plastic slip. She glanced over the course reports, picking out words like 'kind' and 'diligent', then quickly checked the exam certificates. 'Thank you, Debbie,' she said. 'This all looks very good.' Looking up, Anna placed the folder on the table. 'You don't have a reference from your last job?'

'No, I've rung several times, but my ex-employer is incredibly busy, quite often abroad, and I don't want to be a pest. I thought I'd wait until I found something I'm really interested in and then hassle.'

Anna smiled. 'That sounds very sensible. Look, I don't suppose I could hang on to your folder for tonight could I? I could courier it back to you tomorrow and—'

'I'm terribly sorry Ms Jac— I mean Anna, but I've got another interview first thing in the morning and I need it.'

'Oh right, OK, no problem.' Anna tried to gear herself

up into interview mode but she felt far from dynamic. 'So, you're not working at the moment. The agency said you were on holiday, is that right?'

'Yes, I decided to take a few weeks' break before looking for another job. I wanted to go walking in the Lakes and do a bit of decorating.'

That sounded very normal, very ordinary, Anna thought with relief, no mention of Club 18–30 in Magaluf. 'And you didn't want to line anything up before you left your old job?'

Debbie finished making the drinks and brought Anna's over to the table. She pulled out a chair.

'No, I couldn't find anything I liked during my month's notice period and I didn't want to rush into just any old job, so I decided to take some time out and look around.'

Good, she wouldn't just take anything, unlike one of the girls Anna had seen today, five jobs in three years, not a good track record. Anna felt cheered.

'Why did you leave your last position?'

'My last charge started nursery school and I didn't want to be just a housekeeper.'

'I see. 'And you were there for how long?'

'Just over a year.'

'Good.' Anna knew she should be making notes on all this but couldn't be bothered to heave herself out of the chair to go and get a pen and paper. Besides which, she liked Debbie, they had connected, if that was the right word.

'And you've had experience of new-borns, the agency said, of all ages up to nine? Is that right?'

'Yes.'

'What age do you like best?'

'Difficult to say really.' Debbie smiled. 'But if I was pushed, probably I'd have to say babies. I just love babies.' She laughed and blushed and that endeared her to Anna even further.

'Shall I show you round and tell you a bit about the job as we go, Debbie?' Anna asked. 'And you can tell me more about yourself and your previous employment.'

Debbie stood and offered her hand. 'Shall I help you up?'

Anna laughed. 'Normally I'd have said no, but I seem to be stuck in this chair, like a beached whale.' She took Debbie's hand and the young woman pulled Anna up.

'Thanks,' she said. 'I'm not sure I'd have made it without you!' Both women smiled and, leading the way, Anna began the tour of the house.

It was just before five when the young woman turned up at the Harringey Social Services offices. She had walked from the Harbridge estate – about five miles – and was cold and tired. She'd had very little to eat in the last forty-eight hours, surviving on the one pint of milk and loaf of bread that the social worker had left in her fridge. She was weak and still frightened, disorientated by the noise and commotion on the streets after so many months of solitude and silence. She waited for a while across the street, watching the building nervously as people came and went, then she realised, as several lights went out on the first floor, that the place was closing and she had to go in now or not at all. She crossed the road anxiously and approached a middle-aged woman who had just left the building and was standing in the doorway buttoning up her raincoat.

'Excuse me?'

The woman turned. She had a look, the sort of look that people who think they are about to be harassed wear, an impatient, irritated, but none the less wary look. 'Yes?' There was no warmth in her voice and the young woman didn't have the confidence to look her in the eye.

'Is, erm, is the office closed?'

'Yes. We close at five.'

'Do you work there?'

The woman bristled. 'I do, but I'm afraid that there's nothing I can do for you now. If you need to see someone you'll have to come back tomorrow or if it's an emergency there's an out-of-hours helpline you can ring.'

The young woman stared at the floor. 'It's not an emergency. It's just that I was supposed to see a social worker and she didn't turn up. She said she'd bring my money and, well, I've not got anything to eat and . . .' She broke off, her nerve failing her.

The woman snorted derisively, then opened her handbag and took out her purse. She found two pound coins and said, 'If you're going to beg, young lady, at least have the courage to do it openly. Here . . .' She thrust the money at the young woman, who flushed deeply and stammered some sort of reply.

'Go on, take it. If you need the money take it. Only don't come harassing decent people in the street, telling lies. Sit and do it properly like all the rest. Go on! Take the money!'

The young woman did as she was told, clutched the two pound coins in her sweating palm and dropped her head down. Tears stung her eyes.

'I only hope to God that you do something useful with it,' the older woman said, moving off. 'Buy some food. You probably won't though. They never do!'

The young woman stood where she was and the cold, grey concrete pavement blurred in her vision, while the sound of the traffic pounded in her head. She heard the sharp tap of the woman's boots as she retreated off towards the tube, then she dropped the money into her coat pocket and looked up. She wiped her face on the sleeve of her overcoat and set off for home. Home – a small, freezing cold flat in a block littered with junkies and petty criminals. Some home, but it was all that she'd got.

She knew she wouldn't come back here, she would never make a second attempt; the humiliation of doing so would be too much to bear.

When he came in from work, Max found Anna in the small fourth bedroom they had decided would be the nursery. She was sitting cross-legged on the floor, one hand in the small of her back to ease the dull ache that she was permanently plagued with, the other turning the pages of a fabric book. He stood in the doorway, good-looking, charming, urbane Max, and tried to imagine himself pacing that very floor with a squawking baby in his arms, or standing over the cot while it slept. He couldn't; his mind was a complete blank and he wasn't sure if that worried or relieved him.

Anna looked up. 'Hello.'

He blew her a kiss.

'I think I've got a nanny.'

'Really? What, just like that?' He clicked his fingers and Anna prickled with irritation.

'Not exactly just like that, no. I've done four interviews today, three at work and one tonight here, and the girl I saw tonight, Debbie Pritchard, was perfect. Excellent references, bags of experience and very nice, very kind. I think she'd fit in really well.'

'Great! Well done you!' Anna was in charge again. Anna wanted a nanny, Anna found one, it was as simple as that. Max too felt the itch of irritation. 'You don't need a second opinion then?'

'No, not really.' It came out sharper than she intended it to and there was a short silence between them.

Finally Max said, 'I see.' Then, 'When does she start?'

'Well I haven't offered her the job yet, she's got an interview tomorrow so I thought I'd ring lunchtime tomorrow and see how she got on. She said she was interested in the job, that she loved new-borns etcetera, so fingers crossed that she chooses us.'

Max snorted. 'Chooses us? Blimey!'

Anna ignored him.

'Package?'

She sighed. 'Hold your breath.'

Max raised his eyebrow. 'Go on.'

'Sixteen thousand, plus car and four weeks' holiday.'

'Christ!'

'Yes I know, but if she's what we want then that's what we have to pay.' Anna closed the fabric book and dropped it to the floor with a thump. 'I'm sorry, Max,' she said crossly, 'but don't go huffing and puffing about it all now. I did ask you to get involved in the beginning and you refused. All you offered was a second opinion and that was grudgingly. If you don't like it, then tough, you should have done something about it when I asked you.'

'I wasn't aware that you actually asked me, I thought it was more a question of giving me my orders. That's what I took umbrage at, that's why I didn't want to get involved. I don't like being told what to do, Anna.'

'Ha!' Anna lumbered to her feet, the heat of anger bringing a rush of blood to her cheeks. 'Since when did anyone ever tell you what to do, Max? As far as I can see you please yourself. You always have done and you always will do.'

Max lost his patience. 'That's bollocks, Anna, and you know it! If it really was a case of pleasing myself then I certainly wouldn't have come this far.'

'And what's that supposed to mean?' she cried. 'Come this far? What the hell do you mean by that, Max? This far with me? This far with the baby? This far being married? What do you mean, Max? Come on, tell me! What do you mean?' Anna's chest heaved with anger and she felt breathless and faint. She held onto the wall for support and closed her eyes.

Max moved towards her. 'Anna? Anna, are you all right?' He touched her arm, but she shrugged him off. 'Anna? Speak to me!'

She opened her eyes, took a deep breath and shook her head. 'What is there to say, Max?'

He couldn't answer her. There was a silence that seemed to go on interminably, then he turned towards the door and said, 'I'll get on with the supper.'

'You can't; there isn't any. I forgot to get it.'

'Terrific!' He stood where he was for a few moments. Then said, 'I'll go and get a take-away.'

Anna made no comment.

'Any preferences?'

'No.'

He turned and walked out of the room. Anna heard him down in the hall, looking for his car keys, finding his jacket, then the front door slammed and there was silence. She had wanted to call out, to say that she didn't know where all this was coming from, or rather that she did and that it was all because she was frightened that he didn't love her any more. But she had said nothing; once again, Anna had said nothing. She leant against the wall and felt swamped with sadness. She heard his car start up and pull away.

Max was on his way to Sainsbury's. He had decided to buy some fresh pasta and a salad instead of a curry. Anna liked pasta and it would be better for her, give her less indigestion. It was an attempt to make amends for a scene that he knew shouldn't have happened, but whether it would really make any difference he wasn't sure. He wasn't sure about anything any more, not where Anna was concerned. He loved her, but was love enough?

As he turned in the direction of the supermarket, his phone rang and he thought it might be Anna. He hesitated before answering it, knowing that he couldn't face any more anger and frustration tonight. But it kept on ringing and he realised that it could be important, so pressed the answer button. He felt a thrill at the sound of her voice; he simply couldn't help himself.

'Hello Max? It's Chrissy Forbes.'

'Hello Chrissy. How are you?'

'In a stinking mood actually! I've left my copy of the bloody dog food campaign we've been working on in the office and I need to go through it tonight before we see the client tomorrow morning. I know that you've got a copy and I was wildly hoping that you might have brought it home with you and that I could drive over and pick it up. It's just that you live up the road so to speak and the office is one hell of a flog into central London and back.'

Max pulled up at some traffic lights and glanced behind

him at the portfolio in the back of the car. 'As it happens, Chrissy,' he said, 'you are in luck! Wild hope obviously pays off. I've got it in the car with me now, I was going to have a quick look at it tonight myself. I can drop it round to you if you like. You're in Battersea aren't you?'

'Yes I am, but isn't it out of your way?'

'Not at all. I'm en route to Sainsbury's to buy supper. Give me your address and I can be there in about ten minutes.'

'Max,' Chrissy said, 'you are a life saver!' She laughed and gave him her address. 'I'll open a bottle of wine. See you in a while.'

She hung up and Max pressed the end call button on his phone, dropping it on the passenger seat. The lights changed and he pulled away. He would take the work round, maybe go through it with her so that he could have a look at it too and have a quick glass of wine. Then he would get back to Anna. Just a quick glass of wine, Sainsbury's, and straight home. Simple. And it would hardly matter to Anna, she never worried about punctuality. In fact, the way she was when he'd left, a few minutes more would probably be welcomed. She had no time for him at the moment anyway, that much was obvious.

Chrissy was still in her work suit when Max arrived ten minutes later, but she had removed her jacket and kicked her shoes off, padding around her little terraced house in her stockinged feet. As he stepped inside and saw her, relaxed and slightly dishevelled, her breasts obviously without constraint under her black long-sleeved silk T-shirt and her toenails painted vermilion under the sheer black of her stockings, Max got an erection. He was embarrassed by it and stood in the hall with the portfolio in front of him, wondering if perhaps it would be better to leave right now, but Chrissy said, 'I've opened a bottle of Cloudy Bay, it's fizzy and we've got to drink it because it'll be flat by tomorrow.' And he knew it would be rude just to drop and go.

She led Max inside, acutely aware of her effect on him, and poured some ice-cold wine into a long-stemmed tulip glass. 'Here.' She held it out to him and Max put the portfolio down to take what she offered. 'Cheers!'

He smiled nervously. 'Cheers!' Then took a sip. 'Good wine, Chrissy, thanks.'

'It's a pleasure.' She sat down on the sofa and crossed her legs, knowing that she revealed an expanse of stocking-top as she did so. 'It could, of course, be more of a pleasure. Now that I've lured you here to my den!' She smiled and sipped her wine.

Max swallowed. 'You weren't always this direct,' he said.

'I didn't need to be before. As I recall, Max, you never held anything back. I'm not into playing silly games, Max, I'm too grown-up for that kind of thing now. I want you and I'm not going to pretend otherwise.'

Max laughed. 'Chrissy, you are . . .'

She stood and moved towards him. 'I'm what?' She touched his hair. 'Sexy? Outrageous? Resistible?'

'All of those things.'

Her fingers eased down to his ear, then his neck, and he could feel the sharp length of her nails against his skin. His excitement mounted. 'Surely not resistible?' she whispered, darting her tongue out and running it over his lips. She kissed the side of his mouth. 'You're not going to refuse me, are you . . .'

Max kissed her. It was swift and impulsive. He put his hand behind her neck and brought her mouth onto his with one strong movement. She gasped, then kissed him back, pressing her body against him and feeling his hardness. She ran her hands down his back to his bottom and ground her hips down and in towards his crotch. He caught his breath, opened his eyes to look at her, then, as if suddenly gaining consciousness, broke away. He stepped back. 'God Chrissy, I'm sorry, I can't. I just . . .' He stopped.

Chrissy swept her hair off her face and looked at him. She felt the instant pain of rejection, then it disappeared, almost as quickly as it had come, and she knew that this was something she not only wanted, but absolutely had to have. She watched his face, wretched, flushed with excitement, and she realised that this was only the beginning. All good things come to those who wait, she told herself, and smiled.

'It's OK,' she said. 'You would if you could but you can't!' She even laughed; a virtuoso performance.

'You're not angry?'

She moved away from him and reached for her cigarettes. 'Disappointed, yes, I could do with a really good fuck.' She lit up. 'But angry, no. Why should I be? It's not as if you don't want me, is it?'

Max looked away and didn't reply; that was answer enough for her.

'Go on, Max, go and get your shopping.' She walked across to the front door. 'Thank you for delivering the art work, I'm only sorry that you couldn't deliver something else.'

At the door Max stopped and kissed her cheek. 'Chrissy, you are wonderful, d'you know that? Bloody wonderful!'

He walked out and turned to her. 'Can you drop the portfolio on my desk first thing in the morning? That way I can have a quick look at it before you go to see the client.'

'Of course.'

'Thanks.' He stood there, on the pavement, knowing he had to go but not wanting to. 'And thanks for . . . Well, you know, for being so . . .'

'Understanding?' she filled in for him.

He smiled. 'Yes.'

Chrissy smiled back, blew him a kiss, then shut the door. She leant against it and closed her eyes. 'I'm not understanding,' she murmured, listening to him get into his car and drive off. 'I'm patient.'

When Max got home with his bag of shopping an hour or so later, Anna was at the desk in the study checking some documents. She had changed into her pyjamas because her clothes irritated her and she still held one hand on the base of her spine, rubbing at the ever deepening ache.

'Hi!'

She glanced over her shoulder at Max in the doorway. 'Hello. You've been ages.'

'Sorry, there were queues of people.' He watched her for a moment. 'You all right, Anna?'

She winced as the pain in her back moved through to her uterus, and rubbed at her stomach. 'Fine. I think I've got indigestion though. I had a client lunch today and I've had stomach ache all afternoon. Must be something I ate.'

'I'll put the food in the kitchen. Are you hungry?'

Anna stood. She marked the paper with where she had

got up to and followed Max into the kitchen. 'What did you . . . ouch!' Suddenly bending double, she clutched her side.

'Anna!' Max dropped the bag and came over to her. He tried to help her into a chair but she resisted.

'I want to stand,' she murmured, 'it's more . . . ouch! Bloody hell!'

'Christ Anna! What's the matter? Is it the baby?'

Anna took several deep breaths and finally managed to straighten. 'It's that bloody bean soup I had for lunch I should think,' she said through clenched teeth. 'God, that's the last time I have anything like that.' She inhaled deeply, exhaled and stretched her arms behind her back to loosen the tightness in her chest. 'Sorry, Max, but I really don't feel like any supper.'

'No problem. I changed my mind about the take-away and went to Sainsbury's for fresh pasta and sauce. It can go in the freezer if you don't fancy it.' He took her arm. 'Here, sit down for a moment, please.'

Anna shook her head. 'No, really, it's more comfortable if I stand. I've got to finish those documents anyway in a minute, so I'll just stretch my— Oh God!' Anna doubled over again and Max caught her.

'Anna! Are you sure it's just indi—' He didn't finish. Just as he took her hand, there was a small sound, like the popping of an almost deflated balloon, and his shoes, black hand-tooled brogues from Churches, his socks, Italian silk, and the bottom half of his suit, off the peg from Paul Smith, were drenched in water.

'Jesus shit! What the . . .' He sprang back and stared helpless as the floor all around him was soaked.

'My waters . . .' Anna managed to hiss. 'Oh God, my waters have—' She cried out in pain and for the first time in their marriage, Max knew that Anna was in no position to take control.

He grabbed a tea towel off the sideboard and flung it at the pool of water, then he kicked his shoes off and threw them into the sink. He snatched up a roll of kitchen towel, unravelled a wad of it and dumped it on the floor. The pool of amniotic fluid soaked into it and he stared, frozen in panic for several moments, while Anna moaned softly, gripping the table for support.

'Oh God, what next . . .' He unzipped his trousers and pulled them off along with his socks. 'Anna, you stay there . . .' he said hurriedly.

'Don't worry,' she snapped. 'I'm not going anywhere . . .'

'Oh, no, God, of course not. Look, I'll just grab some jeans and clean socks and, erm, get some things for the baby . . . Oh shit! What do you have to take with you?' He stared at her, the nausea churning in his stomach.

'I don't know! I can't bloody remember! Just get my wash bag and . . . Oh God . . .' Anna screwed her face up in pain and Max dashed upstairs. He ran into the bedroom, flung on the first thing that came to hand, a pair of jeans, didn't bother with socks, grabbed Anna's wash bag, realised it was empty, then swiped the glass shelf, knocking everything on it into the bag.

He found Anna's dressing gown, spent a good few minutes looking for her slippers before he remembered that she had them on and ran back down the stairs again.

'Here, I've got everything.'

'I need clean clothes, I'm wet through.'

'Oh God, yes, of course.' He ran back upstairs, found some tracksuit bottoms and a sweatshirt draped over the back of the chair and returned a minute or so later carrying them.

'Can I help you?'

Anna had taken her wet things off and stood naked, shivering and bent double with pain. Max shuddered at the sight of her; he was useless with pain.

'These are yours for fuck's sake!' she said, struggling with the clothes, refusing any help.

'Sorry.' He felt stupid and useless. The pain deepened. Hurrying into the hall, he yanked his coat on, picked up a rug and ran back into the kitchen. 'Here.' He draped the travel rug over Anna's shoulders. 'You have to keep warm . . .'

'Max!' Anna snapped. 'I am not a sofa! Please, take this bloody rug off me and get me my overcoat. It's bad enough having to go to hospital in your sodding clothes, let alone wrapped in a bloody blanket.'

Max blinked several times, he had heard Anna swear only once or twice before, in all the time he'd known her. He rubbed his head, then pulled the rug off her and ran back to the sitting room. He took her coat off the stair post and brought it back to her. She was breathing hard now and her face was set in a grimace, her jaw clenched in pain.

'Right, let's go,' he said, jangling the car keys. He took hold of Anna's arm and she jerked it away.

'I'm not an invalid!' she snarled.

Max said nothing. He opened the front door, helped her, as much as she would allow, into the car and ran back to the house for a couple of dustbin liners.

'What the hell are you doing?' Anna screamed as he started to cover her and the floor under her feet with black plastic.

'Just protecting the leather,' he said harmlessly. 'Sit up a minute, I'll just put this under your—' He stopped sharp as the flat of Anna's palm hit him with a resounding smack across the top of his head. He sprang back. 'Jesus! What in God's name was that for?' He stopped a second time. Anna had started to sob.

Despite the rush to hospital and the sudden spurt of contractions, Anna's baby took a long time to come into the world. Ten hours to be exact. And all that time, Max had no idea what to do.

At first, he watched Anna, sat by her side and tried to hold her hand, rub her back, massage her feet, do whatever she or the midwife asked him to. Then the pain intensified and Max realised that he had never, in all his life, had to endure someone else's pain. He simply didn't know how to cope. It racked him. He was helpless, faint with nausea, exhausted and mentally fatigued by Anna's mood swings. He saw his wife in agony and could do nothing to assuage it. It was the most awful, nullifying and redundant few hours of his life. It reduced him to only half the man he always thought he had been. It undermined his self-confidence and demolished his morale.

In the final hour, Anna had demanded that he leave, not wanting him to witness what she felt was her complete humiliation. He had closed the door of the labour suite and heard her scream, a sound that to him was so far removed from the dream of parenthood that it made no sense at all. He slid down the wall in the corridor and put his head in his hands. That was where the midwife found him, twenty minutes later, to tell him that he had a daughter.

'Would you like to come in now, Mr Slater?' she asked. Max looked up at her with red-rimmed eyes. He shook his head. He mumbled something that she couldn't hear, then he stood, walked out into the car park, breathed in the early morning air and did something he couldn't explain. He thought of Chrissy.

He thought of smooth, cool, smiling Chrissy, with her casual sex and no responsibility, and for a few moments, he wanted her more than he thought possible. Then he dismissed the thought and went back inside to see his baby.

And it was *his* baby. From the moment he arrived in the delivery suite and saw his daughter, Max fell in love. He felt such an extraordinary pull in his chest, such an overwhelming sense of the miracle of life that he was speechless.

'Max?' Anna stretched out to touch him, but she wasn't sure that she had reached him.

'I'm so sorry I wasn't here,' Max said. He took Anna's hand and pressed it against his lips. 'God, she's fantastic Anna!' He leant forward and peered at the odd, misshapen head, all wrinkled and ruddy. 'She's so perfect.' He looked up and Anna smiled. 'So incredibly perfect.' He gently kissed the baby's head and held the tiny, pink-cotton-wrapped bundle close to his chest. Anna, too, longed to feel his embrace.

'You want to call her Maya?'

She nodded.

'I think it suits her,' Max said. 'Maya Jacob Slater.' Then he stood and took her across to the window to look out at the new day. 'Maya, this is your world,' he said quietly. 'Welcome to it.'

And for some reason, when Anna should have felt elated and ecstatic, she felt lonely. It seemed that Max had moved a fraction further away from her and that now, more than ever, she had no idea how to get him back.

*   *   *

Debbie Pritchard was in the bath when the phone rang
later that morning. She was getting ready to go out,
although there was no interview to go to, that had been
purely fictitious. A bit like some of her references, only
she had had them so long now that even she had come to
think of them as real. She stood up, reached for a towel
and wrapped it around herself, plodding through to the
living area of her flat to answer the call.

'Hello?'

'Hello, is that Debbie Pritchard?'

'Yes.' She didn't recognise the voice and felt immediately nervous.

'Debbie. Hi, my name is Max Slater. Look, you don't
know me, but my wife Anna interviewed you last night
for a job with us?'

'Yes, yes of course.'

'Well, the thing is, Debbie, I'm ringing because we'd
like to offer you that job and it's to start immediately, if
you're still interested. You see Anna had the baby early
this morning, a little girl, and, well, we need to get things
organised straight away and—'

'Gosh, this morning!' Debbie said. 'Oh how exciting!
What's she called?'

'Maya.'

'How lovely I'm delighted for her, I mean, for you
both.'

Max could see why Anna had liked this woman, she
sounded totally genuine. 'Thanks.'

There was a moment's pause, then Debbie said, 'I'd love
the job, Mr Slater. I thought about it last night actually and
it's exactly what I'm looking for. I can phone and cancel
my other interview and start today if you like. I could
maybe come to the house and get the cot ready and shop

for a few things? Anna said she didn't have much in the way of stuff for the baby.'

Max heaved an audible sigh of relief. Thank God for that, he nearly said. The idea of him charging round Mothercare and battling with a cot had filled him with horror. As bowled over as he was by his daughter, he had never seen himself as a particularly hands-on father. 'Debbie,' he said, 'that would be marvellous!' On the other end of the line, he even smiled. 'I am at the hospital right now, but I'm going home to wash and change for work. Perhaps you could meet me at home in, say, an hour and a half and I'll give you a set of keys and some cash. Anna will be coming home tomorrow so it would be great to get things ready by then. Is that OK?'

'Yes, that's great,' Debbie said. She dropped her towel and reached for her dressing gown from the back of the chair. 'I'll be there at eleven and thank you, Mr Slater, I'm looking forward to working for you and Anna.' She hung up.

In the car park of the Chelsea and Westminster Hospital, Max sat for a few moments and wondered why he felt so relieved to be handing responsibility over to someone else, and in the living space of her studio flat, Debbie Pritchard hugged her arms around herself and smiled. A baby girl; it was practically fate because that was exactly what she would have liked herself.

Chapter Six

Will Turner sat in his study on the phone and rubbed his left knee. 'Andrew, you couldn't hang on a minute could you?' he said. 'I think I'll transfer this onto the conference line.'

'Yup, no problem.'

He replaced the receiver and pressed the button on his telephone, then stood up. 'You still there, Andrew?'

'Yes. Where was I?'

'The draft agreement for High Tech. Page seven, paragraph two.' Will moved away from his desk as Andrew McKie read out the relevant passage. He stretched his left leg and bent to rub his knee again, crossing over to the window as he did so. He had run too far last night, nearly sixteen miles, and his left knee ligament was stiff and sore.

'Does that sound better to you, Will? We amended clauses eight and nine to the figures you wanted.'

Will looked out of the window at the two gardeners planting a row of espalier pear trees along the south-east wall of the garden. He counted how many had gone in.

'Will?'

'Sorry Andrew. Did you say clauses eight and nine?' He reached over for his copy of the agreement. 'You've amended that to fifteen percent and nine percent respectively, yes?'

'Yes.'

Will glanced out at the garden again. There was something not quite right about those trees. He narrowed his eyes and held his fingers up.

'And we've added a new paragraph directly after that, Will, that should give you a bit of a let out if—'

'Bloody idiots!'

'Sorry? Will?'

'Sorry Andrew, not you, it's those blasted people outside. Christ! They call themselves gardeners. They couldn't grow a carrot in a heap of manure. Jesus!' He stomped back to his desk. 'Look, sorry Andrew, but can I call you back in an hour or so?'

Andrew McKie sighed. 'I'm in a meeting this afternoon, Will, and we've really got to get moving with this. The purchaser's lawyers are breathing down our necks and . . .' He stopped. The line had gone dead. 'Bugger,' he muttered and hung up.

'Sam!' Will strode across the expanse of lawn down towards the east wall of the garden. 'Sam? What the hell's going on? I thought I told you that these needed to be planted at least ten feet apart.' He arrived at the wall where his gardener, Sam Perkins, and his mate were digging and planting.

'What are you doing man?' He paced between each tree. 'There's barely eight feet between this one and that, and . . . five, six, seven . . . Jesus, just seven feet here! What's going on? Didn't you bring a measure out with you? When I say ten feet, Sam, I mean ten feet and nothing less.'

'Sorry, Mr Turner, I thought we was measuring it right.

I didn't realise you wanted 'em measured like that. We'll
dig 'em up and start again, won't we Bri?'

Bri, who was twenty years younger than Sam and less
concerned about his job, said nothing. He scowled and
finally, after Sam had kicked him, nodded and managed,
''Course, if that's what 'e wants.'

'Yes it is, Brian!' Will said sharply. 'It's exactly what
I want. They won't grow properly less than ten feet
apart. Surely you should know that. You've got a bloody
diploma in landscape gardening, for Christ's sake!'

'We didn't do nofing about fruit though,' Brian said in
his defence. 'It was all crazy paving and clematis.'

'Yes, well, I see.' Will was suddenly embarrassed. What
the hell was he doing, storming round the garden shouting at people like some Lord of the Manor? It had never
been his style at all. He dug his hands in his pockets and
said, 'The fence looks good.' He leant forward and tugged
at the wiring. 'Nice and secure that. Good work.'

'Thanks, Mr Turner,' Sam said. 'We'll get on then.'

'Yes, of course.' Will turned and walked slowly across
the grass back towards the house.

'Moody git!' Brian said.

'He's all right,' Sam answered him. 'He's had a lot of
trouble. He weren't never like it before an' I dare say
I'd be a bit the same if I'd had what happened to him
happen to me.'

'Guilty conscience if you ask me.'

'Well I didn't ask you, sonny!' Sam snapped. 'And mind
you don't go round saying things like that neither. It's a
bloody great shame all that business and I don't want to
hear otherwise, all right?'

Brian dug his spade deep into the soil. He didn't
answer.

'I asked you a question, sonny!'

'Yeah, all right,' Brian said.

'Good. Let's get on wiv these trees then.' Sam looked up towards the house. 'A bloody great shame,' he muttered, then he knelt and started to dig up the first tree they'd planted.

'Andrew? It's Will. Sorry, where were we?'

'Will? Are you all right? What on earth was that all about?'

Will ran his hands through his hair. It was long and wavy, too long, it needed a cut. 'I don't know to be honest. The gardeners have planted the pear trees too close together and for some reason I really lost it.'

There was a silence on the other end, then Andrew said, 'Why don't you think about getting away for a while, Will? It would do you good.'

'No. Nice try, Andrew, but no. I've no desire to go anywhere, I just want to stay here and get on with things.'

Andrew knew better than to labour the point. He and Will Turner had been good friends for a decade. It had started as a solicitor–client relationship and moved on quickly to friendship when the men discovered they had a lot in common. Lately it had shifted, very subtly, to something more trusting. Andrew was older than Will, a good thirty years older, and because Will had no parents Andrew had found himself, particularly of late, trying to fill that gap.

'We were on page seven paragraph two,' he said. 'You had checked the changes to clauses eight and nine and I was about to explain the new paragraph directly under those.'

Will sat down at his desk and placed the draft agreement in front of him. 'OK Andrew, fire away!' He picked up a pencil and as the older man talked, he made small notes in the margin that could be typed up by his secretary later.

When the call was finished, Will wandered through to the kitchen to make himself a coffee. It was mid afternoon and the house was cold and silent. He had a lady from the village, Sheila, who came in every day to manage things, but she left at lunch time so that he had the house to himself. It hadn't always been like that; she used to stay until she had to collect her kids from school and sometimes she brought them back with her. But now the thought of company, of other people rattling around the house with him, was unbearable.

Will poured boiling water onto some instant coffee and added a splash of cold tap water. He took the cup to the window and gazed out again at the garden. The trees looked better now, they were the right distance apart and the wall was beginning to take shape. He sipped. The coffee was awful but it was a long time since he had enjoyed the taste of anything. Perhaps Andrew is right, he thought, perhaps I do need a break, but whether Andrew was right or not was irrelevant; he knew that he would never take it.

He left the view of the garden and wandered back to his study to check that things were in order for his secretary. Jenna came in for a couple of hours a day, late afternoon, when he had finished all his work and was invariably out running. She typed up letters, filed things away, handled the post. She was young, attractive and pleasant but that made no difference.

Will avoided her, just as he avoided everyone else in his life.

His cup still in his hand, he walked back into the hall and noticed that the Turkish rug wasn't straight. That was something that never would have bothered him before, but now all life's trivial details seemed important. He put his cup down on the hall table, then bent and shifted the rug. As he did so, he dislodged something small and white and, kneeling down, he picked it up and realised what it was. He closed his eyes. It was a button, white mother of pearl, one of *her* buttons.

Dropping it on the floor, Will stood and walked out of the hall, up the stairs and into his bedroom. He took off his clothes and pulled an elastic bandage over his left leg to give it some support, followed by an old pair of track bottoms, a thermal top and a fleece. He bent and tugged on some socks, then walked downstairs to the pantry and found his running shoes by the back door. He put them on, laced them up and stood for a few moments, stretching his calf muscles, his quads and his hamstrings. Then he opened the back door and stepped out. He didn't lock up, Jenna would be there any minute, he put his head down into the wind and started his run. He didn't know where he was going, not an exact route, and he didn't know how far. Tonight he just wanted to run, for as far and as long as it took, because running was the only thing that eased the pain.

Max was in the shower when Debbie arrived at the house. He came downstairs dripping wet with a towel round his waist, opened the door, briefly introduced himself, told her to make herself at home and hurried back to the bathroom. Debbie took her coat off, went into the kitchen quite prepared to clear up a mess of breakfast things and found it immaculate. She warmed to Max immediately.

She made herself some tea and was just finishing it when he came down, dressed in a Prince of Wales check bespoke suit, a pale pink shirt with cut-away collar, gold cufflinks and a Kenzo tie. The look was tailored but creative, city with a dash of the left bank, and it was a style that Max had elevated to an art form. He was an attractive man and Debbie acknowledged that fact to herself.

'Would you like tea, Mr Slater?'

'Oh, thanks Debbie,' he said. 'And it's Max, please. Mr Slater makes me feel so old.'

Debbie smiled. She poured Max a cup of tea, handed it across, then turned to wash up her own mug.

'Why don't you use the dishwasher?' Max suggested.

'Oh no, it's only one cup and it'll take less than a minute.'

Max watched her as she dried her hands on a tea towel. Yes, he thought, she was exactly the sort of girl Anna would hire; medium height, plump but not unattractive, a nice smile and homely clothes all from M&S.

Debbie looked up. 'Do you have a list for me?'

'A list?' Max looked suddenly perplexed.

'I thought you might have a list of what you wanted me to do and things you wanted me to get?'

'Oh God, no! Should I have had? Anna didn't say, she just said phone you and—'

'No, no it's OK, I don't need a list. If you want me to go and buy the baby's layette I know exactly what to get, I've done it all before, but if there was anything particular, I mean . . .'

'No, nothing. Please, go and get whatever you think

we'll need. I know Anna has a few things in the drawer, so have a look at what she's got already and buy the rest. You must know what makes are better than others etcetera, far more than we ever would. I'll leave it up to you.' Max took his wallet out. 'I withdrew some cash this morning, I've got three hundred pounds. Is that enough?'

'Yes, I'd have thought so, plenty. We only need the basics at the moment.'

He held the money out and Debbie went into the hall to get her purse. 'I keep a separate purse for my charges,' she said, taking the cash and tucking it away in a red plastic wallet. 'I usually keep all the receipts and give them to my employer at the end of each week. Is that all right?'

'Yes, of course.' Max almost smiled. Supernanny had arrived. 'Right, I'll get going then,' he said. 'I'll probably come back this afternoon to catch up on a bit of sleep, before I go to the hospital.' He took a bunch of keys off the side. 'Here, have Anna's keys for the moment. Maybe you could get a set cut for yourself while you're out?'

'Yes, of course.'

'And get a cab for today, could you? I haven't had time to get insurance for Anna's car yet but I'll ring from the office this morning. OK?'

'Yes, fine.'

Max had the faint impression that Debbie was humouring him; oddly, she seemed to have the upper hand. He made for the front door. 'Oh, here's my card, with the office number on. If you need anything urgently then ring, OK?'

'Yes, thank you.'

At the door he stopped. 'I don't know what hours you'd agreed with Anna but . . .'

'Seven till seven,' Debbie said quickly. 'But I didn't start till eleven this morning so I'll stay late tonight to make up the extra hours.'

'There's no need,' Max said. 'I'm not worried, I'm sure you'll be working hard enough from tomorrow onwards.' He opened the door. 'You're welcome to come to the hospital with me later if you like, to meet Maya.'

Debbie blinked rapidly several times. She seemed surprised.

'Oh gosh, I'd love to!' She stopped. 'I mean, if it's not intruding or anything.'

The thought hadn't even occurred to Max. 'Not at all,' he said. 'Not in the least.' Why on earth would it be intruding? God, the last thing Anna would want was Max on his own, sat there for hours just staring at the baby and talking about work. 'You come! Anna will be delighted to see you.' He smiled, said a brief goodbye and left the house.

Debbie stood in the silence for a moment, a silence that after tomorrow would no longer exist, then without another thought for anything except the new baby, went up to the nursery to make a start on constructing the cot.

Andrew McKie was just on his way to a meeting when the phone rang. He was about to leave it, then remembered that he hadn't transferred his direct line through to reception and so walked back to answer it. He picked it up and said, 'Hello, McKie.'

There was a short silence on the end of the phone, then he heard her voice and immediately came round the desk and sat down. It knocked him for six. He couldn't help it, just the sound of her voice, the small, frightened words brought it all back to him and his chest ached.

'Of course I will,' he said. 'Please, don't worry, I'll sort it all out for you. Where are you?' He reached for a pen. 'No, don't tell me if you don't want to. Yes, of course I understand, just tell me where you want me to send the money.' He wrote down a post office address. 'No, I won't tell anyone . . .' He broke off, at odds with his conscience. 'Are you sure you don't want me to tell— OK, if that's what you want.' He knew he couldn't go against her wishes; it wasn't fair. He sighed. None of it was bloody fair! 'Yes I will,' he said, 'right away. Yes, cash. But tell me, are you all right? I mean, are you—' He didn't bother to finish. There was no point; she had hung up.

The young woman replaced the receiver and turned the collar of her coat up against the cold. She glanced behind her to check that she was alone and stepped out of the tube station into the damp morning air. She was permanently cold, chilled right through to her marrow, and her nose ran, constantly, with a miserable stream of mucus. She dug her hands into her pockets and felt the change in there. Seventy-five pence she had left, seventy-five pence to keep her alive until some money came through. She ran the coins through her icy fingers. It was enough. When you'd lost everything that had ever mattered to you, she thought, what difference did having a few coins make in life? Absolutely none.

Chapter Seven

Anna sat up in bed, washed and changed into the clean nightdress and dressing gown – pink sateen – that Max's mother had brought in for her and cursed herself silently for being so disorganised. She should have asked Max to bring a few things in on the way to work; she should have asked him to get Debbie to pack a small bag for her and Maya, but no, she had completely forgotten and had, as a result, had to accept Max's mother's offering, along with the half an hour of subtle chastisement that went with it.

'Of course when Max was born,' Jennifer said, 'I couldn't afford not to be ready. It was my job, you see Anna – running the home, looking after Max and my Peter, God rest him. It was my life and it was done properly.' There was a pause, while this particular message sank in and Anna ground her teeth. 'Should you be cuddling her so much, Anna darling? I wonder if it wouldn't be better to put her down for a while? Babies know, you know, they cotton on from a very early age and once you get into bad habits, then they're very difficult to break.' She stood and peered in at Maya's face pressed close to Anna's chest. 'She's asleep bless her. I'd put her down if I were you, Anna. No you see, if I hadn't been ready, Anna, had my bag packed and everything left in perfect order when the time came for Max to arrive, then I'd have been stuck, I didn't have anyone to help me. And Peter, well, he would never have known what things a woman wanted, not like the men do today – know far too much really if you ask me, but then that's modern life for you, isn't it?'

Max's mother helped herself to one of the deluxe M&S chocolate biscuits she'd brought for Anna and stood to peer at the baby again. 'She's just like Max,' she said. 'Exactly the same.' She sat down. 'A pity your father can't come over, Anna, a great shame. He must be upset, missing it all . . . Oh, here, let me help you, Anna darling, I'll take little Maya for you . . .'

'No, no it's all right.' Still sore, Anna climbed carefully off the bed and placed Maya in the clear plastic trolley cot. 'It's fine thanks, Jennifer. You're right, she should be put in her cot, so I'll leave her there while I go to the bathroom.' She slipped her feet into her slippers, took one of the biscuits and, smiling through gritted teeth, made her way down the ward and out into the corridor to find an unoccupied bathroom.

'My father upset,' she murmured. 'Ha! That'll be the day! He couldn't give a stuff.'

'You OK, Mum?' one of the midwives said.

'My name is Anna!' Anna answered sharply, then said, 'Sorry.'

The midwife smiled. 'It's only natural. Have a few minutes on your own, it'll put things in perspective.'

Anna shuffled off to the bathroom, shut and locked the door and sat down on the bath chair with her head in her hands. Why did Max's mother always have to bring up Anna's father? Why? Anna hadn't seen him since she married Max six years ago; they spoke once a year at Christmas and frankly even that was enough. He had married a woman thirty-five years his junior just a year after Anna's mother had died and Anna had never forgiven him. Anna swallowed back a lump in her throat, then gave up the pretence and let the tears come. Before she knew it there was a deluge and she sat in the NHS bathroom crying her eyes out.

Max had come home mid afternoon, when Debbie was out shopping, feeling stressed and exhausted. He had announced the baby's arrival at work that morning, then immediately regretted it as scores of people filtered into his office offering congratulations and expecting a jubilant reply. He knew he should have been jubilant, euphoric, ecstatic even, but he wasn't. He hadn't been able to face giving a blow-by-blow account of the labour and had passed it off as 'safe', whatever that meant. People kept asking him how he felt and although he knew he loved Maya, he wasn't at all sure about anything else. All he was aware of at that moment was exhaustion and an overwhelming sense of depression at the thought of seeing his mother that evening.

He poured himself a drink when he got in, but changed his mind and decided to go straight to bed. He undressed, took a shower and lay down under the duvet with the curtains drawn. It took him a long time to relax, to clear his mind, but eventually he managed it, and finally, he fell asleep.

Debbie came in at four thirty, laden with bags. She was well in control of the situation and that was exactly how she liked it. She had collected her sewing machine earlier in the day and had chosen some fabric for the nursery curtains that afternoon. Walking straight through to the laundry room, she unpacked the things she had just bought for the baby and piled them into the washing machine with some non-biological powder and some sensitive-skin conditioner; she had a thing about washing everything for new-born babies. She didn't bother to check what powder Anna had, she knew what she liked and from now on that would be what they used. That done, she collected up the nursery fabric, her sewing machine and her needlework basket and placed them on the kitchen table. She went upstairs, a tape measure round her neck, a notebook in her hand, to measure up. Finally, ten minutes later, she came down to the kitchen, made herself a cup of tea, cut the fabric out and began to make the nursery curtains.

Max woke with a start. It was dark, there was a light on somewhere outside his room and he could hear the sound of a sewing machine. He lay very still, overwhelmed with anger and disappointment. It was a childhood feeling and it flooded back to him, choking him with its intensity.

She had sewn, his mother, she had cooked and cleaned and washed and ironed. Her house was immaculate, you could have eaten your dinner off her kitchen floor, she used to tell him. Every inch of her home had been scrubbed and bleached and disinfected. Every tiny insect had been squashed, every spider's web crushed, every surface polished and every particle of air freshened with some kind of lavatorial smelling spray. She would work for hours in the house, cleaning and polishing, and she would spend whole afternoons sewing lace doilies or running up a toilet-roll cover to match the curtains in the bathroom.

But Max's mother had never played. She had never

laughed or sat down to paint great splodges of colour with Max, regardless of the mess. She had never watched *Blue Peter* with him or done his homework with him. She had never come outside on a warm summer's evening to watch him ride his bicycle in the cul-de-sac, or planted things with him in the garden. She was always too busy, too busy being busy.

'Don't you dare touch!' she would shout, swiping hard at Max with a damp tea towel and catching him sharply on the back of the legs. 'Get your filthy hands off!' She would smack him for not taking his shoes off and pinch him if he didn't fold his clothes properly as he got undressed for the bath. Her hands were always rough and chapped and smelled of bleach, but he never held them, they were never still long enough to hold.

Max sat up. He listened to the constant whine of the sewing machine somewhere downstairs and physically shuddered. He reached over, switched on the lamp and climbed out of bed. He had never, not once, in all his years as a child, had any attention, any real love. How the hell was he going to find it in him to give something he had no experience of? He pulled on some trousers and a T-shirt and walked out. Should people with unhappy childhoods have children? he wondered. He didn't know the answer. He went downstairs.

'Debbie?' He had almost forgotten who she was and what she was doing there.

Debbie glanced up from her sewing. She smiled, but when Max didn't return her smile, she looked momentarily embarrassed. She switched off the machine, the little light went out and Max slumped against the wall. He sighed with relief. 'God,' he said, rubbing his hands over his face, 'I wondered what the hell was going on. I couldn't work it out; I'd forgotten that you were here.'

Debbie fingered the curtains nervously. 'Sorry,' she murmured, 'I wanted to get on with these, I—'

'No, no please don't apologise.' He came into the room. 'I must have been disorientated, I never sleep during the day, it's thrown me completely.' He walked across and switched the kettle on, glancing at the kitchen clock. 'Christ! It's nearly six o'clock! Anna will be wondering where the hell I've got to. I'll just make a quick cup of tea then I'd better get going. D'you still want to come?'

'Please. I got something for the baby and for Anna, I—'

Max clapped his hand to his forehead. 'Bloody hell! I've forgotten to get her something. I haven't even got any flowers.' He darted out of the kitchen into the hall and rifled in his briefcase. 'I'll give the florist a quick ring and see if they're still open. I've got the number in here somewhere, in my Filofax I think . . .' He found a card and dialled the number on it from the hall telephone. 'Bugger! It's an answerphone; they're closed.'

Debbie stood and went into the hall. She picked up a Mothercare bag and held it out to Max. 'Here,' she said, 'take this for the baby and I've bought several bunches of tulips, they're in a bucket in the laundry room. I could arrange them and put a ribbon round them if you want.'

Max looked at her aghast. 'Good Lord no! I couldn't possibly take the things that you've bought for Anna.' He shook his head and went back into the kitchen to make the tea. 'It's a nice thought though, Debbie, I appreciate it.' Debbie had followed him in and began to fold one curtain over the back of the chair, smoothing the material and making neat the pleats on the heading. He went to the fridge for milk. 'Would you like a cup?'

'No thanks, I've just had one.' She stopped folding and looked at Max. 'I really don't mind, you know, giving you the gifts.' She didn't mind, that much was true. It made her feel good to think that the first thing Maya would cuddle would be something that she had bought. 'It's only a small teddy and a few flowers. It would help you out of a tough spot and I'll get something for Anna to come home to tomorrow.'

'You don't have to get anything at all, Debbie, it's terribly kind of you to have gone to all that trouble.' It was kind, but Max was missing the point. It was also clever. It placed Debbie in a position of power but he couldn't see that at all; he was too consumed with embarrassment and guilt. In all honesty he wanted to leap at her offer, but his pride wouldn't let him. 'No really, I couldn't possibly . . .'

'I honestly don't mind and there might not be anything open now. Anyway it means you don't have to waste any more time, we can go straight to the hospital.'

Max looked at Debbie. Her face was open and eager to please and it would have been rude not to accept her offer, or so he convinced himself. 'If you're absolutely sure, Debbie . . .'

'Yes, of course.'

'Then thanks, I really appreciate it.' He smiled, one of his warmest, most charming smiles. 'Can I take you up on the offer to put a ribbon round the flowers?'

'Yes, no problem.'

'Great! I'll leave you to it then and go up and get myself changed. We'll aim to leave in, what, ten minutes? OK?'

'Yes, fine.'

Max took a final gulp of tea and threw the rest down the sink. 'What have you been making by the way?'

'Curtains, for the baby's room.' Debbie held up the one finished curtain and a pattern of pink and purple teddies danced on a background of turquoise fluffy clouds.

Max swallowed. Anna was a strictly no-fuss checks and stripes woman. He smiled again, this time less warmly and charmingly. 'Gosh,' he said, 'aren't they jolly? Well done you.' And unable to think of anything else to say, he went upstairs to get changed.

Anna was trying to feed the baby when Max and Debbie arrived. Maya was cross and tired and wouldn't latch on properly and Anna sat stiff and unyielding, dark shadows under her eyes, a fractious baby in her arms and an expression of grim determination on her face.

'Your mother's here,' she said to Max, hardly lifting her face. 'She's gone to get herself a drink. She's been here all afternoon.'

Max sat down on the edge of the bed. 'God Anna, poor you.' He touched her arm. 'Are you OK?'

'Do I look OK?' Anna snapped. 'Maya won't feed properly, I've been talked at and subtly told off for absolutely everything you could think of from my job to the state of the house and why didn't I decorate it myself instead of costing you all that money by getting people in and, God, I know I love her Max and I know that she's true and deep down kind at heart, but if she utters one more word about how I have to put Maya down and let her cry a bit to stop myself from spoiling her, then I'm going to scream.'

'Well tell her then. Tell her to shut up, for God's sake!'

Anna shook her head. Jennifer may have been his mother but he had very little patience with her. 'Don't be silly, Max, she means well and . . .'

'You're too kind, Anna! She can be an old battleaxe and it's only you that puts up with it. Everyone else tells her to—'

'Everything all right, Anna darling?'

Max stopped and turned as his mother appeared, as if by magic, at the end of the bed. Anna nodded and blushed.

'Hello Mother,' Max said, standing to kiss his mother's cheek. 'Did you manage to get yourself a drink?'

'No, I could only find a machine and I didn't have any loose change.'

'Here, I've got some.' He dug in his pocket at the same time that Anna reached for her handbag and Debbie pulled her purse out of her bag.

Max glanced at Anna and held down the urge to laugh. They were all so keen to get rid of her that they were falling over themselves with loose change. 'Loads of the stuff,' he said. 'A piggy bank's worth. Here, here's a couple of pounds, go and find a cup of tea, you must be gasping.'

Debbie pulled a *Hello!* magazine out of her bag. 'Would you like to have a look at this? I got it this morning.'

Jennifer glanced at Debbie.

'Oh sorry, Mother. Debbie, this is my mother, Jennifer Slater. Mother, this is Debbie, our new nanny.'

Jennifer nodded. It wasn't her habit to shake hands with staff. 'How do you do?'

Anna held the baby out and said, 'Debbie, would you like to have a cuddle and see if you can calm her down a bit. She's been really grumpy all afternoon.'

'Yes, of course.' Debbie stepped forward and took the baby, who stopped grizzling almost immediately.

Anna sat back and breathed a sigh of relief and Max's mother said, 'Well it's amazing what a difference it makes with someone who knows what they're doing.'

Max cringed, Anna bristled and, exchanging looks, they completely missed the expression of joy and longing that came over Debbie's face as she gazed down at baby Maya.

'I'll get my tea then,' Jennifer said, 'now that the baby is in capable hands.'

'You do that, Mother,' Max said.

'And take your time . . .' Anna murmured under her breath as Jennifer disappeared down the ward. She looked at Max, who shrugged but made no further comment.

'I got you these,' Max said, changing the subject and taking the tulips that Debbie had arranged, very nicely he thought, with a pink gingham ribbon, out of a carrier. 'And this for Maya.'

He took out the bear, perhaps not quite what he would have chosen himself, and handed it over. Anna took it. She held it and looked at it very carefully, at the soft fur, the pink bow tie, the brown felt paws and soppy expression, and for a moment he thought she was going to say that it wasn't to her taste and could he take it back. He glanced up at Debbie, but she had wandered off with the baby, probably to give them both a bit of space.

'Thank you, Max,' Anna said. Her face had softened and she smiled at him. 'You chose this?' She held it up and waved one of its paws at him. He flushed and nodded. 'It's brilliant!' He arched an eyebrow. 'No, I mean it! The fact that you went out and got something yourself means a great deal. It's Maya's first teddy and it's from you. Thank you.'

Max held up his hands. 'Hey! Don't get carried away. I'm glad you like it, but I'm sure there'll be plenty more by the time she's one.' He laughed, to cover his acute embarrassment, and took the flowers off the bed. 'Shall I get a vase for these?'

'No, sit down and hold my hand. The nurse will do it later.'

Max looked uneasy.

'Please?'

He sat and took Anna's fingers in his own. They sat in silence for a few minutes, then suddenly Anna said, 'Are you happy?'

Max was startled, then uncomfortable. 'Yes, erm, I suppose so.'

Anna looked at him. 'It hasn't been easy, the last six months, me pregnant, the partnership, you working all hours, but it'll be better now, Max, the three of us together, I'm sure of it.' She smiled. 'If we can just dodge your mother that is!'

Max smiled back, but he thought his face might give away the effort it cost him. He didn't know if he had the energy or the desire left to play happy families. 'Of course it will,' he said. 'Of course it will.'

The house was dark and empty when Max got home. It smelt of washing powder and fabric conditioner and there was the faint lingering odour of bleach where Debbie had disinfected the kitchen floor to remove any traces of Anna's waters. It made him feel sick.

He went straight to the fridge to open a bottle of beer and took a sip, walking with it in his hand through to the sitting room. He felt depressed and alone. So this was it, this was the big parenthood thing, this aftermath of confusion was the birth experience, this insecurity, this longing for he didn't know what was his future. He sat down on the edge of the sofa in the dark and thought about Chrissy. He didn't want to think about her, it wasn't a conscious decision, she had just slipped into his mind as easily, he imagined, as she would slip into his life. She was there, cool, detached and undemanding.

Standing, he walked into the hall, roaming the house like a stranger. He glanced at his reflection in the hall mirror, at his tired, hang-dog expression and said, 'You are thirty-six Max, come on, get a grip.' But the moment he said it was the moment that he realised something. As much as he loved Anna, as strong as his emotions for his daughter were, he still felt trapped. He was *only* thirty-six, he was too young to be snared by something he wasn't sure that he wanted. He was too young to be worn down by parenthood, to have the sort of expression he saw on other men's faces, the sour, dissatisfied look. He took another sip of his beer and as he turned away from the mirror, his phone rang. He took it out of his pocket and answered it.

'Hello?'

'Max? It's Chrissy.'

He watched his face in the mirror and saw it change. It visibly changed and he looked younger, more alive.

'I know it's probably not the right time, but I was wondering if you might like to come over and have a drink. Wet the baby's head?'

Max hesitated, but only for one brief second. He wasn't thinking; after today, he didn't want to think.

'Yes, yes I would.'

Chrissy smiled on the other end of the phone and he heard the smile in her voice. 'Good,' she said. 'I'm ready when you are.'

It was done.

Max ended the call, walked out of the house, got in his car and drove to Chrissy Forbes. She was waiting for him, she had got what she wanted. And Max, Max had got more than he could have imagined.

Chapter Eight

The fourth battalion of the Royal and Blues pulled into Winchester Depot in convoy after an eight-week training exercise in Canada. The lorry at the front drew to a halt and Private Darren Woodman jumped down off the back of it with the rest of his platoon. They headed up towards the barrack block.

'Jesus! I can't wait to see my missus, I'm gonna shag 'er senseless tonight. Eight bloody weeks without it, she'll be gagging for it.'

'Shut up, Banks! We don't wanna know about your sex life, ya dirty bastard!'

'You're just jealous mate.'

'Go on!'

Darren walked on ahead of the banter and caught up with the sergeant.

'All right Woodman?'

'Sergeant.'

'You doing anything nice this weekend? Going home to family?'

'Going home to see my mum, Sergeant, and my girl-friend. Have a few drinks with me mates. Usual thing.'

'Very nice.'

'Woody?'

Darren turned. Carlson, one of the other soldiers from his platoon, ran to catch up with him. 'I got us a lift with Stead. He's taking you, me and Billy. All right?'

'Yeah, great! Thanks!' The sergeant walked off and Darren said, 'Where're you being dropped?'

'Ealing. I'll get the tube up to King's Cross from there. Get out there with me if you like. We could maybe have a few drinks up the West End before I get me train.'

'Yeah, OK, you're on!'

'Right, let's get this kit cleaned then, Woody me old mate! The sooner we do that, the sooner we can piss off out of here.'

Darren sat in the corridor outside his room and listened to the chat. He had his head down cleaning, had done his weapons and had them checked and was now finishing his kit. He was tired, the flight was catching up with him and he had a sick churning in the pit of his stomach at the thought of ringing Debbie. He didn't know what she was going to say and, Christ, if his mum ever found out what had happened, she'd go loopy! Jesus! What the hell had he been thinking of, hitting her? He must have been out of his tree.

'You nearly done there, Woodman?'

Darren looked up. 'Yes sir.'

Lieutenant Pope, the platoon commander, squatted down to Darren's level and picked up a piece of kit. He looked at it, turning it over in his hands, and said, 'Well done. Quick too. You must be eager to get away, Woodman.'

'You could say that sir.' Darren smiled.

'How do you feel it went, Darren, this exercise?'

'Personally, sir, I thought it went pretty well. There

were a couple of team cock-ups but I was pleased on the whole, sir, I got a lot out of it.'

Lieutenant Pope smiled. 'Yes, I thought you did. You've matured, Darren, you put in a good performance out there and I think it's time we started thinking about what next.' He stood up again. 'Come and see me when you get back off leave, will you?'

Darren grinned; he couldn't help himself. 'Of course sir!' he said.

'Good. And have a great one.'

'I will sir.'

Darren watched Lieutenant Pope disappear up the corridor. He finished his kit, packed it away and grabbed his stuff for the shower. He'd already decided of course, he'd thought it through on exercise, he had to do what was right, take care of her and stuff. But Christ, if this promotion really came off then he'd be made! It could really come together for him – wife, baby, new job and married quarters.

In the shower room he pulled off his tracksuit and stepped under the hot powerful stream. Maybe, just maybe, for once in his life, things could work out for him; he was young, he had it all to look forward to. He smiled and lathered his body with the Calvin Klein shower gel his mum had bought him. God, he thought, suddenly filled with a brittle confidence, he couldn't wait to see his mum's face when he told her.

Changed into civvies and smelling of the matching CK aftershave, Darren made his way across to the NAAFI for a drink and to make his phone call. It was late afternoon and he knew she didn't finish work until seven. He took his wallet out of the back pocket of his jeans and found the slip of paper she had written her work number on, along with his phone card. Then he bought a can of Coke and went to the booth. He opened the drink, took a swig straight from the can, swallowed, then belched quietly. He put his card into the slot, dialled the number, the line rang and he waited. It was answered.

'Hello? May I speak to Debbie please?'

There was the sound of a screaming child in the background and the faint echo of a television. 'Debbie?'

'Yes, Debbie Pritchard.'

'Oh God! You mean the nanny Debbie? No, you may not speak to her, I'm afraid she upped and left two months ago. She wouldn't come in and work her notice and left us completely in the shit.'

'So she's not there?' It was a stupid thing to say, he realised that as soon as he'd said it.

'No, she bloody well isn't here, I've just said! Are you thick or something?' There was a crash, it sounded as if it was right by the phone, then a loud scream, a child's.

'You wouldn't know where she's gone would you?'

There was a brief silence. 'Sorry?'

'You wouldn't know where she's gone would you? You don't have a forwarding number for her?'

'No I bloody well don't! She didn't ask for a reference and nor was she likely to get one for that matter. The last week she was here she was positively dangerous. She didn't know what the hell she was doing. It's probably a blessing that she left, because the way she was behaving I'd have had to sack her sooner or later. Anyway, who the hell are you?'

'I'm a friend.'

'Really? Well you'll have her home number then, won't you? Ring her there!' The line went dead.

'Hello? Are you—' Darren stopped. 'Shit!' He slammed down the receiver and left the NAAFI. Outside in the cool air, he finished his Coke and thought about what to do. He wasn't sure he did have her home number, she always rang him from work, used her employer's phone to save money. He thought he'd written it down on a piece of paper somewhere but where he'd put it he had no idea. Perhaps he should ring directory enquiries, he knew where she lived, he'd been there often enough. Or was she ex directory? He headed back to the barrack block, his earlier confidence fading.

In his room he rifled through his drawers and his diary but found nothing. Carlson, just out of the shower, put his head round the door. 'You ready then, Woody?'

'Yeah, just got a few calls to make in the NAAFI.'

'Borrow Stead's mobile, you dick! You don't need to go to the NAAFI.'

'Nah, I want a bit of privacy. Thanks for the offer though, I'm sure Stead appreciates it!' He ducked as a towel came in his direction. 'Hey Carlson?' He went to the door and called after his mate.

Carlson turned, in just his underpants. 'Make it quick, Woody, I'm freezing me bollocks off!'

'Remember Debbie?'

'Yeah.'

'You wouldn't know what I did with her phone number, that first night we met, would you?'

'You are joking, aren't you Woody? I was as pissed as a fart and you didn't come back, if I remember correctly, you dirty bastard!'

'Yeah, right.'

'Try that poncy jacket you was wearing. The ferret skin, or something . . .'

'Moleskin!' Darren smiled and went to his wardrobe. He found the jacket and searched the pockets. In the inside pocket there was the scrap of paper with his own, almost illegible handwriting on it. Bingo, he thought, and tucked the paper into his address book, heading straight back to the NAAFI. His stomach had begun to churn again. When he got there, the phone was in use, so he waited for several minutes trying to rehearse in his head what he was going to say. Once it was free, Darren dialled Debbie's home number and heard the answerphone click on.

His mind raced frantically as the message played, then he said, 'Hello Debbie? It's Darren. I just got back off exercise in Canada and I'm coming up to London. Look, I want to see you. I'm sorry, you know, for all that stuff last time, I got it wrong and well . . .' He broke off. He was silent for some time, tongue-tied and embarrassed. The tape recorded on and he said nothing. He swallowed, his mouth suddenly dry. There was a bleep and the phone cut off. 'Bugger!' He re-dialled, waited for the answerphone and made a second attempt. 'Debs? It's me again. Look, I've been thinking and I acted like a real prat, I know that now and I'm sorry, I really am. I want to work things out, Deb, I'm sure we can. I'm getting a lift up and I sort of wondered if I could crash with you? If you get this message before . . .' He looked at his watch. 'Before five thirty, then give me a ring at the depot.' He reeled off the number of the depot switchboard, then said, 'Look, I really want to see you. OK? I mean it.' He hung up. His palms were sweating and he was short of breath. That was the most he had said to any girl, ever.

Making his way across to the barrack block, he reckoned he would cancel drinks with Carlson. It wasn't that he didn't want to go – a couple of months ago he'd have leapt at the chance and still did fancy a night out to be honest. But now he'd made his mind up, things were different. Now he had to get things sorted and he had to do it tonight. If they got it all worked out tonight, then tomorrow they could tell his mum.

Max was dog tired. He had been up five times in the night. Not actually really helping – with Anna feeding the baby, what in reality could he do? Perhaps that was half the problem, he had been up and around, but useless, surplus to requirements, and even when he had insisted that Anna go back to bed while he changed Maya, she had screamed inconsolably and he'd had to call Anna in the end for another feed.

Five times. Five times of being told that there was nothing that he could do, except get glasses of water and make tea, five times of feeling inadequate. And then it was up at seven, shower and shave, cutting his chin because he could hardly see straight, then dress and go to work, feeling like a complete zombie, while Anna and Maya slept on through the morning.

He would have to move into the spare room sooner or later, he couldn't take much more of this. He'd had a month of it now and he was ready to drop. A whole month of constantly waking in the night, of endless crying, colic Anna called it, of feeling peripheral. A month of going to work wondering how he would get through the day, of never having an evening meal in peace, of the house looking eternally shambolic, of an oddly pervasive smell lingering all over the place, in the bedrooms, the bathroom, the sitting room, an odour that was a mixture of sick, dirty nappies, sterilising fluid and soap powder. A month of Anna's hormones making her erratic and difficult, of him constantly trying to fit in, to be there and failing miserably. What was the point? There was never any peace, any solitude, he was always tense . . .

'Max?'

He opened his eyes.

Chrissy lifted her hips and Max's limp penis slithered out of her. 'I don't really see the point,' she said, looking down, 'do you?'

Max shook his head. 'No. Sorry.'

She moved away and stood up. She was a magnificent sight naked – firm and lean, tanned all over. She had round, pert buttocks, very slightly muscular, and breasts that tilted upward with large, dark nipples. As she turned, confidently aware of the image she presented, she played with her breasts for a few moments, then glanced at Max's crotch again. There was no reaction – nothing.

'Oh well,' she said, shrugging her shoulders, 'it was worth a try.' She reached for her underwear and shirt, and dressed while Max lay on her bed, propped up against the pillows, and closed his eyes.

'Max!' Chrissy said sharply. 'Having a bad day in the erection department I can cope with, but having you fall asleep I cannot. WAKE UP!'

Max instantly sat up. 'Jesus! What the . . .' He saw Chrissy and rubbed his eyes. 'That was unnecessary,' he said. 'You didn't have to shout, I wasn't asleep.'

'Liar! You were just drifting off.' She came across to the bed. 'Max, I'm sorry sweetie, but you have to make up your mind what you want. I won't have you coming round here to catch up on some bloody sleep, it's not fair! I deserve more than that.' Max reached for her hand but she pulled it away. 'I mean it, Max,' she said. 'I don't want to be just your escape from domestic boredom. I want an affair, an intensely sexual, can't keep our hands and mouths off each other affair. I don't want a quick one and then a couple of hours' sleep or watching the footy together on the telly.' She took a step back. 'You see my point, don't you Max?'

He nodded.

'I want it all. I want to get on in my career and my life and I want to have fun, loads of it. I don't want babies, I don't want any of the domestic thing. I want to be spoilt, not spend my life spoiling someone else. I am not a wife and mother type, Max, and I don't want a limp cock. I want hot sex.' She moved another step back. 'You see, I know what I want and I'm sorry, Max, but I think you have to decide what you want too.'

He stared at her. Her face was flushed from sex and from losing her cool and her nipples were erect where they had rubbed against the fitted silk of her shirt.

'I don't need to decide,' he said. 'I already know.' Chrissy raised an eyebrow. 'I want the same as you.'

Her eyes went to Max's groin. 'And what about Anna?' she said, keeping her eyes fixed as she undid her shirt and bra and then her skirt. 'What does she want?' It was a daring question, but she reckoned she had Max in a good position. Her assertiveness had excited him. She dropped all three items to the floor and stood naked.

'Anna?' Max said. He knelt up and reached for Chrissy. She stepped into his embrace and he pulled her breasts towards his mouth. 'I really don't know what Anna wants.' Chrissy reached between his legs. He moaned. 'I just don't know.'

'I want to make this work!' Anna cried, flinging an electric breast pump down onto the bed. 'But I just don't seem to be able to get it right.' She was close to tears. 'I have to make it work, Debbie, I've got to go back to my job next week and I have to make it work.'

Debbie stood with Maya and handed her across to Anna. 'You're tired,' she said, 'and stressed about going back to the office. Give it time, it'll work, I'm sure it will. You just have to keep practising. Here, feed Maya and then have a go at expressing the side that she doesn't take.'

Anna took the baby. She latched the tiny rosebud mouth onto her nipple and sat back, taking a deep breath to try to relax. She felt the familiar let-down reflex and closed her eyes.

'Thanks Debbie,' she said, 'I really don't know what I'd have done without your help these last few weeks.'

Debbie shuffled some magazines, tidying them into a pile.

'I desperately want to get back to work, to stimulate my brain and get some sort of life back, but at the same time I can't bear the thought of leaving Maya.' Anna looked at Debbie. 'I feel terribly relieved to have you working for me, Debbie, knowing that I can trust you.'

Debbie glanced up. She smiled, very briefly, then went to the carrycot by the side of the bed and began to strip the sheets off it.

'Oh God, while I remember it, Debbie, I couldn't have the number of your last employer, could I? I thought I'd just touch base with them, let them know how you're getting on; just a formality really.' Anna stroked Maya's head as she suckled. 'Have you seen much of them?'

Debbie was silent for a moment. She finished tucking a clean cot sheet into the carrycot, then stood straight and said, 'Just the once. I baby-sat for them a few weeks ago.'

'Oh, how nice. How were they all?'

'Fine. It was really good to see them.'

'Excellent. Well, if you could leave me the number, then I'll give them a ring over the next few days.'

'Yes, sure.'

Debbie walked out of the bedroom with the dirty linen and Anna gently placed a sleeping Maya on the bed next to her. She applied the pump to her breast once more, switched it on and took another deep breath to relax herself. She felt the let-down reflex again and for the first time, the pump and Anna both worked. Thank God for Debbie, Anna thought, she really knows what she is doing.

The young woman carefully picked up the trailing red geranium in its small plastic container and tapped the bottom of it. She squeezed the sides of the pot and gently lifted the plant out, holding it by the stem and keeping the root ball untouched. She scooped out a hole in the compost big enough to take the root ball, then she placed it in, and firmed the soil all around it. She stood back, looked at the arrangement so far and smiled.

She had two window boxes for the front balcony here, one to actually go under the kitchen window and one to attach to the iron railings. She had already planted a pot to go by the front door and in the narrow slice of sunlight that the front of her flat got each morning, she was content that things would grow very nicely. It pleased her.

A pink verbena next, she decided, liking the eclectic mix of colour and texture, then a silver helichrysum and finally some white trailing petunias. She lined the pots up and worked quickly, scooping out compost, firming it and enjoying the feeling of warm soil in her hands. When she had finished, she turned to the next window box and planted what was left of her selection from the garden centre, then she went inside, filled her watering can and came back out with it. She watered, first the pot by the door, then each window box in turn, slowly, letting the water seep in, darkening the compost. She was in no hurry and she wanted to make sure that the plants had a good soaking to start with. The young woman knew, from experience, that things needed to get off to a good start if they were going to have any chance in life. That done, she scratched an itch on her face, leaving a streak of soil there, and went inside, closing the door behind her and wiping her hands on her dungarees before filling the kettle for a cup of tea.

The young woman had been in her flat for several weeks now and since the money came through from the lawyers she had started to make it into a home. She had plants everywhere; plants made a home, she thought, gave it life and she liked to nurture things, to look after them. She had scattered rugs over the threadbare carpet, rugs that she had got from the housing association, and she had put up posters of paintings that she particularly liked, Paul Klee, Gustav Klimt and the most beautiful reproduction of a fifteenth-century Russian Madonna and Child. She felt content. She wasn't happy; the young woman could hardly remember happiness, but she was settled, which was enough.

The kettle boiled and she made herself a cup of tea, but as she came into the hall, she saw a figure at the door through the frosted glass panel and stood absolutely still, pressing herself back against the wall. There was a loud banging and her heart began to race.

'Are you in there? Open up! I know you're in there. Open the door.'

The young woman pressed herself back tighter against the wall, her palms flat and sweating against the peeling wood chip. She closed her eyes. The figure bent, she heard the letter box rattle and stifled a sob.

'I know you're in there, there's no point in pretending.' The voice was hard and rough, full of anger. It poured in through the letter box and rebounded off the walls, each word making the young woman flinch. 'You can't hide from me, you know, you'll never be able to hide from me. I will always find you. Always!' She started to cry.

'Fuck it! Open the fucking door!' There was a kick, the front door rattled, another kick and the young woman cried out.

'I knew you were in there. I knew it! Come out, you fucking murderess! Come out and face me!'

She sank down to the floor, with her head in her hands, weeping uncontrollably.

'Murderer!' There was a loud smash as the pot by the front door was thrown against the wall, then the window boxes. 'Open the fucking—' There were voices, men, a scuffle. The young woman stopped weeping and listened, holding her breath to stop the sobs. 'Get off me!' she heard. 'Take your hands off . . .' She jerked back as the front door was kicked again and put her hands up to her face. 'I'll be back . . .' she heard, the voice fading. 'You won't escape me, I'll be . . .' There was no more. She opened her eyes and sat there, huddled and shivering.

The young woman had rarely been happy but she was often frightened. Now she was terrified.

*　　　*　　　*

Debbie opened the door of her flat and immediately saw the red light flashing on her answerphone. She walked in, dumped her bag on the table and went past the machine to hang her coat up. As she did so, she pressed play. The first message was from her mother; she ignored it. The second made her stop what she was doing and stand still. She caught her breath. It was from Darren. She turned to listen, a dull thumping anxiety starting in the pit of her stomach. The third message was from him too. As it played on, she looked at her watch. It was five twenty, Anna had let her go early, seeing as it was Friday and she wasn't back at work yet, so there was still time to ring him. She heard the number but didn't register it. What the hell did that mean – I'm sorry and I want to work things out?

Debbie sank down on the arm of the sofa, the coat hanger still in her hand. She felt sick, her palms had begun to sweat and she instinctively reached up and touched her left eye. He was sorry? She gently rubbed her finger over and over the patch of skin just under the eye socket, the area that had several weeks ago been livid with a bloody purple and black bruise. She took a couple of deep breaths, then stood and went to the phone. She replayed the messages, listened to them one more time, then she erased them. She took a hand-sized purple velvet elephant out of her bag and held it close to her chest. He was sorry. Silently, she began to cry.

Darren jumped out into the road and flagged down a free taxi. He narrowly missed an oncoming car, which blasted its horn, and he swore violently at it. Carlson, only just able to stand up, watched from the pavement, outside the Roundhouse on Garrick Street, Covent

Garden. He cheered when Darren secured the cab and staggered over.

'You first, yeah?'

Darren helped Carlson in. 'No way. I'm gonna put you on your train, mate, or you'll never get home.' Darren climbed in after Carlson. 'King's Cross first, then Lavender Hill.' He slammed the door. 'Can you wait for me at King's Cross?'

'You're better off getting another cab, mate!' the driver called into the back. 'There's never any shortage.'

'Oh, right.'

Carlson's head had slumped back against the seat and he'd closed his eyes.

'Good night was it?' the cabbie called.

'Yeah, it was all right.' Darren was still reasonably sober. He hadn't planned to go with Carlson, he'd more or less made up his mind to go straight to Debbie's, but then Carlson had gone on and on about not wanting to go out on the piss on his own and how important it was to stick with your mates, so in the end Darren had agreed. He had agreed to a couple of pints and now it was after ten. A couple of pints to Carlson meant at least six. Darren rubbed his hands over his face. He felt lousy. He was tired and his mind felt fuzzy, unclear. Perhaps he ought to get a couple of cans to take round to Deb's flat; it might ease things a bit, give him a bit of confidence. He looked out of the window at a blur of lights and his stomach began to churn again.

Debbie heard the main door buzzer as she stepped out of the shower. She looked at her watch and felt instantly alarmed. Drying herself, she pulled on her nightdress and dressing gown, stepped into her slippers and tried to pretend that she hadn't heard anything. As she went into the kitchen to make herself a hot drink, it sounded again and she knew who it was. Standing with the kettle in her hand, she was motionless, not knowing what to do. The buzzer sounded a third time, it was more insistent and Debbie walked over to the intercom.

Later, when she thought about that night, she couldn't remember why she had pressed the button, she could remember only what had happened afterwards. She knew she hadn't wanted to see Darren and yet that made no difference, she still opened the door for him. Perhaps it was fear, perhaps it was something altogether different, a need for him, a need to be loved. Whatever it was, she opened the door and a few minutes later, he was there, inside her flat, the same handsome, dazzling young man who had the last time made love to her and hit her, both in the same night.

He held a four-pack of lager and a bottle of wine.

'Here,' he said, handing them over to her as he came in. 'And I got you these.' He held out a box of Quality Street.

Debbie said nothing. She took the beer and wine into the kitchen and placed them on the work surface. She turned and Darren was watching her. He dug his hands in his pockets. 'I know you're angry,' he said, 'and I don't blame you. I acted like a right pillock last time. I'm sorry, Deb, I really am.' He moved a step forward and Debbie took a pace back. She was pressed against the wall. 'God! You're scared of me aren't you?'

She didn't answer.

He hung his head. 'Jesus! I've made a right frigging mess of things, haven't I?' They were silent for a few moments, then he looked up. 'I want to make it up to you, Debbie,

I really do. I've had a lot of time to think, while I've been away, and I've realised how stupid I was. I should never have hit you, I know that, and I should never have said all those things. I wasn't thinking straight, it was a shock, the baby and stuff, and I just couldn't take it in. I was drunk. I thought you'd done it on purpose to trap me, I mean what with us only going out a few weeks and . . .' He put his hands to his face. God, this wasn't going to work! He felt the tears well up in the back of his throat. 'Look Debbie, I want us to have the baby, all right, I want to be a dad to it and to look after you. Christ! What more do I have to say? Please, talk to me, Debbie, tell me that it's OK, please . . .'

Debbie dropped her hands down by her sides. She had been clenching them together and the blood rushed to them now, making them tingle. Darren moved towards her and she didn't resist. She let him hold her, let him lay his wet face on her shoulder and all the time she was thinking, *I cannot tell him, he must not know.* Darren pulled back and looked at her.

'Do you forgive me, Debbie? Can I stay?' He moved his hands down across her back, stroking her, comforting her. 'Say you forgive me, Debbie,' he murmured. 'Please say it . . .'

Debbie nodded. She reached up and touched his hair. How could she not forgive him? Just touching him thrilled her, just being close to him made her lose track of herself, made her imagine that she was someone special, not ordinary, plain Debbie Pritchard. And he loved her, even if he hadn't said it she knew that he loved her and that he wanted to take care of her. How could she hold out, despite her pain?

Darren caught her hand, kissed it and gently led her

towards the bedroom. There, he sat down on the bed and pulled her down beside him. 'Is it OK? I mean with the baby? I don't want to hurt you in any way.'

Debbie touched the skin under her eye, it had become almost a reflex action. Darren moved her fingers away and kissed the spot that he had bruised. 'I won't ever hurt you again, Debbie, I promise you.' He believed it too, until the next time. He untied her dressing gown. 'So? Is it OK?'

She smiled. 'Yes,' she said, 'it's fine.' She closed her eyes and let him undress her, let him kiss and caress the soft roundness of her belly and let him make love to her. Of course he would never hurt her again, he wanted to protect her, her and the baby. She closed her eyes and let her mind go blank. She could think of nothing because her thoughts were too ugly to bear.

Afterwards, he made her tea and brought it back to bed. 'I don't suppose you want a drink, do you? A glass of wine?'

'No. I'll have a chocolate though.'

Darren smiled. 'I did something right then?' He got the box of Quality Street and opened it, finding the green triangle. 'My favourite,' he said. 'You can have it.'

'Thanks.' Debbie unwrapped the sweet and popped it in her mouth. Darren watched her. She had pulled her dressing gown on but he could see the skin on her chest, faintly pink where he had kissed it. She was lovely. Not beautiful, but nice looking, she had a pretty smile, kind and warm. And she dressed nicely too. She was never tarted up like some of the trollops on the camp but she always looked smart, had her hair brushed and her shoes and handbag matching. His mother was going to love her. Darren found her another green triangle and then went to get himself a lager.

'So, how's your job?' He came back to bed and sat on the edge of it in his jockey shorts, drinking from the can.

'My job?'

He was pissed off about this, but he didn't want to make too much of it, not yet. 'Yes, your job,' he said. 'How's it going?'

'Fine.'

Darren placed his thumb and forefinger on Debbie's chin, tilting it towards him. He applied a small amount of pressure. 'I rang the number you gave me last time, your work number, and they said that you didn't work there any more. Some woman with a screaming child said you just buggered off. Is that right?'

Debbie said nothing. She avoided his eye.

'Deb?'

'Yes, that's right.'

Darren could feel the small intense sting of anger in the pit of his stomach. 'Why?' His voice was cold and Debbie was instantly wary.

'Because I was too upset,' she said. 'My face was all bashed in and I didn't know if the distress had damaged the baby. So I left. I didn't turn up again; I couldn't face it.' She looked at him. It was a lie of course, but she was surprised at how easily it rolled off her tongue.

Darren flushed and backed down. He dropped his hand away from her face and clasped it round his can. 'I'm sorry.' He stared at the floor. 'I just don't want you to lie to me, Debs, I couldn't stand it if you . . .'

She touched his arm. 'I got another job,' she said. 'I took some time off until my face healed, then I got another job, for a lawyer in the City. That's why I said my job was fine. It is, I quite like it.'

Darren raised his head. 'You won't have to work, once the baby arrives. You can live with me, we can get married quarters.'

'Married quarters?'

Darren grinned. 'If you want to.'

Debbie looked away. Why couldn't this have happened weeks ago? Why? Why not back then, when everything might have worked out, when there was at least a chance of a happy ending?

'Debbie?'

Darren was smiling. He took one of her hands in his and dropped down onto his knee. Debbie felt as if her heart would burst with grief. 'I must look bloody ridiculous in me underpants with a tinny in one hand.' He flicked her chin and she turned back to look at him. 'Do I have to do the whole thing?'

She forced a smile and her face ached.

'Debs, will you marry me?'

Debbie swallowed back a hard lump that stuck in her throat.

'Come on, Debbie, my knees are killing me!' Darren laughed, then pressed Debbie's hand to his mouth. 'Debs, please, say you'll marry me, please. I know we can make it work, the three of us, you, me and the baby, I just know it. I'm gonna go for promotion at work, Debs, and if I get it we could live pretty comfortably in married quarters.' He kissed her hand again. 'I know I can be a bit of a dickhead and that I lose my rag every now and then, but that's not much is it? Please Debs, what d'you say? Eh? Will you marry me?'

Debbie was still smiling, the expression frozen on her

face. She couldn't do or say anything.

'Debs? Please?'

In the end she just nodded; it was the only movement she could make. Darren beamed. He jumped up and kissed her, then he drank down his lager, crushed the tin in one hand and chucked it up in the air, catching it on the way down. 'I'm gonna ring my mum! God, she's gonna love you, she really is! She's been going on at me for ages about settling down and she's gonna be thrilled, what with the news of the baby and everything. I'm her little boy, you see, her favourite and—' He stopped to catch his breath. 'Debbie? Are you OK?'

Debbie had crawled down under the covers and lay on her side with her knees curled up in the foetal position.

'Debbie? Are you all right?'

Debbie said, 'Yes, I'm fine, I'm just really tired, that's all. I think I ought to get some sleep.'

'God yes, of course, the baby must take it out of you. Sorry love, I didn't think.' He came over to the bed and tucked the duvet round her legs. Despite her misery, Debbie felt cosseted and liked that feeling. Darren bent and kissed her forehead.

'You get some sleep now,' he said. 'I'll turn the lights off and watch a bit of telly with the sound low. You don't mind that do you?'

'No.' She watched Darren switch the lights off and the television on. 'Darren, I've got a bit of a problem,' she said quietly, 'at work.'

He walked back to the bed. 'What is it?'

Debbie rolled onto her back and half sat up. 'My boss wants to ring my old job to get a reference. If I give her the number, the chances are that Madeline, the woman you spoke to, will bad mouth me to Anna and it might spoil things. I really quite like this job and I'd like to keep it . . .' She glanced at him. 'I mean at least until I get too big to carry on.'

Darren thought for a moment. 'Does your boss know anything about the last job? Like where it was etcetera?'

'No, nothing. I started straight away, as Maya – that's Anna's baby – came early. There's never been the chance for them to ask.'

'Well give her my mum's number then, she can ring there.'

'Your mum?'

'Yes, we'll speak to her tomorrow, when we go to tell her about us and the baby.'

'But why would your mum . . .'

'Because she'd do anything for me, my mum.' He smiled. 'I've got her wound round my little finger!'

Debbie frowned but he took her hand and said, 'Now look, you mustn't worry, OK? My mum'll do it, I know she will. All we have to do is explain it to her, she'll understand; she's terrific like that.' He glanced behind him at the television and saw that the football had started. 'Now come on, you said you were tired, try and get some sleep. It'll be all right you know.'

Debbie slipped back down under the duvet and closed her eyes. For some peculiar reason she believed him, perhaps it would be all right. She heard the sound of the football in the background and felt reassured by it. That was the last thing she remembered; within minutes she had fallen asleep.

Chapter Nine

The doorbell rang at nine fifteen and Max went to answer it. He was dressed, casually, in immaculate jeans and a cashmere poloneck sweater. It was his mother.

'Hello, Max darling.' She came into the house without waiting to be invited and kissed him on the cheek. Her lips were dry and the kiss unnatural. 'You're up early. Shouldn't you be having a lie-in on a Saturday morning? You work so hard, darling, I'd have thought that you deserved at least a couple of extra hours in bed at the weekend.' She placed her handbag on the hall table and took off her coat. 'Is Anna not up yet?'

In the kitchen, Anna, who could hear every word, seethed silently. 'I'm in here, Jennifer,' she called. 'I've been up since six actually.' She smiled as Max's mother walked into the kitchen to offer another of her affectionless kisses. 'I've even cleaned the oven.'

Max was shocked. 'Have you?'

It was a lie, but it sounded so impressive that Anna went through with it. 'Yes, I did it at seven.'

'My word, you're becoming really quite domestic!' Jennifer said. 'Are you sure you're feeling well?'

Anna smiled grimly. 'I was,' she replied, but the sarcasm went over Jennifer's head.

'Where's the baby?' Jennifer asked. 'Is she in any kind of routine yet?'

'Maya is asleep, and no, she's only six weeks old, so she has no routine, except the one she chooses.'

Jennifer pursed her lips. 'May I go up and see her?'

'Of course,' Anna said. 'Shall I come with you?'

'No, no. I know my way by now, Anna darling.'

'Right.'

Jennifer made for the stairs and Anna followed her out into the hall. She said, 'It's terribly good of you, Jennifer, to come round and look after Maya for me. I really appreciate it.'

Jennifer nodded.

'I shouldn't be too long this morning, I'll just whiz up to Harvey Nics and then Selfridges and M&S at Marble Arch. Is that OK?'

'Anna darling, of course it's OK. You go off and enjoy yourself, I'm quite happy here at home looking after the baby.'

Anna nodded and Jennifer went on up the stairs.

'You go off and enjoy yourself . . .' she muttered under her breath in the kitchen. 'Enjoy myself! Trudging round the shops looking for something that will cover my large post-natal bottom and colossal lactating bosoms and be suitable to meet clients in at work on Monday.' She switched on the kettle and dropped a tea bag into a cup.

'Mutter, mutter!' Max said, from behind the paper.

'Well it's hardly my idea of fun, Max! I don't like shopping at the best of times, but post-natal and hormonal on a Saturday morning in Knightsbridge and Oxford Street is likely to be pure hell. Plus there's your mother thrown into the bargain.' Anna made her tea, put a cube of sugar into it, along with a slice of lemon. 'Having to suffer her smug comments and open sarcasm is frankly a bit much, especially when you could easily have—'

Max put the paper down. 'Don't start, Anna! We went through all this last night OK? I have things to do.'

'What things?'

'Things at work. I have to go over a pitch, catch up on some paperwork, bill clients, do some stuff that I haven't been able to do this last month because I've been so exhausted and trying to get home early to help you with Maya. Is that good enough for you? Look, you have a nanny, you could have asked her.'

'I think Debbie deserves a day off and I'm not about to ask her to give it up so that I can go shopping. Besides which, I would have thought you might like to spend a bit of time with your baby. I don't think I've seen you pick her up for days.'

Max folded his paper, drank down his coffee and stood up. 'Maya is six weeks old. All she needs is you for milk and comfort and Debbie for her other practical needs. She does not need me, Anna, I am superfluous, or hadn't you noticed?'

Anna could feel a full-scale row brewing, but she couldn't back off now. There were things that needed saying; this lethargy had gone on long enough. 'You are only superfluous, as you say, because you choose to be,' she said. 'You could make yourself needed if you wanted to.'

Max shook his head. 'Don't be bloody-minded, Anna. The baby doesn't need me and you don't need me. It's plain to me. I don't know why you can't see it yourself.'

'No I can't see it.' Anna was losing patience. 'What

do you mean I don't need you? Of course I need you! I needed you this morning, didn't I?'

'What? For a bit of baby-sitting?' Max's face was set and his mouth was a thin, hard line. 'You do not need me, Anna, not in the way that you used to.'

'I do!' Anna was close to tears.

'No you do not. I am not the bread-winner any more; you earn as much as I do and could easily support yourself. You don't need me for love and affection, you get that from Maya – all the love and affection you will ever need you can get from her. You don't need me to help you, you've got Debbie for that, your super-efficient nanny, and as for sex, well, you just don't need that in the way that I do. In fact I doubt whether you remember what it is, do you?'

'Don't be facile, Max! I've hardly been in a position to have sex recently now have I?'

'Haven't you? Not penetration maybe, but the rest of it, the touching, caressing, holding, kissing, stroking each other, sucking and licking each other . . .'

'That's enough, Max!'

'No it isn't enough, Anna!' Max snapped. 'That's where you're wrong.' He walked past her out of the kitchen and into the hall. He grabbed his car keys and his jacket while Anna stood in the doorway and watched him. Then he turned and said, 'It isn't enough at all.' He walked out of the front door and slammed it after him.

Anna glanced up the stairs and saw Jennifer at the top. How long she had been standing there Anna had no idea. There were a few seconds of silence, then Jennifer said, 'I can't seem to find that lovely soft purple velvet elephant I bought for Maya, Anna. Have you seen it?'

Anna took a very deep breath and let it out slowly and silently. 'Is it not in her cot, Jennifer?'

'No. I've checked her toy box as well and it's not there.'

'Maybe it's in the car. I'll look when I go out.' Anna attempted a smile. 'Don't worry, I'm sure it'll turn up.'

'Oh, I'm not worried,' Jennifer said. 'But I do so hate irresponsibility where personal belongings are concerned. Max always looked after his things, and when he was little, I looked after his things for him. You know I really think . . .' But Jennifer didn't get to say what she really thought; Anna had walked away.

Debbie left her building on Edge Road and saw the number fifteen bus just pulling into the stop twenty yards up. She broke into a run, then stopped suddenly, glancing over her shoulder to check that Darren wasn't watching her from the flat. He wasn't, so she sprinted up to the stop, jumped onto the bus as it was moving off and flashed her travel card. She found a seat and slumped down in it.

God, it was a relief to be away, to have five minutes' peace, even if it was only a trip to Sainsbury's to buy dinner for tonight and some flowers for Darren's mum. Ever since last night Debbie had had the feeling that she was caught in some kind of ever increasing spiral. Things were going round at such a phenomenal rate that her head thumped and she could hardly think straight. The lies were mounting and every now and then she would be thrown by a moment of intense panic at being found out and it would make her breathless and faint. Of course Darren just thought it was the baby and he would hold her and talk to her gently and kindly. He would hold her in a way she had never been held before, with such tenderness and affection, and she knew that even though it was a lie, it was the best thing that had ever happened to her. She laid her head against the window of the bus and sighed.

At the stop before Sainsbury's, she jumped off the bus and made her way along the pavement, her feet already aching in her best court shoes, ready to go to Darren's mum. She turned into the supermarket car park, stood for a moment to see where the pedestrian walkway was and, locating it, crossed to weave her way between the cars. At the entrance to the store, she checked in her handbag for her Reward card and, looking up, only a few cars away, she saw Max.

She knew it was him immediately. He was an attractive man, he dressed beautifully and people noticed him; Debbie was no exception. He climbed out of his car, a big, expensive one, one that Debbie wasn't allowed to drive, and opened the door of a black sports car. He leant in, placed his hand on the breast of the woman driving and kissed her. Debbie froze. His hand travelled under the woman's top; the kiss continued.

Someone knocked into Debbie and she dropped her bag. The contents spilled out everywhere – loose change, lipsticks, panty liners, pens, cough sweets, purse, credit-card wallet and a small, soft purple velvet elephant. There was a brief commotion as several people tried to help her retrieve her belongings from the road and Max pulled himself away. He turned and looked straight at Debbie.

They stood there for several moments, staring at each other, then Chrissy called out, 'Max darling, we are wasting time! You have to get to work and I have to get to the gym. Now, are you going to get in or do I have to drag you into my car to have my wicked way with you!' She laughed, a sharp, high-pitched noise that didn't sound at all natural, and Debbie turned away.

She walked blindly into the store, took the wire basket that an assistant at the door handed her and wandered blankly past rows and rows of things that she didn't really see. She found herself in the baby aisle and stopped, reassured by the familiarity of nappies and baby food. She wondered for a moment if anyone in the world really knew the truth, then she took a tube of cream for stretch marks down off the shelf and put it in her basket. She made her way back to the entrance to choose Darren's mum a bunch of flowers.

Outside, in the car park, Chrissy said, 'What's the matter, Max? I feel at the moment a bit like a bad smell.'

Max turned. 'I just saw our nanny,' he said. 'She was over there. She looked right at me, at me and you.'

Chrissy reached for the car door. 'Get in Max,' she said. 'And stop being melodramatic!' She slammed the door shut and held the steering wheel with both hands. Max went round to the passenger side and climbed in. He sat for several minutes, staring into space, fiddling with his hands, until Chrissy said, 'Oh for God's sake, Max! Buck up will you!' She pressed a cassette into the stereo. 'I really don't see what your problem is. So the nanny saw you and me together, big deal! So what if she tells Anna?'

'So what if she tells Anna!' Max threw his hands up. 'God Chrissy, don't you ever think of anyone other than yourself?'

Chrissy inspected her nails. 'As a matter of fact, Max, no I don't. But as I said, I don't see what all the fuss is about. You were the one who told me that you'd made up your mind what you wanted and that it wasn't wife and baby. It seems to me that fate has just done you a favour.' She switched her engine on.

'You really don't understand, do you?'

'Understand what?'

'Understand . . .' Max began, but he broke off. She didn't understand that although he knew he didn't want to stay with Anna, he couldn't bring himself to leave. That even though he wanted Chrissy, wanted her all the time he wasn't with her, he just wasn't ready to make that commitment. She didn't understand that knowing what you wanted didn't make it happen.

'No Max, you are right, I do not understand. Now, I'm going to go home. If you want to make a fuss about your nanny then fine, do it, and I'll go home on my own.'

Max sat where he was for a few moments, then opened his door. 'I need to think,' he said. 'I need to think this through.' He climbed out of the car. 'Sorry, Chrissy. I'll call you, all right?'

Chrissy said nothing. She revved the engine, very hard, Max slammed the passenger door and she drove off, with a screech of tyres and her stereo blaring. She glanced at Max in her rear-view mirror, standing in the cold – beautiful, wonderful, still unavailable Max – and she knew that she had to have him. Forbidden fruit; nothing was as good as what you couldn't have.

When Debbie got back to the flat, Darren was ready and waiting for her. 'You're late,' he said, taking the shopping bag from her. She flushed and found herself apologising nervously. Darren took some chocolates out of the bag, along with the flowers that Debbie had had wrapped, and left the rest of the things for her to put away. 'Hurry up,' he snapped. 'The cab will be here any minute. Are you wearing that jacket?'

Debbie glanced down at her casual rain jacket with its fur-trimmed hood. 'Should I wear my coat then?'

He nodded then, relaxing slightly, said, 'That's nice on you, but I'd like Mum to see you at your best.' He smiled. 'She's going to love you, she really is.'

Debbie nodded and finished unpacking the shopping. She left a packet of biscuits out and opened them when she'd put everything else away. She offered one to Darren, who said, 'Should you be eating those? My sister-in-law piled on four stone when she was pregnant with her first and she's never lost it, silly cow. She's like a tank now, stuffs herself the whole time.'

Debbie took one, nibbled the corner of it, then threw it away and emptied the rest of the packet into the biscuit tin.

Darren smiled. 'You look nice,' he said. 'Your hair is lovely like that.' He reached out and clumped a bunch of her hair in his hand. 'It must be the baby, making you bloom. I read somewhere about that.' The buzzer for the main door sounded and he said, 'Right, that's us then.' He picked up the flowers and chocolates. 'You got everything, Debs? Handbag, keys?' She nodded. 'Good, let's go.' He opened the door for her and took her arm on the way to the lift. At the lift he let her go first, pressed the button for the ground floor and held her hand as the lift doors closed. He opened the main door of the building, she went out first and waited for him on the pavement. He helped her into the cab, gave his mum's address and got in after her, slamming the door.

'Comfortable?' he asked.

'Yes, thanks.' And she was. Despite his moods, the way he snapped at her and nagged her, she was comfortable. She was being looked after, he wanted the best for her and for someone who had spent her life looking after other people, it was a very nice feeling for a change.

Darren's mum was small, plump and dark. She was well dressed, liked to look after herself with a weekly trip to the hairdresser's, and a manicure if she and Doug were going somewhere posh. She had been a secretary once, before she met Doug, and she had a nice telephone manner. She liked to cook, kept a neat semi-detached in one of the better parts of Croydon and she was devoted to her sons. She had three of them and she cherished them all, did everything a mother would want to do for them, from ironing their underpants to making sure that they never went without the latest Nike trainers or Calvin Klein T-shirt.

Darren was her youngest son, and although she would never admit it to the others, he was the one she loved the most, her favourite, and despite the fact that she tried to cover it, there were many times when it showed. He was smart, a bright boy who had gained five GCSEs, and had done a course in car mechanics at the local tech. He had gone into the army at eighteen and made his mother very proud when the Queen Mother had visited his regiment in '96 and spoken a couple of words to him on parade. She had photos of it. He loved her back, Darren did, and that was probably what made the difference; she would have done anything for him. He wrote to her on exercise and sent her postcards from his holidays in Tenerife and Majorca. He always went home on leave and although he towered two feet above her, he hugged her and kissed her cheek in a way that neither of the other two boys had ever done.

This morning, the morning that her son was due back on leave, Nora Woodman was in the kitchen, making an apple pie. She had her sleeves rolled up to the elbow and her face was flushed with the heat of the kitchen and the effort of concentration. Every now and then a few beads of sweat would break out on her forehead and she would wipe them away with a small embroidered handkerchief she kept in the pocket of her apron. She was expecting Darren for lunch, she had his two brothers coming, all four of the grandchildren and providing nothing untoward happened at the brewery, Doug would also be home early from his shift to join them for the main course.

It was half past eleven when the doorbell sounded. Nora tutted irritably, wiped her hands on her apron and went to the back door. It was very probably Doris from two doors up, she often called in for coffee and a chat on a Saturday morning. She stuck her head out and called, 'Come on round the back, Doris!' Then left the door open and went on with her baking. She held an immaculate pie up in the air to cut round the edge with a sharp knife, and glanced over her shoulder as she heard footsteps.

'Oh my God!' she cried, dropping the pie with a thud onto the table. A crack split the pastry in two. 'Darren!' She ran across to the door. Darren beamed, scooped her up into a bear hug and kissed her cheeks. Landing back on her feet, she took a pace back to look at him.

'Darren! What on earth are you doing here so early? I didn't expect you for . . .' She shook her head, not finishing her sentence, a habit she had. 'And you've lost weight. Oh my word, look at you! You're all skin and bone.' She shook her head again and squeezed his hand, still smiling. 'Still, it's good to see you, Darren love, and you're quite brown, aren't you? You got a bit of a tan in Canada then? I hope you used that sun screen I got you—' Suddenly she stopped and looked behind him. 'Darren? You've brought a guest?'

Darren looked behind him and reached out for Debbie's hand. He pulled her forward. 'This is Debbie,' he said, 'my fiancée.'

Nora let out a gasp. Her hands flew up to her face and she shook her head again. 'Dear God Darren, I don't believe it! You're getting married?'

Debbie flushed. Her face pulsated with the rush of blood to the skin and she looked down at the ground.

'You're getting married?' Nora cried again. 'Darren, I can't believe it. Wait till you father hears, he'll be staggered. My word, I can hardly believe that you'd find anyone to take you on.' She looked at Debbie. 'Come on in Debbie, please, come in. I'm absolutely thrilled, I can hardly take it in. My little boy is getting married!' Darren pulled Debbie further into the room but she was stiff with embarrassment and nerves.

'Well you must be a brave girl, that's all I can say.' Nora laughed. 'Taking on this great hulking idiot.'

'Mum!'

Nora laughed again. 'So you're getting married then, I just can't believe it.'

Darren smiled. 'Well you'd better! We're going to do it right away. We thought June time maybe. We want to be settled before the baby comes.'

There was one last brief moment of happiness, when Nora looked at Debbie, her face wide open with smiles, then the meaning of what her best loved son had just said hit her and the smile froze for a couple of seconds, then withered and died.

She stared first at Debbie, then Darren. 'The baby?' she said, quietly and slowly. 'Are you telling me that Debbie is pregnant?'

Darren, still grinning, had entirely missed this swift mood change. 'Yup!' he said. 'Wonderful, isn't it!'

Nora took a pace back, felt for the chair behind her and slumped down into it. 'Wonderful?' She stared at the two of them, then her eyes filled with tears. 'What will the neighbours say?' She shook her head. 'You'll want a registry office and no fuss and they'll all know . . .' She clasped a hand to her mouth. 'How could you do this to me, Darren?' she murmured. 'After all that I've given you, how could you let me down like this?'

Darren stared at his mother. He had a look of hurt confusion on his face, like a boy who has done wrong but can't understand what. He dropped Debbie's hand and moved across to the chair, squatting down. 'Come on, Mum, it's a mistake, that's all. It's just happened a few months early. We'd have had a baby anyway, it's just come a bit sooner than we'd planned. There's no point in jumping off the deep end, I mean, at least we'll be getting married, not like Shirley's Maureen. What is it? Five now and still not managed to get Dave down to the registry office.' He patted his mother's knee and stood up. 'We're delighted,' he said, deciding to play his trump card. 'But if you're too upset to be pleased for us then we won't stay, Mum, we'll get on with things ourselves and—'

'No, of course I'm not!' Nora stood up. 'It's just a bit of a shock, that's all, it'll take a while to get used to, becoming a mother-in-law and a granny, all in the same year.' She put her hand on Darren's arm. 'Please, sit down and I'll make some coffee. Don't go rushing off because I'm upset, please, stay.' She took her handkerchief out of her apron and blew her nose. 'It just takes a bit of getting used to, that's all! I'm old-fashioned, I don't think the way you youngsters do nowadays.' She held out her arms. 'Of course I'm pleased for you, Darren my love. Come on, give me a kiss and then we'll have a drink to celebrate.' Darren glanced behind him and smiled at Debbie, then he hugged and kissed his mother. 'And you too, Debbie.' Debbie stepped forward and Nora placed two rather cool kisses on her cheeks. 'Congratulations, my dear,' she said. 'Welcome to the family.'

Nora went across and put the kettle on. 'So, when's the baby due?'

Debbie placed her hand instinctively on her stomach. 'I'm sixteen weeks,' she said. She knew her dates by heart, even though they no longer existed. 'The baby's due in September.'

'Well, an autumn baby!' Nora said. 'How lovely.' But she was thinking, I wonder how long it'll be before she shows? I wonder if we can have a discreet service at St Anne's with fifty or so guests before she looks too pregnant. Nora took off her apron, glanced at the pie and decided it would have to do, crack and all; she had other things to think about. She turned the oven on to heat up and prepared the coffee. 'We'll have it in the front room,' she said. 'Do you drink coffee, Debbie, or would you prefer tea?'

'No, coffee is fine, thank you,' Debbie said.

She speaks nicely, Nora thought, and she's very presentable. 'Why don't you take Debbie into the front room, Darren, and I'll bring the coffee through,' Nora suggested.

'OK. D'you have any of those home-made biscuits, Mum?'

'Of course. Go on now, take Debbie through.'

Darren put a gentle hand in the small of Debbie's back and guided her out into the narrow hallway and then into the front room. 'She loves you,' Darren said, 'I knew she would.'

Debbie tried to smile; she wasn't nearly so sure. It was cold in the front room, immaculately tidy with a three-piece suite in maroon Dralon, three neatly arranged side tables and a row of small china animal figures on a shelf above the fireplace. Darren knelt to light the gas fire and Debbie shivered.

'It'll soon warm up,' he said. 'And it'll be baking in here this afternoon, with all the family, kids an' all.'

He glanced up. 'You all right, Deb?'

She nodded.

'Well, try and show it a bit then will you?'

'Yes, sorry.' The door was open and she felt inhibited. The phone rang; Darren went into the hall to answer it.

'Hi Derek! Yeah, just arrived.' He put his hand over the mouthpiece. 'Mum,' he called, 'it's me big bro!'

Nora hurried to the phone. 'Hello, Derek! Yes, fine thank you love. Sorry? What time did you say? Midday? Oh no, that's fine. No, bring it, I've got one, but Phil's little one is still in a high chair, isn't she? Yes, do that, thanks, Derek love.' There was a pause and Nora twiddled with the telephone wire. 'Oh yes,' she said. 'He's on very good form. He's got a bit of news actually. No I can't tell you!' She laughed and Debbie heard the tension in her voice. 'He'll tell you when you get here.' She glanced over her shoulder at her son, standing by the gas fire, his hands in his pockets, so grown-up and yet still in so many ways just a young boy. 'Sorry love, what did you say?' She tried to concentrate on the phone conversation but her mind kept wandering. She thought Debbie looked tired and sad, too sad for a young woman just engaged to be married. 'I don't know, Derek, I'll ask him.' Placing her hand over the mouthpiece, Nora said, 'Derek wondered if you fancy a trip up to the pub later? He'll ring round and get a few friends along.'

Darren looked at Debbie; she shrugged. 'It's fine by me,' she murmured. She was gently getting drawn into this family.

'Great!' Darren said, grinning.

'Darren says that's a terrific idea, Derek my love. You go ahead and fix it up and we'll see you and Lesley later.' There was a pause. 'What? Oh, it's chicken casserole and apple pie.' Nora smiled. 'Of course it's Darren's favourite,' she said. 'You know very well how I like to spoil my boys.'

Chapter Ten

At 7.00 am sharp, Max heard the doorbell go and knew it was Debbie. He was anxious to see her, to try and gauge her reaction to him. If she was hostile then she'd have to go. Whatever he decided about Chrissy, and he still had no clear idea, he didn't need any outside interference. Debbie knew too much and knowledge was dangerous.

'Is that Debbie?' he called to Anna from the bathroom.

'Yes. She's got keys, but she always likes to ring anyway before she comes in.' Anna was dressed and sat applying her make-up at her dressing-table mirror. It was her first day back at work and she was edgy but trying hard not to show it. She turned as Max came out of the bathroom. 'I said I'd just leave her to get on with things. Maya isn't awake yet and it's better if I just slip out I think.'

'And you're quite happy about leaving her alone in the house in charge of Maya despite the fact that she hasn't given you a reference yet?'

Anna sighed. 'Max, we've been through all this once already. Yes I agree with you that we must have a reference and that it was sloppy of me not to have followed it up more promptly, and yes I am perfectly happy to leave her here with Maya. For goodness' sake, Max! We've been cheek by jowl for the last six weeks, I think I know her well enough by now to trust her.' She turned back to her reflection and noticed that the red blotchy rash she always got when emotional had spread from her chest up to her neck. 'Oh Christ, look at my neck! This is the last thing I need. I've got three client meetings today and a meeting with Andrew about my fee structure.' She reached for her foundation. 'I look a complete fright.'

Max came over to the dressing table and stood behind Anna, looking at her in the mirror. 'Anna, your neck is the least of our considerations. Listen to me. I am not at all happy about you leaving Debbie alone in the house with the baby, OK?'

Anna spun round. 'And you choose seven o'clock in the morning to let me know this. Great! Thanks Max, this is just what I need on my first day back at work.'

'Don't blame me, Anna, I'm not the one who spent most of the weekend either holding the baby or sitting in front of my laptop working. I would have discussed it earlier only you haven't exactly been available, have you?'

Anna glared at him. 'So what do you want to do? What . . .' she glanced at her watch, 'with fifteen minutes to go before I have to get out of the house, do you propose that we do about this situation? That I cancel my day and stay here with Maya? That I take her with me to the office or that we leave her here on her own and pop back at lunch time to check on her and give her a bottle.'

'Don't be facetious, Anna, I'm not suggesting any of those things.'

'Then what the bloody hell are you suggesting, Max?' Anna snapped.

At the bottom of the stairs, Debbie stood motionless and listened.

'That we ring my mother. If I call her now, then she

can be over here by the time I leave for work and she can stay until you get back.'

'Your mother?'

'Yes.'

'But I thought you had no time for your mother. I thought that you had her here only under sufferance and that any contact with her was torture. Certainly that's what you've always said.'

'I know what I've always said, Anna, and that doesn't really change. But she'd help us out if we needed her to and I think we need her to. At least until we can get a reference from Debbie and if she doesn't give us a reference, then at least until we find someone else.'

'We? I'm sorry Max but I wasn't aware that you had anything at all to do with this nanny.' Anna looked at her watch again and suddenly jumped up. 'Bloody hell! It's seven fifteen and I've got to go. If it really means that much to you, Max, then go ahead and organise your mother.' She pulled on her jacket and checked the back of her tights. 'I cannot believe that you're doing this at this stage of the game but I really don't have the time to argue about it. Go ahead and call Jennifer, but if she hasn't gone by the time I get home from work then I really am going to lose my patience.' She stormed out of the room and down the stairs, picking her laptop and briefcase up off the floor in the hall. She opened the front door.

'Erm, Anna? I'm sorry, but I wondered if I could have a word?' Debbie was hovering at the entrance to the kitchen.

Anna turned and sighed.

'I've got that number you wanted,' Debbie said quickly. 'My old employers. They said to ring any time.' She walked into the hall and gave Anna a slip of paper.

Anna's mood lightened. 'Thanks Debbie, I'll call them today.' She pulled the door wide and glanced behind her before stepping out. At the top of the stairs was Max, so she looked up at him, waved the bit of paper that Debbie had just given her in the air, and left the house. Despite this small triumph, she felt miserable. She was angry, upset and really quite desperate at the thought of leaving her precious baby in the care of someone else.

Debbie finished stacking the dishwasher and switched the kettle on to make up some formula feed. She dropped a tea bag into a cup at the same time and reached for the sugar bowl in the cupboard, but her hands were shaking and it slipped through her fingers, chipping the rim as it hit the work surface and scattering lumps of sugar. She put her hands up to her face and held them there for a moment, forcing back the tears. Then she ripped off a piece of kitchen roll, wiped her eyes and blew her nose. She had to be strong, despite all that had happened, she couldn't crumble now.

So Max wanted her out. She poured boiling water into some bottles and made her tea. She wasn't stupid, that's what all this manoeuvring his mother in meant. He wanted her out because she knew his secret and he was sweating about it. But he wasn't going to get her out, not now, not ever. *She* had Maya now and no one was going to separate them. Debbie's face softened for a moment as she thought about Maya. She felt the familiar tug in her breast. It was an ache, an exquisite pain when she thought about her baby. And Maya was *her* baby. She had been in Debbie's arms from the first day she was born; she was as much *her* baby as anyone else's. Debbie sipped her tea, both hands clasped round the mug, her fingers cold and numb, slowly responding to the warmth of the cup. Yes, Max wanted her out, but just this once Max wasn't going to get what he wanted. He could have a fight if he asked for one, only Debbie had the ultimate weapon and if it meant keeping Maya then she was more than prepared to use it.

Nora Woodman sat in her kitchen looking at her weekly copy of *Family Circle*. It was three in the afternoon and she hadn't strayed far from the phone all day. There was no way she was taking the chance of having Doug answer it, this was her thing and she was going to see it through. She flicked to the end of the magazine, having hardly read a word of it, and wondered where she'd put that packet of cigarettes her sister Margaret left last Tuesday. She didn't smoke, not regularly of course, but she liked one now and again, especially when she was under pressure. Nora got up and rummaged through the odds and sods drawer in the sideboard. She found the packet and lit a cigarette from the gas ring. It tasted awful but it calmed her nerves a bit. She sat down again and drew the magazine towards her for a second look. The phone rang. Nora jumped up. In the hall she cleared her throat and put out the cigarette, then she lifted the receiver and said, 'Hello?'

'Hello, may I speak to Madeline Watts please?'

Nora felt sick. 'Speaking,' she said.

'Mrs Watts, this is Anna Jacob, I believe my nanny Debbie Pritchard told you I would be phoning?'

'Yes she did. How can I help you?'

'I just wanted to touch base with you really and check that everything was all right when Debbie left. She's been with me for six weeks now and I've been very happy. She seems extremely capable and I—'

'Oh she is,' Nora said. 'She's a lovely girl, very efficient, very capable.'

Anna frowned. For some peculiar reason this didn't sound quite right, the answer was too quick. 'And everything was all right when she left?'

'Perfectly, yes. We were sorry to see her go, to be honest.'

Anna relaxed slightly; this sounded better. 'Were there any particular strengths or weaknesses you could identify?'

Nora was caught momentarily off guard. She hadn't been expecting a full-scale reference. 'Not really, not that I can think of off hand.' She paused and tried to think back to the folder that Debbie had shown her. 'She was always punctual, kind, patient and she was very good with the baby.'

'The baby?'

Nora closed her eyes. Lying did not come naturally to her and she was extremely uncomfortable. 'I mean my youngest. We always call him the baby, but of course he was eighteen months when Debbie joined us. Yes, that's right, eighteen months. She had him from eighteen months until he went to nursery four days a week just after Christmas. He's now . . .' She stopped for a few moments to check the calculation, then swallowed and said, 'Two and a half. He's now two and a half.' Her mouth was painfully dry and the taste of tobacco was making her feel sick.

'Great! And you were perfectly happy?'

'Oh, erm yes. Perfectly.'

'It's good to hear that, as my daughter is only six

weeks old and it's so hard to leave her. It's really put my mind at rest, Mrs Watts, to know that you were happy. Thank you.'

Nora recoiled. That bloody stupid boy! She had an overwhelming desire to blurt out the truth, but Anna suddenly said, 'I'm terribly sorry but I have to go. I have a call waiting. Thank you again for talking to me, Mrs Watts. Goodbye.'

'It's fine,' Nora said. 'Goodbye.' The line was disconnected. She sat down on the bottom stair and put her head in her hands. She had always known he had a temper, always, but by God she'd tried to curb it, all his life she'd tried to teach him the consequences of it. And now here she was, covering for him again, just like she'd covered for him before. Telling some woman that a girl she had only just met was a perfectly good, responsible nanny, someone she could trust with her tiny helpless baby. And all because her son had lost it and let fly with his fists. Bloody stupid boy! If Doug ever found out, if his brothers ever knew . . . Nora dropped her hands away and stood up. She had done it now; there was no going back. She went into the front room and took a bottle of sherry out of the cabinet. It was half past three in the afternoon, but she didn't care. She poured herself a large measure and drank it down in one go, then she refilled her glass. I hope to God that what I said was right, she thought, looking out of the lace net curtains to The Avenue beyond. I hope to God that this Debbie is all she seems, because if she isn't and something terrible happens . . . Nora shivered and thought of her own darling grandchildren. I would never, she thought, draining her glass a second time, never forgive myself.

*   *   *

Anna came in from work early. It was four thirty, she was tired, anxious about Maya and had a case full of papers to go through that night. She wanted to feed Maya, have a bath and be on her own for a while.

The house was silent. 'Debbie?' she called, feeling irritated that there was no sign of anyone. She started up the stairs. 'Debbie, hello? I'm home!'

'Anna?'

Anna swung round. 'Oh, hello Jennifer. Where's Debbie?'

'She's out in the garden with the baby. I asked her to keep out of the way until I'd had a word.'

Anna's mouth dropped open. 'I'm sorry?'

'We need to talk, Anna, there are things that should be brought to your attention and I'm afraid that I am going to have to be the one who does it.'

'Jennifer, can't this wait? My breasts are killing me and I need to express some milk.'

'I don't think so,' said Max's mother, tight-lipped.

Anna sighed and walked downstairs. 'I'll make some tea, shall I?'

Jennifer frowned.

'All right, let's get on with it then. Where d'you want to go? Is the sitting room all right?' Anna opened the door and bent to pick the baby rug up off the floor. 'What's up?' she asked, turning to face Jennifer. She was fast losing patience.

'I am not impressed with your nanny, that's what's up, Anna.'

'Really?'

'Yes really. She treats that baby as if she were her own.'

'And?'

'And what? Isn't that enough cause for concern? Something's not right, Anna, she's been caressing and cuddling Maya all day, she's hardly left her alone and she talks to her as . . . well, as if she were her own baby.'

Anna said nothing. Her face was unreadable but an intense, irrational jealousy had sprung up in her chest. 'I would rather that she spoilt Maya with love than ignored her, wouldn't you?' she managed to say calmly.

'Would you? Well I don't think it's right. The girl is a nanny, not a mother, and believe me, Anna, you'll have problems when that little one is older if you don't watch out. She'll go to Debbie at every turn and she'll think she's her—'

'Don't say it!' Anna snapped. Jennifer stared. 'Let's just drop it, shall we, Jennifer? I am Maya's mother and she will be in no doubt about that fact as she grows up.'

Jennifer said nothing.

'Was that all you wanted to say?'

'No. I found the purple elephant that I gave Maya.'

'Good.' Anna was having trouble keeping her voice even.

'It was in Debbie's handbag.'

Anna sighed. 'Look Jennifer, I'm sure there's a perfectly reasonable explanation for that. Did you ask her what it was doing there?'

'What what was doing where?' Max stood in the doorway and looked at his mother and Anna squaring up against each other either side of the fireplace.

'We are having a discussion about Debbie,' Anna said. 'It doesn't concern you.'

'Yes it does,' Max said. 'What the hell's been going on?'

'I am trying to tell Anna that I don't think things are

quite right where Debbie is concerned and she is choosing to ignore me.'

'Anna?'

'This is none of your business, Max.'

'Yes it is. I asked my mother to come here today because I was worried about leaving Maya alone with someone we don't have a reference for, no matter how good she seems, and if she has something to say, Anna, then I think you should listen to it. Mother is a completely impartial observer.'

Anna held down a derisive snort. 'Actually,' she said, making a big effort to sound calm, 'I telephoned Debbie's last employer this afternoon and was perfectly happy with what Mrs Watts had to say. So we do have a reference, Max, a first-hand verbal one.' She shot a sidelong glance at Jennifer. 'Also I have listened to what your mother has to say, Max, and in her opinion Debbie is too fond of the baby. In mine, I would rather it was that way than not fond enough. And finally, there is some misunderstanding about a cuddly toy, which I have no doubt your mother will fill you in on. It is of no interest to me, OK? As far as I am concerned there is nothing more to say. I have no problem with Debbie, she is my employee, so I think that should be the end of it, don't you?'

Anna swept towards the door. She pulled it open and marched out into the hall. On the bottom step, with Maya in her arms and flushed with embarrassment, was Debbie. Anna looked at her. There was no doubt that she had been listening and it gave Anna an odd sense of unease.

'Hello,' she said. 'Shall I take Maya?'

'I was just about to bath her.'

'I'll do that.' It came out sharper than Anna had meant it to and Debbie flushed again. Anna took her baby and she smelt of Debbie's scent, a light, flowery perfume. It came again, an intense, almost blinding stab of jealousy. Anna cradled Maya to her breast and walked away into the kitchen. She sat down on the chair and unfastened her shirt to give Maya a feed. There was one nagging thought that kept going round and round her head. The purple elephant had shown up in Debbie's bag, there was bound to be an explanation for that, some reasonable excuse. But whatever had happened to the exquisite small white duck that Anna herself had bought? From the moment she had put it in the cot next to Maya, it had disappeared and she had never seen it again.

The baby suckled, Anna rested her head back against the wall and closed her eyes. It had vanished, she thought, like the babygros and the white bib with Maya's name embroidered on it, vanished into thin air. Or had it? Anna sighed heavily. Did things just vanish or were they deliberately lost? Things that Debbie might not like, for instance. Anna dismissed the thought the moment it popped into her head. She was being paranoid, ridiculous! She opened her eyes and looked tenderly down at her daughter. She was jumping to conclusions.

Or was she?

It was just after five by the time Debbie made it into the West End. Anna had let her go early but she wasn't pleased; she had wanted to put Maya in the bath. Bath time was the most relaxing, wonderful part of the day and she resented missing it. It was going to be her time, now that Anna was back at work, her time with Maya to play and to soothe and she had been looking forward to it all day.

In Selfridges, Debbie stood still for a few moments

and had a good look round the cosmetics hall. She spotted several well-known brands and headed in that direction. Red, that was the colour she was looking for, a deep, ruby red, with a slight sheen. She approached one counter, looked at the lipsticks, and reached for two or three to try.

'Would you like to try those, madam?' A smart, heavily made-up assistant looked at her.

'Yes, please.'

'Please have a seat.' She adjusted the mirror on the counter to Debbie's height and handed a cotton-wool pad across, doused in make-up remover. 'If you'd like to remove your own lipstick.'

'I'm not wearing any.'

'Just rub the pad over your lips anyway, it'll freshen them up.' Debbie did as she was told and the assistant came round to the front of the counter to apply the lipstick with a small, thin brush. Debbie watched her. The colour was ghastly against her skin, it made her mouth look like a wide bloody gash in her face, but it was the right colour, definitely the right match. The assistant moved away. 'Very nice,' she said. Debbie stared at her reflection. Lucky she wasn't vain or she might just have believed the woman. It was shockingly bad.

'I'll take it,' she said, 'thanks.' Then she wiped the pad hard over her mouth a second time and removed every last trace of the revolting colour. The lipstick was wrapped, she paid for it and dropped it into her bag. That done, she felt better. She walked out of the shop and across Oxford Street to catch the bus.

On the way home, Debbie slipped her hand inside the bag and felt the shape of the lipstick in its expensive packaging. The fight with Max was on and it was a fight that she was going to win. She closed her hands over it and crushed the box. She had already lost one baby and she sure as hell wasn't going to lose another.

Chapter Eleven

'You killed your baby
You are so mad
You killed your baby
You are so bad . . .'

The young woman walked through the estate, her head
down, her shopping bag gripped tightly in her sweating
hand. She ground her teeth as she walked, her jaw locked
together. The children ran after her chanting, pulling at
her coat, throwing small stones. She walked faster, the
grey, heat-steeped pavement blurring as her eyes filled
with tears.

'You killed your baby
You are so mad
You killed your baby
You are so bad . . .'

She started to run. The children ran after her and she
put her hands up to her ears. 'Stop it!' she cried. 'Please,
stop it . . .' But the children chanted louder, enjoying
the chase, enjoying their brief moment of power. She
ran faster, the taunt followed her.

'You killed your baby
You are so mad . . .'

She ran into him and stopped. She saw his face, let out
a cry of terror and put her hands over her face.

'Murderer,' he hissed, then he spat at her. It was warm
and wet on the back of her hand and it made her shudder
with revulsion. She stood stone still, her eyes squeezed
tight, her hands covering her face and her whole body
rigid with fear.

She lost track of time. She had no idea how long she
stood there or what time it was when she opened her eyes
and let her hands drop limply to her sides. They had gone,
all of them, and she wondered for one awful moment if
she had imagined it, but then she saw the mucus on
her hand and she shook it violently. The blob of spittle
dropped to the ground and lay on the pavement, glisten-
ing in the sunshine. The young woman lifted her head, she
eyed the flats on either side of her, the empty cul-de-sac,
then cautiously she moved on. Her heart pounded inside
her chest, it pounded so hard that the vein on her neck
stood out and pulsed with blood. She walked on.

'There is nothing to fear,' she murmured. 'There is
nothing to fear . . .' But as she said it she knew it wasn't
true; there was everything to fear. There were times when
she was frightened even of herself.

Anna called Andrew McKie at nine in the morning and
left a message on his voicemail to tell him that she was
working for a couple of hours at home and would go
directly to the meeting at the client's offices and see him
there. He called her back at nine thirty, concerned that
she was all right.

'I'm fine,' she said, closing the door of the bedroom to take the call. 'I just wanted to oversee some things here this morning, check that everything was in order.'

'Are you having problems with childcare, Anna?' His question seemed innocent enough, but it had a hidden agenda. It was the cardinal sin, for working mothers, to have problems with their childcare.

'No, no problems at all, Andrew.' It was halfway towards the truth. There wasn't a problem that Anna could actually put her finger on, it was more a sense of unease, which could just as well be hormones and tiredness as anything else.

'You've prepared the documents?'

'Everything's ready. I checked through it all last night.'

'Good, I'll see you later then.'

'Thanks Andrew. I'll be there at midday sharp.' Anna could hear Maya's cries and went to hang up.

'Oh and Anna?'

'Yes?'

'If you do have problems, don't let them fester, eh? Take it from me, get them cleared up now.'

Anna felt close to tears. Andrew had a way of talking to her more like a parent than a senior partner and it gave her the overwhelming urge to want to cry on his shoulder. It was definitely hormones and tiredness.

'Thanks Andrew,' she said, 'I'll see you later.' She hung up, listened to Debbie's voice soothing her baby and walked straight out of the bedroom into the nursery.

'I'll take her, shall I?'

Debbie was standing by the window with Maya in her arms. She was rocking her gently and singing. Anna bit down a sudden rise of anger and reached for the baby. 'I think she needs a feed.'

'I thought you'd left,' Debbie said. She took in Anna's track bottoms and T-shirt. 'Aren't you going in today?'

'I'm going to work at home this morning, spend a bit of time with Maya. I've got a meeting at midday, so I'll leave around eleven thirty.'

Debbie handed Maya across and Anna watched her face as she did so. She caught the briefest glimpse of a light that went out in Debbie's eyes.

'You couldn't pile some washing in the machine could you, Debs, while I feed Maya?'

'Yes, of course. I was going to do it in a few minutes anyway. Would you like a cup of tea while I'm in the kitchen?'

Anna softened. Debbie was so kind and willing, and in her heart Anna truly believed that it was better that Debbie cared too much for Maya than not enough. Only maternal jealousy was proving much harder to cope with than she had imagined. She felt suddenly embarrassed at having snapped a few moments ago and said, 'Debbie, I'd love a cup of tea please.' She smiled. 'I'll feed Maya in my bedroom. Could I possibly have my tea in there?'

Debbie smiled back. 'Of course,' she said. 'I'll bring it up in a few minutes.'

Anna bent her head and kissed Maya's brow, breathing in the distinctive warm scent of baby skin. 'Thanks,' she said absent-mindedly. She made her way to her bedroom and left Debbie alone in the nursery staring down at her empty arms.

Down in the kitchen Max finished his toast and coffee and took his things across to the dishwasher to load it. He was on edge and resentful. Anna had insisted he cancel his mother that morning, then suddenly decided to stay at home for a couple of hours, and the idea of Debbie alone with Anna was making him decidedly anxious.

As Debbie came into the kitchen with her arms full of dirty laundry, she said, 'Good morning!'

Max ignored her, pretending to be busy with the dishwasher, and toyed momentarily with the idea of telling her to keep quiet. But he wasn't a rude man and he didn't deal with things like that. His best chance, indeed his only chance of keeping things on a level for the moment was to keep quiet himself and deny everything. It was her word against his. He straightened and looked right at her, then smiled and said, 'Good morning Debbie.' She smiled back and went into the laundry room.

He listened to her loading the washing into the machine next door for a moment, then walked out into the hall to call goodbye to Anna. He shouted up the stairs, acting with far more confidence than he actually felt, and picked up his briefcase from the hall table. He left the house. As he walked down the front path to his car, he glanced over his shoulder at his home and for some strange reason, the sight of this neat Edwardian villa, tastefully modernised inside and well-kept outside, filled him with sadness. He pressed the alarm pad on his key ring, the BMW bleeped and Max looked forward. It was the only way to look.

Debbie dumped the remainder of the pile of washing onto the floor and walked into the sitting room in time to see Max's car pull off. Satisfied, she went into the hall, took the lipstick she had bought last night out of her bag, and carried it back through to the laundry room. She took one of Max's hand-made shirts out of the machine, one she had always disliked, and spread it out on the floor. Twisting off the top of the lipstick, she smeared a slick of bright red onto her fore-finger and ran the finger around the inside collar of the shirt. She did the same around the neck button and the shirt tails, then she found a pair of Max's underpants and smeared inside the waist band and along the crotch with another slick of red lipstick. She put the pants back into the machine, stood to wash her hands and, with the shirt under her arm, replaced the lipstick safely back in her handbag.

She climbed the stairs.

'Anna?' Popping her head round the door, Debbie saw Anna sitting on her bed with Maya on her lap. 'Anna, I'm sorry to bother you,' she said, 'but I was wondering if you had any stain remover? I'm not sure how to get your lipstick off Max's shirt.'

Anna narrowed her eyes. 'My lipstick?'

Debbie stepped into the room. 'Here.' She held the shirt out and Anna leant forward for it. 'It's a pain to try and get out as well,' she went on. 'I don't know why cosmetics companies don't tell you that when you buy them, I . . .' Debbie stopped. 'Anna? Are you all right?'

Anna's face had drained of all colour. She held the shirt in her hands and stared down at the bright red lipstick on the collar.

'Anna?' Maya had started to whimper, so Debbie reached for her and lifted her off Anna's lap. Anna sat there, barely noticing that the baby had gone. 'Anna, are you OK?'

Anna's head jerked up. 'Yes, yes I'm, er, I'm fine.' She cleared her throat. 'Thanks, Debbie. Leave the shirt with me, I'll sort it out.'

Debbie held the baby close to her chest. 'Shall I get Maya dressed?'

There was no reply.

'Anna? Shall I get Maya dressed?'

'Oh yes, sorry, please, if you wouldn't mind, yes.' Anna continued to stare down at the shirt. She had an image in her mind, an image that wouldn't budge. It was the face of Chrissy Forbes; the perfectly made-up, laughing face, with the blond hair and bright red, glossy lips.

Debbie walked out of the room and still Anna sat, staring at the shirt in her hands. A few moments later, she got to her feet, stumbled into the bathroom and, leaning over the sink, was violently sick.

Anna wiped her mouth on a towel and stood straight. She stared at her reflection in the mirror over the sink, the harsh overhead lights making her look older and more haggard than she really was, then she turned away. An intense feeling of panic made her breathless as she went down the stairs to the laundry room. There she knelt on the floor and yanked the dirty washing out of the machine, rifling through it, searching for Max's clothes. She found the underpants, saw the lipstick and clasped her hands round the fine white cotton. She hung her head for a few moments, closing her eyes, then she let out a sob and tore at them, ripping them completely down the centre seam. 'You bastard!' she screamed. 'You fucking cheating bastard!' She began to cry.

Up in the nursery Debbie heard Anna's scream. She stopped what she was doing and listened for a few moments, but there was nothing more; it was followed by silence. She held Maya's tiny hands in her own and looked down at the innocent face. She felt bad. She didn't want to hurt Anna, she didn't want to cause any pain, but it had to be done. Max had to go. It was her or him, and if she'd judged it right, it was going to be him.

*   *   *

Andrew McKie waited in the reception of the High Tech Computer Games Company and flicked through a copy of *Newsweek*. Every so often he glanced at his watch. Anna was late; it was very unlike her to be late and he was worried. He glanced at the clock on the wall above the reception desk and double-checked the time. He stood up.

'Hello, I'm sorry to bother you, but there haven't been any messages left for me by Anna Jacob have there? Any messages that might have gone to the wrong place and not got through to me?'

The girl on reception checked the notes on her pad, then rang up to the main offices to ask. She replaced the receiver and shook her head. 'No, nothing I'm afraid.'

'OK, thanks.' Andrew took his phone out of his brief-case and dialled Anna's home number. He heard the answerphone click on but didn't leave any more messages; he had left three already. He then rang Anna's mobile again. He was told that the phone was switched off and swore under his breath. He left a final message with the Vodaphone recall service, then put his phone away. At that moment Will Turner arrived.

'Andrew! Sorry I'm late. Have you been waiting long?'

'No, about ten minutes or so.' The two men shook hands and Andrew thought how habitually sad Will had grown, and what a waste it was, for someone who used to be so happy.

'Did anyone get you a coffee, Andrew?'

'I was offered.' Andrew smiled at the girl on reception. 'But I declined. I've been waiting for Anna Jacob to arrive actually. She seems to have been held up. Shall we hang on for her or would you like to get started?'

Will looked at his watch. 'Andrew, forgive me, but

would you mind if we cracked on? I was rather hoping to be back in Sussex by mid afternoon. Can we get on without Anna?'

'Without Anna? Yes of course.' Andrew was embarrassed. He was also internally very cross.

'Good.' Will opened the door through to the main offices and held it for Andrew. 'It's good to see you, Andrew,' he said. 'Just the sight of you makes me feel sane again.'

Andrew McKie smiled, but the comment depressed him. Why, he thought, when Will Turner had everything to look forward to, did that have to happen to him? But he didn't have any answers. No one, he thought, ever did.

Anna climbed out of the taxi and paid the driver. She smoothed the front of her dress, one she had bought at the weekend, a navy silk fitted shift dress with matching jacket, and checked her shoes, kitten-heeled slingbacks from L K Bennett. She had extra-sheer stockings on, her face was lightly made up and her hair washed and blow-dried. Catching sight of herself in the plate-glass window of Debenhams, she had to admit that for a hormonal, post-natal, betrayed wife, she looked pretty damn good. The thought boosted her morale for about twenty seconds, then her hands began to shake again. She gripped her handbag tightly and headed across the road to the offices of Max's advertising agency.

'I've come to see Max Slater,' she said to the receptionist. 'I'm his wife, Anna Jacob. He's expecting me.' It was a lie, but Anna wanted the advantage of surprise, so when the receptionist went to dial Max's extension, she said, 'He's in a meeting. He told me to just go on up.' She glanced at her watch. 'D'you mind? I don't have much time and I have to give him this.' She held an envelope up and the receptionist nodded. She handed Anna a pass and Anna made her way over to the lifts.

Up on the top floor, Anna walked through the open-plan floor space, affronted by the hubbub and noise of activity on either side of her. She hated such exhibition-ism. Why the hell couldn't they keep their business private, she thought, instead of opening it all up for the world to see? Typical advertising.

At Max's glass-walled office – one of the three enclosed spaces on the top floor – the blinds were down and a meeting was in progress; the glass wall screened by a white calico blind. Anna stood for a moment and took a deep breath. Then she opened the door. There, seated on two black leather sofas, with a mass of creative work laid out on a table between them, were Max and Chrissy Forbes. There was a tense air of concentration in the room and Anna felt for a moment that she had interrupted something intimate.

'Anna!' Max jumped up. He was in his shirt sleeves and as he stood, he swept his hair back off his face with his hand, one of his nervous gestures.

Anna looked at Chrissy. She was smiling, red lips stretched across her white teeth. Anna left the door open behind her and stepped into the room.

'Max,' she said, turning to look directly at him. 'You are a dishonest, conniving bastard!' There was a perceptible hush in the office space beyond. 'And Chrissy?' Anna looked at her. 'It is Chrissy, I presume, who you've been having an affair with? The lipstick certainly matches. Is it just husbands you like to sleep with or is it anyone?'

There was a snigger behind her and for the first time Anna noticed the silence outside.

'What the hell is going on, Anna?' Max demanded. 'What on earth are you talking about?'

'You tell me,' Anna said coldly.

'Tell you what? I've no idea what you're talking about.'

'Max?' Chrissy turned to Max, who was grey and sweating.

'Surely you're not going to deny it, Max?' Anna snapped. 'It's written all over your face, over both of your faces actually.'

'Deny what?' He was holding out on the ignorance plea and nothing was going to shift him.

'Oh for God's sake, Max!' Anna suddenly cried. 'I know! I know about you and Chrissy. I know that you've been fucking your ass off while I've been working towards a partnership and giving birth to our baby. I know! I know all about the cheap sordid deception and the pathetic attempts to cover it up.' She was shouting now and her voice was full of tears.

'How do you know? Who told you?'

'No one told me. They didn't have to.' Anna slung the envelope with Max's shirt and pants in onto the table. 'Don't insult me, Max, by pretending that it hasn't been happening.' She stared at him. 'Please Max, I'm not stupid.'

Max hung his head. 'It's not like it seems,' he said. 'It's only just started, it doesn't mean anything, it's over . . .'

'Max!' Chrissy interrupted. 'Max, that's not true. That's just not true. Tell her the truth, Max.'

Max looked at Chrissy, then at Anna. He had beads of sweat on his forehead and they glittered in the intense halogen lighting. He didn't know what to say.

Anna watched him. The desire to lash out at him was so strong that she had to grip her handbag with both hands to stop herself from hitting him. She began to shake.

'The truth, Max?' she said, swallowing down a hard lump in her throat. 'You don't know the meaning of the word. You've been lying to yourself and to me for so long that you no longer know what truth means.' Anna felt tears and knew she had to get out of there. She looked at Max, at his impotent figure. Clever Max, oh so clever Max, caught out. Then she turned and walked out of his office. All through the open-plan space of the top floor there was a watching silence. It followed her down to the lifts and enveloped her. She pressed the button, the lift came and as she stepped inside it, she started to sob.

Anna walked blindly along Oxford Street, jostled by the crowds, oblivious to the noise and the stares. Her face was wet with tears, they streamed down her cheeks and dropped off her chin onto the neck of her silk dress leaving small dark stains. Her nose ran and she wiped it every now and then on the back of her hand. Finally, near Marble Arch, she saw the orange light in a taxi and shouted, stepping out into the road to hail it, narrowly missing a car.

'You all right love?' the driver asked.

Anna nodded. She wiped her face on the sleeve of her jacket and sniffed loudly. 'Clapham please,' she said, her voice strained, 'near the common.' She climbed in and slumped back into the seat. Reaching for her bag, she took out her phone and switched it on. It bleeped and rang; she had four messages. They played automatically.

'Hello Anna, this is Andrew. I was wondering if you could give me a call on the mobile. It's eleven forty-five and I'm already at High Tech. There's something I wanted to check before we meet Will Turner. Speak to you in a few minutes. Thanks.'

Anna sat forward. 'Oh bugger!' she cried, rifling in her bag for a tissue. She blew her nose and looked at her watch. 'Bugger, bugger, bugger!'

'Hello Anna, this is Andrew again. It's eleven fifty-five. Where are you? Give me a call, OK?'

'Hello Anna, Andrew again. Please ring me.'

Anna put her hands up to her face. 'Oh God,' she murmured. 'Oh shit!' She listened to the final message from Andrew again and dialled home. The answerphone was on but she knew that Debbie could hear the messages. 'Hello Debbie, it's me. If you're there, please give me a ring urgently on my mobile, OK?'

She leant forward and tapped on the glass partition. 'Sorry, could you take me to Chiswick, instead of Clapham? I've just realised that I should be in a meeting there.'

'Whereabouts in Chiswick love?'

'Near the bridge.' Anna's phone rang.

'Yup, no problem.'

She answered it. 'Hi Debbie, thank goodness you're there. Look, can you do me a favour? Can you get over to Chiswick with my briefcase? The address is . . . Oh shit, I can't remember the street name. It's High Tech Computer Games. Ring directory and they'll give you the number. You can ring them for the address. I should be there in about twenty minutes. OK? Great, thanks Debbie.' Anna disconnected and rang Andrew's mobile. He answered immediately and she swallowed down the urge to cry when she heard his voice. 'Andrew, hi, it's Anna. I'm sorry, Andrew, but I've had a crisis that needed to be dealt with. Yes, yes I'm . . .' She swallowed hard and wiped the tears from her face. 'I'm fine, honestly. Yes, I'm on my way now. Can you remind me of the address?'

She took out a pen and a small bound notepad. She wrote the address down. 'OK, got that. Thanks Andrew. I'll be there by one fifteen.'

'High Tech Computer Games,' she called to the driver, leaning forward again. 'They're at fifty-eight Walden Road.'

'Right.' The driver glanced at her in his rear-view mirror. 'Shouldn't be more than twenty minutes love.'

'Thanks.'

Anna sat back and stared blankly out of the window, until the cab drew up outside her meeting place.

Andrew McKie was in reception at one ten waiting for Anna. She had sounded so appalling on the phone that he was worried sick. He saw her cab pull up and hurried out onto the pavement.

'Anna?' Helping her out, he stared for a few moments at her face. She looked devastated; that was the only word he could think of. 'Anna, are you sure you want to do this? You look terrible, what the hell has happened?'

Anna faced him. In the daylight her face, tear-stained and ashen, seemed to have aged ten years. 'Max has been having an affair,' she said. 'I found out this morning.'

'Oh Anna.' Andrew took her hand. 'Anna, I'm so sorry.' He looked at her. 'D'you want to go home? Have some time off?'

'No.' She squeezed his hand for an instant then gently eased her own away. 'Thanks, but no. I need to work. I've got my nanny meeting me any minute with my briefcase and I'm all prepared for this meeting.' She rubbed her hands over her arms and shivered. 'Could we go inside, Andrew? I feel a bit chilly.'

'It's the shock,' he said, opening the door for her. 'I'll get you some tea ordered.'

Anna turned towards the girl on reception. 'Can I freshen up?'

'Yes, of course. The ladies' is just through the main doors on the right.'

'Thanks.'

Anna headed for the main doors and Andrew called out, 'D'you want me to ask your nanny to wait?'

Anna nodded. 'Please. She'll have Maya with her.' Then she disappeared into the cloakrooms to try and repair her face.

Will Turner finished reading through the documents in front of him and reached for the phone on the conference table. He dialled reception. 'Is Mr McKie still down there?' he asked. 'Good. Tell him I'll come down and join him please.' He stood, pulled on his suit jacket and said, 'I'll go and see what the delay is.' Several of the management team seated round the table nodded. 'And I'll order more coffee on my way down. We'll break for, what, ten minutes?' There was a murmur of assent. 'Fine. We'll reconvene the meeting at one thirty. Thanks everyone.' He left the room.

On the way down to the lifts he asked one of the PAs to get some more coffee and biscuits taken into the conference room and a couple of bottles of mineral water, then he called the lift, saw it was on the ground floor and decided to walk. He took the main staircase and arrived unnoticed, as no one ever seemed to take the stairs. There was a small huddle of people in the seating area and as he stood and watched them, he heard the fragile but unmistakable cry of a tiny baby. He froze. A shiver started in the base of his spine and travelled all the way up it, setting his teeth on edge. He closed his eyes, but his head spun and he felt himself sway. Forcing them open again, he stood where he was, unable to move.

'Will!'

Andrew was by his side within seconds. 'Will, Anna Jacob has arrived.' He put his hand gently on Will's arm and Will somehow managed to move forward. His hands shook. Andrew glanced briefly behind him. 'Why don't you go on up, Will, we'll join you in a couple of minutes.'

The cry came again and Andrew could almost feel Will's reaction it was so strong. 'Anna's nanny came to deliver her briefcase,' he said, trying to keep his voice casual. 'She brought Anna's baby with her.'

Will nodded. He stared down at his hands. 'I'll see you upstairs,' he murmured.

Andrew watched him. 'Yes, we'll be up in a minute.'

Will turned, and with an effort that exhausted him, he climbed back up the stairs to the fourth floor.

'You OK, Mr Turner?'

A girl with a tray of coffee stopped as he leant against the wall. He didn't recognise her for a moment, she looked completely alien. Then he managed to nod and her face became familiar again. 'I'm fine thanks, Sharon, I just felt a bit faint, that's all. A bit of the flu still hanging around.'

She looked at him. 'I'll get you a glass of water,' she said, and taking the tray of coffee through to the conference room, she thankfully disappeared. Will took several deep breaths, stood straight and smoothed his jacket. A year, he thought, it had been a year and one tiny cry could catapult him back into a quagmire of grief and confusion.

Chapter Twelve

Anna took a taxi from her meeting straight home. She didn't want to go, but Andrew insisted. She was in no fit state for work, he thought, but she seemed to be the last person to see it.

'Take some time out, Anna, for God's sake,' he said.

'But Andrew, I've only been back at work a day, after six weeks off on maternity leave.'

'Exactly. We've coped for this long, we'll cope a few days more.'

She turned to him as she climbed into the cab and her face was stricken. 'I need to work, Andrew. I shall go insane if I have to sit at home and think about all this.'

'Then work on marking up this agreement and courier it in when you've done it. And get your secretary to send some more work home. Don't come into the office, Anna, trust me, these things need time. Shutting it out won't make it go away.'

Anna looked strangely at him for a moment and he thought that he might have over-stepped the mark; he was fond of Anna, but she was difficult to get close to.

'Thanks,' she said, 'I appreciate your concern.'

Andrew slammed the door and the taxi pulled off. Concern, he thought, it wasn't really enough. He headed back to the building and saw Will Turner at reception, raincoat over his arm, ready to go. It was clear that he couldn't wait to get away.

'Was Anna all right? She looked terrible and she didn't seem to be ... well, quite as cut and thrust as she usually is.'

Andrew shook his head. 'She's OK, but only just. I think she might need some time off, she—'

'You don't need to explain, Andrew,' Will interrupted. 'I've known enough pain and grief to recognise it in someone else.' He was haunted by her face and by her vulnerability. It had got to him in a way that he hadn't expected. 'I've every sympathy for her.' He smiled, but as with all his smiles, it was only half there. 'How old is the baby? She must be, what, a few weeks? It was a girl wasn't it?'

Andrew was momentarily surprised. He said, 'Good guess.' Then he remembered and, embarrassed, swiftly changed the subject. 'Were you pleased with the way the meeting went?'

'Yes.' Will looked away for a few moments, then said, 'Is it marital? The upset? I've asked about her husband a few times, but she's never very forthcoming.'

Andrew shrugged. He wasn't very good with personal information, found it hard to discuss. It was an occupational hazard, client confidentiality and all that.

'Must be,' Will said, then, 'Good.'

Andrew frowned for a moment. He didn't understand what was good, but dismissed it as meaning the conclusion to the meeting.

Will picked up his briefcase. 'I look forward to seeing her again soon,' he said.

Andrew proffered a smile, but it belied his concern. He

hoped to God that she'd be up to it. 'We'll be in touch,
Will,' he said, 'to finalise things. I'll get Anna to set up a
meeting with you.' The two men shook hands and walked
out of the building together.

When Anna got home, Debbie was in the garden with
Maya. They were sitting on the grass, under the shade
of a rather old and tired apple tree. Max had wanted
to pull it up when they had landscaped the garden, said
it was barren and fruitless, but Anna had insisted they
left it. She was glad of that now, it was in blossom and,
looking at it with her baby under it, she had a brief sense
of solidity, of permanence in a world that had suddenly
turned upside down.

Anna stood at the kitchen window and watched Debbie
for a while. She didn't want to admit it, but she had
to, she had to acknowledge now that Jennifer did had
a point. Debbie looked serene. She looked complete,
content, totally absorbed by Maya and Anna wondered
if perhaps that was more than it should be. She opened
the back door, Debbie looked up and waved and picked
Maya up to bring her over to Anna. She gave it no more
thought. Holding her best loved thing in her arms, Anna
realised that from now on there would be little time to
think about things like that.

'Shall I give her a feed?' Anna asked.

'If you want, but I've got enough stored breast milk in
the fridge if you want to chill out for a while.'

Anna stroked Maya's cheek with her fingertip. 'No it's
fine,' she said, 'I'll take her to the nursery and sit up there
for a while.'

She walked away and Debbie suddenly felt the empty
space in her arms. 'Would you like anything?' Debbie

called out. 'Can I bring you a drink up?'

'No thanks,' Anna replied, glancing over her shoulder. 'Have a break yourself. Go out and have a lunch hour if you like.'

Debbie bristled; she resented being made redundant, even if it was momentarily. But Anna didn't see her reaction; she was halfway up the stairs by then.

In the nursery, Anna sat on the small primrose yellow sofa and gently laid Maya in her lap. She rested her head back against the cushions and closed her eyes. She felt the tears well up again, but there was no anger this time. Here, alone with her baby, she felt completely defeated. She felt small and used and bereaved. At a time in her life that should have been joyful, she had only grief. At a time that should have reflected the hard years of work and trust, she had nothing.

'The trouble is, you see, that I love him,' she murmured to Maya. 'Just like I love you.' She let the tears come. 'I can't help it, it's instinctive and I can't stop it, it just goes on and on . . .' She bent forward and kissed Maya's head, then her face collapsed and she began to cry.

Anna was in the study when she heard the front door. It was mid afternoon, warm for April, and as she sat at her desk, marking up the draft agreement from the meeting, the noise made her jump and she realised that she must have drifted off to sleep. She felt momentarily disorientated and confused, then she heard Max's voice and her whole body froze.

'Anna?'

He stood in the doorway but she didn't turn to look at him.

'Anna, are you all right?'

She said nothing.

'Anna, talk to me, please.'

The papers in front of her blurred and she knew she was crying. She put her head down and squeezed her eyes shut tight. There was a silence behind her and then Max said quietly, 'Anna, please don't cry. Anna, I'm so sorry, I really am.'

She swung round and turned on him. 'You're sorry?' she cried. 'Sorry?' She stood up, sending the chair crashing back into the desk. 'Don't give me that bullshit, Max! You weren't sorry when you were in bed with Chrissy, were you?' She stared at him, her face wet with tears, and he looked back at her, his eyes pleading.

'No, of course you bloody well weren't. Don't insult me, Max. You're not sorry for what you've done, you're only sorry that you've been found out.'

'No, it's not like that!' Max countered. 'I am sorry, I'm sorry for all the hurt and pain and for not being what you wanted me to be.' He threw his hands up. 'God, I'm sorry for this whole fucking mess that we seem to have got ourselves into.'

'We?' Anna shook her head. 'We? Are you blaming me, Max? Jesus! That is unbelievable!' She stormed past him, shoving him out of the way and walking into the kitchen. There she stood for a few moments, gripping the sink and staring out at the garden to try and calm the massive rage that had sprung up in her chest. Max made the mistake of following her.

'I didn't mean that you were to blame,' he said. 'I meant—'

'I don't care what you meant!' Anna jerked round. 'I want you out of here, Max, I want you to pack your bags and get out of my house and out of my life.'

He shook his head. 'You don't mean that, Anna, you're just upset, confused. You can't mean—'

'Don't tell me what I mean,' Anna shouted. 'I want you out. You've no right to be here any more, Max, you're not a husband and you've never shown the slightest interest in being a father. You're just a sitting tenant and I want you to get out. I want you to fuck off to be precise!'

Max tensed. 'Don't be rash, Anna,' he said. 'We can talk this through, try to work something out. I have always tried to be there for Maya, you know that, even when I was no bloody use at all. Come on, please Anna, there's no need for all this . . .'

'For all this what? Anger? Upset? What did you want, Max, a nice little cosy scene, with the three of us trying to work out some sort of rota? I have Max on a Monday, you have Tuesdays! For God's sake, grow up!'

'No, I didn't mean anything like that. Please Anna, calm down, let's at least try to talk.'

'Talk about what? What is there to talk about, Max? You are leaving, now, and that's all I'm prepared to say.'

Max stared at her. 'I am not going anywhere,' he said. He clenched his jaw and stood his ground. If he walked out, what chance was there of her ever having him back? 'This is my house too, Anna, and I'm not leaving you and Maya.'

'Yes you are! You're going to do the decent thing for once in your life and get out.' She moved forward towards him. 'You're not staying, Max, I can't even bear the sight of you here.'

She tried to shove past him again, but he grabbed her arms, gripping them tightly and holding her rigid for a moment. 'You've got no right to kick me out, Anna, and you know it,' he cried. 'This is half my house and I pay half the mortgage. I can stay if I want to. I'm not leaving you and I'm not leaving my baby.'

'Oh really,' she shouted, breaking free. In an instant, and without thinking, she slapped him hard across the face. Calm, sensible, strong Anna. She slapped him as hard as she could, the blow made a sharp cracking sound as the bone in her hand hit his nose and Max staggered a few paces back. His nose started to bleed.

'Jesus!' he cried. He shrank back, angry and confused, but deep down conscious of the fact that this was what he deserved. 'I think you've lost it, Anna. You've gone over the edge.'

'Oh have I?' she slung back at him. 'And I wonder who the hell pushed me!'

They stood there for a few moments, locked in rage and pain, then Anna collapsed back against the wall and started to sob. Her body folded in half and she wrapped her arms tightly around herself, racked with grief.

Max stared on, helpless. 'Oh Christ, Anna,' he murmured. Walking to the sink, he ran the tap and doused his handkerchief in cold water, putting it up to his face. Then he took some tissues from the box and walked across to her. 'Here.' He held them out and when she didn't take them, dropped them on the floor next to her. 'You really want me to go?'

She nodded, still weeping.

He stood there for a while longer, desperate for her to change her mind, to at least talk to him, but she said nothing.

'If it's what you really want, then I'll go and pack an overnight bag,' he said. He walked towards the door. 'You need some space.'

She kept her head down, unable to stop sobbing.

'But it doesn't mean I'll leave. I'll be back tomorrow. Perhaps we can talk civilly then about what to do next.' He stood there for a moment, unsure of whether to touch her or not. He decided against it and walked out into the hall. At the foot of the stairs, he saw Debbie.

'Don't pretend that you haven't heard all this,' he said. 'You were listening, you can't fool me.' He walked forward towards her and stopped, just inches from her. She pressed herself back against the wall. 'I don't know what your problem is, sweetheart,' he said, his voice just above a whisper, 'but I'm on to it, OK? I'm on to you.' He looked at her, keeping his gaze unfaltering. 'I hope you're satisfied!' Then he moved past her and went on up the stairs to pack a bag.

Debbie waited in the nursery until she heard the front door and was sure that Max had gone. Then she checked on the sleeping baby and went downstairs to find Anna.

'Anna?' she said gently. 'Anna, Max has gone.' Anna sat huddled against the kitchen wall, her face buried in her hands. She made no move.

'Anna, can I get you some tea or something?'

Anna lifted her head. She rubbed her hands over a face that was swollen from weeping, and stood up. Her legs felt weak and she had to hold onto the wall for support.

'Thanks,' she said. 'Tea please, with sugar.' She pulled a chair out and slumped down onto it. 'I'm sorry that you had to witness that.' She was cold and reached for a cardigan that hung over the back of the kitchen chair. 'Life can be so ugly sometimes.'

Debbie busied herself with the tea and made no reply. She didn't feel guilty – Max had asked for it – but she did feel sorry for Anna, a casualty of war.

'Is Maya all right?' Anna asked.

'She's fine. Asleep.'

'Good. I'll have my tea and then I'd better get back to my work.'

Debbie stirred the pot and poured out a cup. Anna took the mug and warmed her icy fingers round it. 'I'll be in my study,' she said. 'Give me a shout, would you, when Maya wakes up?'

'Yes, OK.' Debbie watched Anna go. She would do no such thing of course, she would wait until *she* was ready to hand the baby over. She smiled. Things were beginning to work out even better than she could have imagined.

In her study, Anna sat down at her desk and took a couple of very long, deep breaths, then she opened the papers in front of her and glanced down at where she had left off. She looked at the work. Work, she thought, all this work. She put her head in her hands for a moment. She didn't want to do it, she wanted to curl herself up in a tight ball and shut the world out, shut the pain out, but she had to, if she was going to survive this, then she had to work. Work would save her.

She re-read what she had been doing. She was in the middle of redrafting a clause in the agreement regarding the provision of a guarantor for the purchaser and had a brief look at the notes she had made during the meeting.

'Blast,' she muttered under her breath. She had made a note about the seller, but couldn't remember what it referred to. She tried to think back, but the whole meeting had begun to blur and she honestly couldn't remember. She picked up the phone, went to dial Andrew McKie, but changed her mind. It was unprofessional to ring with such a minor query, it made her look incompetent. 'Bugger!' She doodled a bit on the pad and re-read the notes. It had to be irrelevant, she decided, she would definitely have made more notes if it wasn't. Anna continued with the redrafting as she remembered it and went onto the next point in the agreement. But her heart wasn't really in it, she just didn't have the concentration level, her mind was all burned out. But work, she kept telling herself, would help; it always had in the past.

Max sat in his car outside Chrissy's small terraced cottage in Battersea and listened to a CD. It was seven o'clock, he had been driving round for hours since leaving Anna and had ended up here. Chrissy was in, he could see the lights on in the bedroom and the sitting room, and every now and then he caught a glimpse of her figure in the window, but he didn't want to knock yet, he couldn't face it, not yet. He could have gone to a hotel of course, or to his mother's, and still could. He wasn't sure why he was here really, except that in thinking he had wanted her all these weeks, he felt now he ought to at least give it a go. He leant forward and turned the volume up. This was a track he particularly liked; it reminded him of being happy and for a moment he was transported back to that time. Then his phone made its irritating little musical noise and he was catapulted back to the present and the grim reality of what had happened that day.

'Hello?'

There was a brief silence on the other end and for a second he thought it might be Anna. 'Hello, Max Slater.'

'Hello Max, it's me.'

It was Chrissy and the disappointment was crushing.

'Hi. The line's not very good, Chrissy, I can't hear you very well.'

'But I should think you can see me quite well,' Chrissy said, 'if you look up at the house now.'

Max turned to look out of the car. At the main bedroom window, with the light behind her, Chrissy stood in a cream lace thong and several ropes of pearls that hung provocatively between her naked breasts. She had the phone to her ear and smiled at Max. She wound some pearls round her finger and brushed them against her erect nipple. Almost as if he had no control over his body at all, Max had an instant erection.

'Are you going to sit out there all night, Max?' she said.

'I'm not sure.' He continued to watch the window.

'How about if I take this off?' In the window Chrissy fingered her underwear.

'What, now? In front of the neighbours?'

'Yes, now.' There was a silence and then the line went dead. Max dropped his phone and saw Chrissy turn her back to him. She bent, so that her tanned, rounded bottom was in full view, and slowly peeled the lace thong down over her hips and thighs. She turned and stood in just the pearls. Then she blew him a kiss and drew the curtains. Max sat for a few moments more, then, overwhelmed by her audacity and her brazen sexuality, he climbed out of the car. This was what he had wanted, wasn't it? This was what it had all been about. He went to the boot for his overnight bag, walked up the path and knocked on the door. He waited several minutes before the door was opened and Chrissy, quite impervious to the passers-by on the pavement, stood naked before him.

'Come in,' she murmured, leaning forward to run her tongue over his lips. 'Or should I just say come?'

Max stepped inside and was enveloped by her. Her scent, her body, her sex. It was a warm, unreal sensation, and he gave himself up to it. But in the back of his mind there was the faintest echo of a voice that said, *Is this all there is?*

Chapter Thirteen

Chrissy liked to come to consciousness slowly. She liked that half-sleep, half-waking period of the morning, when she was warm and content, wrapped in her Egyptian-cotton-covered duvet, her limbs still loose and relaxed, her mind still empty. She liked this part of the day more than anything else, more, in fact than the sated feeling of sex. And, as she rolled over onto her back that morning and touched the solid, muscular shape of Max's thigh, she wondered if it could get any better.

Then the alarm went off. A sharp, electronic bleep, louder than anything she had ever heard before, filled the room. It screamed in her head. Max sat up in bed, fuggy, unshaven and irritable, slammed his hand down over the small clock he had put on the bedside table the night before, and said, 'Fuck. It's six thirty.'

He climbed out of bed, opened the curtains and switched on Chrissy's radio, re-tuning the dial and turning the volume up. Radio One blared out, he staggered into the small en-suite bathroom, used the toilet, turned the taps on full, splashed his face with cold water, did a quick teeth clean, then gargled with mouthwash and spat noisily into the sink. He pulled on Chrissy's silk dressing gown and came back into the bedroom.

'D'you want tea?' he growled.

Chrissy sat up. 'Max!'

He was halfway out of the door, and turned. 'Oh shit, sorry.' He came back to the bed, bent forward and kissed her full on the mouth with his nauseatingly sweet minty breath. 'Sorry. Good morning. I'll go and make the tea, bring you one up.'

Chrissy shoved him away, he staggered back and she jumped out of bed. 'Max, what the fuck do you think you're doing?'

He looked at her, not fully awake, and frowned. 'Getting up, going down to make tea?'

She let out a scream of frustration and stormed into the bathroom, slamming the door behind her.

'Chrissy? What did I do?'

She yanked open the door. 'What didn't you do, you mean.' She pulled on a T-shirt and climbed back into bed. 'Firstly Max, I do not have to get up at six thirty, I do not have a meeting this morning at eight o'clock. Secondly, I do not listen to Radio One. Turn the bloody thing off! Thirdly, I do not want to listen to you pee every morning, fourth, that's my dressing gown, fifth—'

'All right!' Max snapped. 'I get the message. Sorry, I'll draw the curtains, make you some tea and bugger off. I can shower at the office.' He pulled off her dressing gown and threw it down on the bed, yanked the curtains together again, then walked naked out of the room. Chrissy put her head in her hands and closed her eyes.

Moments later Max put his head round the door. 'Do you want milk and sugar?' he asked.

Chrissy dropped her hands away, saw his face and smiled. 'Sorry,' she said. 'I didn't mean to snap. I just can't bear rude awakenings in the morning.'

'That's OK. What do you want? Tea or coffee?'

'Tea please, with lemon, remember?'

Max sighed. 'I remember.' He forced a smile and left the room. How could he forget? She reminded him every time he put the kettle on. She took Earl Grey with lemon and half a teaspoon of organic sugar; put the tea bag in and leave it for a minute, no more because it was too strong and no less because all you got was the bergamot and not the flavour of the tea. Squeeze the lemon before you drop the slice in so that the tea has a good lemony flavour and add a splash of cold water so that it doesn't have to stand for ages in order to be cool enough to drink.

He padded down the stairs in semi-darkness. Then there was the coffee to consider. It had to be fresh – no instant, that wasn't good enough – and it had to be just the right amount in the cafetière; if there was too much coffee she could taste it, it was too strong, and she liked hot milk, done in the microwave . . . Max turned on the lights in the kitchen and went to fill the kettle. He turned on the taps and stood for a moment paralysed by the memory of making bottles for Maya. He reached over, turned the taps off and closed his eyes. I wonder what she's doing now, he thought. I wonder who's making her bottles. He swallowed hard, took a deep breath and tried to put the thought out of his mind. He got on with making the tea.

When Max had disappeared downstairs, some semblance of calm came back to Chrissy. She lay back down and pulled the duvet up round her chin. She closed her eyes. Having Max was all very well, but having him in her two-bedroomed cottage in Battersea was not going to work. If she took him on, she wanted the whole Max package – the house, the car and the share options. Max was a good catch, even to someone who had never contemplated marriage. His career was at its height, he earned one hell of a whack, he was well-connected in the industry, attractive, clever, charming, well-dressed . . .

Chrissy's list went on and as she rolled over onto her side, she let it grow in her mind until he came up with the tea and she said, 'So, what do you do next, Max?'

He took a sip of his tea 'Next? Well, get dressed and go to work I'd have thought. Any other ideas?'

Chrissy sat up. 'Don't be glib, I mean it Max. You need to think about what you're going to do next. How you're going to play this thing with Anna.'

'Chrissy, I can't even think about what I'm going to have for breakfast, let alone make decisions about my future. Give it a rest will you? Let's leave things for a while, let them settle and then think about it.'

'But why? You'll only have to make the same decisions in a month that you could have made today.'

'Chrissy, I haven't got the energy to make decisions, that's why. All I can think about is going across tonight to pack a few more bags and moving enough of my stuff in here to be comfortable.'

'Moving your stuff in here?' Chrissy was shocked. She hadn't expected to be put upon; it just wasn't part of her make up to be put upon. 'Max I don't think—' She stopped. His face had changed and was unreadable. She realised that she was on a fine line between getting her own way and getting nothing at all. 'You're right,' she said, folding her arms across her chest to display her breasts to their best advantage. 'Let's not talk about it now, we've got better things to do.'

Max sighed; he had no impetus for sex at all. 'We don't have time,' he said.

Chrissy went forward onto all fours and moved up the bed towards him. She stopped with her face over his crotch and took him in her mouth. Max ran his hands down the length of her body and between the cleft in her buttocks. She moaned and rolled her wet, warm mouth over his growing erection. 'It won't take long,' she murmured lifting her head and moving slowly up to straddle him. Her breasts were level with his face and he caressed the warm, scented flesh.

'No . . .' he said, catching his breath as she lowered herself onto him. He moaned with pleasure as she ground her hips down and round. 'Just long enough . . .'

Anna woke long before Maya cried out for her morning feed. She sat up, careful not to disturb the sleeping baby next to her, and climbed wearily out of bed. Taking the plate and cup from the bedside table, she carried them downstairs and put the kettle on for tea. Maya had been awake on and off all night, feeding every hour and a half, and it was only at 3.00 am, when Anna realised that she hadn't eaten anything at all yesterday and that her milk supply was probably depleted, that she got up to make a sandwich and a cup of hot milk. She solved the problem. The last feed at four had finally satisfied Maya and she was still asleep now at seven.

But Anna felt crummy. She felt hungover without having touched a drop of alcohol. Her eyes burnt and she moved slowly, not really in full control of her limbs. She made a slice of toast, some tea and took them back upstairs to the bedroom. Sliding into bed under the duvet, she drank a few mouthfuls of tea, ate half the piece of toast and, laying her head back on the pillows, closed her eyes for a moment. Without knowing anything more about it, she fell instantly asleep.

The second time Anna woke, it was with a start. She heard a door close in the house and sat up. Maya had gone and her first emotion was overwhelming panic. She leapt out of bed, ran round it to check Maya hadn't fallen out, then ran out of the bedroom shouting for Debbie. Debbie appeared moments later with Maya in her arms and Anna stopped dead, putting her hands up to her face. Unable to stop it, she began to cry.

'Oh God, I thought something had happened, I thought . . .' The sobs were uncontrollable. She didn't want to cry, she didn't even know why she was crying, but the weeping came up from her chest and overpowered her. 'What the hell were you doing?'

Debbie stood where she was and her face flooded with a deep blush. 'I'm sorry,' she said quietly. 'I let myself in, heard Maya crying, and took her away to wash and change her. I was just going to bring her back. You were fast asleep, I thought—'

'I know,' Anna murmured, suddenly embarrassed, 'what you thought.' She fumbled in her pyjamas for a tissue and blew her nose. 'I'm sorry, Debbie, I got a terrible fright, I didn't know what had happened.'

There was a silence, then Debbie held Maya out. Anna shook her head. 'I must get dressed,' she said. 'You take her downstairs and give her a bottle. I'll have a quick shower and then come down to express some milk. OK?'

Debbie nodded and made for the stairs. 'I'm sorry, Anna, I didn't mean to upset you.'

'No, I know you didn't.' They smiled at each other,

then Anna went into the bedroom. Maya let out a cry
of hunger and Debbie held her close. 'It's all right, little
one,' she whispered. 'I'm here. I'm always here.'

Anna showered, washed and dried her hair and wrapped
herself in a towel. She was just applying some make-up
when the front doorbell sounded. She carried on with
what she was doing, assuming that it was probably just
the postman, but there was a knock on her bedroom
door, she called out and Debbie came in.

'Anna, I'm sorry,' she called out towards the bathroom,
'but there's someone here to see you.'

Anna popped her head round the door. 'Who is it?'

'He says his name is Will Turner.'

Anna was confused. 'Will Turner? Are you sure,
Debbie? Are you sure he said that?'

'Yes, definitely.'

Anna experienced a stab of panic. He wanted her off
the deal, that's what it was, he'd come to tell her she was
sacked. 'Oh God,' she murmured, closing the door behind
her. She leant against it and tried to breathe calmly.

'Anna?' Debbie crossed to the door and knocked gently
on it. 'Anna, what shall I tell him?'

Dropping the towel, Anna reached for her dressing
gown and untied her hair. 'Tell him I'll be down in a
minute,' she said coming back into the bedroom. 'I'll just
get dressed.' Debbie left and Anna opened her wardrobe.
She took out her new lightweight black wool suit, a white
silk shirt and some black shoes. She rummaged in the
drawer for some underwear, found the relevant items and
pulled them on. She dressed quickly, her whole body stiff
with anxiety, slipped her shoes on and went downstairs.
She didn't think to check her appearance in the mirror. If

she had she might have realised that she had forgotten to finish her make-up, had not checked her tights for ladders and still had all the shop labels on her suit.

She walked into the sitting room and found Will Turner there, standing by the fireplace, looking at her photographs. He seemed to dominate the room, his height and build making everything look small and inconsequential.

'Will?'

He turned and Anna tried to smile. She barely knew this man, had met him only on a handful of occasions over the past few months, and his presence in her house made her decidedly uneasy. What on earth was he doing here?

'Hello Anna.'

She held out her hand and he took it, only he didn't shake it, he held it for a few moments, then dropped it and put his hand in his pocket. He looked embarrassed and ill at ease.

'Can I get you some coffee?'

'No, no thanks Anna. I was passing and I . . .'

'What? From Sussex?'

'No, I was on my way to a meeting and I drive through Clapham, on the A3 and, well, I was worried about you yesterday and I . . .' He broke off and glanced down at the floor for a few moments. 'I just wanted to see if you were all right. You and the baby.'

Anna blinked. 'Maya?'

'Ah, that's her name. Yes, I mean, you looked so distraught and I . . . I didn't want you to worry about work and . . . well . . .'

He stopped mid sentence and Anna waited for the rest of it. She waited a couple of minutes and nothing came, so she said, 'Are you sure you won't have coffee?'

'No, no thanks. I've got to go actually. My driver's waiting for me outside.'

Anna frowned. Was she missing something? Was there a point to all this? 'I see.'

Will looked at her, suddenly intense. 'Do you?'

She glanced away. She didn't actually, she didn't see at all and it made her very nervous. She said, 'Was everything all right at the meeting yesterday?'

'Yes, fine.' Will glanced at his watch. 'I really must go, I've got another meeting this morning and . . .' Again he broke off and Anna expected something else, but nothing was forthcoming.

In the hall, he turned to her. 'If you ever need anyone to chat to . . . you know, if things get a bit . . .'

'Yes,' she said. 'Thanks.' She had a fleeting sense that this was some kind of clumsy, impulsive pass, but dismissed it almost immediately. It was highly improbable. 'I'll see you out.'

'No, really, don't bother. You get on with what you were doing.' He opened the front door. 'Bye Anna,' he said.

'Goodbye.' She wrapped her arms around her and watched him walk down the path and climb into some sort of big, sleek car. It had a driver with a peaked cap and for some reason, as she closed the door, that made her smile. A pass indeed! She shrugged and wearily climbed the stairs. It wasn't just improbable, it was completely impossible.

Andrew McKie walked into the office and was told he had a call waiting. 'Who is it?' he asked his secretary.

'It's a young woman,' she answered. 'She's in a call box and she's been waiting for about three minutes now.'

Andrew hurried over to his desk and picked up the receiver. 'Hello,' he said. 'Are you all right?'

There was a brief silence on the other end, then he heard her weeping.

'Where are you?' he said. 'Please, tell me where you are and I'll come and get you. Please, don't cry, please . . .'

The young woman held her hands up to her face in the cramped, stale-smelling phone booth in Crouch End and struggled to gain control of herself. 'I don't know what to do,' she whispered. 'I'm frightened, he knows where I am and—'

'Who knows?' Andrew demanded. 'Tell me who you're frightened of.'

'I can't . . .' The young woman pulled some toilet paper out of her pocket and wiped her face with it. Hearing his voice made a difference, it gave her a bit of comfort at least.

'You're getting the money though? There's no problem with the money, is there?'

'No, no it's fine. I'm just scared, that's all. My social worker has disappeared, I've tried to contact her but she's just gone. No one's seen her since the day that she moved me in and—'

'Calm down a little. Come on now, perhaps she's just moved onto another case, perhaps—'

'No! She's disappeared! I rang them and they've got no record of me, all the systems went down the same day and they've lost all trace of me. I could disappear too and no one would know, no one would care and . . .' She started to cry again and Andrew felt angry and helpless.'

'Look, let me get involved, please, let me talk to someone.'

'No, no you can't! You mustn't!'

'Well can't they move you? Have you complained? If you're being harassed, then they should move you, they should—'

'But they've got no record of me!' she cried. 'I don't exist!'

Andrew swore under his breath. Bloody social services were a totally inept bunch. 'Please let me ring them, let me speak to someone and—'

'No, no really, I don't want you to get involved, I don't want anyone involved.'

'Then let me tell—'

'No!' the young woman interrupted. 'Please don't, please don't tell him.'

'But why not, he could help, he'd get you away from there.'

'No!'

Andrew frowned. He could hear the fear in her voice, but it didn't make any sense. 'OK, if that's what you want. What can I do? I must be able to do something.'

'No, nothing.' She began to sob, she couldn't help herself. Her money was running out and she didn't want to let go of the sound of his voice.

'Please, let me do—' Andrew stopped. The line started bleeping and he said, 'Hello? Are you there? Are you . . .' It cut off. 'Bugger it!' he snapped. He replaced the receiver. 'Bugger it!' he said again and as he swore, he realised that this was one of the rare times in his life that he was at a loss to know what to do.

When Will had gone, Anna went up to her room and lay down on the bed for a while, staring blankly up at the ceiling. None of it made sense, she was numb and confused, not thinking straight at all. Everything that had happened had become muddled up in her mind, she had no sense of the sequence of events, and images and words floated in and out of her head with no pattern at all.

She knew she had to work though, and an hour later, she got up. Her eyes burnt with lack of sleep and her face sagged with the burden of emotion. She went down into her study, collected up the agreement she had been working on and put it in her briefcase. She took her raincoat out of the hall cupboard and left it by the front door with her handbag and briefcase.

'Debbie?'

Debbie appeared from the kitchen. She looked at Anna with her shoes on and her things ready by the door and said, 'Are you going to work?'

'No, I'm off to the beauty parlour!' Anna laughed, in a high-pitched, manic way. 'Should have done it sooner, eh?' She picked up her things.

'But I was going to make lunch,' Debbie said. 'I thought you were staying here today.' It was a lame attempt, but Debbie didn't dare say anything more. It wasn't up to her to comment on Anna's behaviour, but she certainly didn't look fit for work. She looked dishevelled – creased and untidy. She had forgotten to finish her make-up and her face had a strange blank look to it with just foundation on. Her suit was crumpled, her shirt hung out over the waistband of her skirt and her tights had a ladder in them.

'I have to get to work,' Anna said. 'I need to earn a living.' She opened the front door. 'I'll be back this evening.'

Debbie worried for a few moments about what to do, but she left it too late and before she could say anything, Anna waved and disappeared out of the door, slamming it

hard behind her. She heard the baby cry and all thoughts
of Anna instantly evaporated. She went immediately up
the stairs to see to Maya.

Anna made it to the office just before lunch time. She
was oblivious to the looks she received as she walked
through reception and carried on to the lifts unaware.
At her floor, she got out, went down to her office and
dialled her secretary.

'Hello Pam, it's Anna. Could you pop down and collect
a document from me? Thanks.' She hung up and took the
papers out of her case. She glanced up. 'Oh, hi.'

Pam stood uneasy in the doorway, taking in Anna's
appearance. 'Anna, shouldn't you be at home? You don't
look well.'

'I'm fine,' Anna said. 'Here. The latest draft of the High
Tech agreement. Could you type it up, Pam, and circulate
it to the names attached?'

'Don't you want to check it?'

'No, give it to Lucy, Andrew's junior, she can proof it.
I've got a couple of clients to see this afternoon, so I'll be
out until tea time. If you could have my copy ready for
me by then?'

Pam took the agreement. 'Anna, I'm sure you'd be
better off at home, I'm really not sure that—'

'Pam, I'm fine!' Anna said sharply. 'Please, just get on
with the work.'

Pam left the office. Anna never snapped and she had
never looked so distressed, so unkempt. Instead of return-
ing to the secretarial office, Pam walked on down the corridor to see Andrew McKie. He was in the meeting room.

'Mr McKie, I'm sorry to bother you, but may I have
a word?'

'Is it urgent, Pam?'

'Yes.'

Andrew stood up, made his apologies and stepped outside the room.

Pam said, 'Anna's in her office and she seems to be in a bit of a state. She's talking about visiting clients this afternoon but by the look of her she should be at home. I think she's a bit unsteady, Andrew, I don't want her to make a fool of herself.'

Andrew glanced at his watch. 'I'll have a word.' He stuck his head round the meeting-room door and said, 'I'm afraid I have to see someone, I'll be about ten minutes. Sorry about this. Pam will get you all some more tea or coffee.' He shut the door and hurried down to Anna's office.

'Anna!' At a glance Andrew took in Anna's appearance and her anxious state. He picked up her bag and raincoat and said, 'Anna, go home please.'

She stared at him and the muscle in her jaw twitched. He knew she was on the brink of tears. 'Anna, you are a brilliant lawyer, you've got nothing to prove. Please, go home until you've got this thing sorted out.'

Anna stood up. She took her coat and bag from Andrew then, without a word, left the office. She looked at no one on the way out, she kept her head down and forced the tears back. As she left the building, she caught a glimpse of herself in one of the plate-glass windows and saw what a state she was in. She was deeply ashamed; it was the final humiliation and there was no further left to fall.

When Anna got home the house was empty. It had a peculiar deserted air, the washing up had been left in the sink, the nursery was untidy, Maya's things were scattered all over the place and Anna felt a vague sense of unease.

'I'm being paranoid,' she said aloud, as if actually speaking the words made them more concrete. She climbed the stairs, taking her jacket off as she did so, undressing on the way to the bedroom. Once there, she slipped off her skirt, drew the curtains and climbed into her still unmade bed. She pulled the covers up round her chin, closed her eyes and, exhausted, fell asleep.

Andrew McKie was working late. His wife didn't like it, but to be honest, tonight it was a relief; a relief to lose himself in the finite detail of the law. Life could be messy at times and when he was reminded of that mess, like today, he found great solace in the neatness and precision of his work. He had a great deal of it to get through – he was likely to be there for hours – and to cap it all, the High Tech agreement that Anna had been working on had just landed on his desk.

'That was quick,' he said to Pam as she delivered it.

'Anna brought it in this morning, it's been checked and has gone out to the list of names attached. It went out by courier about three this afternoon.'

'Good, well done Anna.' He drew it towards him and had a brief look at it. 'I'll give her a ring later,' he said. 'Check that she's all right.'

Pam had her coat over her arm. 'Will there be anything else?'

Andrew smiled. 'No, thanks Pam. You get off and I'll see you tomorrow. Have a good evening.' He watched her leave and had the smallest twinge of envy; long gone were the days when he could leave the office at six, even if he had wanted to.

It was just before seven when his phone rang.

'Andrew McKie.' It was the lawyer for the buyer of High Tech. 'Yes I have, Mike, I've got it right here, I was just about to look at it.' Andrew pulled Anna's re-drafted agreement out from under a pile of papers. 'It's in front of me now. Yes, yes I did, I . . .' Andrew broke off. 'Yes, I've found the new clause, no, no you're right, I remember the discussion clearly and we did agree that the guarantee should be mutual. No, no it isn't here, I'm afraid that . . .' He broke off again. 'No, it's not a deliberate attempt to go back on what was agreed, not at all. No we don't have a problem with a mutual guarantee, I think that somewhere along the line in the meeting my colleague has misunderstood what was going on and made the wrong notes. No, I really don't think . . .' Andrew took a deep breath. 'Anna Jacob is an associate partner and she's never made a mistake like this before. I apologise, yes I'm afraid that she was, no, not at all well, shouldn't have been there really. No I realise that it's no excuse but, yes I will, I'll get it amended straight away and courier you a new draft first thing tomorrow.' He made a note of what had been said on his copy of the agreement. 'Yes, of course, thank you for your patience. Goodbye.' He hung up and drummed his fingers on the desk. 'Bugger!' he said aloud. The first thing he had to do was amend the agreement, the second was to ring Anna. What the hell could she have been thinking of? Why hadn't she checked it with him if she'd been uncertain about any points? He sighed, switched on his PC and got on with the amendment.

The phone rang by the side of the bed and Anna woke with a start. She was confused for a few moments, disorientated. The house was in semi darkness and silent, and as she reached for the receiver she switched on the lamp which somehow only served to heighten the silence.

'Hello?'

'Anna, it's Andrew McKie.'

Anna sat up. 'Hello Andrew.' She looked out onto the landing and noticed the darkness.

'Anna, it seems that the guarantee clause in the High Tech agreement was wrong. We had discussed in the meeting that the guarantee needed to be mutual and there was no mention of—'

'Sorry Andrew, could you hang on a moment?' Unnerved by the darkness outside her room, Anna couldn't concentrate. She climbed out of bed and walked into Maya's room. It was exactly as it had been earlier, still untidy, still empty. She called downstairs; there was no reply.

Going back to the phone, she said, 'Andrew, look, I'm sorry but there seems to be something wrong here. It's . . .' She glanced at her watch and caught her breath. 'Jesus Christ! It's seven thirty! Where the hell are they?'

'Anna?'

'Andrew there's no sign of Maya and the nanny, they've been gone all afternoon, they . . .' She dropped the phone suddenly and ran into the nursery again. Searching the drawers, she saw that several babygros had gone, Maya's fleece, then noticed that her teddy had gone from the cot, along with a couple of blankets. A sob escaped her. Biting her hand, she willed herself to be calm; she was no use unless she was calm. Picking up the phone again, she said, 'Andrew I think they've gone, I think . . .' She couldn't get her breath. 'I think the nanny's taken her, I . . .'

'Anna stay calm!' Andrew called down the line. 'Just stay calm, try to breathe and stay calm. I'll be there as quick as I can.' He hung up and stood, grabbing his raincoat and briefcase. He turned off his PC, but left his desk as it was, he would have to come back to it later. Hurrying out of the office, he gave no more thought to anything other than Anna Jacob.

Anna was sitting by the front door when Andrew arrived. She had every light in the house on. She heard him knock, pulled open the door and then turned away immediately. 'I thought it might be them,' she murmured.

'Anna, have you heard anything?' She shook her head and sat down on the hall chair again.

'What makes you think that Maya's been taken? Have her clothes gone?' He knew nothing of this kind of thing, he was stabbing in the dark.

'A few things, yes.'

'Has the nanny got a phone?'

Anna nodded. 'It's switched off.'

'Has her pram gone? Anything else?'

Anna stood up. She wrapped her arms around her and walked the length of the hall. 'A few of her clothes have gone, along with her blanket and her teddy. Four of her bottles have gone, enough to keep her going, the pram has gone and so has my car.'

'Your car?'

'Yes, the nanny's taken my car as well.'

'Did she say she might be going out for the day?'

Anna turned. 'For God's sake, Andrew! Would I be scared senseless like this if she had?'

Andrew rubbed his hands wearily over his face. 'Call the police,' he said. 'You can't take any chances, Anna, call them right away.'

She stopped pacing and came across to the hall telephone. 'Who do I ring?'

'Ring nine-nine-nine, they'll put you through to you local station.'

Anna picked up the receiver. She dialled, the line connected, rang and a key went in the front door.

'Debbie?' Anna dropped the phone back and ran to the door. She yanked it open, with the key still in the lock.

'Jesus Christ!' she cried. 'Where the bloody hell have you been? I've been worried out of my mind!' She pushed past Debbie and reached into the pram for Maya. 'You stupid girl!' she shouted, turning on Debbie. Her face was creased with tears of anger and relief. 'You stupid irresponsible girl! I was just about to ring the police.' She walked inside with the baby and went straight upstairs.

Debbie stood on the doorstep and hung her head. Tears sprang to her eyes. 'It was so nice we went out for the afternoon. I took the baby to the seaside for some fresh air. I tried to ring, but there was no reply. I did try, honestly, you can call one-four-seven-one, I did try, I . . .' She broke off and fumbled in her handbag for a handkerchief.

'I'm sure you did,' Andrew said. 'But quite understandably, Anna has been worried sick. You didn't leave a note or ring the office to let her know where you were going or what time you'd be back, and your phone was switched off.'

Debbie blew her nose.

'I'm sure that you didn't mean any harm but I'm afraid that in the present circumstances, with so much hurt and upset in the house, it might have been more prudent to stay put in the garden. Anna is bound to be upset, she is very distressed at the moment.'

Debbie was crying openly now and Andrew wasn't at all sure what to do. 'Look, why don't you get things organised and then make us all a cup of tea? I'll go and talk to Anna. OK?'

Debbie nodded and blew her nose again. Andrew went upstairs.

'Anna?'

Anna was in the bathroom, running a bath for Maya. 'She'll have to go Andrew,' she said, glancing over her shoulder as she began to undress Maya on the changing table. 'I'll give her a month's notice in the morning and start looking for someone else straight away.'

Andrew sat down on the edge of the bath. 'Don't be hasty, Anna,' he answered. 'Everyone makes mistakes. The girl is thoroughly upset, she tried to ring but there was no reply and I honestly don't think—'

'I've been out of my mind with worry, Andrew, I—'

'You've been out of your mind, full stop, Anna.'

Anna turned abruptly.

Andrew looked at her. 'Anna, you need a break. You are not thinking straight, you've had one hell of a shock and you need some time out. What happened this afternoon was unfortunate, but on any other occasion you probably wouldn't have even known about it. Debbie would have been at home by the time you got in from work and all that would have been said was we had a nice time at the seaside today.'

'You're saying that I'm over-reacting, is that it?'

Andrew sighed. This was not a conversation he particularly wanted to have; it was getting a little too close for comfort. 'Without wanting to offend you, Anna, yes, I do think that you might have got things mildly out of perspective, but then you are under a great deal of pressure emotionally and it's hardly surprising.'

Anna rubbed her hands over her face. 'So you think I

should say sorry for shouting, forget the whole thing and take a couple of weeks off, right?'

'I think you'll handle it in your own way, Anna, and you're always fair. But yes, I do think a couple of weeks' break will help you to sort things out, even if it's just in your own mind.'

Anna made no answer, she gently lifted Maya off the changing table and lowered her into the warm bath. 'Is this professional advice, Andrew?' she asked without looking at him.

'No.'

She glanced sidelong at him. 'Thank you,' she said. 'You're right, I'll try to get away.'

Andrew sat and watched her for a few minutes. It seemed both odd and strangely reassuring to see Anna Jacob, sharp, cool, calculating lawyer, tenderly bathing her baby. He thought of the house in Portugal, it popped into his head and he spoke suddenly, without thinking. 'Will Turner has a house in Portugal you could use. He's never there, bought it for investment really and I manage it, as a friend. It's got everything you might need, especially with a baby. Microwave, washing machine, tumble dryer, that sort of thing. It'd be far better than a hotel.'

Anna looked up. 'Will Turner? Oh no, thanks Andrew but I don't think so.'

'Why not? He never uses it and in fact he'd never know if you were there or not. It would do you good, really give you a chance to think things through. Consider it at least, will you?' Andrew was a great believer in holidays. Some people didn't put much store by them, but he had always considered them an essential part of modern-day life. To get away was, for him, the antidote to stress.

'OK, thanks Andrew,' Anna said, 'I'll think about it.' But she had no intention of doing any such thing. She lifted Maya out of the bath, wrapped her in a towel and laid her on the changing table.

'I must get back to the office,' Andrew said. He stood. 'Did you get the redraft of the High Tech agreement by the way?'

'Yes.'

Something in his voice made Anna turn. 'Problems?'

Andrew hesitated for a moment, then said, 'Yes, there was a problem actually, that's why I rang you this evening.' It was obvious that she hadn't heard a word he had said earlier. He went on. 'You omitted to make the guarantee in clause nineteen mutual to both parties. It was discussed in the meeting but never made it into the agreement. I had the purchaser's lawyers on the phone this evening asking if we had done it deliberately. They're pretty upset about it.'

Anna flushed deep red and looked away. 'I made a note, but couldn't understand it when I came to re-draft. I should have rung you, I knew I should have.' She shook her head. 'God Andrew, I'm deeply embarrass-ed. How incompetent!' Biting her nail, she said, 'I can't believe I did that. I've never made a mistake like that before.'

'Don't beat yourself up about it, Anna, it happens. Like I said earlier, everyone makes mistakes.' There was a brief silence, then Anna had the grace to smile.

'I must go,' Andrew said. 'Really. I've got work to do.'

'Redrafting the High Tech agreement?'

'Yes.'

Again Anna flushed and Andrew patted her arm as he

went out of the door. 'Think about the Portugal thing, won't you?'

'Yes, I will.' Anna picked Maya up, snugly wrapped in her towel, and held her, kissing her brow. 'Goodbye Andrew, thank you, I mean, for everything.'

He made for the stairs. 'That's perfectly all right, Anna,' he said. 'Goodbye.'

She watched him descend, heard him go into the kitchen, exchange words with Debbie that she couldn't catch, and leave the house. The front door slammed and he was gone.

'Anna?' Debbie came up the stairs. 'I've made tea, would you like some?'

'Yes, please.' Anna looked at Debbie. 'I apologise Debbie,' she said quickly, 'for flying off the handle like that. I was worried and upset.'

'No, it was my fault, you deserved to be upset, I shouldn't have gone off without telling you. I'm sorry, I had no idea it would distress you so much.'

Anna shrugged. 'A misunderstanding,' she said. 'Best forgotten.' She went towards the nursery. 'I'll just get Maya ready for bed, then I'll come down.'

'OK.' Debbie felt the need to hang around. Maya was smiling at her and the urge to pluck her out of Anna's arms was a powerful one. 'D'you need a hand?'

'No thanks,' Anna said over her shoulder. She didn't say any more – there was no need to – but she also didn't see the look on Debbie's face. Debbie went downstairs thwarted and Anna carried on oblivious.

A short time later, while Anna sat on the sofa feeding Maya, Debbie brought her some tea and said, 'Mr McKie mentioned that you might be thinking of going away for a few days.'

'Did he? Is that all he said?'

Debbie stood by the door. 'No actually, he said if I could persuade you to go it would do you good.'

Anna smiled. 'He's very predictable,' she said, 'and very tenacious. He obviously thinks I should go away and won't give up until I do.' She glanced up. 'What do you think? Would it fit in with your plans, Debbie?'

'What? To come with you, you mean?'

Anna blinked rapidly. She looked away, acutely embarrassed for a moment, and then said, 'Oh, uhm, yes, of course.' But it wasn't of course; it wasn't what she had meant at all. She had been asking if it would suit Debbie to take holiday at that time, only now it had been misconstrued there was no going back.

'Yes it would actually.' Debbie glanced behind her and bent to plump a cushion on the armchair. Her need to get away was so great that she was frightened it would show in her face. 'I can come any time at all. My passport is in order and I've no plans that can't be cancelled.' She stood straight and headed for the door. 'Just let me know where and when,' she joked. Anna forced a smile.

Outside the sitting room, Debbie slumped back against the wall and took a deep breath. To get away would save her, it would save her sanity and give her breathing space, which she desperately needed. She was choking at present, choking on Darren's mounting concern for her, on his continuous future planning, on his pressure for the wedding, on his very presence on leave in her small one-bedroomed flat. She thought she loved him, but she was being suffocated by him, by his constant talk of her pregnancy and of a baby that didn't exist.

In the sitting room Anna tried to weigh up the situation. She had no desire to go anywhere, but she had made a professional error today, something she had never done before, and maybe Andrew was right – maybe they were all right – maybe she had lost it. Maybe Max's affair had pushed her over the edge. She looked down at her dishevelled appearance and cringed. The phone rang.

'Anna?' Debbie had answered it and came into the sitting room with the mobile handset. 'Anna, it's Max.'

Anna started and Maya flinched. She broke off feeding and whimpered. 'Tell him I'm not here,' Anna said.

Debbie held the phone out. 'Anna I can't. He knows you're here, he says he's outside in the car. I'm sorry . . .'

Anna handed Maya across to Debbie and fastened her shirt. She took the phone and switched it on. 'Yes.'

'Anna, it's me. We need to talk.'

'No we don't, Max. There's nothing to say.'

'Anna please, I'm sorry, I really am. We must talk, I want to explain.'

'There's nothing to explain. It all seems pretty straightforward to me.'

'Anna, you can't just ignore this, you must talk to me. I won't go away, Anna, this won't go away. We have to sort things out, we have to—'

Anna hung up. She clenched her jaw to stop the tears and dialled Andrew McKie's mobile. 'Andrew,' she said, when the line connected, 'it's Anna. If this house really is free, then I'll take it, if that's OK.' It was impulsive and unconsidered, but she didn't care. She couldn't face Max, she had to get away from him. How could she talk about things now, when it was all still so raw? 'Tell me where to book my flights to and I'll do it right away.'

She stood and walked out into the hall where she found a piece of paper and a pen. 'OK, yes, I've got that. Thank you. I'll let you know when we travel.' She put the handset back in its cradle and looked at Debbie who was standing in the hall with a grisly, hungry baby. 'Here, let me take her,' Anna said, reaching for Maya. 'You'd better get off home,' she continued, 'and start packing a case. We'll leave as soon as I can get flights. Is that OK?'

Debbie smiled. 'It's fine,' she replied. 'It's absolutely fine.'

Chapter Fourteen

'What the hell do you mean you're off to Portugal?' Darren said, standing in the middle of the sitting room, his hair wet and a towel round his waist. 'You can't just up and off like that! Not when I'm on leave.'

'I've got no choice,' Debbie replied, dragging her suit-case out from the store cupboard in the hall. 'It's work.'

''Course you've got a choice, you say you're not going, that's what!' Darren was really riled. First it was her refusal to let him come with her to the doctor's for a check-up this week and then she hits him with this. 'And what are you going to do about seeing the doctor? You're supposed to have a check-up on Friday.'

'I'll rearrange it,' Debbie said, lugging the suitcase into the bedroom. She left it on the floor by the side of the bed and knelt to open it. 'It's only a check-up.' He came to the door of the bedroom and she said, 'Look Darren, your parents are going to be here in half an hour. You'd better get a move on if you want to get down to the off-licence before they arrive.'

He scratched his head. 'How long are you going for?'

Debbie shrugged. 'A week maybe, ten days. I'm not sure yet, Anna's booking the flights tonight; I said it wasn't a problem.'

'Wasn't a problem?'

Debbie stayed where she was, kneeling, out of his way. He made her nervous in this sort of mood and she automatically took up a defensive position. 'No, it isn't a problem,' she said quietly. 'I'm getting paid my full salary, I'll have no expenses for a week or so, no travel and no food costs and it's easy work. I thought you'd be pleased. We might get a chance to put a bit of money away.' She was rarely outspoken about anything but this trip was hers; she had to go. She had to get away. Standing, she edged round the outside of the room and went out into the kitchen. 'I got a chicken pie from M&S on the way home. I'm going to do that with new potatoes, beans and carrots. Is that all right?'

Darren, still shaken by the whole idea of Debbie going off to Portugal and leaving him alone, followed her into the kitchen and watched her take the shopping out of its carrier bags and lay it on the small Formica table.

'Can you carry the table into the sitting room for me?' she asked.

He nodded, but didn't seem to hear her. 'Can't you make an appointment at the doctor's for tomorrow? Then I can come with you before you go away.'

Debbie's hands stopped moving for a few moments.

'I should be there. I'm the baby's dad, aren't I?'

Debbie froze. There was something in that last question that frightened her. She took a few moments to compose a reply, then turned and said, 'I doubt if I'll be able to get an appointment at such short notice, but I'll ring them in the morning. OK?'

Darren looked at her. She held her breath, but he smiled. 'All right,' he said. Oh God, she thought, how had this all happened? How had she got herself in so very, very deep? The front door buzzer sounded and it made them both jump. 'That's my parents,' Darren said. 'You'd better let them in while I get dressed. We don't want them to think that we're up to no good.'

Debbie smiled. They separated and she went to the door while Darren disappeared into the bedroom.

Pressing the intercom, she spoke to Nora, then released the door lock and went out to the stairs to wait for them. She could hear Nora talking and Doug's vague replies.

'Hello!' she called out.

They came round the corner, up the last flight of stairs and Nora beamed. 'Debbie, I've got wonderful news!' she said, hurrying to embrace her soon-to-be daughter-in-law. 'St Anne's is free! Saturday July the fifteenth at two pm. Reverend Splice has managed to fit us in.' She didn't mention that it was worrying her sick that Debbie would be showing too much and that they would have to try to cover it up if she was. She held up the two carrier bags she had in either hand. 'So we need to get organised,' she went on. 'And I've got everything in here.'

Doug reached Debbie and kissed her on the cheek. Nora took her arm, blissfully unaware of the drowning panic that engulfed her. 'Come on,' she said. 'Don't look so awe-struck! I said I'd get things moving, didn't I? Just wait till I tell Darren, he'll be over the moon!'

Debbie tried to look pleased, raising her eyebrows and making small furrows on her forehead. Over the moon, she repeated dismally inside her head. Oh God, he'll be over the moon.

Max walked up the small path to Chrissy's cottage and dug in his pocket for the spare key that she'd given him.

There were no lights on and, despite the fact that he was late in from work, he was obviously the first. He went inside, sniffed the lingering odour of last night's take-away curry, and dumped his stuff on the floor, going immediately to the window in the kitchen to let some air into the house. He turned on the lights, took a beer out of the fridge and went into the sitting room to switch on the TV. He was tired, upset at not having spoken to Anna and generally pissed off. The place was a mess, not that he could be bothered to tidy it, and he hated being alone. He aimlessly channel-hopped for a while, drank his beer, festered in his bad mood, then, closing his eyes, drifted off to sleep.

He woke, a short time later, with the oddest sensation in his left ear. Putting his hand up to it, he swotted impatiently at whatever it was and turned onto his side. It was only as he did so that he encountered a body next to him. He half-opened his eyes.

'Hello,' Chrissy whispered. 'Didn't you like my tongue in your ear?'

Max sat up. He stretched and rubbed his hands wearily over his face. 'Is that what it was?' he mumbled irritably.

Chrissy uncurled her long body from the sofa and stood up. 'You're in a good mood tonight. What are we celebrating?'

'Ha ha! Very funny!' Max reached for the beer he hadn't finished and swigged down a couple of mouthfuls. 'What shall we have for supper?'

'Who knows?' Chrissy looked at him, tired and creased on the sofa, and although irritated by him she didn't show it. It was early days and there was plenty of time to shape Max the way she wanted him. 'Why don't we have a shower together, get dressed and go out for dinner? Hmmm? It would do us both good to go out together and a nice warm relaxing shower with a massage afterwards might just—'

'I had a shower earlier at the club,' Max snapped. 'And I really haven't got the energy to ponce myself up to pay through the nose for my dinner.'

'Ah,' Chrissy said, 'it really is a bad mood. I thought it might just be lack of sex.'

Max glanced up at her, then went to the kitchen to get himself another beer. 'Many things this relationship lacks, Chrissy,' he said spitefully, 'but sex is not one of them!' He took another bottle of lager out of the fridge.

'That was uncalled for,' Chrissy said from the doorway. 'You know the score, Max, if you don't like it, you don't have to stay.'

Max turned. She was right, he was here of his own free will and the last thing she needed was him carping on at her. 'I'm sorry,' he said, 'I guess I'm just missing my things, my habitual way of life.'

She came across to him and put her arms round his neck. He folded her in to him and breathed in the scent she wore, warm and spicy, full of sex. 'It's different for both of us,' she murmured.

'Yes, yes it is.'

Chrissy moved out of his embrace and took the beer from his hand, drinking a mouthful. 'Maybe getting a few more of your things might help?' she suggested.

'Maybe.'

'Perhaps the sooner you break your old ties the better?' She trod lightly; she didn't want to be seen to be pushing, but Max needed a bit of a shove. 'If you had a few more of your personal possessions around you it might make

the break feel cleaner, might help you feel better in your
own mind about things. We'd need a bigger place though.
Maybe something in Chelsea Harbour.' She turned away
to let this sink in. Bending to look in the fridge, she said,
'Now, supper, let me see . . .'

Max dug his hands in his pockets and watched Chrissy
fiddle about with bits of old vegetable in the bottom of
the fridge. He could see that her heart wasn't in it and
frankly nor was his. Would cutting a clean break with
Anna make him feel better? Was that what he really
wanted? He had thought it was, had been consumed
with a desire for freedom, but now he had it, what did
it all mean? Coming home to an empty house that wasn't
even his, constantly on the move for the next experience,
sex, dinner out, massages and foreplay in the shower. He
sighed and turned to look out of the window at the small
patch of brick that Chrissy called a courtyard garden. A
few terracotta pots and a bench. Even the sex didn't feel
as good as it used to.

'How about pasta with some mushrooms, green beans
and cauliflower?'

'Cauliflower?'

'I bought it to make cauliflower cheese a couple of
weeks ago. It's a bit black in places, but I can chop those
bits off.'

Max shrugged. 'I'm not terribly hungry to be honest,'
he said, being not in the least bit honest. He was starving.
'I might just go up to bed and read for a while. I'm
bushed.'

'OK. I'll settle for a glass of wine and a Pot Noodle in
front of the telly then.' Chrissy looked at him. 'Are you
sure you don't want to go out?'

Max had a sudden flash of memory – the same scene,

different people, different kitchen and the roles were reversed. But the words were the same, almost exactly the same. Why had he always been so insistent about going out? What was there with going out anyway? 'No, sorry Chrissy, I'm just not up to it,' he said.

She shrugged. 'OK.' Switching on the kettle for her Pot Noodle, she took a bottle of wine from the wine rack and reached into the drawer for the bottle opener. This will have to change, she thought, skewering the cork and popping it out of the bottle.

'Night Chrissy,' Max said. 'See you in bed.'

'Yup, see you in a while,' she replied. This has definitely got to change, she determined, pouring a large glass of Fetzer and taking an enormous rage-calming gulp. The wine hit the back of her throat and warmed down inside her neck, right down to her stomach. She let out a breath. This, she told herself, taking a Pot Noodle from the cupboard, peeling off the lid and pouring on the boiling water, will not happen again. She took her wine and her supper into the sitting room, and sat down in front of the television, cross and alone, to eat.

Will Turner sat in his study and stared out at the garden in the dusk. He should have been working, he had a whole stack of things on his desk to do but he couldn't concentrate. He was tired and his mind was a jumble of thoughts. He hadn't slept well last night, but that was nothing unusual – he rarely slept well. He had woken in the night thinking that he heard a baby crying in the house, and the pain and fear had been so acute that he'd had to get out of bed and walk around for a while to ease it. It had happened before, it was nothing new, only this time he could hear the cries so clearly that they felt as if they were coming from right beside him. And that scared him. It scared him that his emotion was still so raw that it could twist his mind and make him imagine all sorts of things that were no longer there.

Will stood up. He stretched his legs, which got stiff so quickly from all the running, and walked across to the window. The fruit trees had taken root and were growing well. There was a scattering of blossom on them, pale pink and white, and it lifted his spirits just to see it. He thought about Anna Jacob and that too lifted his spirits. He wondered when he was going to see her again. She intrigued him, with her legal, pointed manner and yet her vulnerability so close to the surface that he felt he could almost touch it. Brittle was the word that sprang to mind, like an eggshell, brittle and so easy to crack.

He heard the front door and turned from the window, wondering who the hell it was calling on him without an invitation. He heard the housekeeper's footsteps along the passage and braced himself for her opening the door.

'Will, there's a delivery for you,' she said, just putting her head into the room, 'you have to sign for it.'

Will sighed irritably. 'What, at half past six? I'd have thought most drivers would have knocked off by now.' He hadn't ordered anything and had no intention of signing for anything, but that wasn't Sheila's problem. He would have to sort it out himself. He walked out into the hallway and saw a man in blue overalls at the door. 'Can I help you?'

'I've got a delivery for Turner,' the man said. 'It's from the States. I'm sorry it's so late, mate, but I couldn't find the place earlier and had to put you to the back of me work sheet.'

'I'm sorry, but to the best of my knowledge I haven't ordered anything.'

'Well it says here Turner. Is this Calcott Manor, Widbry, West Sussex?'

'Yes.'

'Well that's what I've got written down.'

'Here, let me have a look. You don't know what it is, do you?'

'Yeah, it's some kind of garden equipment for kids. It's custom-made in the States apparently. It's . . .' The man broke off. Will had walked away. 'Oi! I gotta deliver it, mate! It's all paid for, you just gotta . . .'

Halfway down the passage, Will stopped. The dizziness came, then the struggle to breathe. Sheila appeared at his side and he managed to say, 'Send him away. Let him deliver the stuff and send him away, please . . .' He stumbled on blindly towards his study. Once there, he sank onto his knees and closed his eyes, concentrating hard on breathing. He struggled for a few moments, fighting to get the air into his lungs, then he brought it under control. He began to count it through, breathing in, slowly, counting up to ten. He held it, then let the breath out, counting again to ten. The dizziness started to clear. He kept going, counting and breathing, slowly, slowly, slowly. He opened his eyes.

He remembered now, she had ordered it, a whole play area. She had ordered it and it had never come. Will looked up as Sheila knocked on the door.

'Here,' she said, 'I've brought you some tea.'

He took it, supporting himself on the desk as he got to his feet. 'Thanks.' The tea was hot and very sweet; it made him wince. 'Did that driver leave the stuff?'

'Yes, I got Sam to organise it. They took it to the barn to store it.'

'You have it, Sheila.'

Sheila flushed. 'Oh no, Will, I couldn't possibly have it, I . . .' She stopped and, embarrassed, looked down at her hands. 'You can send it back, get your money back.'

'It's paid for, Sheila, I had it specially made.' He looked at her. 'How old are the children now?'

'Eight, six and five.'

'They'd love it. Have it, Sheila, get Sam to bring it over in the Land Rover. Please.' He turned away from her and walked across to the desk. Picking up some papers, he left his mug on the edge of the desk and sat down. 'Thanks for the tea.'

Sheila collected the mug. In the doorway, she stopped and said, 'If you're sure, Will.'

He didn't look up. 'If you don't take it I shall leave it to rot in the barn. I don't ever want to see it.'

Sheila looked at him for a moment and wished there was something she could say or do to ease his pain, but there wasn't. Not for the first time, she uttered a silent prayer of thanksgiving for her own children, then she left Will to get on with whatever he was doing and went to see Sam about delivering the play frame.

Will sat where he was, papers in hand and the words blurred, making no sense at all. Nothing made any sense at all. He thought about April, about children playing on the grass, little girls in summer dresses, cherry blossom, asparagus and days that had begun to stretch long into the evenings. He thought about spring and new beginnings and he felt sadder and more hopeless than he had for a very long time. Every time he tried to forget, at every turn there was something there to remind him. It was hopeless, it would always be there, that pain, that terrible grief and guilt and helplessness, it would be there for the rest of his life.

Will dropped the papers on his desk. He walked up to his room, dragged a big canvas bag out of the wardrobe and started throwing things into it. His trainers, deck shoes, shorts, T-shirts, sweater. He packed quickly and simply; just the necessities. When he had finished, he zipped it up and carried it downstairs.

In his office, he called Andrew McKie, left a message on his voicemail and asked him to e-mail any urgent queries regarding the High Tech deal. He wrote out several cheques, one large one for cash, and some brief instructions to Jenna. She was to handle everything, work as many hours as it took and e-mail him with any problems. He asked her to cash the cheque and use it when required. Then he packed his laptop away and left his desk as it was. He didn't have time for tidiness.

In the kitchen he found Sheila.

'I've decided to go away for a while,' he said.

She glanced at his bag. 'How long for?'

He shrugged and even though they were the same age Sheila thought he looked so young and so lost at that moment that she wanted to hug him like a child. 'Are there any specific instructions? While you're away?'

'No, just keep things running for me would you?' He laid a cheque on the table. 'There's a month's money, so that you don't have to worry, and Jenna will have cash if you need it.'

Sheila nodded. She wanted to say that it wasn't going to help – to run away – that it hadn't helped before and that all the pain was still here when he got back, but she didn't. Whatever she felt she kept to herself, Will Turner didn't invite intimacy. 'Thanks. You'll call and let us know when you're coming back will you? So that I can get the house ready, get some provisions in.'

'Of course.' He picked up his bag. 'I'll see you,' he said, turning to leave.

Then Sheila did something very uncustomary; she hurried up to him and kissed his cheek. 'Take care,' she said.

'Yeah.' Moments later he was gone.

Sheila went back to the sink and wondered where he was going; she wondered if he even knew as much himself. She doubted it. He had hardly known anything since it all happened, he was a man just existing. And that was no life for anyone.

Chapter Fifteen

Anna slipped her seatbelt through the loop in the orange child's seatbelt and fastened it loosely round her waist. Debbie handed her Maya, she sat the baby on her lap and strapped her in safely too. The seatbelt sign came on, an announcement was made and they started the last of their descent into Faro.

'We've made it,' Anna said, leaning over to look out of the window. 'I have to say that I'm quite looking forward to it now.'

'Me too,' Debbie said, 'despite the set-backs.'

The spur-of-the-moment trip away had taken several days to arrange in the end, with flights almost fully booked because of half-term week, Andrew unable to contact the management for the house and Darren kicking up a fuss about Debbie leaving him alone. It had taken so much hassle in fact that Anna had sorely doubted going and had been on the verge, several times, of cancelling the whole thing. But now, with the blue evening sky spread out before her and the sun bouncing off the water below, she was relieved that she had seen it through. This was her first proper holiday for two years and she was quite surprised at how excited she was. Bugger Max, she thought, as the plane tilted and made a wide arc in to land. Bugger Max and bugger Chrissy, they can both go to hell! There was a gruelling sinking feeling, a sharp bump, the screech of brakes and they were down.

Anna smiled. It was the first genuine smile, for herself, in over a week.

The hire-car company were waiting on the other side of customs with Anna's name written on a piece of card. 'It would seem that Andrew has taken care of everything,' Anna commented to Debbie as they followed the representative to the desk and then out to the car park. They unloaded their luggage, a bag each and three for Maya, stacked up the car and climbed in. 'The sales guy said we can follow him,' Anna said. 'He's in a red Fiat apparently, so keep your eye out for . . .' Anna slammed the car into gear and reversed out of the parking space at top speed. She accelerated hard and moments later caught up with the sales guy. 'For a young man in a red car!' She swung out behind him, onto the right side of the road and glanced behind her at Maya in her hired car seat. To look at her baby filled her with both exquisite joy and overwhelming sadness. What had Maya done, to find herself in the middle of such an emotional mess? Anna drove on. And what, she couldn't help asking, had she?

It was just after six when Anna and Debbie drove into the Val de Lobo estate. It was marked by a wide stone arch and consisted of cool leafy boulevards with houses set back in lush, scented gardens. They were still following the man in the red car, who had slowed and indicated, pulling into the side of the road. Anna pulled in after him and wound her window down.

'You have the address?' he asked.

Debbie passed Anna her handbag and she pulled out her travel package. She handed over the slip of paper with the address of the villa on and the young man nodded, then smiled. 'Is very nice. Very nice road. Come, I show you.'

'Sounds promising,' Anna said. 'Thank God again for Andrew.'

They drove on, for only a few minutes more, down past the beach and right onto the back of the golf course. At a set of black wrought-iron gates, the red car slowed, stopped, then its hazard lights came on. Their guide jumped out of the car, spoke into an intercom on the white pillar and then turned, showing them the thumbs up. He grinned, the gates opened and, jumping back into his car, he drove into the grounds of the house. Anna followed.

'Blimey!' Debbie murmured beside her.

The villa was low and white, with a salmon-pink terracotta tiled roof and a long terrace that swept the length of it. The windows and doors had dark wood shutters and pink bougainvillea trailed over the whitewashed walls in abundant colour. The gardens were lush and green, cool and leafy in some spots, brilliantly sunny in others. When the iron gates shut behind them and Anna took in the whole place, she had the wonderful feeling that she had been suddenly closed into a sanctuary. She opened the car door and sat for a few moments, breathing in the cool, fragrant air, then she climbed out and walked up the steps onto the terrace of the house. The front door opened.

'Hello, Mrs Jacob?'

A dark woman in a light blue dress and white apron

stepped out of the villa smiling and Anna held out her hand. They shook.

'I am Millou, I look after the villa for you while you are here. Meester Andrew phone me and tell me you arrive today. And you have baby?' She looked past Anna towards the car, where Debbie was lifting a sleeping Maya out into her arms.

'Ah, how lovely, you have tiny baby!' Millou swept past Anna, down the steps towards Debbie and the baby. She was beaming and making clucking noises with her tongue. Anna laughed. She watched Millou take the baby, still clucking, and carry her, carefully and tenderly, up the steps into the villa. She followed.

The inside of the house was white and cream, white marble floors, cream calico sofas and white walls. The wood was East African, dark and heavy, chiselled into intricate patterns on the table tops and legs, and the only colour was from the hand-woven cushions and rugs.

Millou gently placed Maya into a special baby seat on the floor, stood and indicated a green glass jug of Sangria and two glasses. 'Please,' she said, 'have something to drink.' She smiled at Anna, then at Debbie and lastly beamed at the still sleeping baby. 'Oh, she so beautiful!' she cried, clucking again, and Anna laughed once more. It felt good; it was the first time she had laughed in days. 'Come, some Sangria. And welcome,' Millou said. 'Welcome to Portugal.'

Max drew up outside the house in Clapham and sat for a few moments with the engine running, uncertain of whether to go in or not. It didn't feel right somehow, with Anna away, it felt intrusive. But then she *was* away and she hadn't told him where, just that she was going and that if he wanted to pick up any stuff, the next ten days were the time to do it. He switched the engine off, knowing that he had to get it over and done with, and wondered yet again where she might have gone. He had been obsessed with it all day, ever since he'd got her e-mail. He didn't like not knowing what she was doing, it worried him; it distanced her and he wasn't at all sure he liked the idea of that. If he was honest, he might have admitted that he missed her, but he wasn't able to be honest with himself. Yet.

Climbing out of the car, Max locked it and walked up the path to the house. He took out his key, put it in the lock and let himself in, going immediately to the alarm and deactivating it. The house was dark and silent. They had only been gone since lunch time, but already it had that unlived-in smell, musty and airless, and it felt empty. He wandered through to the kitchen, turned on some lights and looked in the fridge. Immaculate, not a rotting bag of salad in sight. He opened a couple of cupboards – neat and orderly, no binge buying, just enough of everything – then he sat down at the kitchen table and put his head in his hands. All those things, he thought, all those minute, unnoticeable things that were just part of living with Anna. Her cleanliness, her sense of order, her desire to have things right. He had lived with those traits every day for the last seven years and yet not once had he noticed how much they contributed to the smooth running of his life. He remembered his shock at making himself some scrambled eggs at Chrissy's a few days ago and cracking an egg which gave off such a stench that he had to fumigate the kitchen. Four months old it had been – not just one, but the whole dozen, four months and one week out of date. He shook his head. He had joked last night, asked Chrissy if she kept old vegetables because she felt sorry for them, because they didn't have a pension or private health insurance, but she hadn't laughed. 'If you don't like it,' she'd said, 'you don't have to stay.' It had become a bit of a refrain that one.

Max stood. He walked out of the kitchen, turning on lights as he went, stopped to look in the sitting room and smiled at the precision of its arrangement. It had taken them weeks to get it right, to hang all the pictures and arrange the bits and pieces. He had the creative eye, Anna had the sense of perfection, and they made a good team. The result was pretty stunning.

He went upstairs. In the bedroom, he paused for only a couple of minutes, finding it too painful to stay. He took a bag from the wardrobe, unhooked several hangers of clothes, knelt to grab a couple of pairs of shoes, then walked out. He did it all without switching on a light. Finally he stopped at the nursery. The small, simple room with its garish, inappropriate curtains that Anna had taken in her stride with only thanks and praise for Debbie and relief at not having had to do them herself. Max felt suddenly overwhelmed with shame. He could have done them. He could have chosen a Designer's Guild fabric from the book Anna liked and ordered a pair to be made. He could have put up the cot and at least done something to contribute. But he had done nothing. God, that must have hurt Anna. He went into the room and picked up the teddy that Debbie had bought and he had given to his daughter. It was a sad, pathetic, cheap-looking thing, which, he thought, was apt. He dropped it back into the cot, the smallest bit hurt that Anna had left his one gift to Maya behind, and then a great deal irritated with himself for such terrible self-pity.

He moved on, down into his study, finding the things

that he wanted: a current biography he was reading, his files of work, his DNAD awards and a photograph of his father. He put them all in the bag and went back into the hall. The red light was flashing on the answerphone. Max pressed it and his mother's voice filled the silence of the house. He slumped back against the wall. God, Jennifer! No one had told Jennifer!

'Hello, Anna, Max darlings, it's me!'

Max put his hands up to his face. It was as if she were in the room with him and he broke out into a sweat.

'I'm just calling to see if I might come up tomorrow to see you all. It's been over a week and you know how much I miss little Maya. I've got some photos by the way. You must see them; they're beautiful. Anna, you look radiant and Maya is exquisite. Funny though, I don't seem to have one of you, Max. We must rectify that soon and have one of you all. Anyway let me know tonight will you, darlings, I'm desperate to see my gorgeous granddaughter. Hope I haven't used all your tape. Lots of love. Bye for now!' The phone clicked, the tape whirred into rewind and Max took out his handkerchief to wipe his face.

All his life Max had wanted his mother's approval and love. He had wanted her attention so desperately over the years that he had done everything he could think of to impress her, and yet here she was, wanting pictures of his family and longing to see them all. Here she was, overriding all her criticism of Anna, all her coolness towards him in order to be part of his family. A family he had literally just tossed away. Max stood straight and took a couple of deep breaths. He would have to ring her tonight, tell her the truth, explain what had happened, if he could find the words. He smoothed his jacket, picked up his bag and went through the house, switching off the lights he had turned on just half an hour ago. He stood in the darkness for a few moments before he opened the door and looked around him. So this was what he had come to, a dark empty house and a bag full of his possessions. It was nothing, when it could have been so much.

Vilamoura was lit up and teeming with people when Will Turner docked his thirty-foot Nicholsan at its mooring on the far side of the marina. He switched the motor off and jumped down onto the walkway, handing a thousand escudos each to the two young Portuguese lads who had guided him in. They shook hands and wished him well, disappearing quickly up the gangway towards the shops and bars of the marina complex, laughing and joking as they went. Will watched them go and remembered some time in his past when he had had such energy and enthusiasm for life. It made him feel tired. He smiled. Hell, he was tired! He had been on board for three days now, sailing hard around the coast, just him and miles of ocean, clouds and wind. He had eaten poorly, living off cans and fresh fruit, biscuits and tea and he realised, standing there in the warm, with the lack of motion underfoot and the absence of the elements beating over him, that he was ravenously hungry and needed a bloody good wash. He decided to lock up the boat, cover it and pack a few things in a bag. He could either take a room at the Marine Hotel for a couple of days and plan his next trip or go back to the boat. He would see how he felt after a few beers and a good meal.

A short while later, Will found a restaurant in the marina that looked reasonable and sat down, ordering himself a beer and asking for the menu. He liked good food, but he had never been one for pretentious restaurants. A good steak and chips washed down with a few glasses of red wine did very well for him and if it came with a fresh green salad and a decent vinaigrette, then frankly he was happy. He ordered exactly that from the menu, asked to see the wine list and chose a half bottle of Dāo to go with it. He sat back, watched the holiday life and smiled at a gaggle of young girls in skimpy tops and short skirts who had singled him out for their fleeting attention. He borrowed a paper, read a few pages, then his meal arrived and he ate. He had forgotten how good food could taste.

His steak finished, he chatted with the waiter about boats for a while, ordered a coffee and a Portuguese pastry and took out his mobile phone. He switched it on, realised that he probably would have to check into a hotel as its batteries were running low and he needed to recharge it. He could also pick up any messages on his PC while he was there and send a couple of e-mails himself. He asked for the bill, dialled Andrew McKie's home number, feeling the need to make personal contact with a friend, and swore under his breath when he got the answerphone.

'Hello Andrew, it's Will. Just to let you know I'm in Portugal for a few days. I've been sailing and thought of you and Marjorie and the last time we were on the boat together. I'm going to check into the Marine Hotel for a couple of days so you can reach me there if you need to. Sorry not to have spoken to you. Hope you're both well. Bye.' He ended the call and switched the mobile off.

The waiter, who was hovering with the bill, said, 'The Marine Hotel is full, sir, my brother he manager there and they have a big conference.'

'Oh damn. What, no rooms at all?'

'I don't think so. I ring now for you if you like.'

'Thanks, that'd be great.' Will glanced at the bill, laid some cash on the plate and drummed his fingers on the table-top while the waiter went off. His good mood had instantly evaporated. He didn't like change, that was his problem, he didn't like anything new; it unnerved him. He always went to the Marine Hotel, he knew it, they knew him, it had everything he needed and he was blowed if he was going to go anywhere else and find it not up to scratch.

The waiter came back shaking his head. 'I talk to my brother. They got rooms from Friday but not today.'

Will handed him the payment and said, 'Thanks for trying anyway. And thank you for dinner, it was excellent. Keep the change.' Then he stood and started back for the boat. He hadn't always been like it, of course, he had been quite adventurous once, travelling the world on his own with a backpack. But that was before it all happened. That was before he realised how vulnerable he was, how much danger there was out there and how fragile life could be.

He stepped down onto the walkway and headed for the boat, only another night on board really didn't appeal. Then he thought about the villa. He had wondered about it many times over the past few days, had already decided to call in there on the way back to the airport to check it was being managed properly, but now he actually thought about going there for a few days. He hadn't been before, not at all in the last year – he hadn't been able to face it, yet another place he had once been happy. But he had to get over the difficulty some time and it would be better than any old hotel. At least it had everything he needed.

Will made his decision. Turning on his heel, he walked away from the boat and back towards the marina. He would get a taxi up on the main road and call Andrew from there as well, let him know he was at the villa. He felt better about it already. And increasing his pace, he headed for the taxis, a long hot shower, warm, clean towels and a normal-size bed.

Andrew McKie opened the door and let Marjorie go in first. She took off her shawl and laid it over the back of the Regency chair in the hall.

'Marjorie!' Andrew removed it and hung it up. He saw no point in spending a great deal of money on antique furniture if his wife was going to drape her clothes all over it.

Marjorie turned and smiled. 'You're getting pernickety in your old age, Andrew,' she said. 'You'll have to watch it or you'll become a grumpy old man!'

He smiled.

'Cocoa?'

'Please. I'll just go into the study and check my messages. Call me when it's ready, will you?'

She nodded and went into the kitchen. Andrew walked along to his study. This house was far too big for just the two of them, but Andrew loved it. It was furnished with impeccable taste – not his, Marjorie's – and it gave him, every time he entered it, a feeling that he had really made it. Once a hungry ambitious young boy from a council estate in Glasgow, now here in Kensington after an evening at the theatre, about to go into his book-lined study for a bit of work. He smiled and touched the hand-painted wall. Perhaps more than a *bit* of work, but then nothing came without its price.

Andrew pressed the answerphone replay button first and listened as he switched on his PC. The first couple of messages were social, he would leave them for Marjorie. The third was from Will Turner and it made him stop and sit down. The next was from Will again and this time Andrew reached for the phone. He picked up the handset, flicked through his phone book and found the number he was looking for. He dialled, let the line ring for some time, glanced at his watch and realised it was hopeless. The management offices would be closed and there was no other way to contact Anna.

Marjorie knocked on the door and put her head round. 'Cocoa's ready.' She frowned. 'What's up?'

'I arranged for Anna Jacob to go to Will Turner's house in Portugal. She left this afternoon. Now I get a message from him to say that he's in Portugal and on his way to the villa tonight. I wondered what the bloody hell had happened to him, he's been gone for several days.'

Marjorie came in. 'Oh dear.'

They were silent for a few moments, then she said, 'Why did you suggest the villa anyway?'

'Well he never goes there, he wanted to sell it earlier this year and I persuaded him to hang on to it for a couple more years as an investment. I thought it would be better for her than a hotel, what with a young baby and nanny etcetera.'

Marjorie reached out and patted his arm. 'You were right, Andrew. I'm sure it'll be OK.'

He shook his head. 'I'm not so sure, Marjorie. It's embarrassing at the least, damaging at the worst.'

'Damaging? Whatever makes you say that?'

'Two fragile people, insecure and alone.' He sighed and stood up. 'Well, one thing is for sure – there's nothing I can do about it now, so I might as well come and have my cocoa and then get on with some work.'

'Andrew, you're not going to work now are you? It's twenty past eleven!'

He smiled. 'Someone has to pay the cocoa bills, Marjorie.' He linked his arm through hers and they went back to the kitchen for their bed-time drink.

Maya was awake and so was Anna. It was after midnight, Anna had gone to bed at ten, but had been woken by Maya at eleven and was still trying to settle her. She had fed her, changed her and walked around the room with her, making gentle soothing noises, but nothing seemed to work. So now, in desperation, she got up to make herself a drink and to sit outside on the terrace. It was very warm and she wondered if a little cool air might make the difference.

In the kitchen she made tea with a slice of lemon and, carrying Maya into the sitting room, pulled open the huge sliding glass door that led onto the terrace. She stood in the doorway for a while, the breeze that came in off the sea cooling both her and the baby. She leant her head against the cold glass, Maya wrapped in a blanket in her arms, and closed her eyes. She could hear the sea, a faint lulling noise in the distance, but nothing else. Nothing except the soft breath of her baby and the steady pulse of her heart.

Will's taxi drew up at the drive to the villa and he climbed out, handing a note across to the driver and not waiting for his change. He shinned over the gates noiselessly and landed with a soft thud in the drive. He had keys to the house but no remote for the gate. Walking up the steps, he noticed a small window on the first floor open and was immediately irritated. He would have to see the management tomorrow. That was shoddy and irresponsible; anyone might get in. Silently opening the front door, he stepped inside the house, his deck shoes soundless on the marble floor, and went towards the sitting room. It was a bright night, almost a full moon, and he didn't need to switch on any lights. He rounded the corner into the wide white room that looked out over the sea and stopped dead in his tracks.

There at the window was the vision he had always feared might one day come back and haunt him. She was standing in the moonlight, the wind blowing her nightdress and the baby in her arms. He dropped his bag, it hit the floor with a thud, and he let out a cry, a half-strangled cry of fear.

At that point Anna opened her eyes and turned.

Chapter Sixteen

Will reached out to the wall. The dizziness came, it swamped him and he held on tight, gripping the solid reality of brick and plaster. He started counting, his breath coming in spasms as he struggled to bring it under control.

'Oh God!' Anna laid Maya on the floor and ran across to him. 'Will?' She recognised him almost immediately she turned the light on. Her brain, still reeling from the shock and fear, had somehow clicked into motion and she had subconsciously placed his face. But she was confused and shaking as she went to him. She knew him, but she had no idea what he was doing here.

'Are you all right?' She made to touch him but he jerked away. He couldn't speak, couldn't draw the breath in, his face was ashen and his lips were blue. Anna did the first thing that came into her head: she ran to the kitchen, turned the cold tap on full pelt and filled the plastic bowl in the sink. She picked it up, ran back into the hall with it and threw it at Will. He flinched, his whole body juddering as if she'd slapped him, and then he gasped, taking in a mouthful of air. He started to breathe with long, hard rasping sounds as each breath went in. Anna stood helpless.

'I'm sorry, I . . .' He stopped and dropped to his knees, the breath coming more easily now. Minutes later, he slumped against the wall and attempted to smile at her. 'I'm sorry,' he tried again, after another lapse of time. 'You gave me such a fright, I wasn't expecting anyone to be here . . .' He broke off. 'I'm slightly asthmatic, nothing serious, I have a problem when I get stressed . . .'

'You gave me one hell of a scare as well!' Anna was suddenly annoyed. Her fear, then panic, had given way to anger. 'What on earth are you doing here? Andrew said you never came here, he convinced me that—'

He held up his hands. 'I don't. It's just . . .' He broke off and looked at her. 'I'm afraid it's just one of those incredible coincidences.'

Anna looked away. She blushed, not prettily, but a deep flush of blood that flooded her face and neck, making her body break into a sweat. She was silent for a few moments, then she picked up Maya. Cradling the baby, she said, 'I'm sorry. I'll pack now and leave first thing in the morning.'

She moved past him, but he reached up and touched her arm. 'Please, don't rush off. Let me explain.' She turned and Will got to his feet. 'I haven't been here for a year or so, I hardly ever come, but I keep a boat on the marina in Vilamoura and I've been sailing for the past few days. I needed a shower and a good rest and my usual hotel is full so on the spur of the moment I decided to come here. It's me who should be apologising, for creeping in and scaring you half to death.'

'Actually it was you who seemed to be scared half to death,' Anna said. 'If you don't mind me saying so, I was worried about you for a few moments. Don't you have a puffer?'

Will dug in his pocket. 'Here.' They both smiled. Will noticed that she smiled with her whole face and that her eyes shone. He liked that. 'I'm not actually, in medical terms, asthmatic, it's purely stress, but they gave me an inhaler anyway, to keep me happy. I never use it, I forget it's there. Look,' he said, 'I desperately need a wash, I should think that I'm stinking you out here and . . .'

Anna pulled a face. 'I didn't like to say anything but . . .'

Will looked suddenly embarrassed and she smiled. 'No, not at all, I was only joking.' He smiled back. They seemed to be standing there doing an awful lot of smiling but it didn't occur to either of them that it might look faintly ridiculous.

'Look, why don't I go and have a shower and then we can have some tea and decide what to do next. OK?'

Anna nodded. 'I'll make the tea,' she said. 'It's the least I can do.'

'Deal.' Will picked up his bag. 'What rooms are being used?'

'I'm in the master bedroom, well I assume it's the master suite, the one with the four-poster bed . . .' Anna blushed as she said it, feeling terribly presumptuous. 'But I can change the sheets now and let you have that one if you—'

'Don't be silly,' Will interrupted. 'I wouldn't dream of it. You stay put.'

'And my nanny is with me. She's in the blue and white room, on the far right.'

'Oh yes. Is there anyone else, parents, cousins, friends?' Again Anna blushed and this time Will smiled. 'Only joking.' He headed for the stairs. 'I'll be down in twenty minutes or so.' Anna nodded and he disappeared up, leaving her to watch him as he went.

*   *   *

In the guest room on the left wing of the house, Will sat down on the bed and put his head in his hands. His stomach was churning with the most noxious cocktail of emotions he had experienced for a long time. He had been frightened back then, genuinely scared, and for a few moments he wondered if he was losing his mind. He had thought it was her, he had thought that she was there in the room with him and it terrified him. She and Anna were the same type, not particularly alike, but the same build, both blonde and slim. Both alone and vulnerable. The similarity between them was apparent now and he wondered why the hell he had never noticed it before. Or perhaps he had, he had just never admitted it to himself.

Will shook his head and stood up. This was bizarre. He was soaked and yet he'd hardly noticed it, neither of them had. Something had happened then, something weird, a connection, if there were such things, a strange, intangible connection. He stripped off his clothes and walked naked across to the bathroom. And that was another thing, he thought, turning on the shower, it was a bloody long time since he had had an erection.

Clean and changed, Will made his way downstairs, leaving the lights off. He found Anna and Maya in the kitchen, Maya still wide awake, rocking very gently in a baby seat, Anna, now dressed in shorts and a T-shirt. There was a warm, sweet smell in the room and a kettle was simmering on the cooker.

'I put the croissants that Millou left for us in the oven,' Anna said, 'but there's no jam I'm afraid, I'm not that organised.'

'A veritable feast, even without the jam.' Will sat down

at the table. 'I would offer to show you where everything is, but I don't know myself.'

'That's OK, I've pretty much found what I need. Tea or coffee?'

'Tea please.'

Anna made the tea in mugs with the tea bags she had brought from home. 'Terribly British,' she remarked, taking the mugs to the table, 'I've brought my own tea bags.'

Will smiled.

She then took the warm croissants out of the oven, put them on plates and took those over too. She moved Maya's seat closer to the table so she could see what was going on and finally sat down. 'It feels like breakfast,' she said. 'I can't believe it's only one am, it feels like seven thirty.'

'That's because you're on holiday. There's no sense of time on holiday, not like there is at home.'

There was a whimper from the floor. 'Well,' Anna said, bending towards Maya. 'There never used to be, but now, who knows? I shouldn't think this one's little body clock stops on holiday.' She picked the baby up and Maya made the funny little 'O' shape with her mouth that she always made when hungry.

'Oh dear, she needs feeding. I'm sure she can smell what I'm eating and wants it right away.'

'Do you want to feed her now?'

Anna looked away. She wasn't prudish, she'd had a sensible, discreet attitude to breast feeding all along, but there was something about feeding in front of Will that made her uncomfortable. Perhaps it was his attractiveness, perhaps just the fact that he was a man she didn't know well. 'I'll wait until we go up to bed,' she replied, hoping her embarrassment didn't show.

'Shall I hold her while you eat your croissant then? She looks as if she might be getting a bit cross.'

Anna was surprised. 'Would you mind?'

'Not at all. I'd like to.' Will stood and reached for the baby. 'What's she called again?'

'Maya.'

'That's right. I'd forgotten. Pretty name.' He took her and held her, turning her expertly to face her mother so she wasn't alarmed. She turned her head, puzzled, and looked up at him, then she smiled and made a baby satisfaction noise.

'Born to flirt!' Anna said. They both laughed and Will walked Maya over to the window while Anna ate. For several days she had been virtually forcing food down in order to keep up her milk supply, but now she didn't have to force down anything. The croissants were sweet, flaky and buttery and they melted in her mouth. She ate two, drank her tea and was licking her fingers and wiping the last crumbs off the plate when Will turned back.

'Good Lord, that was quick!'

Anna laughed. 'I was hungry. I didn't realise just how hungry until I tasted the croissants.' She stood and took Maya back. 'Look, I really will move out tomorrow and let you have the house to yourself. I'm sure the management can find us a decent hotel.'

Will looked at her. She had crumbs down the front of her T-shirt and butter on her chin. She looked tired and tousled and maternal with Maya on her hip and yet so sexy that it startled him. 'No, I won't hear of it,' he answered. 'I'll kip here tonight and go back to the boat tomorrow. It would be unforgivable of me to let you go and find somewhere else, with the baby and your nanny in tow. No, I absolutely insist that you stay here. Really!'

Anna stared at him for a moment, then smiled. He looked rather odd with his earnest expression and open honesty, odd and pleasing. 'We'll talk about it in the morning,' she said, 'but thanks for the offer.' She carried her plate to the sink and left it there. 'Goodnight Will,' she said.

'Goodnight Anna.'

She went upstairs to bed, climbed into it and banked the pillows up behind her to feed Maya. But as she glanced down at the baby, Anna saw that she had dropped off to sleep. So she laid her in the cot and went to bed. Switching off the light was the last thing she remembered. She was asleep as soon as her head hit the pillow.

When Anna woke the following morning, the sun was streaming into the room and Maya was making tiny gurgling noises in the cot next to her. She felt different to how she had felt for months and, sitting up, she realised that she felt refreshed. She glanced at her watch.

'My word, it's nine o'clock!' She leant forward and peered over into the travel cot. Maya smiled up at her. 'You little star, Maya Jacob, you've slept your first night through!' Anna grinned; no wonder she felt refreshed.

Pulling on her dressing gown, she drew back the curtains and threw open the French windows, stepping out onto the balcony. She looked at the rolling, lush green landscape of the golf course and in the distance the glittering blue sea. 'You should see the view, Maya,' she called over her shoulder. 'It really is spectacular!'

She stood in the warm morning sun for a while, tilting her face up to it, then she looked down at the gardens below and caught sight of a young man in white shorts and T-shirt laying out the blue-and-white-striped cushions on the chairs around the pool. She watched him for a while, watched him water the huge terracotta pots, clean the pool terrace and finally put up a large white canvas umbrella over the teak table. She saw Millou come out, speak to him and hand him a basket. He began to lay the table with silver and glasses and Anna went inside.

'This is some place,' she whispered to Maya, then she sat down on the bed and pinched herself very hard.

Will was on the terrace drinking coffee when Anna came down. He was chatting to Debbie, who spoke quietly back to him, not quite able to meet his eye and plainly intimidated by the situation. Debbie stood as Anna walked out onto the pool terrace, relieved to see her, and said, 'Shall I take Maya while you have your breakfast?'

Anna registered the feeling that she was loath to give Maya up, but quashed it. Debbie needed to be employed, she realised that.

'Thank you,' she said. 'Have you eaten?'

'Oh yes, Millou made me an omelette.' Debbie took Maya and cuddled her, looking down at the radiant little face. 'I'll take her into the shade,' she said, 'on the veranda.'

Anna nodded. She watched Debbie go and joined Will at the table.

'Good morning.'

'Hello.'

'Did you sleep well?'

'Actually I slept wonderfully, for almost eight hours. Did you?'

Will shrugged. 'I never sleep well, but I slept OK.'

Anna wondered why momentarily, but it would have been impertinent to ask. She sat down.

'I think your nanny was relieved to be let off the hook,' he said. 'She seemed to be a bit uncomfortable talking to me.'

'She was probably a bit overwhelmed.'

'Coffee?' Anna nodded and Will poured her a cup. 'Overwhelmed by what?'

Anna was taken aback for a moment. The question was so arrogant it seemed out of character. 'By all this! Come on, don't tell me you can't see that.'

'I don't notice it to be honest.'

Anna shook her head. She was irked by him. 'I think that's arrogant,' she said, unable to hold down her irritation, 'to be blasé about such conspicuous wealth.'

Will looked at her. 'You're cross,' he said. 'I'm sorry, I don't mean to be arrogant, but to be honest with you I don't notice very much in my life.'

'Then that's sad,' Anna concluded.

Will drank his coffee in silence for a few minutes. He stared out at the sea in the distance and wondered when it had all stopped meaning something. 'I think you're right, I think it is sad,' he said. 'I guess I've come to the conclusion that none of it really matters. All this . . .' He spread his hands. 'It's not important.'

'It's not if you've got it!'

Will suddenly laughed. 'Oh boy, am I glad you're on my side, Ms Jacob, I should think you're a formidable opponent.'

Anna smiled. She wasn't irritated any more, she could understand where he was coming from, but it did make her wonder how someone who had everything could be so poor.

Will finished his coffee and said, 'Now, what would you like for breakfast? Millou cooks a wonderful omelette, we have fresh fruit, pastries, rolls, bread, cereals . . .'

Anna held her hands up and laughed. 'Just a roll and coffee will be fine, thank you.' Will passed her the basket and she took a roll.

'Millou found the jam, I see.' Anna helped herself to butter and cherry jam. 'It looks delicious.'

'I made it myself,' Will said. Anna narrowed her eyes. 'OK, OK, I confess, it's shop-bought, but it was worth a try to impress you.'

'I'd have been more than impressed, I'd have been stunned.' They laughed and Anna said, 'I was thinking, about you moving out, and I wondered, erm, if it's all right with you, whether we couldn't both use the house for the next few days, sort of share it. I'd really hate it if you moved out on my account, I mean it is your house and if you still insist that we stay, well maybe that would be a good compromise.'

Will looked away. He had been in isolation for so long now that the thought of company unnerved him, but he had to admit that the idea appealed. Anna was an attractive woman.

'You're not sure,' Anna said. 'I'm sorry, it was presumptuous of me. Look, let's stick to plan A and I'll find somewhere else. I don't want to impinge on your space and—'

'No! No, it's not that, you're not *impinging* – great word by the way – it's just that . . .' He stopped. What was it exactly? Just the unfamiliarity of it really. He thought for a few moments about sharing his house, then about sharing it with Anna, and surprised himself by how much he actually liked the idea. He didn't continue his sentence and in the end said, 'Actually, I think it's a good idea. It would be nice to have some company and—'

'And having a tiny baby around will drive you completely nutty. It's OK, I understand! It was a daft idea, I can see that, let's just—'

'No really! It wasn't daft, it was a good compromise. I like the thought of Maya around.'

'You do?' Anna narrowed her eyes. She stared at him for a while and realised – just as she had realised on that unexpected and extraordinary visit he had made to her house – that Will was very earnest. He meant what he said.

She puzzled over that fact for a moment, then he said, 'Come on, let's do it, for a day or so at least.' He stood up. 'I don't want to hear any more about it, OK? It's decided.' He dropped his napkin on his plate and pulled a cap on. 'How about I show you round a bit this morning, drive you over to the food markets in Quarteira, show you where to get bread and stuff?'

'No I couldn't possibly take up your time like that. We'll find our way round eventually, please, I don't want to put you out and—'

'Anna.' Will shook his head and smiled. 'Anna, let's just be honest with each other shall we? I offer because I want to. If you don't want to come, just say so, no offence. Let's be straight, please, I'm not very good at these polite gestures.'

Anna smiled back. 'OK. Yes, I'd like to come. Thanks.'

'Good.' He turned to go.

'Will?' He glanced back over his shoulder. 'Do you really mean it, about being honest and straight with each other?'

'Yes, yes I do.'

'Then you've got jam on your chin,' Anna said. And laughing, she ducked as he picked up his napkin and threw it at her.

Nora Woodman sat in the hall with the phone in her hand. She had taken it off the hook and put it back so many times in the past hour that it was ridiculous. Either she had to get on and make the call or she should stand up and forget it completely. She hated herself for dithering, but there was so much at stake and she really wasn't sure she was doing the right thing. That stupid boy! If it hadn't been for Darren's lack of control then she wouldn't even be in this situation. It was like opening Pandora's box. What would she do if she gained a knowledge that she didn't want? What would she do if her fears turned to reality?

Nora sighed. She glanced down at the number Debbie had given her as a cover and finally made her decision. She would ring; it was her moral duty to do so. She dialled, went through to reception and asked for Madeline Watts. Her call was connected immediately.

'Madeline Watts!' said a sharp voice on the end of the line. Nora's nerves faltered for a moment, then she said, 'Hello, Mrs Watts, my name is Nora Woodman from Kids R Us nanny agency and I'm ringing to check up on one of our applicants, a Miss Debbie Pritchard. Would you have a minute to discuss her with me?'

There was a brief silence, then, 'I do have a minute, but that's all.'

'Thank you.' Nora's hands began to sweat. 'How long did you know Debbie Pritchard?'

'Two and a half years.'

'And were you happy with her as a nanny?'

Again there was a pause. 'I was happy, yes, to a certain extent. But it's the same with all these girls, you know, they appear caring and efficient when you're there, but God knows what they get up to when you're not. The children liked her, she seemed happy with us, but then one morning she just left, walked out and to be honest that's coloured my opinion ever since. That and . . .' Mrs Watts broke off. Nora wiped her hands on her skirt.

'And what, Mrs Watts?'

'That and the false references.'

Nora caught her breath. 'False references?'

'Yes, I'm afraid so. When she walked out I was furious! I thought it was highly irresponsible to be frank and I was also very disappointed in her. I was so upset, in fact, that I decided to check her references to see if this had happened before, and lo and behold two of them turned out to be bogus.'

'I see.' Nora could hardly speak. Out of the box the demons rose up. 'In what way? Made up completely?'

'Yes. Her qualifications are bona fide, as is the first reference, but the second two are complete fiction. I contacted the agency, of course, the one who had supplied her to me, but she had moved on. All I can say is that I'm glad that you've got the foresight to check because I hate to think what those false references might be covering up.'

'Quite.' Nora felt sick. She heard Mrs Watts take a breath, ready to mount another attack, and said quickly, 'Well thank you for your time, Mrs Watts. I appreciate it.' And immediately cut her off. She replaced the receiver and, trembling, leant against the wall. So there it was.

Her head was filled with all the terrible thoughts she had unleashed, and the knowledge that she hadn't wanted to acquire lay heavy on her shoulders.

Max steered his mother smoothly through the cool white tables at Conran's Mezzo, following the waiter and nodding every now and then to the odd person that he knew. They stopped at a discreet table in the corner and Max pulled out his mother's chair for her. She sat, took the menu and opened it without saying a word.

'Would you like a drink, Mother?'

Jennifer lowered her menu. 'A gin and tonic please, young man,' she said to the waiter. 'And make it a large one. I'm going to need it.' The waiter nodded and Max winced.

'A mineral water for me please,' he ordered. 'Sparkling, with a slice of lime, not lemon.'

He picked up his own menu and perused it. Jennifer was firmly hidden by hers. 'I hope this expense-account lunch is not to butter me up regarding your disgraceful behaviour, Max,' she said loudly, keeping the menu in place. 'I do not condone affairs, never have done and never will do. The sooner you leave that trollop and go back to your wife the better if you ask me.'

'She is not a trollop, Mother!' Max snapped.

Jennifer put down her menu.

'And could you please keep your voice down,' he hissed. 'This place is full of ad men.'

'I don't care if it's full of archbishops, Max! Your behaviour belongs in the gutter and I'll not have you try to buy my silence with a lunch.'

Max glanced hastily round the room, held down his irritation and took another tack. 'Mother, I brought you here to try to explain what's happened, not to have a row about it, and I thought you might like a lunch out. It's ages since we had some time together.'

Jennifer snorted derisively. The drinks arrived and she took a large gulp of hers before Max had even been given his. 'That's hardly my fault,' she said.

'No, you're right, it isn't, it's mine. I work long hours and recently I've been rather taken up with—'

'Screwing around!' Jennifer finished for him.

'That wasn't quite what I was going to say,' Max answered. He was beginning to regret this whole idea. He had suggested it on the phone last night to calm Jennifer down; she had been in such a state that it was the only thing he could think of. He had imagined that they would be able to talk about it sensibly and that an expensive restaurant would take a bit of the sting out of things. But he had been wrong. She was tense and acerbic and her anger boiled dangerously close to the surface. The last thing he needed was a scene in the middle of Mezzo.

'Look Mother, let's not row here, please. I know how you feel, you told me as much last night, and I realise that it's all been a bit of a shock for you, but it's been a bit of a shock for me too. I had no idea that Anna would react the way that she did and I—'

Jennifer put her glass down. 'You what, Max? You thought she might say: oh dear, silly you! Never mind, we all make mistakes.' She bent and took up her handbag, an ancient, stiff, black lizard-skin affair, with a gold clasp and bamboo handles. She had had it for decades and Max wondered briefly if she still had that old tin of travel sweets at the bottom of it. She took out a packet of cigarettes, laid them on the table and replaced her bag on the floor. 'Would you kindly ask the young man for a light,' she said.

'This is a no-smoking table, Mother,' Max replied.

'By the looks of it, this is a no-old-people restaurant, but I'm here aren't I? Please ask, Max.'

Max did as he was told, was informed by the waiter that this was a no-smoking part of the restaurant but was given some matches nevertheless. Jennifer lit up, the waiter scowled, and Max said, 'I didn't know you had taken up smoking again.'

'I haven't. I just feel like it right now,' Jennifer replied. She took a long drag and turned to look round the restaurant. Max watched her. She had never been a happy woman, but now she looked thoroughly miserable. Max experienced a stab of guilt.

'I miss little Maya,' Jennifer said suddenly, turning back. Her face had softened and her eyes glittered with unshed tears.

'I know I nagged Anna, that she didn't do things the way that I would have done, but I was fond of her, Max, in my own way, and she's kind, kind and clever. I was proud of that – that you had got yourself a clever, accomplished wife. And well, then little Maya was born, what, only eight weeks ago, and my life changed. All of a sudden I felt important again and needed and when I saw that tiny baby in hospital I knew that I had a role to play, an important one. I was a grandmother and I've looked forward to that for so long . . .' Her voice wavered and a tear rolled down her cheek. Max was acutely embarrassed.

'None of the work, you see, none of the struggling to keep it all together because your father never lifted a finger, never even made a cup of tea, not in all the thirty years we were married. None of the struggle to work through the miscarriages – seven of them – and to carry on so that you didn't see it, covering it up, all the pain and not telling your father because he didn't like a fuss. None of the struggle trying to make it look good, to be in control.' She wiped her face on the napkin and left a smear of beige make-up on the white linen. 'There's none of that, just the love. With Maya there's just the holding and cuddling and buying things and being with her.' She smiled. 'I was there when she first smiled you know. I was there.'

Max sat silent and stared down at the starched white tablecloth. The waiter came and went. 'You never told me,' he murmured.

'Told you what? About the miscarriages? Why should I have done? You were too young to understand and when you grew up a bit it wasn't relevant. That part of my life was over.'

'But you were always so distant, so, so busy and clean and always doing things. You could have said it was a struggle.'

'Could I?' Jennifer finished her gin and glanced round for the waiter to order another one. 'And what would that have achieved, Max? I was busy because I had to be, because I had no help, there was only me to do all of it and because if I didn't do something I would have gone insane with grief and disappointment.'

'But seven miscarriages! I just can't believe that you've never said anything.' Max felt affronted by this confession. He felt left out and hurt. 'Why didn't you ever say?'

'Because it was private,' Jennifer snapped. 'And some things are best left unsaid.'

'Then why now?'

Jennifer looked at her son. She reached out and took hold of his arm, her fingers surprisingly strong. 'Because

I want to explain, I want you to know that I love my granddaughter, I love her like she was my own child, Max, and if Anna leaves you and I don't get to see her then . . .' She glanced away for a moment, her face distraught, then she turned back to him. 'Then God knows what I'd do,' she said and for a moment, Max froze.

Sheila heard the front door and dried her hands on her apron. She went to answer it.

'Registered delivery for Mr Will Turner, can you sign for it?'

'Hello, where's Reg?'

'He doesn't do the registered.'

'I see. Can you hang on a minute? I'll call Mr Turner's secretary. He's away and his secretary signs for all his post.'

Sheila went across the hall and along the passage to Will's study. She knocked. 'Jenna, there's a registered letter. Can you sign for it?'

Jenna nodded, stood and followed Sheila out into the hall. 'I'll put the kettle on, Jenna. Would you like a coffee?'

'Please Sheila.'

Jenna went to the door. She signed for the letter, looked at the envelope and went into the kitchen.

'Anything important?'

Jenna shrugged. She read the frank and said, 'It's from the trustees.' The women looked at each other.

'You'd better e-mail him,' Sheila said. Jenna nodded. 'And let's keep our fingers crossed.'

Chapter Seventeen

The young woman went to the post office and queued up at the counter, glancing nervously over her shoulder as she waited. At the front of the queue, she showed her card and said, 'Hello, I've come to collect my post.' The old lady behind the counter smiled and handed two letters across. The young woman forced a smile back; it took a great deal of effort. She tucked the letters down into the front pocket of her dungarees and walked out into the warm early-morning sunshine.

Some distance from the post office, in the shade of a tree, she stopped and took the letters out to look at them. The first one was from Andrew McKie, she recognised his hand writing, the second was a white Conqueror envelope with a typed name and address. It instantly unnerved her. She was tempted to open it straight away, but she knew she wasn't safe; she was never safe out on the streets. So setting off again, she held both letters in her hand and walked as fast as she could. It was a mile and a half to the Harbridge estate but she was home in under fifteen minutes.

Inside her flat, the young woman locked the door behind her and sat down on the floor. She left the letter from Andrew – knowing that was money – and opened the other one first. She saw the solicitor's heading and her name, in plain, legal black and white, and her heart began to pound. She read on.

We are writing to inform you that Mr Andrew McKie has recently been in touch regarding the release of certain funds in your name and although he is the main trustee of your estate, we felt it prudent to notify the other trustee, more as a matter of courtesy than anything else, that you now have access to your funds. We trust this is acceptable to you.

Yours sincerely,

B.J. Myers, Senior Partner

The young woman stared at the letter for quite some time, but she didn't see the words – the thoughts were racing through her mind too fast to see anything concrete on the page. She started to sweat, and wiped damp palms on the threadbare rug underneath her. She had to move, she had to get out. She couldn't be found, not by him, not by the other one, and if she had been frightened in the past it was nothing compared to the terror the thought of that gave rise to. She picked up Andrew McKie's letter and tore it open; it contained two hundred pounds in cash. She stood, put the money in her side pocket and went into the bedroom.

She had very little to pack, it would all go in the rucksack. She began to lay things out on the bed, quickly and efficiently, and once she had everything there, she packed it all neatly into the bag. She was ready.

That was the only good thing to have come from her time inside, the lack of desire for material things. When they had stripped her of everything else, she found that she still had her mind and spirit intact and from that point on, she knew that they were all she really needed.

Opening the door of the flat, she hitched the rucksack up onto her back, glanced right and left to check that she was alone, and stepped out. She knew where she was going and she knew what she had to do. She would confront the fear, take the advantage and watch him. She slammed the door shut behind her and went on her way. For the last time.

Anna jumped out of the car as they rounded the corner into the market area of Quarteira and leant in for her straw bag. The traffic was bumper to bumper, the car park was full and crowds of people spilled out of the covered markets onto the roads, dodging the three-wheeler vans laden with produce.

'Where shall I meet you?' she asked Will.

'I'll walk up with Maya and see you in the fruit market.'

'Are you sure that's OK?'

'Of course it's OK!' he said. 'There's no point in both of us trudging miles from the car. Besides which if you get the shopping done we can have longer for coffee and pastries.'

'Right.' Anna blew Maya a kiss, slammed the door and darted across the road towards the markets. Will watched her go. He loved to watch her; he loved the way that her body was so well put together with such natural grace and the way that her hair moved and shone and blew over her face in the wind, making her cross and causing her to push it out of her eyes and sigh irritably. He loved her hands, they were never still; she talked with them, or stroked the baby when she held her. She was extraordinary, he thought, such a balance of dynamic energy, intelligence and reasoned calm. Anna measured things, she kept them contained until she was ready, until she had thought them through and reasoned them out and yet she was such fun, with such a spontaneous sense of humour, that he couldn't remember a moment in the last week when he hadn't been laughing.

Anna jumped onto the pavement, turned to look back and Will waved. She looked momentarily puzzled at his delay, there was a sudden loud symphony of screeching horns behind him, and Will realised he'd set up a traffic jam. He hurriedly shifted gears, grated them, jerked forward and finally moved off. Glancing in his rear-view mirror, he saw Anna laughing at him before disappearing inside and it made him feel good.

Anna shopped prudently. She liked to taste the grapes and strawberries, squeeze the melon, check her peaches, choose her tomatoes individually and generally make a right pain of herself at the stalls. But she got what she wanted and she was a good judge of produce, she knew a perfectly ripe tomato when she saw one. She had shopped for the fish first – sea bass and some giant prawns to barbecue – and now she was selecting newly cropped asparagus, salad and potatoes. She bought what she wanted and no more, despite the stall holder's insistence that she should have a whole kilo and not just three quarters, then she went outside into the sun, stood for several minutes watching the traffic of Portuguese shoppers and decided to start along the sea front towards where Will would have parked the car.

Halfway along, she saw him. She stopped, stood where she was and put her bag down on the ground. He was sitting on the low brick wall that separated the pavement from the drop down onto the beach and he had the pushchair facing him. He had expertly put the sun shade up so that it covered the whole of Maya and he held her tiny hands in his. He was singing to her and she was responding with such delight that it made Anna's heart ache with love. She watched for some time. She watched his face, his smiles and rapt expression and she realised that he was totally oblivious to the passers-by, completely unselfconscious in his desire to please the baby.

She had the oddest feeling. It was a slow dawning, a sort of peculiar knowledge that she thought she might have had all along, but not recognised until now – the knowledge that he really was the most attractive and remarkable man. She looked at him again, taking in the whole man. The tall, athletic frame, the faded and worn but effortlessly stylish clothes. His face, hopelessly unshaven, tanned and wrinkled, and his smiling eyes.

She picked up her shopping again and walked along to him.

'Hello, are you having a nice time?'

'Ah ha! Mama's here.' Will stood and took the shopping from Anna. She took hold of the pushchair. 'Coffee?'

'Please.' They turned and headed for the cobbled walkway in the shopping precinct and Anna said, 'It's funny how easily we slip into little routines. Shopping, then coffee and cakes. It's become a bit of a ritual, hasn't it?'

Will smiled. 'Yes it has. I have to confess I rather like it.'

'So do I.' Anna bent forward over the pushchair. 'And so does Maya, judging from all those smiles you get from her.' She turned to him. 'You're very good with her, Will.

I don't know why but I get the impression that you've done it before.'

Will had been looking at Anna and thinking how nice her skin was with just a light colour from the sun and how young the freckles on her nose made her look. He registered what she said and in that moment he remembered. He remembered it all, it flooded him and he had no control over it. He turned away from her and stopped.

'You go on, Anna,' he managed to say. 'I've forgotten something. I'll be with you in a few . . .' He didn't finish what he was saying, he simply strode away, leaving Anna confused and alone on the pavement.

Anna stared after him. He walked fast, not watching where he was going, and knocked into someone, righting them and apologising, then walking away at a greater pace. He disappeared into a side street and Anna stood there still, her hands gripping the pushchair, the urge to cry suddenly rising up and threatening to overwhelm her. She swallowed hard and pushed Maya on. At the small café they usually stopped at, she went inside and ordered *café con lette*. She didn't want a cake, she didn't really even want the coffee, but she felt she had to order it, to do something normal, in the light of such bizarre behaviour. She took the coffee and sat down outside in the sunshine, but she didn't enjoy it. The warmth had suddenly gone out of the day.

In a side street Will stopped and put his hands up to his face. He had never cried, never, and that was the problem, or so his doctors said. He couldn't let it out and so it wouldn't let him go. He took several deep breaths and his head started to clear. There was no dizziness this time, just the images, the wonderful, achingly sad memories and the terrifying picture that he could never get out of his head. He rubbed his face, massaging his temples with his fingertips, and opened his eyes. In his pocket he found his puffer, he opened his mouth and pressed it twice, releasing the Ventolin. He took a sharp intake of breath, stood still for a couple of minutes and then began to feel better. He wasn't genuinely asthmatic, he knew it, they all knew it; he wouldn't be able to run the way he did if he was. But there were times when a shot of Ventolin did the trick and one of those times was now.

Standing straight, he ran his hands through his hair and walked back towards the precinct and Anna. He hadn't worked out what to say yet, but whatever it was, it wouldn't be the truth.

'Hello.'

Anna turned. 'D'you want a coffee?' She got up, her purse at the ready, and Will touched her arm.

'Sit, let me get you one.'

'I'm fine,' she said tight-lipped.

He pulled out a chair. 'No you're not. Honesty, remember? You're upset and I don't blame you. I'm sorry for just marching off like that, it wasn't anything weird, it was an asthma attack. Not a bad one, thank God, but the last thing I wanted to do was collapse at your feet again gasping for breath.'

Anna turned to him and he took off his sunglasses to look at her face. 'Anna, I'm sorry, but it embarrasses me. I don't want you to see me in a state.' She softened. He could see it, her whole body relaxed and he was relieved. 'Come on, let's have a coffee and a cake. I shan't feel that my morning is complete unless we do.'

'OK.'

'And this afternoon,' he said, digging in his pocket for

some change, 'for our last afternoon, how about I take you out on the boat for a sail round the coast?'

Anna was surprised. 'Well, I, erm, I . . .'

Will stood. 'I'll get the coffees, you think about it.'

He went inside and Anna mulled the idea over but she was just as uncertain when Will returned with the drinks. He handed her a coffee and a crisp filo pastry shell filled with egg custard and sat down. 'You're not sure,' he said, without offence. 'We know each other, we've had dinner together the last week, spent some time in each other's company and you like me – well I hope you do – but spending several hours on a yacht in the middle of the ocean with me might be a bit much, right?'

'Go on.'

'Only the idea of being on a yacht really appeals, as it quite rightly should, it's a bloody fantastic experience! You feel the wind – pure clean wind, purified by the Atlantic – blowing right through you, the sun is warm and you can taste the salt on your lips. It sounds perfect, the motion, the calm, the excitement of tacking and hoisting the sails, the whole thing sounds wonderful, if only. If only you can work up enough confidence to trust me for a few hours. Yes? Am I close?'

Anna smiled.

Will held up his hands and pulled a face. 'What if he has an asthma attack? What if you feel sea sick? What if he gets on your nerves after five minutes and you're stuck with him for the whole afternoon? And why should you be enjoying yourself when you've just been through a really crummy time?'

Anna said, 'It's funny, you know, but I do think that. I can't help feeling guilty. It's extraordinary, isn't it? I find out Max is having an affair, he leaves me—'

'You asked him to leave I think,' Will interrupted, 'or so you said.'

'Yes, sorry. I ask Max to leave, I come away for a rest because I'm so distraught and then I feel guilty because I'm having such a nice time. It's like I don't deserve it. It's really odd!'

'So you'll come then?'

'I'm not at all sure how we got round to it, but yes.' She smiled again. 'Yes please, I'd love to come.'

'And Maya?'

'Is it safe? For babies I mean?'

'Perfectly and I've got a baby life jacket.'

'OK then. Yes please for both of us.' Anna bit into her cake. It was sweet and creamy and in three mouthfuls she had eaten it.

'Shall we go?' Will asked.

'You haven't eaten your cake.'

He pushed the plate across. 'You have it, Anna, there's nothing nicer than seeing someone enjoy what they eat.'

'I'm not sure if that's a compliment or not,' she said, taking the cake and biting into it. 'It might imply that I'm greedy.'

Will laughed. 'There's nothing wrong with excess Anna, in the right context.'

Anna blushed, although she wasn't quite sure why. Perhaps it was the thought of excess and Will and its subtle sexual overtones. Perhaps it was the intimacy of being teased. Whatever it was, she wasn't going to think about it now. The fact that she felt it was quite enough to be going on with.

Debbie was on the veranda when she heard the car. She had been sitting there for the last hour or so waiting for them to return, and now that they had she picked up her book and strolled down the steps towards them.

'Hello. Shall I take Maya inside?'

'Oh hi Debbie! Yes, yes please.' Anna climbed out of the car and leant in for the baby. She unstrapped Maya, lifted her out and held her for a few moments. 'We're going sailing this afternoon,' Anna said. 'We'll have a quick change of clothes, pack a picnic lunch, and get off about midday. It was midday, wasn't it, Will?'

Will turned. He had the bag of shopping which Millou had come out of the house to take off him. 'Yes, midday. Is that OK?'

'Lovely.' Anna smiled and Debbie watched her. She didn't like it. Anna didn't need anyone else, she just needed Debbie to look after Maya and if she was on her own then she needed Debbie all the more. Anna turned and said, 'Are you all right, Debbie? You look a bit pale.'

'Yes, I'm fine. Shall I take Maya to the beach while you go sailing?'

'Oh, no, no we thought we'd take Maya with us. All that fresh air will do her good. You have the afternoon to yourself, Debbie, I'm sure you could do with it.' Anna smiled down at the baby and didn't see the emotion that wrung Debbie's face. When she glanced up, Debbie had managed to bring her anger under control.

'Are you sure that it's safe, for a baby on a yacht?'

'Oh yes, Will's got a baby life jacket.' Will joined them. 'Haven't you, Will?'

'Haven't I what?' He looked at Debbie.

'You've got a life jacket for Maya, haven't you? And it's quite safe for a baby on board?'

'Yes, perfectly.'

'What about all the sun?' Debbie said. 'You'll have to be very careful to make sure she doesn't get sun burnt or wind burnt.'

'She'll be fine,' Will said. He kept his eyes on Debbie and something in the back of his mind stirred.

'As long as she doesn't get a chill,' Debbie countered, 'being out in the wind all afternoon.'

Anna looked up. 'She couldn't get a chill could she?'

'She might, if she's not wrapped up the whole time. I mean the wind is very cold out at sea and . . .'

Will gently touched Debbie's arm. 'She'll be fine, Debbie, I'm sure of it. Now why don't you take her in and organise a bag for the outing and then we can get off.'

Debbie bristled. She removed her arm from his touch and reached out for Maya. Anna handed her across. Again Will watched Debbie and again something odd registered in his mind. It bugged him, he couldn't think what it was. Debbie took Maya inside and Will said, 'Anna, Millou wants to know what you've bought us for supper, so she can do some preparation while we're out.'

'Of course, I'll come in and show her.' Will held his arm out and she tucked hers through it. 'This is the way to live,' Anna said, and she couldn't help admitting to herself that she had been just the smallest bit seduced by it all.

An hour later, the lunch had been packed into the car, Maya was safely strapped in, Anna had a hold-all full of everything they could possibly need and Will stood very patiently by the car while she emptied it out trying to find Maya's sun hat.

'I'm sure I put it in,' Anna said, 'yesterday, when we

went to the beach, and I'm sure that she had it on when we came back. I just can't think what's happened to it. Debbie? Are you sure you haven't seen it?'

Debbie shrugged. 'She shouldn't really go without a hat, not with the glare of the sun off the water.'

'Anna, we can stop at the marina and buy her another one,' Will said. 'There's loads of shops there. Really, it's not important.'

'Yes it is!' Anna snapped. She stopped, pushed her hair off her face and shook her head. 'Look, I'm sorry, you're right, it's not important. We'll stop and buy another one.' She began to shove everything back into the bag and Will climbed into the car. He started the engine. Anna threw her bag on the floor in the back and climbed in as well. 'We'll be back about six tonight,' she called out to Debbie. 'Enjoy your afternoon off.'

Debbie nodded and held up a hand to wave. Anna glanced behind her at the baby, and then looked back at Debbie. 'I'm sorry I got upset about the hat,' she said, as Will swung the car round in the drive and pulled off. 'It's just that I hate it when things go missing and that dress I bought Maya the other day seems to have disappeared completely. It's so frustrating, Will, it makes me think I'm going loopy.'

'Not going loopy, you are loopy! You've just had a baby; everyone knows that your brain has shrunk.'

Anna hit his thigh. 'Which explains why I am coming on a sailing trip with you presumably.' They both laughed.

As they turned out of the drive onto the road, Debbie walked back up the steps towards the house. She took Maya's small, frilled white sun hat out of her pocket, went round to the side of the house where the large wheelie bin was, lifted the lid and dropped it in. It joined the pink and white smocked dress Anna had bought a few days ago, still wrapped in tissue and lying in its bag from the shop. It was jealousy and spite that did it, and the almost obsessive need to be the one and only provider for Maya.

The sun was beginning to drop in the sky and the wind had taken on a slight chill as Anna sat in the cockpit of the boat, drinking tea – made with her own tea bags – and eating biscuits. They had dropped anchor off the coast at Lagos and the boat rocked gently from side to side, lulled by the waves. Will was fiddling with the main sail, apparently something had broken and he was fixing it, but Anna was too relaxed to be bothered with what exactly. She was happy to leave it up to him and to just sit back and watch. It was something she had never done before, being the capable one in her marriage, and she realised now just how hard it had been, always having to be the one who knew how.

She glanced at Maya, asleep in her carrycot, protected from the sun and the wind by a makeshift canopy that Will had constructed out of an old sail, and blissfully content. She smiled.

'What are you smiling at, Anna Jacob?'

'Nothing much. Just enjoying seeing you work and drinking my tea. Here, have a biscuit.'

Will took what was offered and slid down next to Anna. He picked up his mug and took a sip. 'Good tea, thanks.'

'What was wrong with the sail?'

Will smiled. 'Do you really want to know?'

'No.' Anna kicked off her shoes and tucked her knees up under her.

'Good, because it's very boring.'

'What I'd really like,' Anna said, 'is some whisky for my tea and for you to tell me something about yourself. I've bored you for hours over dinner about the merits of being a lawyer and exactly how I made associate partner, each painful step, and of course with the whole Max story, but you . . .' She turned to look at him. 'You haven't told me anything. Just the bare essentials.'

Will stood and reached into one of the lockers. He took out a bottle of single malt and unscrewed the cap. 'A bit of a waste in tea, but . . .' He poured some into Anna's mug, then his own. 'Who cares?' He replaced the cap and put the bottle down.

'What d'you want to know, Anna? You know how I got started, the fact that I built an IT company out of a schoolboy obsession with computers and acquired several other companies along the way to add to it—'

'Like High Tech Computer Games, which you are about to sell,' Anna interrupted.

'Exactly. You know that I'm single, thirty-six . . .'

'Why?'

'Why what? Why am I thirty-six? I don't know, I guess it's just one year after another and they add up and before you know it, there, you're nearly middle-aged and—' Will stopped. Anna had placed one of her long cool hands on his face and turned it towards her. His whole body was still at her touch, he dared not move.

'Why are you still single?' She reached up and kissed the side of his mouth. 'When you plainly shouldn't be . . .' He felt a moment of such physical intensity that it hurt, then he took her hands away, held them and pulled her in to him. He kissed her. His lips were dry and tasted of salt and Anna kissed him back, licking the salt off them. She didn't think about what she was doing. She was miles from the shore, miles from reality and she wanted him so much that the place where Maya had grown ached for him. Will kissed her neck, he kissed the hollow beneath her neck where her shoulder bones started and where the sun had turned them a pale golden brown. He tugged her shirt down over her arms, careless of the buttons, eager to get at the skin that tasted so warm and scented, and Anna moaned and closed her eyes and lifted his T-shirt to run her hands over his taut muscled back. She dipped them down, down beneath the waistband of his shorts where his cool skin warmed, and Will pulled away.

'Anna, are you sure?'

She looked at him, traced the curve of his mouth as he faintly smiled at her and shook her head. 'I'm not sure but I don't care. It feels too strong to deny.'

He wound his fingers into her hair. 'Yes it does.' He kissed her again, then bent his head to her breast, easing the fabric of her bra across her nipple.

Anna flinched for a moment. 'I'm still feeding . . .'

Will kissed her and licked her skin. 'I know. It doesn't matter,' he murmured. He unzipped her shorts and eased them down over her hips, along with her pants, then he pulled Anna up to him and she straddled him, her shirt open, his mouth on her breasts. She fumbled for a moment, trying to release him. 'You need practice,' he whispered, pulling free and doing it himself. Anna felt him, she ran her fingers over the hot hard skin and then lifted her hips and lowered herself on to him. It took them both by surprise. The simplicity of the act and the complexity of the feelings made Anna shiver with pleasure. She cried out and Will held her tight against him. Then she began to move.

*   *   *

'The thing about boats,' Will said, pulling the rug closer in around them, 'is that they're usually pretty chilly.' They lay together, clothes in disarray, half on, half off, a blanket under them in the cockpit of the boat, a couple of rugs over them. 'We could go inside,' he murmured, kissing her hand, 'and use the bunks.'

'What, so soon?' Anna ran her hand down Will's stomach to his groin. 'Good Lord, that's rather a quick recovery isn't it?'

Will grinned. 'Is it?'

'Stop being coy!' She moved to stretch and rolled over onto her back. 'There is something truly wonderful about being out here under the sky. It makes me feel very free.'

Will stroked her hair. He couldn't stop touching her. 'You are free, Anna, you are free to do whatever you want.'

'No, not really. I used to think so, but not now. We all have constraints, even if we can't see them.'

'That's not true. You can do anything you want to if you just let yourself.'

'I don't think so.'

Will propped himself up on one elbow. 'Don't shake your head like that. I mean it! You are free, Anna, it's your life, you can live it how you want to. If you wanted to give it all up, law, London, Max, and live with me in Sussex, nothing could stop you.'

'Is that an offer?' she teased.

Will thought for a moment, then he sat up. 'Yes it is actually.'

'Hey! You've taken all the blanket!' Anna tugged the rug back over her.

'Anna? Did you hear me?'

Anna pulled the rug up to her chin. 'I heard you,' she said quietly, 'but I was trying to change the subject.'

Will turned away. They were silent for a while, then Anna said, 'Will, I was only joking, asking if it was an offer, I didn't mean anything by it. Please, don't take me seriously and—'

'And what? Get upset by your flippancy? Anna, I don't make a habit of bringing women out to my boat and making love to them, in fact it's been a long time since I've felt enough about anyone to want to touch them like that and well . . .' He broke off and ran his hands through his hair. 'Look, shit, this is all going wrong. I should have thought about it first, considered it. Look Anna, I think you are, well, I've always found you attractive – unbelievably attractive actually – and well, I came to your house, remember, in a rather gauche attempt to offer a shoulder to cry on and that was the beginning, when I found out about you and Max, and that attraction has deepened. It's . . .' He searched for the right words and all the time Anna watched him, not at all sure if she was happy or distressed at his words. 'It's grown and I can't believe that I've met you because for a while I wondered if my life was ever going to be happy again and . . .'

Anna sat up too. She fastened her shirt and pulled the rug round her shoulders. 'And now this has happened,' she interrupted. 'We've met and had a wonderful time together, made love, which was, even by my standards, pretty damn good . . .'

Will smiled and Anna took his hand. 'Will, I'm not trying to be glib, but let's take it one step at a time, shall we? Let's go home and see how things develop. If this is real, Will, then what's the rush?'

They both turned as Maya woke and made gurgling

noises in the carrycot. Anna pulled on her shorts and moved across to the baby. Lifting Maya out, she carried her across and sat down, leaning forward so that Will could pile some cushions behind her back. 'She's hungry,' Anna said.

Will stood. 'Shall I make some more tea?'

She looked up at him. Was this real, she wondered, this whole thing? This attractive, kind and sensitive man, with his villa and yacht, wanting her, liking Maya, being so earnest and serious about her. 'No, no more tea thanks,' she said. 'And you don't need to disappear inside while I feed Maya, unless you want to.' Anna undid her shirt and Will sat down. He watched her with the mechanics of buttons and clips, he saw her breast and the baby's tiny rosebud mouth latch on to her nipple, and was strangely moved by it. He touched Anna's skin and felt the warmth there.

'Anna, I . . .' He wanted to tell her, he wanted her to know everything.

'Don't talk,' Anna said quietly. She rested her cheek against the hand on her breast, then turned to kiss it. 'Please, just touch me.' He stroked her skin and bent to kiss her neck. 'When she's settled can we go inside?' Anna whispered.

'Yes.' He had forgotten his need to explain, he had forgotten who he was and what had gone before. He could think only of Anna – of Anna and Maya and himself.

Max was in a foul mood. Jennifer had been on the phone again, twice that day, his pitch meeting had been a disaster and to top it all, he'd had instructions from Chrissy to drive down to some country house party in Sussex for

the night. It pissed him off, it really did. As if he didn't
have enough to wear him out at the moment, without the
whims and fancies of a thirty-something single woman
who had only herself to think about. He packed his
briefcase with notes from the meeting, along with the
art work – in the hope of going through it all some time
this weekend – then he picked up his overnight bag, took
his jacket off its hanger and slipped it on. With any luck,
leaving at this time the traffic in town wouldn't be too
bad and he would make it down past Guildford before
the rush hour. He activated the voicemail on his phone
and walked out of his office.

'Good night!' he called out collectively. There were a
few replies but most of the open-plan office were too
preoccupied to pay any attention to him. It wouldn't go
unnoticed though, he thought, early leavers were always
noted down.

In the underground car park, Max pressed his key ring,
his BMW bleeped like an old friend and he opened the
passenger door, throwing his bag onto the front seat. He
climbed in, feeling at once more relaxed in the cool,
leather interior, and slipped his favourite CD into the
stereo. He started the engine and reversed out of his
space. As the car filled with Mozart his mood improved.
Perhaps tonight wouldn't be too bad after all, as long as
Chrissy's friends behaved themselves.

Hitting the A3, however, at five thirty was far worse
than he could have imagined. It was bumper to bumper all
the way down Putney High Street and very slow moving
until he was well clear of Kingston. At Guildford he hit
the rush hour full on and it took him over an hour to
get clear of that. By the time he got out onto the A283,
he was back in a foul mood, his shoulders ached and

he had been driving for two and a half hours. He pulled in at a petrol station and bought himself a can of Coke and a chocolate bar, then asked directions for Kirdford, wrote them down and got back in his car. He checked the map, reckoned on another half an hour tops and ate his chocolate driving along.

But the directions were poor. He found Kirdford, which turned out to be a very small village with a complex network of lanes and large houses set back in big gardens. After that he was lost. He drove round for an hour, tried to ring from his mobile, but there was no network coverage, and was just about to find the nearest pub for a drink and something to eat when he spotted the house. It was up a long drive, well hidden from the road, and it had the smallest name plate he had ever seen. It was a fluke that he'd found it at all really, he had chosen the drive at random to turn round in, but now he was here, he drove on up to the house and parked. His mood improved, but only marginally. He climbed out, grabbed his bag, locked the car and went up to the double front door to knock.

Chrissy opened it.

She was wearing a long silk kimono and Max blinked a few times, not expecting this at all. 'Hello, I'm sorry I'm late.'

She shrugged and smiled, holding out her arms. Max stepped into the hall and she kissed him, tangling her fingers in his hair. 'Hmmm, nice welcome . . .' He dropped his bag, kicked the front door shut with his foot and felt the shape of her body under the kimono. He pulled away. 'My word, what's this?' Chrissy opened the kimono and despite his mood, Max had an instant rush of blood to his groin. 'Ah, you're not ready yet.'

She laughed. 'Of course I'm ready!' She was completely naked underneath except for a pair of very high-heeled, satin backless slippers.

Max blinked. 'But isn't this supposed to be a dinner party?' He stared over her shoulder to check no one was looking as alarm bells started to ring in his head.

Chrissy laughed again. 'Don't be such a prig!' She kissed him. 'Come on,' she said, 'I've got a surprise for you.' She slipped the kimono off and turned to walk away. Max watched the sensuous movement of her buttocks and began to sweat. It wasn't that he didn't find the sight erotic – who wouldn't? – but it somehow just didn't feel right.

'Chrissy? Where is everyone?' He started to follow her. 'I thought you said this was a dinner party.'

'It is. You'll see, come on.' She walked across the black-and-white-tiled hall, her heels clicking, her flesh quivering. Max undid his tie, and began to unfasten his shirt. He followed her through a door and along a stone passage, through a kitchen and into a boot room. She opened one last door and the heat hit him instantly. They were in the pool room. Chrissy turned. 'D'you like it?'

He glanced round. A Roman pool, floodlit, a sauna at one end, teak deck chairs, terracotta pots and a huge basket of laundered white towels. Around the edge of the water and in the shallow end, five of Chrissy's friends lounged and swam, all, like her, completely naked.

Max did a double take. He took a step backwards, the intense heat bringing beads of sweat out on his forehead, and banged into the door. 'Look Chrissy, I . . .' He shook his head, feeling behind him for the door handle. 'Chrissy, this really isn't . . .' He swallowed hard, deeply embarrassed by the scene. 'This really isn't my thing. I'm far too old for all of . . .' He broke off again on locating the door handle and twisted it to open the door. 'Sorry,' he said, 'but I'll give it a miss.' He pulled the door, took another step back into the passage and let the door slam behind him.

'Who's the square, Chrissy?' one of the men called out.

Chrissy bit her lip. Frankly she was getting a little bit pissed off with Max's new found puritanism. He had changed over the past few weeks – the bright star that was once Max had dulled, got a bit tarnished, and she was getting bored. She stood, torn between going after him and drinking a glass of champagne in the pool. The hedonistic side of her nature won out. She slipped into the water and swam a width across to the other side. The man who had called out to her handed her a glass. 'You didn't answer me,' he said.

Chrissy took a sip of fizz. 'The square?' She shrugged. 'No one in particular,' she said.

Max walked back through the empty house and out to his car. He was seething, not really with Chrissy, but with himself, for ever getting involved in something that was so meaningless. He climbed into the BMW and drove away, without even a backward glance. Several miles later it hit him. He stopped the car and put his head in his hands. For the first time since it had all happened he realised the full extent of what he had lost.

The drive back from the boat was quiet and relaxed and Anna had a feeling of contentment, a feeling that she hadn't had for a very long time. She was tired, but she felt right with the world. She felt good. She liked the way that Will made contact every now and then, stroking her hand or touching her leg, it was as if he was trying to reassure himself that she was there, and real. She liked everything about him if she was honest with herself, but she couldn't be honest, she couldn't admit that, not yet. Trust was something she was a little short of.

As they pulled into the drive, she said, 'I'm almost sorry to be back, even though I know we've got Millou's sea bass to look forward to.'

'Me too.' Will parked the car, climbed out and went to get Maya out.

'It's OK,' Anna said, 'I'll take her. You unpack the car.'

'Doesn't sound very fair to me.' He smiled and went round the back of the car, unloading the bags and picnic hamper. He took it all up the steps and dumped it on the veranda. Then they both went inside.

'I'm going to check my messages and have a quick shower,' Will said. 'What time do you want to eat?'

'Immediately! I'm starving!'

He laughed. 'Eight? Eight thirty?'

Anna looked at her watch. It was six thirty now and she desperately needed a bath and some time to reflect. 'Eight thirty,' she said.

'Drinks at eight then.' Will headed for the stairs. He started up, then stopped, turned and came back down. He took Anna's face in his hands and kissed her. Then without another word, he disappeared upstairs.

In his room Will peeled off his clothes and left them in a heap on the floor. He walked across to the bathroom, turned on the shower and stepped under it. It felt fantastic. He felt fantastic. He soaped himself and started to sing, quite tunefully for someone who had no ear for music whatsoever.

His shower finished, he wrapped a towel round his waist and decided to check his messages before getting dressed. He switched on his PC, connected and looked at his e-mail. He had three messages. He read the first two and started on the third. He sat very still. It was from Jenna and he read it again and again. Then he dropped his head in his hands.

A short while later he took some clean clothes out of the drawer and threw them on. He wasn't really thinking, but he knew that he had to get out of there, that he needed some space and time to think. He paced the floor for a while, wondering what the hell to do, what to say to Anna, then he gave up trying to think and went along the corridor to knock on her door. She opened it wearing a towel, and blushed, glancing at her watch.

'Sorry, am I late?'

'No, not at all, it's just that, well, I don't think I can do dinner tonight, I've just had a call and I've got to go and see someone.' He avoided looking at her face. 'I'm sorry, Anna, I really am. I know it's our last night, but I just can't get out of it. It's stuff to do with the house, the management agent actually, he's got some problems with the house and apparently I need to sort them out before I leave. Why he couldn't have rung sooner I don't know. Still . . .' He shrugged. 'I really am sorry.'

Anna fingered the edge of her towel. She was disappointed but didn't want to show it. 'It's fine,' she said. 'Please don't worry . . .'

'But I do! I hate leaving you.' He took her hand. 'I was looking forward to tonight, I really was.'

Anna shrugged and behind her Maya began to cry.

She looked over her shoulder and said, 'I'd better go to her.'

'Yes, of course. Look, I'll try and get back for coffee, OK?'

'Yes, fine. Really, I don't mind.'

'And at least we're travelling together tomorrow.'

'Yes.'

Will reached forward and kissed her cheek. 'Good.' He dug his hands in his pockets and immediately turned to go. It was almost as if he couldn't wait to get away from her. 'See you later then maybe?'

She nodded and, walking back into her bedroom, closed the door behind her and went across to pick up Maya. She held the baby and gently rocked her to soothe her. Maya closed her eyes again and relaxed in Anna's arms. 'I wonder what that's all about?' she whispered. 'It seemed a bit odd or am I just being paranoid?' She smiled and kissed the top of Maya's head, carefully placing her back in the cot. 'Yes, I know, I'm just being paranoid. Thanks Maya.' She walked over to the window in time to see Will drive off. 'He's very self contained,' she said aloud to herself and, having said it, realised that it wasn't something she disliked.

Chapter Eighteen

Max sat on the bottom stair in the hall and waited for his mother to get her handbag and put the finishing touches to the house. She had been cleaning all morning. Anna had a cleaner of course, but she wasn't good enough for Jennifer, particularly because – as she kept reminding Max – so much was riding on this homecoming. He had to get it right, she told him, and a clean and tidy house was the first step.

'There now, I've put flowers in your bedroom and just dressed those gorgeous new curtains that you ordered so that the pleats fall exactly right. We want Anna to see them in pristine condition, don't we?'

Max nodded wearily.

'And you've ordered the food? It'll be here at eight?'

'Yes Mother.'

'And you've put champagne in the fridge?'

'Yes Mother.'

Jennifer stopped fiddling with the mirror above the hall table and glared at Max's reflection in it. He caught her eye. 'There's no need to say it in that tone, Max, all I'm trying to do is help.'

Max stood. 'I know, Mother, and I appreciate it. Thank you. Now, shall we get going?'

'Yes, of course.' Jennifer pulled on her cardigan and put her bag over her arm. 'You will ring me, won't you Max, when you get home and let me know how little Maya is?'

Max walked out after his mother and locked the house up. 'I'm dropping you at Clapham am I?'

'Max!'

He turned. 'What?'

'You will ring me, won't you?' She put her hand on his arm. 'You will let me know how Maya is?'

He looked down at her fingers, no longer chafed from work, but still rough and cold. 'Yes,' he said, 'I'll ring you.'

'Good.' Jennifer went down the path towards Max's car and waited for him to open the door. He pressed the alarm pad and reached for the passenger door handle. As he did so, Jennifer grasped him once more with her vice-like grip. 'Don't mess it up, Max, will you?' She stared at him and he wondered if her eyes were properly focusing. 'You won't mess it up?'

He lifted her hand off him and swung open the door. 'No Mother,' he answered, 'I won't mess it up.' But even as he spoke, he had very little confidence in his reply.

Nora had made up her mind to tell her son about his fiancée as soon as she saw him that afternoon; she had been working up to it for days, but as she saw him waiting for her by the taxi rank at Waterloo, she was immediately full of doubt. How could she tell him? What was she going to say? There was no proof that there was anything wrong. Fudging references – people did it all the time, didn't they? And what would he think of her nosing around? It was hardly an easy thing to admit, snooping behind people's backs.

Darren was waiting at the taxi rank, a scowl on his face. Nora didn't park the car, she simply pulled over, hooted the horn and he saw her, throwing his kit bag over his shoulder and striding towards her. He didn't smile.

'Hello love,' she said.

He chucked the bag in the back and climbed in. 'All right?' was all he said.

Nora shifted gear and moved off. She knew his moods and knew this one was a maelstrom. 'What time is Debbie's flight due in?' she asked, in an attempt to make conversation.

'It lands at four twenty,' Darren said.

'Right, good, so as long as we're there by four thirty we should be OK.' She smiled. 'Plenty of time,' she went on. 'We can have a coffee if we've time, or I can drop you off and go and have a wander round the shops on my own.'

Darren stared out of the window.

'And you're all right to get the tube back are you? You don't want me to wait, because I can . . .' Nora's voice trailed away as Darren turned to her and withered her with one of his looks. Of course he didn't want her to wait, he wanted to speak to Debbie on his own. Stupid to even have mentioned it. 'No, better I leave you to it,' she murmured. Nora concentrated on driving for the next few minutes, then changed the subject.

'You've lost weight, love. Not training too hard I hope.'

But Darren didn't seem to have heard her at all. 'I'll bloody kill her,' he said. 'She pissed off to Portugal and I've not heard a word from her since.'

Nora pulled up at the junction and glanced nervously at him. 'Don't do anything silly, Darren love, don't go upsetting her now, will you?'

He didn't answer. He went back to staring gloomily out of the window. 'She'd better have a bloody good excuse lined up,' he said. 'I'm not taking any more shit from her, I tell you. I've had enough!'

Nora kept her hands firmly on the steering wheel. Whatever thoughts she'd had of telling him about the references had vanished. She was silent for a few moments, silent and still. A queue of cars formed behind her and she glanced in her rear-view mirror at them. She was in it up to her neck and she knew it. 'It'll work out, Darren love,' she said, but it was more for her own benefit than for his. 'I'm sure it will.' Then she saw a space in the traffic ahead and accelerated out into it.

The flight attendant came round the aircraft checking seatbelts and made sure that Maya was strapped in safely. The plane was due to land and already Anna could feel her nerves kick in. She glanced across at Will who was reading and envied him such calm. Hugging Maya a little tighter, she stared over the top of the baby's head at him and wondered. He hadn't made it back for coffee last night and had said nothing about his meeting. It seemed a bit secretive, but then Anna had come straight from a marriage where everything was shared. She brushed her lips over Maya's sweet smelling soft hair and felt the sharp ache that any thought of Max gave rise to. She closed her eyes.

'You all right, Anna?' Will reached out and touched her arm. She opened her eyes and looked at him.

'Yes, fine, thanks.' She read the concern on his face.

'I'm not a great flyer. I'm looking forward to making it safely back onto firm ground.'

Will nodded. 'And once on that firm ground?' He raised an eyebrow. Anna smiled. She was pleased to be reminded of how much he wanted her, it gave her depleted confidence a boost, even if it was the faintest bit oppressive.

'I'll think about what you've said . . .'

'What I've offered.'

'Yes, what you've offered.'

Will took her hand. 'Good. You know, Anna, I think our lives are about to change, both of them, and for the first time in many years, that fills me with hope.'

Anna smiled again, this time more warily. 'Let's wait and see,' she said.

Once through baggage reclaim, with Maya settled and in her pushchair, Anna headed for the green channel and an end to her extraordinary experience abroad. Debbie pushed the trolley behind her and checked in her handbag for some change for the tube. They emerged into the main terminal and the first person they saw was Max.

Anna stood still; the shock of seeing him rendered her motionless for a moment. Debbie had to pull up sharp behind her to stop hitting her in the back of the legs with the trolley, and her suitcase fell off, with a loud chink.

'Shit!' she said. Anna turned. 'That was my pottery from Loulé.'

Max ducked under the barrier and hurried across to help. He lifted Debbie's bag back up onto the trolley and said, 'Come on, the car's this way.'

Anna didn't move. Just the sight of Max filled her with anger and confusion.

'Anna?'

She looked at him. 'What the hell are you doing here, Max?'

Max's nerve faltered. People were having to redirect to get past Anna, the pushchair and the trolley and he was embarrassed. He hated scenes and this looked as if it was going to turn into one. 'I've come to take you and Maya home,' he said. 'That's where you belong, home, with me.' He went to take hold of the trolley to move it out of the way.

'Leave it!' Anna snapped. Max stepped back. How dare he just turn up and start taking control like he had some right to be there. 'I'm not going anywhere with you, Max, and you seem to have forgotten but it's no longer your home.'

Max dug his hands in his pockets and took up a defensive stance. He looked far braver than he felt. 'It is just as much my home as yours, Anna, and I'm not moving out. Please Anna, come home, I want you home, at least so that we can talk—'

Anna cut him short. 'There's nothing to talk about,' she snapped.

'Yes there is!' Max was trying hard to keep his voice under control. 'We've got to work this out, Anna, we've got to try at least, for Maya's sake. I want you home, I want to explain, I want to say . . .'

'Say what?' Anna glared at him and beneath her glare, Maya looked up at Max and smiled.

Max reached out and touched her face with his finger-tip. He thought, God, she's grown so much in just a short time. I am missing her life, it's going by and I'm not even part of it. He longed to hold her, but knew Anna wouldn't let him and it made him angry, but not with Anna, with himself.

'What is there to say, Max?'

Max looked at her. 'That I'm sorry?'

Anna stayed very still. How could he say he was sorry? Was that it? Sorry? I fucked about, deceived you, undermined your trust, lied to you, shattered your confidence, obliterated your morale and I'm sorry. She looked away. One part of her wanted to hold him then, to cling to him and tell him that it was OK, sorry was OK, everything was OK, but she knew in her heart that it wasn't enough.

'Sorry isn't good enough.'

'Then what do you want me to do?'

'I want to go home to my house on my own.'

Max shook his head. He felt hopeless. 'I'm not leaving you, Anna.'

'Then I'm not going home,' she said.

Max moved towards her. 'Anna, stop this please. Just stop it all. Let's just go home now, please Anna.' He was desperate to make her understand, to make her see that if only she'd give him the chance he *could* make it up to her, he *would* make it up to her. He would prove that he was sorry, more sorry than she could ever know. 'Anna, please, come home.'

But Anna's mouth had become a hard, tight, unforgiving line. The more he pleaded, the more confused she became, and in turn the more angry and upset. Was that what he thought, that a few nice words, a few pleas and promises of contrition would make it all go away? She shook her head. 'I am not going anywhere with you, Max!'

'Anna please! Look I'm sorry – how many times do I have to say it? – I'm really sorry. I'm trying to make it up to you, I realise what I've lost and what I've done and I've been trying to make amends. Really I have. I've done stuff in the house, in the nursery. I even went out and ordered another pair of curtains instead of that bloody awful pair that—'

Debbie's head jerked up. She looked briefly at Max, then she flushed and turned away.

'Oh Max!' Anna cried. 'How could you?' It was typical, he didn't care who he hurt in order to get what he wanted.

'How could I what? For Christ's sake, Anna! What have I said now?' His mistake was genuine. He was focusing so hard on Anna that he was oblivious to anyone else. He looked at her, then at Debbie, and realised immediately what he'd said. 'Oh God, look I'm sorry, Debbie, I wasn't thinking.' He turned back to Anna. 'Anna please, please listen to me, stop shutting me out and listen.' He took her by the shoulders, but she shoved him away.

'Get off me!' she shouted. 'Don't you dare touch me.'

'What the fuck is going on?'

Both Anna and Max turned and Debbie cried, 'Darren? What are you doing here?' Her stomach took a massive lurch.

'I came to see you.' Darren took hold of Debbie's arm. 'Are you OK? Is this bloke upsetting you?'

Debbie's face flooded again with a rush of blood to the skin. She was immediately anxious and embarrassed. 'No he's not upsetting me,' she mumbled. 'Please Darren, leave it and go away.' She could sense his mood, the undercurrent of anger and violence made her recoil from him.

'Go away?' His temple throbbed as he stared at her.

'Yes, please. This has nothing to do with you.' Her voice rose in panic. 'Leave us, me alone!'

Darren shook his head. 'Leave you alone? What the hell is that supposed to mean? You've been away for ten days, I hear nothing, I've been worried sick and now I've got to leave you alone? What the fuck are you playing at, Deb? We're engaged. You're having my baby, for God's sake!'

Anna spun round. 'You're pregnant?'

'No!' Debbie cried. She put her hands up to her face and willed herself not to cry. This was terrible, it was worse than she could have imagined.

'What d'you mean no?'

She dropped her hands down and a look of fury crossed Darren's face that was so intense it made Debbie start. She took a step back.

'Debbie?' Anna said. 'Are you pregnant?'

'No, I mean . . .' Debbie looked frantically from Darren to Anna and Max. She was frightened, caught off balance and couldn't think straight. 'I mean yes, I mean I don't know.'

'What do you mean you don't know?' Darren pulled her round to face him. 'What d'you mean you don't know?'

'I don't know,' she cried. 'I don't know anything any more, what with you bullying me every five minutes about this bloody baby and your mother going on and on about the wedding! I just don't know what I think or what I'm doing or what's right, I . . .'

Anna said, 'Are you pregnant, Debbie? We all need to know.'

'Anna, this is hardly relevant now,' Max said. 'Please, let's just go home.'

'I told you, I'm not going anywhere with you, Max.

Nowhere!' Anna looked at Debbie. 'I've got to find a taxi,' she said. 'Could you help me with my trolley? Please?' Anna moved off.

Max panicked. 'Anna, come back! I haven't finished, Anna, please, don't just walk away like this . . .'

'Deb?'

'Darren, I've got to go. Get out of the way please.' Darren stood his ground. 'Darren please!' Debbie was on the verge of tears and Darren had such an urge to slap her that he had to clench his fists by his side. He was conscious of people watching, of being in a public place, and so moved out of the way and she pushed the trolley forward.

Max went after Anna. The thought of losing her, of her walking out of his life with their baby, drove him on. He didn't want a scene, but he couldn't let her just walk away.

'Anna wait!' He caught up with her and grabbed her arm, swinging her round to face him. 'Anna, that's my daughter, at least let me see her, at least—'

'Let go of my arm, Max,' Anna said coldly.

'No, not until you talk to me, not until you let me—'

'Let go of me, Max!' Her voice had risen in anger, but in desperation, Max gripped tighter. 'All I wanted to do was go home and now you've spoilt it for me. Couldn't you think of someone other than yourself, Max?' She shrugged her arm free. 'Now please, go—'

'Anna? What's going on?'

Anna turned to see Will striding towards her. 'Anna? Are you all right?'

'Will! Yes, I . . .' Uncontrollable tears suddenly welled up and ran down her cheeks. Max dropped her arm, thoroughly ashamed.

'Anna, the driver is waiting outside; he can take you wherever you want to go. You're welcome to come with me if you—'

'Go with you?' Max stared angrily at this outsider. 'Who the hell do you think you are?'

'It doesn't matter who I am. What matters is that Anna is upset.'

Max couldn't believe he was hearing this. 'Like hell it doesn't matter who you are!' His patience finally snapped. 'Anna?' he shouted. 'What the fuck has this idiot got to do with . . .' But it was too much, he had gone too far. Frantic to hold her back, he had instead pushed her forward, out of his reach.

Shaking, Anna turned away from Max towards Will. 'I can't go home,' she said. 'I can't take all this . . . this anger and distress . . .'

'Then come to Calcott. You can stay as long as you like.'

She was silent, the tears coursed down her face, then she nodded. Will took hold of the trolley. 'Do you want to come to Widbry, Debbie? You can stay at Calcott if you want, or you can make your own way home.' There was an air of such authority about him that Anna just let him take control. She had neither the strength nor the energy to intervene.

Max stood and watched, completely helpless. Calm, rational, reasoned Anna let herself be meekly led and it incensed him. He knew it was foolhardy, but he couldn't stop himself. He cried, 'What the hell are you doing Anna? Who the fuck is this bloke?'

Anna wiped her face on a handkerchief Will handed her and turned to him. 'It's none of your business, Max, and I'm doing what you always do, I'm pleasing myself.'

'Debbie?' Will had all the bags loaded onto one trolley.

Debbie glanced behind her at Darren and he glared at her. His presence overpowered her and she could think of nothing but escaping it. 'I'll come with you,' she answered.

Anna turned. 'You don't have to, Debbie,' she said. 'It's not part of the job.'

'I know.' Debbie pulled her jacket in tighter round her body and looked towards the exit. 'But it's more than just the job,' she said. 'Maya means everything to me.'

Chapter Nineteen

They drove from Gatwick to Widbry in silence. Will didn't have a car seat so Debbie and Anna sat in the back, Anna with Maya on her lap, and Will sat in the front with the driver. Anna wasn't a car person, she knew and cared very little about cars, but she could see, from the moment that she climbed into this one, that it must have been worth a fortune. She smelt the old leather and noted the gleam of the polished walnut dashboard, but Will said nothing about it so neither did she. He wasn't really a car person either, this car was an investment on the advice of his accountant, an asset that appreciated, like so many of the things that he owned.

A couple of miles from Widbry village, they pulled off the main road and followed a network of lanes that seemed to Anna to be directionless, until they came to the wrought-iron gates of Calcott Manor. When Will stopped to open them and they started up the drive, Anna thought, here we go again, and felt suddenly angry with herself at being seduced by such wealth and perfection.

The house was everything she could have imagined it to be, square Georgian, perfectly symmetrical, built in the early eighteenth century out of locally quarried stone, with a slate roof and two acres of gardens. They stopped at the end of the drive in front of the house and still Anna said nothing. Will climbed out, opened the door for her and Debbie while the driver went to the boot of the Aston Martin for their luggage. Anna joined him on the steps of the house.

'Your house is very beautiful,' she said.

'It's a house,' Will replied. 'Just a house.' He lifted Maya up to show her the view.

Anna watched him for a few moments, then asked, 'How can you be so dismissive? So arrogant?'

'It's not arrogance, Anna, it's the truth. I live here because I have to, not because I want to. It's just another thing I own. It is beautiful, yes, but it's not a home, I'm not happy here, I haven't been for years.'

'Then sell it, let someone else enjoy it.'

Will sighed. 'If it were that simple I'd have done it. It's in trust for my children; it doesn't actually belong to me.' He kicked the front door open with his foot. 'It may have escaped your notice, Anna, but I do have a fairly good business brain.'

'You like owning things,' Anna said, holding the door for Debbie and following her into the hall.

Will turned. 'Perhaps,' he answered. Anna took Maya into her arms once inside and stood for a few moments looking at the hall. As she did so, a woman came down the stairs and walked across to Will. They talked, and then Will turned to introduce her to Anna.

'Anna, this is Sheila, my housekeeper. Sheila Wright, this is Anna Jacob.'

In an instant the expression on Sheila's face froze, then she gasped and put her hand to her chest.

'Sheila?'

Will moved towards her and she seemed to struggle for

a moment while Anna stood there puzzled, then embarrassed. But it was only a moment. Almost immediately, she recovered herself and stepped forward, holding out her hand. 'Hello, welcome to Calcott, Ms Jacob. I'm sorry about looking so surprised,' she said, 'but you reminded me so much of someone for a moment that it quite took my breath away. Not in looks, in manner.' She coughed nervously and looked at Will but he seemed not to have heard her, he was directing the luggage.

'And this is?' She looked at Maya.

'Maya, my daughter, and Debbie Pritchard, my nanny.'

Sheila nodded at Debbie, then the gaze wandered back to Anna. She stared for a moment, then glanced away. 'I've got everything ready, Will. Would you like tea in the sitting room?'

Will turned. 'Thanks Sheila. That was quick work, we only phoned from the car an hour ago.' He came and patted her arm. 'Anna? Some refreshments?'

'Please.'

'OK, drinks in the sitting room please Sheila.'

'And will I put the cot for the baby in Ms Jacob's room or with the nanny?'

'Oh, in my room please,' Anna said. She turned to Will. 'That's very organised, having a cot.'

Sheila blushed, but Anna missed it and Will mumbled a reply that she didn't quite catch.

'Shall I take Maya up and get her ready for bed?' Debbie interrupted. 'It's nearly six and she's getting tired.'

Anna hesitated. She and Debbie needed to talk, but perhaps not immediately. 'Yes, thanks.'

Anna handed Maya over and Sheila said, 'I'll show you up, then bring a drink up if you like?'

Debbie smiled. 'Yes, please, I'd love a drink.' Halfway up the stairs, Sheila glanced behind her at Anna again, but Anna didn't see it. She had gone into the sitting room with Will and so missed the sad, perplexed expression that crossed Sheila's face.

In the sitting room, Anna walked across to the window and looked out. It faced the front of the house, the sweep of drive and the lawns that banked it on either side.

'Anna?'

'Is Sheila all right? She looked a bit odd for a few moments back there.'

'Anna?'

'I hope we haven't thrown her, by staying the night. I'm sure she wasn't—'

'Anna!' Will crossed to her and took her hands. 'Anna, I'm so glad that you're here with me, here at Calcott. I—'

Anna broke free. 'I don't know what I'm doing here actually,' she said. She didn't want any more pressure, any more talk in fact. She just wanted peace and quiet and some space. She felt confused; everything was in such chaos. 'I just didn't know what else to do,' she went on, more to herself than to Will. She had to set it straight in her own mind. 'I couldn't go home, I can't go back there if Max is there. I was going to get a taxi, but I hadn't thought about where I could go and, well, then you offered to drive me and I suppose, I suppose it was an escape . . .' She broke off and wrung her hands. 'What a mess!' Turning to look at him, she said, 'You know, just a few months ago my life was so ordered, so neat and tidy. I had everything in its place, I had it under control. And now . . .' She shook her head. 'Now I'm here, and I don't really know why.'

'You're here because you want to be, Anna,' Will said. He wanted to touch her again, but he didn't dare. He sensed her withdrawal and felt the need to bring her closer. 'Anna, in Portugal, last night, I—'

'I don't want to know.'

'But I want to tell you, please Anna, I want to explain.'

Anna shook her head. She walked to the door and said, 'Explain what? Why does everyone feel the need to explain? There are some things, Will, that we just don't need to talk about.' She shrugged. 'I need to talk to Debbie.'

'OK.'

She opened the door.

'Can we have dinner together? I can cook for us, or rather warm something up that Sheila will take out of the freezer.'

Anna looked at him for a moment, uncertain. He was undeniably attractive, as far as she could tell completely genuine and yet, yet somehow it didn't feel right. If things were really over with Max, wouldn't she be a fool to turn away from all this? 'OK,' she said, then she turned and walked out of the room.

Debbie lifted Maya out of the bath and laid her gently on a thick towel on the floor. It was warm in the bathroom and so, drying her off, she let her lie without any clothes on and kick while Debbie drank her tea. She was looking out of the window at the garden when Anna knocked and walked in. Debbie turned.

'Can I have a word?'

'Yes.'

Anna hesitated, then said, 'Debbie, I know it's none of my business, only the thing is that, being your employer,

it is important that I know and I just wanted to ask again
if you might be—'

'No I'm not.'

'Ah.'

Debbie put her tea down and knelt on the floor to dress
Maya. Anna stood uncomfortably by the door.

'Darren's got all worked up about nothing. It was a
false alarm.'

'But you are engaged?'

Debbie fastened the nappy, then gently eased Maya's
arms into her vest and pyjamas. Anna thought that Debbie
did it so much more carefully than she did herself and
felt a moment of guilt.

'Yes, we're engaged,' Debbie said. 'He wants to get
married straight away, but I'm not in any hurry.' She
stood, scooping Maya up into her arms. 'You don't mind
do you?'

'No! Of course I don't mind, I just . . .' Anna stopped.
It struck her suddenly that her relationship with Debbie
was so outside the normal realm of employer–employee
relationships that she wasn't quite sure how to handle
it. Here was this young woman who worked in Anna's
home, cared for her most precious thing, was party to
so much of Anna's life, private and otherwise, and yet
Anna wasn't entitled to know even the most basic facts
of Debbie's personal life. 'I guess I just thought you
might have mentioned it. I mean, I know it's none of
my business, but you must be excited, making plans and
stuff.'

Debbie glanced away. 'Not really.'

'Oh.' Anna didn't know what else to say. 'Well, if you
want to phone, erm, Darren is it?'

She nodded.

'Please feel free to use my mobile. Any time. OK?'

Again Debbie nodded and Anna waited for her to hand Maya over for her feed. She bent and picked the towel up off the floor and waited. She folded it, put it over the hot rail, showered out the bath and still Debbie held Maya. Anna said, 'Shall I take her now, for her feed?'

Debbie held her out. Anna took her and opened the door of the bathroom. She sensed something odd, something hostile, but couldn't quite identify it. So she put it down to the row with the boyfriend earlier and went along to her room. She gave it no more thought. She had enough to think about already, hadn't she?

Max walked into the empty house in Clapham and went straight to the phone. He dialled Anna's office and asked to be put through to Andrew McKie.

'Hello Andrew, this is Max Slater.'

'Max.' Andrew McKie braced himself for an onslaught. He had no idea why Anna's husband would be phoning, but it was hardly likely to be social.

'Andrew, I'm sorry to bother you, but I need your help. Anna has gone off with someone called Will. She flew in from Faro this afternoon and took off at the airport with this tall bloke, rangy, sort of scruffy and—'

'Slow down a minute, Max,' Andrew said. 'What d'you mean Anna's gone off with someone?'

'Someone was with her at the airport and I wondered if you knew who the hell it might be. I've never seen this bloke before, he's not one of our friends and . . . Shit!'

Max was finding it hard to control the tremor in his voice and Andrew heard as much. He said, 'The man in question, you said he was called Will?'

'That's what I heard, but I can't be sure.'

'OK, it sounds right. I think that's Will Turner. Anna has been staying at his house in Portugal.'

'Shit!'

'Don't jump to conclusions, Max, I'm sure it's all perfectly innocent.' Why am I saying this? Andrew thought. This man is an adulterer.

'Have you got his number?'

Andrew hesitated. 'I'm not sure I should give it to you, Max. He is a client of mine and if Anna had wanted you to have it, then she'd have given it to you herself.'

'Andrew,' Max said, 'I don't give a damn what you think. My wife and my daughter have gone off with a man they hardly know and I want to know where they are. OK?'

Max had a point and Andrew could see it. 'Yes,' he said. 'OK.' He glanced at his address file, found Will Turner's number and read it out. 'His address is Calcott Manor, Widbry, West Sussex.'

Max wrote it down. 'Thank you, Andrew,' he said, then he hung up. He didn't think twice about it, he ripped the address off the pad, took up his car keys and left the house.

Max was in love with Anna; he always had been. It was a bit late to realise it, but it was better late than never.

Jennifer held the receiver suspended in mid air even though the line had disconnected. She took another gulp of wine, flicked her ash into the small silver ashtray she had on her lap and closed her eyes. All around her on the hall carpet lay photographs of Maya. Snaps from all angles, in all lights scattered like Jennifer's memories, with no order and no connection.

'Bastard,' she muttered, draining her glass, Max was never there when he should be. She dropped the receiver and left it dangling from the hall table, then stood and stepped precariously in between the pictures, making her way to the kitchen for a refill. 'Bastard,' she muttered again, filling her wine glass and slopping it over the top. She bent her head to it and slurped the excess out of the glass, wiping the spillage with the hem of her apron. She knew she was drunk, drunk for the first time in fifty odd years, yet she couldn't give a damn. Suddenly a stab of pain so intense shot through her uterus that she cried out and doubled up, clutching the kitchen table for support.

'Bastard,' she shouted at the silent house. Then she started to weep. 'Oh my little baby Maya, please God let me hold my little baby Maya one more time . . . Please . . . God . . . please.'

Anna and Will sat on the carpet in the sitting room together, leaning back against the sofa, warming their toes on an unnecessary but wonderful log fire. She was drinking whisky, and kept swirling the amber liquid round and round her glass while Will watched her, close enough to touch her, but not able to. There was something distant about her tonight, something self-contained that deterred him from doing so.

Anna took a sip.

'Is it OK?' Will asked. 'I've got another malt if you don't like it, or some blended whisky. I never know which one is—'

Anna put her hand on his arm and stopped him mid sentence. 'It's fine. Lovely.' She shook her head. 'It's all lovely, all of it. You, the house, the dinner . . .'

'What, shepherd's pie?'

'Yes, although the shepherd was a bit chewy. I've been seduced by it, by you and all of this . . .' Anna spread her arms. 'This luxury. I'm in escape mode, my life has lost all perspective and I've simply run away.'

'There's nothing wrong with that.'

'Isn't there?'

'No, I've been running away for the past year and trying to escape for much longer than that.'

Anna put her hand up to his cheek and touched it. 'Poor Will. You are always so sad. I don't understand it, why someone who has so much can be so bereft.'

'I've got all this and nothing too,' Will said, catching her hand. 'Or I had nothing, until you.'

'Don't say that.' She retrieved her hand. 'Will, I'm confused. This isn't Portugal, this is real and I don't want to make another mistake with my life.' She moved gently away from him. 'I appreciate it, you letting me stay here, you are . . . a very good friend.'

Will stared at the fire. His face changed, something in his expression changed, but it was too dark for Anna to catch exactly what it was. He looked unhappy, or was it more? She watched him for a moment, then glanced away; she just couldn't say. 'Will?' She reached out and touched him. He started.

'Sorry,' he said, 'I was miles away.'

Anna shrugged. 'Somewhere nice?'

'No,' he said. 'In my head, there isn't anywhere nice to go.' And for some very peculiar reason, Anna shivered.

Chapter Twenty

Anna had slept fitfully. She had woken several times in the night, wondering if she could hear someone moving around the house, but was too nervous to get up and investigate. She had brought Maya into bed with her and had lain in the dark, straining to listen for any sound, but finally she had drifted off to sleep, convinced that it was her imagination.

In the morning, she woke early, feeling exhausted but somehow clear-minded. She showered and dressed, once she had fed Maya, and, knocking on Debbie's door, asked if she could leave the baby in Debbie's care while she went to find Will. She had made up her mind about certain things in the night and needed to make some calls. She wanted to use Will's study for a couple of hours because if she was going to find somewhere for her and Maya to rent in London, she needed the use of a fax as well as a phone.

Downstairs, she tried the study first, but finding it empty went along to the kitchen where she heard voices. She knocked and walked straight in. Sheila and a younger woman sat at the table with mugs of coffee, deep in conversation. They stopped, looked at Anna and an uneasy silence filled the room.

'Oh, sorry to butt in . . .' Anna felt herself flush. 'I was looking for Will, I wondered if I might use his study for a couple of hours this morning to catch up with some calls and . . .' Her voice trailed off. The silence had deepened and she was embarrassed. 'Sorry, erm, did I interrupt something?'

Jenna suddenly galvanised herself into action. 'Of course not! Sorry, you must be Anna. Sheila told me all about you. I'm Jenna, Will's secretary . . .' She held her hand out and Anna shook it. 'Come on, I'll take you through to Will's study, I'm sure he won't mind. You can use the phone in there.'

'Thanks.' Anna smiled and Sheila smiled back, but it wasn't an easy smile and it lasted only a matter of seconds before Sheila stood and took the cups over to the sink. Anna followed Jenna out into the passage and along to the study.

Jenna opened the door and said, 'The phone is on the desk.'

'Right, thank you.'

'If you need to receive a fax it's the same number, the machine sorts it out; if you want to send one, lift the back of the phone and instructions are there. I'll be in the kitchen, so just shout if you want help.'

'Right. Thanks again.' It would seem that after the initial hesitation Jenna couldn't be helpful enough.

The first thing Anna did was call Andrew McKie. She was surprised at the feeling of comfort she got from the familiar sound of his voice and said, 'Hello Andrew, it's Anna.'

'Anna hello! How are you? And where are you?'

'I'm fine and I'm in Sussex.' She hesitated. 'I'm, erm, I'm staying with Will Turner.'

'With Will?' Andrew took a couple of moments to digest this piece of information. He realised of course, from Max's call last night, that Anna had left the airport yesterday with Will, but he wasn't expecting her to be staying there. It made him uneasy, but he was Anna's boss and it wasn't up to him to comment on her behaviour. He did however say, 'Max called and I gave him Will's address. I hope that is all right Anna?'

'Yes.' She supposed he had a right to know where she was.

'Have you plans to stay there for long?'

'No, just for a couple of days, until I get things sorted out at home. I was ringing to let you know that I should be back at work by the end of the week.'

'The end of the week? Excellent! We could do with you back, Anna, things have been hectic while you've been away.' Andrew was relieved. A small voice said it was none of his business, but he couldn't deny his concern.

'Is there anything I can be getting on with?' Anna asked. 'I thought I might call in to the office tomorrow afternoon.'

'Why don't we have a meeting at three?'

'Yes, three would be good.'

'I'm out with clients for lunch, but I'll get Pam to put it in the diary. We can catch up with some things then.'

'OK, thanks Andrew, I'll look forward to it.'

Anna hung up. She carefully replaced the receiver and sat down at the large modern desk, running a finger along its smooth, sleek edge. She picked up the heavy silver pyramid paper weight and turned it round and round in her hand, then had a good look at the room. It was different to the rest of the house, there was nothing antique in here, nothing remotely old-fashioned, this was a high-tech, modern working office, with white walls, minimalist furniture, large unframed modern landscapes and a huge, very expensive-looking computer system.

Anna stood and walked across to the fireplace. Either side of it were two filing cabinets, both light blond ash with polished steel drawers, and both had a flowering orchid on the top, in a polished steel pot. It was the plant that caught Anna's attention. She moved over to the nearest cabinet to look more closely at it and noticed that below it, each drawer in the cabinet had a small engraved plate in the centre under the handle. She read them and noted Will's attention to detail.

The cabinet she was looking at was obviously for Calcott Manor and each drawer had its own plate for its function. The first said 'Calcott household', the second 'Calcott accounts', the third 'Calcott staff', the fourth 'Photographs' and the last 'Calcott miscellaneous'. It was the photographs that interested Anna and, glancing over her shoulder, feeling suddenly guilty at her curiosity, she pulled the drawer. It wouldn't open. She noticed then that each drawer had a lock and so tried the drawer above to see if the whole cabinet was locked. It wasn't. Anna frowned. She tried every drawer then, even the accounts and staff records, and every drawer came open except the photographs; the photographs were firmly locked up. Anna moved over to the other cabinet. This one was for Will's company, WT Computer Systems, and again Anna tried every drawer. They all slid open. She sighed, walked back to the desk and took a good, long look round the room. This didn't make any sense. Who on earth would lock up their photos? And why? Especially when everything else was open. It had to be a mistake, or else it wasn't photos at all, but something secret, listed as photos as a decoy. Anna dismissed the thought as ridiculous. Did being deceived make one more suspicious? she wondered. She certainly couldn't remember thinking this much about such trivial things before.

Putting all thoughts of hidden photos out of her mind, she walked over to the door. She opened it, knowing she was in need of some open space and fresh air, and, glancing back at the room one last time, walked out and made her way into the garden. Stepping onto the terrace, she realised something that she hadn't noticed before; outside she felt comfortable, more comfortable than she felt anywhere else in the house.

Max woke up just after eight. His telephone was ringing and it brought him to abrupt consciousness. He opened his eyes, put his hand up to shield them from the bright sunlight and felt in his pocket for the phone. It stopped ringing. 'Shit!' he muttered, and sat up. He felt crappy. Opening the car door, he climbed out – stiff and sore from sleeping in the car seat all night – stretched, then found the nearest tree and relieved himself. He rubbed his hands over his face, looked across at the entrance to Calcott Manor and wondered what the hell he was doing there.

He had come down last night in a fit of fury after the scene at the airport, but on the drive down had realised that he just couldn't go banging on the door of Calcott Manor and demand that Anna return home with him. She had made the decision to leave with this Turner bloke and if Max wanted her back he was going to have to win her round, not bully her into it. So he'd driven to the house and parked off the road in a clearing almost opposite the gates to set up watch. What he thought that would achieve he didn't know, but then it was late, he was tired and he wasn't thinking straight. Of course this morning, in the clear light of day, it all looked rather impulsive and ridiculous and standing there, unshaven, crumpled and exhausted from the lack of restful sleep, he felt a complete fool.

He still wanted to see Anna though and he wanted to find out more about the man she was staying with, so climbing back into the car, he decided to try and find somewhere local to stay, to have a shower and shave and to have a chat with anyone who knew anything about Will Turner.

Ten minutes later, in the centre of Widbry, he found the village pub, the Cricketers, and felt instantly better. Local pubs were a good source of information and this one had a nicely painted B & B sign up over the door. Max parked, locked up the car and knocked on the main door, reassured by the mouth-watering smell of cooked bacon.

The door was opened by a small, plump woman in her mid forties, wearing a blue-and-white-striped apron over T-shirt and long white shorts. Max said, 'Sorry to call so early, but I wondered if you might have any rooms for the night?'

The woman looked at him. She took in the expensive suit, the hair, dishevelled but still recognisably well-cut, the decent shoes and tie, and said, 'I've one left. Did you want it now? I could do you a special half rate for today and full rate from tonight onwards.' The fact that he was very attractive didn't go unnoticed either.

'That sounds fair, thank you. Could I possibly go up and have a shower and then get some breakfast?'

'Of course sir.' The woman was impressed by such

courtesy; you usually only ever got that from Americans. 'Would you like my husband to go and get your bags?'

'Oh, no, thanks, I don't have any.'

The woman looked momentarily surprised, but covered it with a smile and said, 'Right, well I'm Mrs Biggs . . .'

Max immediately held his hand out. 'Max Slater,' he said. 'Very pleased to meet you, Mrs Biggs.'

Again the woman's face registered surprise – very few people introduced themselves – then her initial polite smile widened to an hospitable grin. 'I'll show you to your room, shall I?'

Max smiled back. 'Thank you, I'd like that.'

Twenty minutes later he sat in the small, neat dining area of the pub and glanced briefly at the menu while Mrs Biggs waited for him to choose.

'The sausages are hand-made by the butcher,' she said. 'And the eggs are free range.'

'Sounds delicious!' Max replied. 'I'll have the full English then please, with toast and coffee.'

'Good.' Mrs Biggs noted it down on her pad.

'Lovely place you've got here,' he said, as she cleared the other place setting from the table. 'Always busy I expect.'

'Mostly. Summer trade is the B & B, but winter it's mostly the locals who use the pub and restaurant. What about you, Mr Slater, are you here on business, or just passing through?'

'Just passing through,' Max said. 'I need to see someone at Calcott Manor.'

Mrs Biggs glanced up. 'You're not one of those journalist chappies are you?'

'Journalists?' An alarm bell rang in Max's head. 'Good Lord no! Why would I be a journalist?'

She shrugged. 'Had loads of them last year when the trouble all blew up at Calcott. They packed the place out, made quite a nuisance of themselves actually.'

Max sat forward. The word 'trouble' gave him a definite sense of unease, but he kept his voice as calm and as even as he could. 'What was the trouble?'

She hesitated, looked at Max, then said, 'I'm not one for gossip, but it was in all the papers anyway.'

'It was?' He thought rapidly of the last year's news; nothing sprang to mind.

'Yes, terrible business it was, the whole thing, it quite divided the village.'

He began to feel sick. 'Really? And it involved Will Turner in some way, did it? At Calcott?'

'Oh yes.' Mrs Biggs moved round the table a couple of inches so that their conversation was more private. She was enjoying the fact that she had Max's full attention. 'Some said that it wasn't her fault.' She lowered her voice. 'And others said that it might not have even been her.'

Max was near to exasperation. He had a growing sense of anxiety and very little real information. 'Could you tell me exactly what happened? What *she* did?'

Mrs Biggs tutted, leant a fraction closer and Max listened with a sudden sense of desperation. He knew, with a sick, sinking feeling, that he wasn't going to like what he was about to hear.

Anna had been alone for the past hour. After her calls, and a brief walk around the garden, she had played with Maya for a while, read without really concentrating, and had a solitary cup of coffee in the conservatory. Hot-house plants weren't really her thing and once she had wandered round, glancing at the labels and trying to muster some enthusiasm, she went outside into the garden again to have a better look at it. The sun was shining in between scattered pillows of cloud, it was warm in bursts when the wind dropped and Anna walked across the wet grass, feeling more at ease out here than she felt in the house. The English are divided into people who like gardens and people who don't. Anna, being one of those who did, found great pleasure in Calcott's old-fashioned herbaceous borders, its ancient yew trees, its large diverse kitchen garden and the well-thought-out pattern of it all. She stopped and bent every now and then, touching a leaf or inspecting a flower, sometimes squatting to read the plant labels stuck into the soil. She lost track of time and of where she was, until she glanced up and found herself by a small stone building with a circular slate roof and a timber door, some distance from the house.

'The dovecote,' a voice said behind her.

Anna jumped and spun round.

'Sam Perkins, ma'am. Head gardener.' The elderly gentleman nodded and stood, slightly stooped, wiping his hands on his canvas apron.

'Anna Jacob, I'm a friend of—'

'How do. Seen you earlier, walking round. Thought you liked gardens, I can always tell.'

'I do, I love them. I've got a small garden in London, but it's rather haphazard in comparison to this I'm afraid.'

Sam looked up at the dovecote and Anna followed his gaze. The building looked deserted and unloved. 'Used to be more of it, years ago, but Mr Will, he's not really a gardener and recently, well you know . . .' Sam broke off and looked away, not finishing his sentence. Anna got the feeling that she should know. 'It's a full-time job mind. Even without the extra acre.'

'I'm sure. This building, the dovecote, what was it used for?'

'Doves, ma'am.'

Anna held down a smile. 'Yes, I understand that, but why? Why did they keep doves and why aren't there any now?'

'Kept them for food in the old days, but there ain't no use for 'em now.'

'He shot 'em!' Brian said.

Both Anna and Sam turned.

'That's enough, Bri. Ma'am, this is Brian, my under gardener.'

Anna nodded. 'Hello.'

'But he did, Sam, didn't he? Before my time, miss, he came out one morning with his gun and shot every single one of them. One of the lads who helps out from time to time, you know Dobbo, Sam? He said the mess was chronic. It took days to get rid of them all and some were injured and flew off and then dropped over the estate and it took days to collect them all up. He wanted every one of them cleared away. Didn't care about the carnage. Mad it was, Dobbo said, he was blood mad. Said he—'

'Enough Brian!' Sam snapped.

Anna had wrapped her arms tight around her body and was staring up at the dovecote with horror.

'Take no notice, ma'am,' Sam said, gently touching her arm. Anna jumped and instantly recoiled. 'It's idle gossip. These young lads have got nowt better to do than talk and make up stupid stories . . .'

'But he did shoot 'em, Sam, it's true!'

'Yes he did, he culled 'em. He could no longer look after 'em and so he culled 'em. It's different, lad.'

'Still bloody murder to me.'

'Enough!' Sam suddenly shouted. Anna turned. 'You will not spread malicious rumours about Mr Will like that. You weren't here and you don't know. Now that's the end of it, Brian. Go and get on with what I asked you to do.'

Brian turned. He kicked at a clump of daisies on the lawn and shuffled off. He muttered to himself as he went and Sam, watching Anna's face, said, 'Young uns. They don't know nowt. Think they do, of course, think they know it all.'

'Yes,' Anna said, but she didn't really know what to answer. She dug her hands in her pockets and turned. 'I ought to get back to the house.'

'Aye.'

'Nice to meet you, Sam.'

'And you ma'am.'

Anna nodded and walked off.

Letting herself into the house, Anna called out and Sheila opened the door of the sitting room. She came out, a vase of flowers in her hand, and said, 'Lunch will be ready at one. Would you like to eat with us in the kitchen or in the dining room?'

'Where does Will usually have his lunch?'

'Oh he doesn't—' Sheila stopped abruptly, then blushed. She had been about to say that he rarely ate, but realised how odd that sounded and that it might need an explanation – one she didn't know if she was authorised to give – so she said, 'He doesn't mind, wherever.' But she knew it came across badly because Anna looked at her puzzled, then shrugged.

'I'll have it in the kitchen I guess. If that's all right with Will.'

'If what's all right with Will?'

Anna turned; Will was behind her. She felt undeniable relief at seeing him and said, 'I was beginning to wonder about you.'

'I've been doing a few chores in the village. Are you OK?'

Anna nodded.

'And Maya?'

'Yes, we're fine. Are you going to join us for lunch? I was just telling Sheila I'll have it in the kitchen, if you don't mind.'

Will came across to her. 'Why should I mind? I won't join you, I've got too much to do I'm afraid, but you have lunch wherever you want to.' He touched her arm. 'You must treat Calcott as your home now, Anna.'

Anna glanced down at his hand on her arm and gently moved away. 'Yes, thanks.'

'Good.' He moved on past her and made his way along to his study. Anna watched him go, and although they were meant to, for some odd reason, his words didn't give her any comfort at all.

Sheila coughed. 'Was there anything else, miss?' she asked.

'No, no thanks.'

Sheila turned to go, but Anna stood where she was so Sheila glanced back. She was making a pig's ear out of this whole situation, she knew it but she couldn't help it. It wasn't really the likeness, it was just having a young woman and a baby in the house, it was too terrible, it reminded her too much and the memories were too painful.

'Is there something more, Ms Jacob?' she asked.

'Oh no, nothing. And it's Anna, please.'

'Anna. Right you are.' Sheila went into the sitting room and closed the door behind her. She leant against it, shut her eyes and for the first time in a long while, felt close to tears.

With lunch over, Anna once again found herself at a loose end. Will had offered to take her with him into Widbry to pick up some provisions but she declined, feeling suddenly odd about being alone with him. There was just the slightest bit too much pressure. So she gave Debbie the afternoon off and took Maya for a walk around the garden in the sling before carrying her upstairs for her afternoon nap. She settled her with a bottle, winded her, tucked her up in the cot and went to lie down on the bed. But Anna was restless – restless and uneasy. She pulled on a sweater and decided to have a look round the first floor of the house. She had seen a few rooms last night with Will, but this time she wanted to see everything. She knew it was wrong, to snoop uninvited, but she couldn't help herself. It was more than just curiosity that led her on, it was a need to know.

She left the door of her room ajar and peered into the one next to hers – a guest bedroom. It was furnished much the same as her own, with several antique pieces, round bedside tables covered in cloths that matched the drapes, a thick, quilted counterpane on an old-fashioned bed, and the walls hung with expensively framed prints. She looked, took it in and went on. The room further on was again a guest bedroom, this time less grand, more like a girl's room, with two iron bedsteads covered in white sprigged cotton and an old rocking horse, beautifully hand-carved, that stood in front of the window.

She saw four guest bedrooms in total on that floor, two

separate bathrooms and Will's room, which was much the same as the others, only more masculine, furnished with heavy mahogany furniture and deep blue-and-red-striped and checked fabric. Anna stood in it for a while, wondering what it was that bothered her about the house. She looked round and round that room, taking in every detail, unable to put her finger on it, until suddenly it came to her. It was a house, not a home, and it could have been anyone's. There were no photographs, no books, no personal effects. There was no mess, no clutter, no sign of the paraphernalia of human habitation. There was nothing of Will Turner here, not even his puffer by the side of the bed. She sighed, walked quietly out and closed the door behind her.

She climbed to the next floor, a narrow passage with only four rooms that led off it. The first was a bathroom, recently done by the look of it and pristine in its empti-ness. The second was a small sitting room, very pretty, in pale yellow, and the third and fourth were two connecting rooms. Anna walked into the biggest, a bedroom with just a large double bed, a lady's Victorian armchair and a pine chest. A door on the right led into a smaller room, but this was completely empty. She walked across to the window and opened it, putting her hand out to touch the iron bars over it. This room had been a nursery, that much she was certain of.

Turning, she noticed a single panelled door in the wall, a built-in wardrobe and, unable to stop herself, went to it, placed her hand on the brass handle and pulled it down. She had the strangest sensation as she swung the door open, a charge of excitement, as if she was on the verge of a discovery, and yet a dull sense of dread. She stopped, peered into the darkness and saw a switch. She reached out her hand and flicked it. The wardrobe was flooded with light. Anna sprang back.

'I couldn't part with it all.'

She spun round and saw Sheila standing in the doorway watching her. She put her hand up to her chest, her heart hammering so fast that it felt as if it would burst. 'I . . . I . . .' She turned back to the wardrobe, to the boxes of toys, the rail of baby clothes, the large white polar bear and the brown teddy bear.

She shook her head, distressed and confused. 'Whose is it? Who . . .' Then she saw a tiny pair of shoes, soft pale pink suede, and she turned and ran, pushing past Sheila, down the stairs, her eyes blurred with tears and her thoughts in turmoil. She ran down the first floor, down to her room, and snatched Maya out of the cot. Cradling her baby to her chest, she carried on running, not knowing what she was doing or why. She ran down the main stairs, along the hall and out of the front door. As she ran down the steps and onto the drive she heard the crunch of tyres and looked up just as a car screeched to a halt, missing her and Maya by inches.

'ANNA!' Max was out of the car and across to her in seconds. 'Anna! My God, Anna, what's the matter?' Max pulled her into him and held her, Maya pressed between them. 'Anna, please, calm down, tell me what's . . .'

Anna pulled away. Maya had started to cry, having been so rudely awoken. Anna took several deep breaths and wiped her face on a screwed-up tissue she found in her pocket, all the time jiggling Maya in an attempt to soothe her. 'I don't know, Max, I don't know what I'm thinking, I . . .'

'You're frightened, Anna, I can tell. You're frightened here, aren't you?'

'No! Not frightened, just confused. There are things I
don't understand and I, I don't know . . .' She broke off
and blew her nose. 'I'm getting them out of perspective
I think, I'm . . .' She looked at him. 'Anyway, what on
earth are you doing here?'

'It doesn't matter. Look Anna, you're not getting things
out of perspective, you're right. If you're frightened then
come home with me. Come home now.' Max held her
shoulders and looked at her. 'Listen to me, Anna. What
do you know about this man? Nothing! You've come here
to the middle of nowhere, put yourself in a vulnerable
situation and you know nothing about him. You've put
yourself and Maya in danger, Anna, you've—'

'No! No I haven't. Not danger. There's nothing dangerous here, it's just that I don't know exactly what's going
on, I don't know—'

'You don't know anything. For Christ's sake, Anna! Did
you know that he has all sort of terrible things in his past,
things so awful that I can hardly bear to think about you
being here with him, things that he did—'

Anna looked at Max. 'Max, stop it! Stop making these
accusations,' she said. 'How can you possibly know all
this?'

'I just do.' He didn't want to tell her that he had been
snooping, it was too undignified. 'I know all sorts of things
that I can't tell you.'

'Like what?' Anna and Max turned and saw Will. He
had come round the side of the house and stood looking
at them, his face grim and unreadable. 'What things have
I done?' Anna moved away from Max and instinctively
towards Will but she wasn't conscious of it.

'No,' Max said, 'I'm not going to be drawn into a row
with you. You tell her. Tell her the truth about your life,

about what happened to your sister. I presume she doesn't know any of it.'

'What sister?' Anna said. 'What the hell is going on, Max? Will?'

Will shrugged. 'I'll tell you, Anna, I'll tell you everything you need to know. The truth, not some ridiculous village gossip.'

Max bristled. He didn't like this man and it wasn't just jealousy. 'Tell her in front of me.'

Will looked at Anna. 'If that's what you want, Anna, then fine, if you don't trust me enough to tell you in private, then fine I'll—'

'No, it's not that. I do trust you, I—'

'Then let's go inside and talk.'

'No Anna, don't go with him. Make him tell you out here.'

'Max, you're being ridiculous!'

'Am I? Am I really? Tell her about the dead baby, Will! Tell her about the dead, murdered baby.'

Anna caught her breath. She turned and stared, wild-eyed, at Will.

'Tell her who killed the baby,' Max said quietly, suddenly drained by his adrenaline and emotion. 'Tell her the truth.' He glanced at Will and a look of such hatred and revulsion crossed Will's face that it made Max shudder. He stood his ground, but it was no good. Will moved towards the door and Anna followed. She owed it to Will to give him the chance to explain. Max had had his chance and he'd blown it; he'd blown it big time, when he slept with Chrissy Forbes.

Chapter Twenty-one

Max sat in the kitchen with Maya. He held his baby, one of his fingers tightly gripped by one of her tiny hands, and wondered what the hell he was going to do next. He looked down at her small round face, her wide, clear eyes and he knew that he could never leave her. No matter what Anna decided, he would always be Maya's father and nothing could take that away from him, or her.

He glanced up as Sheila came into the room.

'Would you like a cup of tea or coffee?'

'No, thanks.' He smiled. 'I'd rather just . . . well, you know, sit.'

Sheila watched him for a few moments, remembering such scenes in this very kitchen, and she said, 'A baby is very precious. They change your life completely and at times you wonder why on earth you ever decided to start a family, but they do something to you, they change your perspective and make you see more, not just yourself.'

Max looked at her. 'I know. I wish I'd realised it sooner.'

She sighed. 'You never really know what you've got until it's taken away from you.' Her eyes flickered towards the door. 'And then it's too late.' She turned, put the kettle on the Aga to boil and got on with the washing up.

*   *   *

In the study, Anna sat across the room from Will. It was the most neutral place in the house, and as she sat, she had nowhere else to look apart from at him.

'I don't know where to start,' he said.

'At the beginning?' She wondered about Max in the kitchen and wanted him there. Why, why did she keep wanting Max?

'The beginning is a long time ago, Anna, sixteen years ago. My parents died, as you know, and left me and my sister, Esme.'

'You never told me you had a sister.'

'No. Esme was ten when it happened and she took it very badly. I was twenty. She was away at boarding school by then and the trustees and I saw no reason to disrupt her . . .' He stopped and stared down at his hands. 'In hindsight I don't know, maybe if she'd been here with me, maybe if she had been at home . . .' He looked up. 'She began to hear voices, at fourteen. The school put it down to hysteria, adolescence, an over-active imagination, anything they could think of really. But she got worse and by the time she came home at eighteen, I knew things weren't right. To cut a long story short, Anna, Esme has some kind of mental illness. They couldn't identify it, that was part of the problem – whenever she was seen by doctors she appeared perfectly well but when she came home she'd be . . .' He stopped again, put his hands up to his face and it took him a few moments to compose himself. 'She'd be difficult, hysterical, sometimes violent. I didn't know how to handle her. Then a few years ago Esme seemed to get better. It wasn't sudden, it had been a long slow climb since she was eighteen, but we had her medication right and she had a job, working in London for a restaurant. She was twenty-four and I can honestly say that that year was the happiest year of my life.' He looked at her. 'You wouldn't understand that, Anna, someone who has always had things so under control, so mapped out and achievable. You wouldn't understand what it's like to live with the threat of chaos, all the time not knowing what was going to happen.'

Anna hung her head. He was right. How could she possibly understand that? One crisis and she had gone to pieces.

'But that year, with Esme settled and reasonably happy, was the first time I could remember since my parents died that I wasn't constantly anxious. It *was* happy. I was happy.' He smiled. 'You know Andrew always says that I was driven, driven to make the computer company so successful, perhaps he's right. I had nothing else, you see, just the work and Esme. I buried myself in the business, to escape. I was a computer wizard. My father had started it, selling software, one of the first people in this country to do so, and he was successful, but I was mega-successful. I was driven, I had talent and ambition and nothing else. Anyway . . .' He sighed again. 'It all seemed OK, then Esme met someone. I won't bother with names, but he was one of life's shabby people. He was dishonest and unkind and out for what he could get. Esme adored him and before we knew it she was pregnant. That was when it all went terribly wrong. He convinced her to come off her medication, told her it would harm the baby, which she did. She would have done anything for him. And of course without the pills, Esme got ill again. She became violent, towards me mainly and self-mutilating. She went into hospital, the boyfriend insisted she came out and live here with him and under the health act Esme had the right to discharge herself. She did what he wanted, against my wishes and the advice of her doctors. I had the top floor of the house converted for her, and him, but it didn't work. He stayed a few weeks then walked out. Esme went into premature labour with the shock and distress, four weeks early, and Sophia was delivered by Caesarean section on . . .' Will's voice wavered. He paused and cleared his throat. 'On the tenth of January nineteen ninety-seven. I named her after my mother. Esme would have nothing to do with her. She was . . . She was the most petite, beautiful, incredible thing ever to happen in my life and I . . .' Will stopped. For the second time he put his hands up to his face. He couldn't continue, he sat like that for a long time, struggling to bring himself under control. There were no tears, just pain, searing, breathless pain.

Anna stared down at her hands. She locked her fingers together and held them under her heart where it ached for him.

'I couldn't have loved her any more if she had been mine,' he said.

Anna looked up.

He stood facing her, his face crumpled with distress. 'I went every day to the Special Care Unit, I fed her, changed her nappy in the incubator, talked to her, stroked her through the special openings. And when she made her target weight I brought her home, to Sheila, who was going to look after her. Sophia gave me, in her few short months of life, such exquisite joy, such complete love that I have barely smiled without her.'

Anna just sat and stared.

Will went on. 'I brought Esme home too, but she knew very little about it. The pregnancy had sparked some kind of adverse reaction and she went from bad to worse. I should have known, I should have realised, but naively I kept hoping that it was all going to be all right. I couldn't see how anyone could not love this baby. But Esme didn't. She hated her, she was frightened of her, wouldn't touch her at times and I didn't see it, I didn't see it coming.' Will ran his hands through his hair, then he took out a handkerchief and wiped his face. 'I'm sorry, Anna,' he said, 'but this is very painful for me.'

Anna said nothing but she reached out and touched his hand. He caught her fingers and held them for a moment, then he went on.

'Esme became increasingly distressed. She became hysterical about small things, like the sound of the doves in the dovecote or the lights on the sensor pads for the alarm all over the house. Evil eyes she called them. And she thought the figures in the paintings were watching her. It was horrible, this descent into madness. Some nights I would wake up and find her in my room. She had a white nightdress and she would stand by the window and watch me. She thought she was an avenging angel. It scared the hell out of me. I took to sleeping with Sophia in my room, I bought that travel cot that Maya is in so that I could have her next to my bed. I was frightened, Anna, I lived in a permanent state of anxiety for months, but I never thought, I never thought she would really do anything serious. I never really believed it was that bad . . .' He swallowed. 'Then one night, April it was, April the thirtieth, Sophia was nearly four months old, she was teething and was fractious and Esme couldn't cope with the crying. It got to her, she was in a state about it. Foolishly I went out. I left her alone and . . . God, I've never forgiven myself for that mistake. I left her alone and in desperation, she shook the baby. She shook her so hard that she was . . .' He broke off and turned away from Anna. 'She was unconscious when they found her and she never came round. Esme shook her to death.'

Anna caught her breath. She had known what was coming, she had been preparing herself all the way through for this information but still it hit her like a bludgeon blow.

Will turned to look at Anna, who had barely moved all the time he had been speaking. She had clasped her hands in her lap, her fingers locked tight together, and her body was perfectly still.

'I never told you I had a sister. What could I have told you, Anna, that wouldn't have tainted everything between us? How do I explain something like this?'

'I don't know.'

'I love you, Anna.'

She looked up.

'I see no point in pretending otherwise. You know everything about me so you might as well know that too. I loved you, I think, from the time I saw you in the office with Maya, so sad and vulnerable and alone. I can't explain it, it just happened, and once it had it changed everything.'

Anna didn't want to hear this. She understood it, she thought that in some sense she felt it too, but she couldn't react; she was too numb. 'What happened to Esme?' she asked.

'Esme pleaded guilty to manslaughter with diminished responsibility. She was sent to a secure hospital.'

'And?'

'And I don't know. She will have no communication with me. Nothing at all. I have set up a trust fund for her so that she never has to worry about money and

Andrew is the trustee but he deals only with the hospital administration, not Esme herself. She has shut me and everything to do with me out.'

'I'm sorry. It sounds so trite, to say that I'm sorry, but I truly am. I have criticised you for being arrogant and dismissive and I had no idea of . . .'

'Anna, you were right! I've lost so much but I still have a great deal, a damn sight more than most, so you were right.' He smiled, but it was self-deprecating. 'You made me think. It did me good.' He shrugged and they were silent for a while. 'So there,' he said finally. 'You have the truth. What now? Are you going to leave with Max?'

Anna didn't hesitate. 'No. I'll stay.'

Will let out a breath and stood up. He felt suddenly exhausted and there was nothing left to say. 'I'll be in the garden, if you want me.' He turned towards the door, looked at Anna's face once more, then left the room. Alone, Anna put her head down and cried the tears that Will was unable to.

Later, on the drive of the house, Max stood by his car, reluctant to leave but knowing there was no point in arguing any more. Anna had made her mind up.

'I'll ring you,' he said, 'to make sure you and Maya are OK.'

Anna shrugged.

'I'll be out of the house by tomorrow night, OK? If that's what you really want, I'll find myself somewhere to rent.'

'Thank you.'

'Don't thank me, Anna; it doesn't make me feel any better. I want you and Maya to come back with me, but if you won't, if it really is over, then . . .' He looked at

her and for a moment he thought that she was about to
say something. He stopped and willed her to say it, but
she didn't. She remained silent. 'The house is yours,' he
said. 'I don't want it, not without you in it.'

'Don't, Max!' Anna shook her head. 'Don't make it
worse.'

'Worse for who? You've made your decision, how can
I make it worse for you?'

Anna didn't answer him; she didn't know how to say
what she wanted to. She had made a decision, to stay, at
least for tonight, but everything else was as confused as
it had ever been. She loved Max, she knew that, but how
could she let all that had happened go? How could she
forgive him on just a few promising words? And Will?
How could she leave all that pain and suffering and love
for her? How could she just walk away from all that? She
glanced behind her and said, 'Look, I've got to go in, Maya
is hungry and I need to feed her.' She went up the steps
towards the house.

'Anna?' She turned. 'I'm always here for you, if you need
me. You may not think it now, but I'll prove it to you.'

Anna turned away again; it hurt too much even to
look at him.

Darren waited nervously in the corridor outside the
company commander's office. He bit his fingernails and
stared at the grey wall, his stomach churning. The door
opened.

'Private Woodman!'

He stood to attention as the company sergeant major
marched out. 'Right turn, on the double, quick march!'

Darren was marched in.

'Halt!'

He stopped in front of a desk and stood, his feet hip-distance apart, his hands clasped behind his back. In front of him and behind the desk sat the company commander, Major Black, to the right of him the platoon commander, Lieutenant Pope.

'Private Woodman,' Major Black said, 'you have made an application for special leave over the next three days due to personal reasons. Would you like to explain these "personal reasons"?'

A sweat broke out on Darren's forehead. 'No sir.'

'How am I to process this special application if you do not explain the reason for it?'

Darren stared down at the floor. 'I don't know sir,' he said.

'Would you like to say anything at all to help with your application?'

'No sir.'

'Have you anything to add, Lieutenant Pope?'

'Yes sir. I'd like it to be noted that Private Woodman has an unblemished record with the regiment and that this is the first time he has asked for special leave. I am inclined to trust that this is a highly personal matter that he does not wish to discuss outside his immediate family.'

'Thank you, Lieutenant Pope.'

There was a brief pause, some papers were rustled, some notes made and Darren sweated more heavily.

'Private Woodman.' He looked up. 'On consideration of Lieutenant Pope's recommendation, I grant you three days' leave as of midnight tonight. I hope you will be able to solve whatever problem it is that you have. March him out, Sergeant Major.'

'Sir! About turn! On the double, quick march!'

Darren turned and, ramrod straight, marched out of

the room. Outside in the corridor, he stopped and wiped his face on his handkerchief. The CSM said, 'You were lucky, Woodman. Now go and join your platoon.'

'Yes sir.' Darren let out a sigh of relief and hurried away.

The young woman had bolted the door. It smelt in there, but she didn't mind. She had placed paper towels all over the floor and sat on them, with her back up against the door, her face opposite the small oblong of grimy plastic that served as a window. She had a rucksack with a sleeping bag attached, and inside it, a ground sheet and some basic cooking utensils. She had her clothes, her toothbrush and some water. That was all she needed, that was all she had ever needed. On the floor in front of her, laid carefully and neatly out on the paper towels, she had placed the few things she had brought from her flat. A sharp knife, the one she used for fruit, a roll of toilet paper, a neatly coiled rope and a set of keys. She reached out and touched the keys now, holding them in the palm of her hand and fingering the tiny, intricate teeth. There were three of them, and she knew exactly where they fitted. She smiled. She would have the advantage, she would out-manoeuvre him.

Behind her, the door handle rattled but she ignored it. She had been a nomad for a couple of weeks, nowhere to go, hiding, frightened, but that was all over now; now she had made up her mind. Not knowing caused fear, but if she knew, if she watched and waited and took control, then she could face the fear, confront it and destroy it. She knew what she had to do and, whatever the cost, Esme was going home.

*   *   *

Will had been out running. It had been raining, he was wet and exhausted and under his fleece a film of sweat clung to his skin, making him cold and shivery. He came up the stairs to have a shower, wet and muddy trainers in his hand, and padded barefoot along the corridor. He stopped at Anna's room and put his ear to the door. He heard singing, soft, low singing, and so gently turned the handle and looked in.

Debbie heard the noise and jerked round.

'Oh I'm sorry, I thought it was Anna, I . . .'

She was sitting in the darkness by the cot and the shaft of light from the corridor fell in a slice across her, contorting her face, half illuminated, half in shadow. Will looked at her.

Several times before he had seen something in her eyes that he thought he knew, something that he thought he recognised but couldn't place. It had unnerved him. He saw it again now, that same expression, and this time he knew it instantly. He said nothing, but closed the door and walked on to his own room. In the bathroom he switched on the lights and went across to the mirror. He stared at his reflection and saw the same expression in his own eyes. It was grief.

Chapter Twenty-two

It was odd weather. It had been warm in the afternoon, then it had rained, but the rain didn't clear the air, the moisture seemed locked in and the heat made it cling to everything.

Anna had gone to bed early but she couldn't sleep. She lay for a long time, looking at the dim light of the moon through the drapes and the dark shadows of the room. She was confused and her mind wouldn't settle. Finally she drifted off to sleep around midnight, a light, troubled sleep where she dreamt of water closing over her head and the struggle to get to the surface.

She woke with a start.

She was lying on her front with her face turned towards the wall and as she opened her eyes, she was momentarily displaced and confused. She couldn't focus and so closed her eyes again to try and re-adjust them. That was when she heard it. With her eyes closed and her ears in full sensory arousal. It was a faint rustle, a movement, a swish of fabric. She sat up.

She turned her head immediately towards the cot, and in the darkness thought she caught sight of a figure, just beyond it. Her fright was so great that for several moments she froze. It was dark, the sort of darkness that only the country knows – pitch black, no light outside for miles, no moon and no stars – and as she stared, her heart thudding in her chest, the figure merged into the darkness and she lost sight of it. She blinked rapidly and opened her mouth, but no sound came out. Then she moved; she lunged towards the door and that unlocked her voice. She yanked it open and hollered into the passageway.

The lights were on in minutes and Will was in the room. Anna was at the cot with Maya in her arms but she couldn't speak, she was shaking so hard that she couldn't get the words out. Seconds after that Debbie arrived.

'Anna! What the hell has happened? Anna? What is it?' Will steered her across to the bed and Debbie took Maya out of her arms.

'I think I saw someone,' she said. 'I think I saw a figure, by the cot. I'm sure I did. I saw someone in the room.' She folded her arms in tight to her body to try and stop the shaking.

'Right! Stay here. Debbie, you stay with Anna and lock the door after I've gone. I'll check the house.'

'Shouldn't you ring the police?'

'I'll check the house first,' he said. He walked out of the room and Debbie turned the key in the lock after him.

'I saw something, Debbie,' Anna said. 'I'm sure I did! I saw a figure, then in the dark it seemed to vanish. I heard something too, a movement, the rustle of clothes. I'm sure there was something there, I don't think I imagined it.'

Debbie nodded. She came over to the bed. 'D'you want to hold Maya for a while? It might make you feel better.'

She handed the baby across and Anna looked down at her face. She swallowed the urge to cry. 'Thank God she's OK . . .' She touched the pale, soft skin. 'I did see it!' she said, more to herself than anyone else, then she glanced across at the cot and Debbie followed her gaze. The curtains behind it were thick, heavy drapes that moved, very slightly, in the draught from the window. In the dark they might have looked like a figure, and both women had the same thought. 'I couldn't have imagined it, could I?' Anna asked.

Debbie shrugged; she honestly didn't know.

They sat in silence and waited, until Will came back. 'The house is secure,' he said, 'completely secure. I've checked every room. No one has got in, to the best of my knowledge. Is the window open?' He crossed to the window and drew the curtains. One of the sash windows was open, but only a couple of inches. Anna would have heard someone open it further. 'I doubt whether anyone could get through there,' he said, closing the curtains again. He came across to Anna. 'Anna, are you sure it was real? I mean, after today and all the upset, I just wonder if . . .'

'Are you doubting me, Will? Do you think I imagined it?'

He shrugged. 'I don't know. The mind is a very powerful thing, Anna, and you've been under a lot of stress.'

'Maybe I did,' she said. 'Maybe I'm going mad!' She put her hands up to her face and rubbed them wearily over it. 'It was very real, the image was so real that for a few moments I thought I could have touched it. Then it seemed to fade, in the pitch dark I couldn't see it any more. Perhaps I did imagine it. I don't know . . . I'm confused now . . .' She stood and walked across to the cot. 'At least it didn't upset Maya too much. She seems to have drifted off to sleep again.' She lowered the baby gently into the cot and turned. 'Sorry, I feel rather foolish now. Sorry to have got everyone up.'

Debbie shrugged. 'As long as you're all right,' she said. She went to the door. 'If you're nervous at all, call me, OK?'

Anna nodded. 'Thanks Debbie,' she said. 'I appreciate it.'

Debbie left the room and Anna looked at Will. 'Did I imagine it?' she asked.

'Probably.' Anna hung her head and Will crossed to her, taking her in his arms. 'It doesn't matter, Anna,' he murmured. 'So what if you did? It's been a very long day and you're probably feeling the effects. Now why don't I tuck you up in bed and bring you a cup of cocoa.'

'Cocoa!'

Will smiled. 'OK, how about a whisky toddy then?'

'That's more like it.' Anna smiled back. 'But no, nothing thanks. I think I just need to get some sleep.' Will released her and she went to the bed, climbing in and pulling the duvet up to her chin. Her stomach was still churning and she didn't want Will to leave, but she wasn't going to admit that – she felt ridiculous enough as it was.

'Are you all right now?'

'Yes.'

'Do you want me to stay?'

'No, no thanks.'

Will shrugged. 'OK, I'll just go down and turn the lights off, then I'll go to bed. Are you sure you're OK?'

She nodded.

'Good.' He walked out of the room.

Down in the entrance hall Will opened the cupboard and checked the alarm pad again. It was definitely off but he couldn't for the life of him remember if he had actually turned it on before he went to bed. He had left it off last night, he remembered that quite clearly. He had left it off in case Anna or Debbie came downstairs for a bottle or a drink in the night, but tonight he just couldn't remember what he had done. He had the oddest sensation that he had turned it on, but he wasn't going to let himself believe that, because if he did, then it meant that someone had turned it off. He came out of the cupboard and closed the door firmly behind him. It was still the same pin number, the number they had had for years; he had never seen any reason to change it. He walked along to his study, turned the lights on and wrote a note on his desk for Jenna. It said, 'Tuesday am call Security Systems and get them to key in a new pin number for the alarm.' Then he turned out the lights and left the study.

Walking once more through the house, Will turned off the lights in each room as he double-checked it. He felt uneasy and something else too, something familiar that he couldn't place. He went upstairs and did the same to all the guest bedrooms, peering in, then turning off the lights. Finally he went up to the top floor and double-checked each room there. He never came up here, it pained him too much to see it. He glanced in the bathroom, the sitting room and lastly the bedroom. He saw the wardrobe door slightly ajar and the light on in it, and all at once he recognised the feeling that he hadn't been able to place. He recognised it, in all its painful familiarity.

The feeling was fear.

Darren stayed in barracks despite the fact that he was on leave; he had things to think through and he needed the time alone. The following morning, he got up at five thirty, showered, dressed and took the car keys that he'd borrowed from a friend out of his locker. The car was parked over in married quarters and as he made his way across there he thought about what it might have been like, could have been like, if only things had been different. It made him infinitely depressed.

He opened the car, climbed inside and started the engine. He was determined in his course of action, so determined, in fact, that nothing would stop him.

He had a road atlas and knew where Widbry was – that was the name of the place that bloke at the airport, the one Debs went with, had mentioned – and he'd looked it up yesterday. But Calcott, the other place, he was less sure about. He thought it was probably the name of a house, but there was no way of checking, except physically, so that was what he planned to do. Exactly what he was going to say if he got there he had no idea. He supposed he just wanted the truth, if she was capable of giving it to him. Only that was the real problem. What could he now believe?

'Mrs Jennifer Slater please. To see Dr Mitchem.'

Jennifer stood and hooked her handbag – her best one, the lizard skin with the bamboo handles – over her arm. She lifted her shoulders, put her head back and walked through the waiting area towards the doctor's consulting room. She knocked, put her ear to the door to listen for a reply, heard 'enter' and went on in.

'Ah, Jennifer. Please, sit down.'

She did as Dr Mitchem asked, perching her bag on her lap.

'How are you feeling?'

'Fine.'

'Good.' Dr Mitchem took his glasses off. 'I've had a call from your consultant and he asked me to see you, that's why I've called you in. He said that he spoke to you about your cancer and what was needed – the operation, followed by chemotherapy, but that you refuse to have any treatment at all. I wondered if we might have a little chat about that.'

'It is hardly a subject for chat, Dr Mitchem,' Jennifer said, in her habitual sharp tone. 'My reasons for refusing treatment were explained to Mr Marcus quite clearly at the time and I see no reason to keep repeating myself.'

'Jennifer, your ovarian cancer is fairly well advanced. You need an operation to remove the cancerous ovaries immediately and probably the uterus and then you need chemotherapy to eradicate any more cancerous cells. Without either the operation or the chemo, you will certainly die.'

'Dr Mitchem, we will all certainly die; that is something I have been coming to terms with all my life.'

'Is that what you want? To make a quick exit?'

'Put like that, yes, I suppose it is. When your time's up, Dr Mitchem, I see no point in hanging around, out-staying my welcome.'

Dr Mitchem sighed. 'We could prolong your life by a year, possibly two with treatment.'

'For what purpose?'

'I'm sorry?'

'Why would you want to prolong my life? With all due respect, you don't know everything about me.'

Dr Mitchem changed tack. 'What do your family say about all this? Have you told Max?'

'No, I've not told my son and I have no intention of doing so. It is none of his business when and how I die.'

'Of course it's his business! You are his mother, you have responsibilities, Jennifer!'

Jennifer smiled. 'Dr Mitchem, is it me, or is this conversation rather perverse? The National Health Service is permanently under-funded, you as a practice have to manage your funds very carefully indeed and I have no idea why you aren't kissing my cheek and thanking me. I will save you thousands by going away and dying quietly. Please, don't look a gift horse in the mouth.'

Dr Mitchem shook his head and grudgingly smiled. 'I have never heard that expression used in such a context, Jennifer.' He threw his hands up. 'If you have made up your mind and you are absolutely sure about this, then who am I to argue? We are here if you need us; if you want any more information or anything at all really, don't hesitate to call.'

Jennifer stood up. 'Is that it?'

'Yes, that's it.'

She was glad she had brought her good handbag, it gave her an air of confidence that she didn't really possess. 'Thank you, Dr Mitchem.'

'You'll make an appointment on your way out for next month?'

'Is it absolutely necessary?'

'No, but I'd like to see you. I will arrange some blood tests and make sure that you are managing without too much pain.'

'OK.'

She turned towards the door and Dr Mitchem took one last stab at finding the root of the problem. 'How is your granddaughter, Jennifer? You told me about her last month, she must be – what – six, eight weeks old by now?'

Jennifer turned. Her face had set but it didn't cover her obvious distress. 'She's nine weeks,' she replied archly. 'But as to how she is, I don't know. I haven't seen her for a while.'

'I see.' Dr Mitchem made a note on his pad to call Max Slater. It wasn't conventional, but he didn't really care.

'Goodbye Dr Mitchem,' Jennifer said.

'Goodbye, Jennifer.'

She opened the door and was gone. Dr Mitchem called in his next patient and hoped sincerely that it was just a simple case of flu.

Anna was still in bed when Will came up with some tea. She was awake, lying with Maya next to her and playing, in the silly, absorbing way that people play with babies. She glanced up as he came in.

'Hello. You look tired,' Will said. 'We neither of us slept well.'

'No.' Anna sat up. 'Look, Will, I've been thinking and I really do need to go back home today.'

'Really?' Will stood and went to the curtains. He drew them and let some light into the room, then he fiddled, avoiding turning back, opening the window and tying up the drapes.

'You're upset.'

Finally, he turned, but he wasn't able to meet her eye. 'No I'm not "upset". I don't want you to go, but you must do what you think is best.'

'I know I said I'd stay, but I can't. I honestly can't. I called Andrew yesterday and said I'd be back at work by the end of the week and well . . .' Her voice trailed off.

'Then you must go.'

She looked away. There was a silence between them, then Will said, 'Really, if that's what you want to do, then you must do it, but would you promise me something first?'

Anna shrugged.

'Come for a walk with me this morning. Bring Maya and let me show you Calcott and Widbry and everything you want to leave.' He came over to the bed. 'You can pack your things and we can have one last morning together. How about it, Anna?'

Again she shrugged and Will turned to walk back to the door. 'Think about it,' he said. 'Let me know later.' He opened the door. 'Do you need to use the phone again this morning?'

'No, thanks.'

'Really? Did you find something to rent?'

Anna glanced away. 'I'm going home,' she said. 'Max is moving out and letting me have the house.'

Will couldn't keep the shock out of his voice. 'You trust him to do that? To move out?'

'Yes! I—' Anna stopped. Why was she having to explain herself? Why was this making her nervous? 'I do.' She climbed out of bed and reached for her robe. 'Look Will, I'll come for that walk. Let's go early, then I can—'

'Get away early?'

'No!' Anna was beginning to feel trapped. 'It's not like that, it's just that I arranged to see Andrew McKie this afternoon at three and, well, I might as well get us all settled back in London today, before then, rather than go up and come back and . . .' She broke off, seeing his face, closed and unreadable. 'It just seems more sensible, that's all.'

Will shrugged. 'Whatever you want, Anna,' he said. He walked out and left her alone.

*   *   *

Max was at the Cricketers pub. He woke late and lay in the dark wondering what he was doing and whether perhaps he was actually losing it. He should have gone back to London yesterday, he should be in work this morning, on the phone, organising his removal from the house in Clapham, but he couldn't bring himself to leave Widbry. He was worried, no, more than that – he was genuinely anxious about Anna and Maya and, even if it was futile, the fact that he was just a few miles away from them made him feel marginally better.

At nine thirty, Max got up. He dressed in the same clothes he had worn for two days now and went down to breakfast. He had no set plans, except to ring his mother again – he had rung to let her know where he was last night and had only got her answerphone – and to check his answering service. He thought he might go for a walk, have a good tramp round to clear his head. He ate a full English breakfast, drank several cups of tea and left the pub. It was a warm morning, but overcast and slightly humid. He said good morning to the postman, asked him where the nearest public footpath was and set off. He was in his city shoes, shirt sleeves and his suit trousers, but it didn't bother him. For the first time in his life, Max was totally unconcerned about what he looked like; he had far too much else to worry about.

Jennifer found herself at Victoria train station. It was mid morning and, standing underneath the huge information boards, looking up for a train to Chichester, she realised that she had no clear idea of how she had got there. She had made no conscious decision to come, it had just happened. She had walked out of the doctor's surgery at Esher, driven to the station and got on the next through

train to Waterloo. At Waterloo she had taken out eighty
pounds in cash from a Lloyds Bank cashpoint and climbed
into a taxi for the ride across to Victoria. She had done it
all without thinking, without actually saying to herself, *I
am going to see Maya*. In her handbag she had the address
of the Cricketers pub on a slip of paper and at the ticket
desk at Esher they had told her that the nearest station
to Widbry was Chichester. So here she was, waiting for
a train and knowing in her heart that she was doing the
right thing. She had to see that baby, she had waited so
long and not even the thought of dying was going to
stop her.

Darren drove into Widbry village and saw the pub on his
right. He pulled into the car park, left the engine running
and climbed out. There was a woman by the front door,
watering her hanging baskets.

'Excuse me?'

She turned.

'I'm looking for a place called Calcott. Would you know
if it's a house, or a village?'

'It's a house – Calcott Manor. You need to go out of
Widbry, past the little petrol station and carry on for
about two miles. There's a bend in the road and opposite
a clearing in the woods are a set of gates. That's Calcott
Manor.'

'Oh, right, thank you.' Darren climbed back into the
car and wound the window down. 'It's straight on then,'
he called. 'Out of the village?'

'Yes, that's right.'

He indicated, waved at the woman and pulled out. Mrs
Biggs left her watering can where it was and went inside.
'Hugh,' she called, 'there's something odd going on up at

Calcott. Mr Slater's gone off in a sour mood and there's another bloke this morning asking for the address.'

Hugh Biggs came out from behind the bar where he'd been changing a barrel. 'I hope not,' he said, wiping his hands on a beer cloth. 'There's been enough trouble up there to last a lifetime.'

Max stopped by a stile and leant over it to admire the view. He had walked three miles, much of it on a gentle incline, and the view from up here, on the side of the North Downs, was stunning. He took several deep breaths and filled his lungs with cool air, feeling suddenly hopeful. The peace, the solitude, the feeling of being at one with nature energised him.

Then his phone rang.

Max started. He dug in his pocket, pulled it out and cursed himself for bringing it. The modern-day convenience of being contactable at all times in all places had its drawbacks. He answered the call, saw that the network coverage was low and barked down the line.

'Who? Sorry? Dr Mitchem? Oh right, yes, my mother. What? Sorry? Did you? No I'm not there. It is?' Max was silent and listened to Dr Mitchem speak. He stared out at the view and took in the irony of being in such a wonderful place to hear such terrible news. Despite the odd mix of feelings he had for Jennifer, Max did love his mother. She was also his last link with immortality; her death would inevitably bring him closer to his own. 'No it's fine, I'll come this afternoon.' He glanced at his watch. 'If I leave now I can be there by one.' He swallowed back the sudden urge to cry. 'Yes, thanks Dr Mitchem. I'll see you later.' He ended the call, took one

last look at the view, then made his way back down to
Widbry.

Anna and Will had walked the public footpath through
the Calcott estate and followed it for two miles, along the
lower slopes of the North Downs into Widbry village.
They finished their walk at the end of the car park behind
the village hall, and as Will lifted the pushchair across the
stile, Anna said, 'Thank you, Will. It was just as lovely as
you promised.'

He smiled and climbed over after Anna. 'How about
coffee in the village tea rooms?'

Anna glanced at her watch. 'I'd love to but I really
ought to be . . .' She didn't finish; Will had walked away.
Catching him up, Anna said, 'Don't be angry. I'll be back
to visit.'

He turned to her. 'Will you?'

She hesitated. There was something in his eyes that she
didn't understand and she didn't know how to answer
him. Will said, 'Anna, I've got to pop into the village store
for a couple of things and then to the chemist before we
get back. D'you want to come or wait here for me?'

'I'll wait here.' She nodded towards a bench in front of
the village hall. 'I'll wait on that bench just over there.'

'Fine.' He dug his hands in his pockets and walked
off.

Anna moved towards the bench. She parked the pushchair at the end of it and sat down, finding her sunglasses
and slipping them on. The sun had just started to burn
through the clouds and she was glad she had brought
them with her. Resting her head back against the wall, she
closed her eyes and sighed deeply. She was tired, the sun
relaxed her and her mind slipped easily from conscious

thought. It emptied, and for a few wonderful moments Anna felt suspended from the stress and anxiety that had dogged her for weeks. She dozed off.

A short while later, she opened her eyes and glanced down at her watch. She had been there for five minutes or so and felt stiff in the neck and shoulders. She stretched and wondered where Will had got to, then she turned to look down at Maya.

Her whole body stopped.

For one moment, her heart stopped beating and she lost vision. The blood roared in her ears. Then she cried out.

'My baby . . . I . . . My baby . . . My baby's gone! Oh my God, someone has taken my baby! Oh my God . . . !'

Chapter Twenty-three

Anna ran with the pushchair up through the car park to the main street of the village. 'My baby's gone,' she shouted. 'Please help me, someone please . . .' She ran into a shop, her face stricken, and the manager darted round the counter to her.

'What's happened, love? Tell me what's happened.' But Anna was virtually incoherent.

'My baby,' she kept crying. 'My baby's gone. Someone has taken my baby!'

He took hold of her shoulders. 'Stay here, love, try and stay calm,' he said. 'We'll call the police.

'Trish!' he shouted over his shoulder at his assistant. 'Dial nine-nine-nine!' He gently held Anna's shoulders.

'Where's Will? I must tell him! Where's Will?'

'Try and calm down, love, try and breathe and tell me exactly what's happened.' But Anna ducked away from him. She ran a few yards up the street, then changed direction. She didn't know what she was doing, but the urge to run was overwhelming.

People stopped, the small crowd of shoppers just stopped. A man started to run. 'I'll look up there!' he shouted. Someone else called, 'I'll check behind the village hall.'

Anna began to cry, great sobs racking her body. A crowd formed round her. She was gently led back to the shop. 'Oh God, Maya . . . my baby . . . Oh God . . .' Anna wrapped her arms round her body, still sobbing. She began to shake violently. 'I've got to look,' she wept. 'I've got to go and look for her . . .' but she was trembling so hard that she couldn't move.

'Whisky Charlie four zero, we're approaching the scene now. There's a small crowd, but we'll need back-up.' The squad car screeched to a halt outside the shop and two uniformed officers climbed out. They pushed their way through the crowd, parting the spectators. 'Excuse me, let us through please, thank you.'

Anna looked up.

'Right, hello love, try and calm down now, all right? It's OK, we'll have the situation under control in a few minutes. What's your name love?'

'Anna . . . Anna Jacob.'

'And what's happened? Is it a baby that's gone missing? Come on, try and calm down and tell me what happened. Can you try and tell me what happened?'

'My baby . . . Maya, she was in her pushchair, asleep, I was sitting, dozing in the sun and then I opened my eyes and she was gone . . . I was only dozing, right next to her, outside the hall. I didn't hear anything. It was only a few minutes, five, ten at the most, not even that, just a few minutes and she was right next to me, I had my hand on the pushchair and . . . Oh God! Someone's taken her and I . . .' Anna didn't know if she was making sense; she couldn't think straight.

One of the men who had run off pushed through the crowd. 'I've tried up the main street towards the pub but there's no sign of anyone with a baby. Did anyone see anything? Has anyone any idea of who we're looking for?'

The other officer stepped in. 'Are you involved with this lady, sir?'

'No I'm just trying to help, I—'

'Thank you, sir. Could you step over here and tell me what happened? Exactly what you saw?' The man was led to one side with the officer.

'My baby . . .' Anna began. 'Maya, she's . . . she's nine weeks old, she's . . .' She started to cry again. 'She's so little, she won't survive without me, oh God . . .'

The officer got on the radio. 'Whisky Charlie four zero, there's been a child abduction, it's a baby, female, nine weeks old, from outside the village hall in Widbry.' He looked at Anna. 'What was the baby wearing, love? Can you give me a description of her clothes?'

'Erm, she was wearing a . . . erm . . . a white dress, with embroidered flowers on the front and, sort of . . . oh God . . .' Anna's sobs punctuated her words. 'Sort of shorts, with a frill round the leg and socks, white socks, and . . . Oh God . . .' She wiped her face on her hands. 'I don't know, yes, definitely socks . . . white socks, and she had her sun hat on, I think she . . .' Anna glanced at the empty pram and suddenly put her hands up to her face. 'No, it's there. Oh God, it's there in the pushchair, it must have come off, her sun hat . . .'

The officer spoke into his radio. 'The baby is called Maya . . . How do you spell that?'

'M-A-Y-A,' Anna murmured.

The officer spelt the name out on the radio. 'She was wearing white, a dress, and shorts and white socks. Yes, hang on.' He looked at Anna. 'Is there anything else you can tell us about her? Does she have any birth marks? Did she have a blanket, a shawl, teddy, anything at all?'

Anna shook her head.

'Hair colour?'

'Fair, but she hardly has any. Her eyes are blue, she weighs eleven pounds . . . I, erm, I don't know what that is in metric, I'm sorry, I . . .'

The officer put this information out over the radio. 'They're sending down five more officers to talk to people here, OK? I think what we need to do next is get in the car and just drive round, see if there's anyone we can see that might be suspicious. Is that OK?'

Anna nodded. Someone had passed her a tissue and she wiped her face on it. She had stopped weeping but a numbness had set in, an icy cold numbness. They waited, it was four, maybe five minutes and another squad car arrived with two more officers. The PC who had spoken to Anna first talked to the two who had just arrived, then started to clear a path through the crowd for her. She followed him, hardly conscious of what she was doing. She held her handbag and walked on, seeing and hearing nothing. At the squad car the door was opened for her and she climbed in. She sat in the back and stared out of the window, then a feeling of sudden panic engulfed her.

'I shouldn't leave!' she cried. 'What if she's brought back, I must be there, I can't go anywhere! I have to stay here . . .'

The officer in the front passenger seat turned. 'It's OK. There's an officer waiting here, and someone by the village hall, in case she's found immediately. There's no need to worry, if she's found she'll be taken care of, I promise.' He looked at her, smiled reassuringly and it registered in the back of Anna's mind that he had a kind face.

'We're going to drive round the immediate area now and I'd like you to look closely out of the window, OK? If you see anything, anything at all that looks odd, tell us and we'll stop. Don't be afraid to mention any tiny thing that you notice. All right?'

She nodded and the driver started the engine. As the squad car pulled off and Anna gazed blankly out of the window, Will came out of the chemist's and made his way up to find her.

Superintendent Nigel White saw DS Annie Taylor in the corridor. She was calm and efficient, on her way to set up a new incident room. He may have been wrong giving her a key role in such a major incident, but he had a gut feeling that if anyone was going to handle this properly and sensitively, it was DS Taylor.

'DS Taylor, can I have a word?'

She stopped. 'Sir?'

'I just wanted to run through a few check points with you. The squad car is on its way in with the baby's mother and I need to know that certain initiatives are in place. Have you got a minute?'

'Certainly.' DS Taylor followed him into his office.

'Firstly, has the area been cordoned off?'

'Yes sir. We've got five officers down there at present interviewing witnesses and we've sealed off the main street of the village at both ends.'

'Good. Check points?'

'Yes, on all major roads.'

'OK. Has the helicopter been put up?'

'Yes, Hotel nine hundred is on its way.'

'Dog handlers?

'Not yet. I didn't think they'd be much use in the middle of the village, to be frank sir.'

'It's worth a try, Annie. In a situation like this, anything is worth a try. They'll be able to pick up scents from the pushchair and you never know, we might get lucky.'

'Right, I'll get on to it.'

'Good. And you've called the Child Protection Team?'

'Yes, they were called by control and they're in contact with social services now, checking schedule one offenders in the area. We're also trying to find as much as we can about Mum and Dad. They're separated apparently.'

'Well done. Looks like you've covered virtually everything. What's the ETA of the mother?'

'Don't know, but it shouldn't be long, sir.' DS Taylor's bleeper went off. 'Might be them now.'

'Right, get on to it then. Can you ask the press liaisons officer to get a bulletin out to the local media? I'd like it on the local news at five, radio and TV if that's possible.'

'OK.' DS Taylor made a note of that on her file.

'Thank you, Annie.'

'Sir.' DS Taylor nodded and left the room.

Will ran his hands through his hair. 'I don't understand,' he said again. 'When did this happen? I just don't understand it . . .' He broke off and struggled for breath, digging in his pocket for his puffer.

'You all right, sir? You seem a bit breathless.'

'Yes, I get a bit of asthma, that's all, I . . .' He started to feel the familiar constriction in his lungs, the rising panic. He opened his mouth and used the Ventolin. It took about a minute to work, to dilute the airways, then he took several deep, hard breaths. 'I was only gone about fifteen minutes . . .' He shook his head. 'I can't believe it, I just can't believe . . .'

'I'm sorry sir,' the PC interrupted, 'but could you please tell me exactly what happened, in your own words. Where you've been and when you last saw the mother with her baby.'

'Yes of course, I . . . I went to the chemist, I had to get some things, shaving foam and razor blades, some deodorant . . . If only I'd stayed with her . . . I . . .' Will took a handkerchief out and wiped his forehead. He was sweating profusely.

'Try and keep calm, sir, and explain it all bit by bit, if you wouldn't mind. You went to the chemist, is that right?'

Will nodded.

'What time was this?'

'I don't know, ten, maybe fifteen minutes ago. I can't quite remember.'

'Where did you leave the victim?'

'The victim?' Will shook his head. He felt the tightness in his chest again. 'The victim? Oh God, Anna, I left her on that bench there, just over there . . .' Will pointed to the bench by the village hall and ran his hands through his hair again. The PC watched him. He was upset, distressed, the asthma looked genuine enough, but there was something else, he was edgy, anxious and it looked odd.

'Would you mind just walking up to the shop now and verifying that you were there? They might have a clearer idea of the time, sir.'

'What? To the chemist's? Why? Don't you believe me?' Will shook his head. 'You don't believe me do you? You think I had something to do with . . . Oh my God, I'm a suspect!'

'Calm down, sir, no one is suggesting that you are under suspicion. I would just like you to wander across to the shop and ask someone to identify you. Do you have your receipts?'

'Yes, they're in the bag, I . . .' Will opened the carrier bag and pulled out the items that he'd bought. 'They're here, I had them just a few moments ago, I asked the woman to put them in the bag, I . . . shit! They're not here, I must have dropped them . . .'

'Perhaps we could look for them on the way back to the shop, sir.' The officer motioned for Will to move off. 'Shall we?'

'Yes of course.' Will felt his hands begin to tremble. He shoved them deep into his pockets and knew that the action had been noted.

'I'm just going across to the chemist with this gentleman to verify his alibi,' the officer called out. Will picked up the word alibi and began to wheeze. He followed the police officer through the crowd, which parted silently for them, and along to the chemists. He kept his head down, supposedly looking for his lost receipts, but in reality avoiding the stares of passers-by. His chest was getting tighter, his breathing more laboured as they went into the shop. He went immediately to the till he had been served at and saw that the assistant who had served him wasn't there.

'Hello? Excuse me? There was a young girl on the till a few minutes ago. Fair-haired, slim, about twenty-five or so.'

'Yes sir, Hayley. She's gone home. She only does a couple of hours to help out, nine till eleven.'

'Has she left the shop?'

'Yes.' The woman now on the till glanced at the police

officer, then at Will with open curiosity. She knew Mr Turner and certainly knew of him, poor man. 'Would you like to speak to the pharmacist?'

Will nodded. They waited and for every minute that went by, his chest got a little more wheezy. The pharmacist came out from the back, a small man in shirt sleeves, who said, 'Hayley Walton was the girl who probably served you. She's gone home I'm afraid, but I've got her address, if you'd like.'

The police officer said, 'Yes please. Can we contact her at home this morning, do you know?'

The manager nodded. 'I think she collects her daughter from nursery just after eleven and goes home after that.'

'Right, thanks.'

The police officer turned to go, but Will looked at the older woman on the till and said, 'This is a small shop, you didn't see me in here, did you? I had to wait, there was someone who wanted a prescription but you didn't have it. The girl had to order it.'

The woman shook her head. She would have liked to help, but she couldn't. 'Sorry,' she said, 'I've just come off my coffee break. I take it out the back and I wouldn't have seen anything.'

'Right.' Will nodded and took out his puffer; his breathing was getting worse. He took two puffs, stood still for a minute or so and then took a couple of deep breaths.

'Are you all right, sir?' the PC asked. Will nodded. 'Right. Well if you wouldn't mind, I think it would be a good idea to carry on with your details down at the station.'

'The station?'

'Yes, we'll take you down in the squad car.'

Again Will nodded and they waited in silence for the manager to return with the sales assistant's address.

Sheila saw the police car the moment she opened the front door of Calcott Manor. She looked past the two officers at the white, orange and black vehicle and her heart stopped. She put her hand up to her mouth and took a step back.

'Mrs Turner?'

'No, I, I'm the housekeeper, I manage things, I'm not, he's not married.'

'Your name?'

'Sheila Wright. Mrs.' Sheila couldn't look at them, she kept looking at the police car and remembering – remembering the last time.

'Mrs Wright, is there someone called Debbie Pritchard staying here at the moment?'

'Yes, the nanny, she, erm, she's not here, she . . .' Sheila caught the briefest of looks that passed between the two officers. 'She went out for a walk, she left about an hour ago. Her boyfriend turned up and they went out. She was upset, she . . .' One of the officers went across to the squad car and got on the radio.

'Whisky Bravo three four, we're at the house and the young woman isn't here. Right, got that!' He came back to the steps of the house. 'Which direction did she go in, Mrs Wright?'

Sheila blinked rapidly, then put her hand up to her forehead. 'I don't know, I can't remember, I . . .' She swept her hand out towards the right of the drive. 'I think it was that way, I . . .' She stopped and turned, following the gaze of both officers. Debbie ran towards them. She was flushed and sweating and looked as if she had been running for some distance.

'What's happened? What's going on? It's nothing to do with Maya, is it?'

The officers exchanged a look. 'Maya?'

'Yes, the baby I look after. There's nothing wrong with her is there, I mean, she's not . . .' Debbie broke off, suddenly aware of the look the policeman was giving her. She bit her lip and stared down at the ground.

One of the officers stepped forward. 'Miss Pritchard?'

'Yes?'

'Would it be possible for you to come down to the station with us?'

'Yes, why, I . . .' She glanced behind her as Darren jogged up to them. He too was red in the face. 'Deb? What's going on?'

'I don't know, I . . .'

'A baby has been abducted, sir, and we'd like Miss Pritchard to come down to the station. She might be able to help us, give us some information about the baby that Mrs Slater isn't able to do.'

'Maya? It's Maya? Is it Maya that's gone missing?' Debbie put her hands up to her face. 'Oh my God! It can't be, it . . .' She broke off as her voice faltered. Darren stepped forward.

'Is the station really necessary? Can't you question her here?'

'And you are, sir?'

'Private Darren Woodman. I'm Debbie's fiancé.'

Both officers looked at him. 'Perhaps you'd like to accompany her, Mr Woodman, give her some moral support?'

Darren glanced at Debbie, but she didn't return his

look. She hung her head and avoided his eye. 'Yes,' he said, 'I would.' One of the officers moved towards the car and both Debbie and Darren followed.

'Mrs Wright? We'll send an officer down to ask you some questions about Mr Turner if you don't mind. They'll be here in about twenty minutes. Would it be possible for you to stay here and wait for them?'

Sheila nodded.

'Good.' The second officer moved towards the car. 'Is there anyone else you can think of who might be able to help us with our inquiries?'

She shook her head. 'I don't think so, I can't think of anyone.'

'Well if you can, perhaps you could give us a ring at the station.' He opened the car door and climbed in. The car was silent and rife with tension. 'Right,' he said, 'let's go.'

Sheila watched the squad car all the way up the drive until it disappeared through the gates and onto the main road. Then she went inside and burst into tears.

Jennifer saw the police car before it saw her. She stepped out onto the road and waved it down. She was lost, she was tired and in constant pain.

'Can I help you, madam?' One of the officers opened the window.

'I hope so. I'm lost and I . . .' She stopped suddenly and clutched her stomach, doubling over with a sharp burst of pain. 'Oh sorry, I . . .' She took several deep breaths and closed her eyes. 'It's the pain, it takes me by surprise and I . . .' She stopped again. 'Oh, I . . .'

The officer got out of the car and took her arm. 'Can we give you a lift somewhere?'

'I want to see the baby. I'm lost and I've come to see the baby. I must see her. I've got her things in here . . .' She held up a carrier bag, then dropped it on the floor as more pain gripped her. 'Little Maya it is, I've come all the way from London for her, all the way just for her . . .'

The officer glanced across at his colleague in the car. He picked up the radio. 'Whisky Charlie five six, we've got a woman here in South Street, Chichester, who is talking about a baby called Maya. Wasn't there something on the radio half an hour ago about that? There was . . . is it? Right! No, she's not well, a bit confused . . . Yup OK, got that . . . Bringing her in now.' He climbed out of the car.

'Can I give you a hand, madam? I wonder if you'd like to come down to the station and sort things out there? Have a nice cup of tea and a bit of a rest.'

Jennifer glanced up and snapped, 'I may be ill, young man, but I am not an idiot! Please don't talk to me like I've lost my marbles.' But she let herself be led to the car; frankly she was too tired to be bothered to argue.

Superintendent White stood at the front of the incident room facing fifteen CID officers. It was 3.00 pm, baby Maya had been missing for four hours and they had three suspects in the station. It wasn't enough.

Behind him pinned up was a map of the area, with Calcott Manor marked, along with Widbry village, and Anna's handbag photo of the baby. He had written the names of the three people currently held in the station on the white board, and on the table beside him was an outfit from Mothercare, the same as Maya had been wearing.

'Right,' he said, settling everyone down. 'Let's go through what we know so far. DS Taylor?'

Annie Taylor stood up. 'OK. First, there's nothing, as expected, on CIS for Will Turner, Anna Jacob or Debbie Pritchard, no criminal records at all. The connections are that Will Turner and Anna Jacob – or Mrs Anna Slater – are having a relationship and that Debbie Pritchard has met Will Turner through Anna Jacob, who is her employer.'

'The father? Have we checked him?' White asked.

'We're on to it and at first glance it looks like we might be up for another suspect. We've called his office, a big advertising agency in London, and he's not been in work for the past two days, although he's on his way in now. Anna Jacob also said he was at Will Turner's house, Calcott Manor, yesterday causing trouble. We've sent DC Franks and . . .' she glanced down at her notes, 'DC Perkins up to London to check the home address and the office. I've asked them to get anything they can from colleagues at work. The couple are separated, and not very cordially.'

'Could there be a connection between the father and the nanny? Could they be working together?'

'Unlikely.'

'Right, let's find him. That's the number one priority. Have we done a vehicle check?'

'Yes.'

'And we've got it out over the central computer?'

'Yes sir.'

'Good. What about media? Have we had any response from the local news bulletin yet? It went out at – what – one?'

'Yes. We've got a helpline set up and we've had a steady

stream of calls coming in over the last hour. Nothing to go on yet though.' Annie Taylor made a note on her file and sat down.

Superintendent White glanced behind him at the board. 'OK, Will Turner,' he said. 'What have we got on him?'

DS Granger stood up. 'Right, to start, the relationship between him and the baby's mother is pretty new. Less than a month. They've known each other through work for several months – she's a lawyer and she's been working on a deal for his company – but they only struck up a relationship when they met at his villa in Portugal.'

'Did they arrange to go away together?' White asked.

'No. She borrowed the place and he turned up apparently. It was a coincidence.'

White made a note of this. 'Does it sound credible?'

Granger looked across at DS Taylor. She said, 'We think so, sir. I can't see any reason to doubt that. Why?'

'He might have targeted her, a vulnerable, newly separated single mother, or they might have planned in secret to go away together.'

DS Granger said, 'What if they had?'

'I don't know. It could throw up all sorts of different thoughts. As far as Jacob is concerned, it could be a case of new relationship, rich boyfriend, baby in the way? It might even have been attention seeking. Does the father know about the new boyfriend?'

'I'd have thought so. He certainly knows his wife has been staying with Turner in Sussex so he's probably put two and two together.'

'Jealousy?' White made several more notes on his pad. 'Let's keep all this in mind, shall we? Sorry DS Granger carry on with Turner if you would.'

'Well, Turner was with Jacob this morning, they were

out walking with the baby, then in the village he disappeared off to buy some things in the chemist's. While he was gone, the baby disappears.'

White looked up.

'We're checking with the sales assistant now that he was actually there, but there might still have been time to take the baby and visit the chemist's.'

'Would there? Where would he have put the baby? Were there any signs that he might have been running?'

DS Granger looked at his notes. 'He was apparently sweating and breathless, but he does suffer from asthma and kept using an inhaler.'

'OK, check it with his GP. Did he have an accomplice? Could there be anyone else in the frame with him?'

DS Taylor said, 'Anna Jacob?'

White nodded. 'Maybe? Find out as much as you can about their relationship and both histories. Also get every bit of information you can about the separation from Slater and anyone else who knows the couple. Is there anything else on Turner? Have we got any friends or relatives we can talk to?'

'Says his parents died sixteen years ago and has no other relatives. He's given us the name of a family friend and his lawyer . . .' DS Granger glanced at his notes, 'one Andrew McKie. He's in London and we've got someone on their way up there now to talk to him. He's expecting us.'

'Anything more anyone can add?'

DS Granger said, 'The PC that brought him in said he was very edgy, didn't seem right at all and I'm inclined to agree. He keeps asking when he can go home.'

'Right. When we let him go then we keep him under surveillance. That is a key priority, OK?' Granger nodded.

'That leaves the nanny. Anything on her?'

DS Taylor stood up again. 'Two things. First, when she saw the two officers at Calcott, she immediately asked about the baby. Why? How could she possibly have known something might have happened to her? Second, she was missing from the house, along with the boyfriend, for an hour or so around the time that Maya disappeared and can't – or won't – give any clear indication of where she went. Finally Turner mentioned she had been acting very strangely recently and the mother says she's quite possessive of the baby.'

'No witnesses? No one saw anyone like her in the village?'

'No, nothing yet.'

'Then let's do a house-to-house inquiry. What else?'

Annie Taylor sighed. 'Instinct tells me Debbie's hiding something. I can't put my finger on why, but it's just a feeling. There's something she's not telling us.'

'The boyfriend?'

'He's keeping stum. Just backs her story and keeps saying that he wants to talk to her.'

'Could it be both of them?'

'Could be. He's in the army, based down in Winchester and he's on special leave; I confirmed that with his CO. It could have been planned by both of them.'

'Right.' White stood up. 'We have to think laterally here. We have three people in the station and are pursuing a search for Slater, the baby's father. We haven't been able to rule anyone out of the inquiry as yet and we won't be able to do so until we have found out every little bit of information there is to find on each person on this list here.' White pointed to the board and underlined each name up there. 'But is there anyone else? Is there anything or anyone we might possibly have overlooked? If there is, then get out there and find them. Don't rule anyone out until you are absolutely sure you can do it safely. Plus, there are other things to think about. One, is someone hiding that baby? Two, is someone working with one of the suspects, someone who could have been passed the baby once it had been snatched? As well as the house-to-house inquiry, I want a door-to-door search within a ten-mile radius of the incident.' There was a murmur of assent in the room. 'That's if the baby is still alive.' The murmur died away to complete silence. 'I want dogs in the area and I want every rubbish bin, every hedge, every inch of that area searched for a body. Also I want someone on to the Divisional Intelligence Unit right away and I want them to search the CIS for any histories of baby snatching, any weirdos in the area, anything at all with the same MO, all right? Finally, let's find the husband. I want him here ASAP! If anything comes up from the media coverage, then let me know immediately.' He looked at his watch. 'We'll reconvene in an hour. So come on everyone, let's go! I want to find that baby and I want to find her alive.'

Darren sat with Debbie, still in the side room, and held her hand. He looked at her, but she hung her head. 'I just phoned my mum, Deb, and when I told her what had happened she burst into tears. She says it's her fault, Deb.' He stopped and tilted her chin up, holding it between his forefinger and thumb. He squeezed and it hurt. 'She said that if I ask you you'll tell me. She said to ask you about your references. What's she on about, Deb? What's going on?'

    Debbie started to cry. Tears rolled down her face and

splashed onto her skirt, but she said nothing. 'Where did you go to this morning when I came after you, Deb? I had to run like hell to catch up with you. What were you doing?' He squeezed a little harder. She shook her head. 'Look, I've got a hell of a lot at stake here, Deb. I'm in the army, I can't afford to be involved in a crime. Tell me what's happened, Deb.'

Again Debbie shook her head, but still she said nothing. Darren sat there for a minute or so, then he dropped his hand and stood up. 'Fuck it!' he suddenly shouted. 'Fuck it all!' And he slammed out of the room.

Max paced his office. He walked up and down five or six times, then suddenly he stopped. 'What's he doing?' he said to the DC.

'He's phoning the boss.'

'What d'you mean he's phoning the boss? I told you, didn't I? I told you it was Turner, for Christ's sake! What more proof do you want? He's got a dodgy past, a sister locked away for infantile murder and God knows what else. It's him, for Christ's sake!' Max banged his hand down on the desk. 'Jesus! I told her he was dangerous! I should have stayed on, I shouldn't have left, I—'

The DC stood up. 'Why don't you sit down, sir? There is no point in upsetting yourself.'

'Sit down? Sit down? Are you for real? My baby's been abducted, Maya has gone, my tiny, vulnerable . . .' Max stopped and put his hands up to his face. He was silent for some time, trying to stop his tears, to rein in his anger. He was full of fear and rage, a terrible combination. The police officer stared out of the window and wished himself a million miles from the scene; he had a five-month-old son at home. Finally Max looked up and said, 'I'm sorry it's just that I keep thinking how stupid I was to even have let her go there. I should have stopped her, I should have reported him, the moment I found out about his sister. I should have known that he'd do something like—'

'Mr Slater, I must remind you that no one has as yet been charged.'

'What?' He shook his head and ran his hands through his hair. 'You mean he hasn't been locked up?' Max's anger rose again, quick and fierce. The fear churned in the pit of his stomach. 'I'll make a complaint about this, I swear! I'll write to the bloody chief constable . . .'

He swung round as the door was opened.

'So?'

The other DC stepped into the room. 'Mr Slater, we'd like you to come to the station with us now.'

'Me?' Max's jaw dropped open. His frustration was so overwhelming it threatened to swamp him. 'What the hell do you want me for? I should be with Anna, she needs me!'

'We'd like you to help us with our inquiries.'

'To help you with . . .' Suddenly it hit Max. 'Are you saying that I'm a suspect?'

'I'm not saying that, sir, I'm just saying that we'd like you to come down to Sussex with us and help us with our inquiries. And we'd like to leave now.'

At that moment the door opened and Max's boss put his head round. 'Everything all right, Max?'

'No it bloody well isn't!' Max snatched up his jacket and pulled it on. He was near to tears again and had to take a few moments staring out of the window to fight them back. He swallowed, but the hard, dry lump in his throat remained. 'Sorry,' he said, turning back, 'but I can't make drinks tonight, I have to go out.'

And flanked by the two detectives, he walked out of the office.

Superintendent White walked into the incident room last; most of the CID officers were already there.

'OK,' he said. 'No time to waste. There's been three major developments. Firstly, we've had a call from a Nora Woodman, Darren's mum, who claims that Debbie's been peddling false references. She's given us the number of one of Debbie's former employers, a Mrs Watts, and I want someone up to London to speak to her immediately. We need to question Debbie again. I want to know exactly what she was doing this morning and I want to know exactly where she went. She's keeping silent at the moment and we've got to crack that. Secondly, apparently Will Turner is the brother of one Esme Turner. Last year Esme was convicted of manslaughter for the murder of her own baby. She's supposed to be in a secure wing at Broxwood Hospital, but let's find out if she is. Someone ring the hospital and check. She might even have been released into the community, but the only way we'll know that is to ring Broxwood. I want every detail of that case you can find and I want someone to contact Divisional Intelligence again and get them onto it. I want a profile of her crime.

'Will Turner. There might be a collaboration between him and the sister. DS Taylor, I want him questioned and let's put him under pressure. I want to know why he didn't mention the sister and I want to know every little detail of his relationship with her. And finally we've just had a statement from Mrs Biggs, the pub landlady, saying that Max Slater has been in the area staying at her B & B overnight. He arrived with no bags, used the same clothes, and went for a walk this morning, leaving in a hurry immediately after. He's on his way in, but I want everything you can find on him. I want someone at his office, I want his house searched and we need to question the wife again on the details of the separation. Find out his exact route on this walk and I want a search of the whole area he covered.' He glanced behind him at the photo of the baby, then faced front. 'OK!' he barked. 'Time's running out. We must find baby Maya. Let's go!'

Chapter Twenty-four

Anna came down the steps of the police station as the squad car with Max in it drove up. She stopped. Immediately behind her was Will; they had been released together.

Max climbed out of the car and looked up at Anna. He moved towards her and she stood motionless to take his embrace. He put his arms around her and pulled her stiff, unyielding body in to his. 'Anna, I . . .' He touched her hair and thought that she was beyond him, that he was never going to reach her again. 'Anna, I'm sorry,' he murmured.

Anna laid her face against his chest and closed her eyes. The smell of him, the shape and feel of him, was so familiar and thus so comforting that she let him stroke her hair and soothe, if only for the briefest second, the fear that raged inside her.

'Please God, let us get her back,' Max whispered. Anna said nothing. He felt the touch of a hand on his arm and acknowledged that the moment was over. Gently he released her and stepped back. 'They will find her, Anna, I know they will.' Anna looked at him, she looked at his face and willed herself to believe him. A short while ago she would have believed him, she would have trusted him and taken solace in his words. Now they were empty promises and they echoed inside her head.

'Mr Slater?'

Max glanced behind him at the police officer and nodded. He moved past Anna and on up the steps. At the top he saw Will Turner. He stared, looked the man straight in the face and dared him to look back. But Will couldn't. He averted his gaze and focused on the ground. Max went inside with the knowledge that he had just encountered a coward, but as he glanced back, he saw Anna and Will move off together and that knowledge only filled him with despair.

It was nearly eight when Will opened the door of Calcott Manor. He went straight to the alarm pad, keyed in the new number and the high-pitched bleeping stopped. There was silence – silence and twilight. Nothing could be easily seen, the house was a mass of confused shadows.

Anna shivered.

He switched on some lamps in the hall and opened up the sitting room. 'Would you like tea?'

There were three police officers with him and Anna – two family liaison officers and one CID. At the end of the drive was a surveillance car with CID back-up. One of the officers, a WPC called Shona, said, 'Yes, thanks. Shall I help you make it?'

'No, I . . .' Will stopped. They didn't want him to be alone. 'Yes, OK, thanks.' He opened the door. 'The kitchen's this way. Anna? D'you want to come and warm up by the Aga? You look cold.'

Anna shrugged, but followed them anyway.

'Make yourselves at home in the sitting room,' Will said over his shoulder to the other two officers, 'or in the den.

There's a TV in there if you want to watch something.' He led the way through to the kitchen.

He filled the kettle and put it on the Aga, then he began preparing the tea. He rarely made drinks, he wasn't a domesticated man and he couldn't find things very easily. It irritated him and when finally he opened the fridge and there wasn't any milk, he said, 'Shit! No bloody milk!' and slammed the fridge door shut. He turned. 'Look, WPC—'

'Shona, call me Shona.'

'Look Shona, I'm sorry, but could I have a word with Anna alone? I really think we need a bit of space to take in what's happened.'

'OK, sure.' Shona went to the door. 'I'll be outside if you need me,' she said to Anna.

When the door was closed, Will said, 'Anna? Anna, are you OK?'

She was standing on the opposite side of the room from him, almost as far apart from him as possible, and she held her arms defensively across her body. 'What do you think?' she answered.

Will hung his head.

'Why didn't you tell me about Esme before?' she went on. 'Why did you wait until I was here, until, until I had nowhere else to go and . . .' She broke off. 'Damn you, Will!'

'You think Esme is involved? You think it's her?'

Anna looked away.

'But as far as we know she's in hospital, Anna. How could it be her?'

She turned back. 'I don't know! But what if she's been released, or she's got out somehow?'

Will threw his hands up. 'Anna, she can't get out! She's in a secure hospital, people don't just "get out".'

'And you can promise me that, can you? You can say, for certain, that she can't get out and that she hasn't been released?'

She stared at him but he didn't look back at her; he looked away. There was a silence, then he said, 'I don't know.'

'And nor do I. Jesus, Will, it could be anyone!' She was near to tears again. 'It could even be you.'

Will stared at her. 'Me?'

'Yes! Where were you? You said you were in the chemist's but how do I know that? You were gone for a hell of a long time, weren't you? How do I know it wasn't you?'

'You don't.'

Anna looked at him.

'But the police have released me, Anna, and if they believe me then so should you. They've still got Max there for questioning, it could just as easily have been him.'

'Max? Don't be ridiculous!' she snapped.

'As you said, it could be anyone, and he's still there, isn't he? He was here yesterday, making accusations, angry, upset, it could easily have been—'

'Stop it!' Anna cried. 'Just shut up!'

Will turned away. He was silent for a while, then he said, 'Look Anna, I'm sorry that I didn't tell you about Esme's background earlier, but you know why I didn't, you know that I was frightened of losing you.' He went to move across to her, but she took a step back and he realised it was too soon. 'I'm sorry too that I didn't tell the police about her right away, but I was upset and confused, I wasn't thinking straight. Anyway, I don't see how she can be involved. She's locked up.'

Anna didn't really believe him, but then she hadn't

remembered Esme either, until a couple of hours ago. It was the shock, the distress, it had rendered her almost useless, and ever since she had tortured herself with the guilt of not having mentioned something so vital. She twisted her hands together and Will said, 'I can't bear to see you like this, so anguished and distressed.'

She didn't respond.

'I can't bear it, Anna. I've come to think of you and Maya as my own and if anything happened to her, if something—'

'Stop it!' Anna cried again. 'I can't think like that, Will, I can't even consider for one second that anything might have happened to Maya . . .' She began to cry and Will stood motionless across the room watching her.

'We need milk,' he said quietly, and went out.

'We need milk,' he said again to Shona in the passage-way. 'I'll go and get some.'

'DC Halden will drive you,' she answered quickly.

Will shrugged. 'Whatever.' He went to the back door and found his trainers, sitting on the floor to pull them on. Shona watched him but thought nothing of it. He left his loafers on the shoe stand and took off his jacket, changing it for his fleece. 'I'll go and get him,' he said. 'I think Anna could maybe do with some brandy, there's some in the cabinet in the sitting room if you need it.'

'Right. Will you be long?'

'No. The petrol station in Widbry will be open. We'll get some milk there.'

'Fine.'

Will walked along the passage and out into the hall. The two officers were still there and DC Halden leant against the Georgian walnut table. He stood straight when Will saw him. 'Shona said you'd want to accompany me to get some milk. DC Halden, is it?'

'Yes. Right, I'll drive if you like.'

'Thanks.'

DC Halden jingled his car keys in his pocket and the noise seemed louder than it actually was in the strained silence of the house. He pulled open the front door and said, 'Ready?'

'Yup.' Will walked out.

Max sat in the interview room, his solicitor next to him, and said again, 'I didn't leave because I was worried about my wife and baby staying with a man they hardly knew and who had previously been involved in something so terrible.'

'Being the death of his sister Esme Turner's baby,' DS Taylor said.

'Yes, that's right.' Max ran his hands through his hair. 'I admit that I wasn't thinking terribly clearly, my marriage is on the rocks, I love my wife and all I want is for her to return home with me. I was confused, I went for a walk to try and clear my thoughts.'

'Why did you leave for London in such a hurry, Max? What was so pressing that you had to rush off, at approximately the same time that baby Maya disappeared?'

Max sat straight and his face was unreadable. 'I was on personal business for my mother. You will have to ask her for the details,' he said. 'I am not prepared to discuss it.'

'But we have asked your mother, Max. She was in Chichester this afternoon, she was picked up by one of our squad cars and she knows nothing of the personal business that you say you were seeing to. She denies all knowledge of involving you in her personal life.' DS Taylor stood up and stretched her legs. She walked across the room and turned. 'Max,' she said, 'you are in serious trouble and it really isn't time to start on the ethics thing. I must have the truth, Max, your baby's life is at stake. If you had nothing to do with her abduction, then please, tell us why you left Widbry in such a hurry. It might make a difference between the life and death of your baby.'

Max's face was still unreadable, but the muscle in his jaw twitched. 'May I speak to my mother, in private?' he said.

DS Taylor hesitated for a moment, but only a moment. 'If it brings us closer to finding Maya alive,' she said, 'yes, you may.'

DC Halden drove into the small petrol station in Widbry and switched off his engine. He couldn't park by the shop as the pump was directly in front of it, so he had to park to the side and be content with letting Turner out of sight for the few minutes it took to get the milk. He told himself he was being paranoid – the place backed on to open country and it was pitch dark. If he was going to make a run for it, where the hell was he going to run to except past the car?

He turned the radio on and watched Will get out of the car and go into the shop, then his mobile rang and he dug in his pocket for it, pressing the answer button and finding that the line had disconnected. He fiddled with the phone for a moment, trying the recall button, and then glanced up to check that Will was in the shop. He couldn't see, the man had brought the flower stand in ready for closing and it blocked his view. He climbed slowly out of the car and approached the shop. There was a figure in there, but some of the lights had gone off and DC Halden couldn't make out who it was. He felt the rise of panic and, darting into the shop, found a young mechanic in there and the man who served behind the counter.

'There was a bloke in here!' he said. 'Tall, athletic? Where's he gone?'

'Don't know. He was here a minute ago. He went out the front I think.'

DC Halden ran out of the shop and down past his car to the road. How the hell had Turner got past him? He ran up the road, then turned back and ran to his car. He took out his radio. 'Whisky Charlie five six, this is DC Halden. The suspect has made a run for it. I'm at the Esso petrol station in Widbry. He must have gone up onto the main road. That's the B248, repeat, the B248. I'm going to try and find him now but we need to get a block out on all connecting roads.' He switched the radio off. 'Fuck!' he said, then he got in his car and drove off.

An emergency briefing was called in the incident room. Superintendent White saw DS Taylor in the corridor.

'Annie, you've got to take this I'm afraid, I have to go down to the *South Today* studios to put out a news bulletin for national news.'

'Right, what's the policy decision?'

'We have to trace and find Will Turner as soon as possible. I want Hotel nine hundred up in the air and I want to use infra-red cameras to track the areas of land around Widbry. If he's gone across country, unless he's a bloody experienced runner, we'll find him out there. What about the nanny?'

'We've checked her references, nothing sinister there,

just lying about experience, but there's still no explanation about where she was and what she was doing this morning.'

'OK, keep on her. You also need to issue an all-points bulletin to stop Turner leaving the country. Have we done with Jacob?'

'I think so. I can't see her involvement at all. She's distraught, confused, frightened, all very natural reactions. And there's nothing that gives any indication that—'

White held up his hand. 'OK Annie, if that's what you think, you don't have to convince me.'

DS Taylor smiled grimly.

'Have you got someone at Victoria meeting the next train in from Chichester?' White glanced over his shoulder; his driver was waiting.

'Yes, organised.'

'Good! Look Annie, I've got to go. I'll be back within the hour. Call me if there's any other developments will you?'

'Yes sir.'

DS Taylor nodded, White walked away and, letting out a tense sigh, she went into the incident room.

Andrew McKie sat in his study with the two CID officers from Chichester and waited until Marjorie had poured the coffee before resuming his conversation. She left the milk and sugar on the tray, handed round the cups and silently left the room. She was upset. Ever since she had seen the bulletin on the six o'clock news she had been wretched. She blamed Andrew. She blamed Andrew for ever having introduced poor Anna Jacob to Will Turner and all his turbulent past.

When she had gone, Andrew McKie stood up and went

to the top drawer of his filing cabinet. 'I've got some documentation here regarding Esme Turner that you'll need.' He took out a file and opened it, handing several letters across to the DC. 'The top one is to the legal firm holding Esme's funds in trust,' he said. 'Esme was released from Broxwood secure hospital into the community two months ago. I have been sending money to the postal address in there for her living expenses.' He looked at the DC. 'You might want to use my phone,' he said, 'because I'm afraid that I think she may be involved.'

'Does Mr Turner know about her release?'

Andrew McKie shook his head. 'I wouldn't have thought so. She asked that no one in the family be contacted, but he might have had a letter from the trustees. I'm sure he would have told you if he had.'

'Would he, sir?' the officer asked.

Andrew McKie sighed. Absolute honesty was something he always endeavoured to give. 'Actually, I don't know,' he replied. It was, after all, the truth.

Chapter Twenty-five

Esme had been walking, on and off, for nearly five hours. She had been watching him and she knew, she knew it all. But she was exhausted, her feet ached and she needed a drink. It wouldn't be long now, just a few more miles and she'd be there; she'd be safe. She was in the woods, it was dark, but she had her torch and she liked the darkness, this kind of darkness, alone with the animals and the stars. She trudged on with her rucksack on her back, lighting the way with one small beam, and she felt content. She wasn't frightened any more, all the fear had gone. She had seen the baby last night, then seen what had happened today and it had all made sense. At last, it made sense. All that time not knowing, not for sure, always doubting herself, always afraid. Not any more. Now it made sense, and finally, she knew what she had to do.

DS Taylor turned halfway down the corridor as one of the DCs called out to her.

'We've got Turner on a mobile phone. Says he wants to talk to you.'

She turned and ran back to the incident room. 'Are we taping this?' she called.

'Yes.'

She picked up the phone and pressed the connect button. 'Hello, DS Taylor.'

'Hello, DS Taylor? I'm in the woods around Calcott and I've seen the remains of a fire. It's probably a day old, but there's been someone here and I'm frightened that it could be my sister Esme. I've no idea how, she's supposed to be in Broxwood, but she knows the land round here and she'd come here if she was in trouble. I'm sorry I ran out, but I had to come and check, I had a gut feeling it could be her and I—' The network coverage was bad and the line was breaking up. 'Hello? Hello? Can you hear me?'

DS Taylor looked across at the officer on the other line and he shook his head; he hadn't a clue what was going on either. This wasn't at all what she had expected. Was it for real?

'Yes I can just hear you, Will,' she said. 'Look, if you think it's Esme then I need you to tell me as much as you can about her now. Try and think if there's anything that we should know that might help us find the baby . . . Will . . . Will?' She gripped the phone, putting her hand over the mouthpiece. 'The sodding line's breaking up. Christ, that's all we need.'

His voice came back. 'I can't think off hand, I mean, there isn't anything, except that, well, except that she knows the house and I think she's got a key. I think she might have been there last night and she's not well, she's unbalanced, she . . .'

'What is Esme like, Will? Where might she go if she was under pressure, what might she do?'

There was a silence. The line crackled with distortion and DS Taylor held her breath. 'She'd be here, in the woods, or the grounds,' Will said. 'That's why I came to find her, she'd be here and she could do . . . well . . . anything . . .' The line broke up, his voice faded.

'I'm losing you, Will . . . Hello? Will? . . .' DS Taylor held the phone. 'Shit! He's gone.' She put it down and the whole room stood silent, waiting for it to ring again. It didn't. DS Taylor looked across at the officer on the other line. 'Is he right, d'you think?'

'God knows, although it sounds pretty genuine to me.'

'Has anyone sighted this sister? Any reports at all in the area?' Several officers shook their heads. DS Taylor rubbed her hands over her face. 'Well, Turner thinks it's his sister, that she's in the area and capable of anything. Let's investigate. We need to get . . .' She stopped. In another part of the room, a separate line rang. DS Taylor turned, she looked at the officer taking the call, at his face and a feeling of complete failure swamped her.

He made a note, then hung up. 'There's been a call to WACR, from two boys fishing on the Arun, near Burpham,' the DC said. DS Taylor stood up and the hairs on the back of her neck prickled. 'They found something in the water,' he continued, 'wrapped in black plastic.' His nerve failed him and he glanced for a moment down at the floor. There was a hush and DS Taylor held her breath. She willed him not to say the next sentence, knowing there was no way to stop him. He looked at her.

'It's a body,' he said.

It was dark by the time DS Taylor's squad car reached the stretch of the Arun where the boys had been fishing. She blinked in the glare of the spotlights set up by forensic and climbed out of the car. The grass underfoot was damp and soft and her heels sank into it. She looked across the white tape and the mass of people and saw the black plastic sheeting covering the body. Her first reaction was relief, then guilt for feeling that – whoever it was was going to be missed by someone.

'Ah, DS Taylor.' The pathologist was one she had come across before, blunt, immune to the finer emotions of death. 'Not your missing baby, as you can see.'

'No.'

'She's a white female, in her late thirties I'd have said, who died from a massive blow to the side of the head with a blunt instrument, probably a club, possibly a baseball bat, that sort of thing. She's been dead about two months, but not in the water for more than two weeks. Any ideas?'

DS Taylor shook her head. 'Not off hand,' she replied. 'I'll get a list of missing persons and . . .' She turned as another car drew up, and squinted in its headlights. The superintendent climbed out and came across.

'Not the Jacob baby then?'

'No.'

'Right, where were you?'

DS Taylor turned her back on the body and faced White. That wasn't her case. 'We'd had contact from Turner who thinks his sister is involved and confirmation from the family solicitors that she has been released. She could be on the loose in the Widbry area. He's out looking for her now.'

'Have you checked with the hospital? They'd have a record of where she's living, surely.'

'We're waiting for one of the senior members of the medical staff to get back to us. They apparently need his approval before they can release confidential information.'

White hesitated, but only for a moment. 'Let's get the helicopter with its infra-red cameras up over the area now. Also I want fifty men with dogs in the Calcott grounds. D'you think it could be the sister, Annie?'

DS Taylor shrugged. It was the strongest possibility, but it didn't feel right. She was someone who trusted her instincts and they told her now that this whole thing was too neat. It was too sudden, a solution, out of the blue, introduced by Turner. 'I don't know,' she answered honestly. 'It's a good hunch.' She glanced behind her at the body, hoping to God it was the only one she was going to see tonight. 'And at the moment,' she said, 'it's the only thing we've got.'

Anna sat in the kitchen at Calcott, cold and numb. Opposite her sat the WPC, idly flicking through a magazine, her eyes, every now and then, lifted towards Anna to check that she was all right, or as right as she could be in the circumstances.

The WPC had made coffee but it was untouched, and she longed to smoke to relieve the tension, but she was on duty. Under the table she jigged her knee up and down, up and down while Anna was completely still. The phone rang. It was Anna's mobile. For a moment both women just looked at it on the table, then Anna picked it up and took the call. Her face remained unchanged.

'Anna, it's Max.'

Max stood on the steps of the police station, illuminated by the hundreds of lights on in the building, his phone clutched to his ear. 'Anna, can you hear me?' He was only allowed one call and this was it.

'Yes.'

The WPC looked at her and she mouthed the word Max across the table.

'Anna, are you OK?'

'Yes.'

'I heard that Turner's disappeared. Has he contacted you?'

'No, he hasn't, Max.' She felt the sudden bite of anger. 'Why? What's it to you?'

Max closed his eyes. Was there no way of getting through to her? 'I'm sorry, that's all. If he's involved, if he's . . .' Max broke off. He took a breath and said, 'Look, I'm just sorry Anna, sorry for you, for both of us. I don't want you to suffer any more than you have. I want them to find Maya.'

Anna held the phone close. She pressed it so hard against her ear that it hurt, but it made her feel closer to Max. She could hear his breathing.

'Anna, I love you,' Max said. Anna closed her eyes. She wanted to answer him, to say something back, but what he had done paralysed her.

Finally, she opened them again and said, 'I know.' But Max didn't hear; he had rung off.

'This is useless!' The helicopter pilot glanced sidelong at his co-pilot. 'How long have we been up here now?'

'Twenty minutes, but we're low on fuel.'

'Shit! It's like looking for a needle in a bloody haystack.' He glanced at the fuel gauge. 'We'll give it another five minutes, bear right, then we've got to get back and refuel.'

'Roger.'

Hotel 900 tipped and changed direction.

'Let's go in a bit lower, it might help.'

'You want to risk it?'

'Might as well.'

It dropped in height and the infra-red cameras scanned the ground below.

Esme heard it, only seconds before she looked up and saw its flashing lights, like alien stars in the sky. She had run out from under cover of some bushes and seeing it up there, she froze. There was no reason to be afraid, she had told herself that she would never be scared again, but the helicopter terrified her. She stood still and put her hands over her ears. Her heart hammered in her chest, but she couldn't run. She stood, crippled with fear.

'I've got something, down there! Scan in a bit closer . . . That's it . . . Yes! That's definitely a figure, down there to the right. See it?'

'Yup, got it! Is it the girl?'

'No idea, I can't tell. Presume it is and get onto HQ to report our coordinates. I'll track her.'

'Roger.' The co-pilot radioed into WACR.

'She's moving off again, she's running, keep steady . . .'

Suddenly Esme looked up again and saw it even closer. The terrific noise galvanised her into action and she ran, as fast as she could. She had cover, she had somewhere to hide if only she could get to it. She heard the roar of the engines overhead and it sounded like gunfire. She was petrified. If only she could get to the tree. She ran a bit faster, but there was something behind her, someone behind her. She turned her head, caught sight of who it was and ran as hard as she could. She ran on and on and the noise and her pursuer ran after her.

'We're bloody low on fuel, we're going to have to . . . Shit, she's disappeared! Where the hell?'

'There must be cover down there, some sort of dug-out.

Get on the WACR and give the coordinates. She's gone, completely vanished; that's if it was her.'

'Roger.'

'Wait, there she is! No, hang on, I think it's someone else! Or is it her?' The pilot let the helicopter hover for a few minutes to get a closer look. 'Can you see any more clearly than me?'

'I don't know, I can't tell. Looks different in build. Bigger, taller. Look, shit, we've got to get going. We can't risk staying any longer. Radio and tell them that we think there might be two people down there and one of them has disappeared. OK?'

'Roger.' The co-pilot got on the radio while the helicopter turned, gained height and made its way back to base.

DS Taylor was in the area control room when the call from Hotel 900 came in. She heard it, noted down the grid reference and then swore. 'Bloody typical, just when we thought we'd got something. Shit! Doesn't anything ever go right?' She picked up her notes and slammed out of the room.

'Sir?'

She caught Superintendent White on his way out of his office. 'Sir, Hotel nine hundred have picked up someone who could be Esme Turner but they've just disappeared. They say they think there's someone else down there as well, it could be Will Turner, but to be honest, it could be anyone.'

'Tell them to keep with it.'

'Can't. They've had to go back to refuel.'

'Bugger!' White thought for a moment. 'Have you got the grid reference?'

'Yes.'

'Right, lets move the men and the dogs out there right away.' He looked at his watch. 'I want that whole area searched tonight, inch by inch. If she's out there, then we'll find her.' He looked at DS Taylor. 'We've got to. It's not an option.'

Esme heard the dogs from several miles off. She was in the hollow of an old oak tree, shivering with fright. She had to move and she had to move fast. She emptied out the rucksack and found the keys, the knife and the rope, tucked them all into the pocket of her jacket and stood up. She darted out of the tree, glanced behind her, then up at the sky for the lights, but saw it was clear. She was safe for the moment and she could out-run the dogs. She set off. She didn't need her torch, she knew the ground here, tree by tree, it was where she had been happiest. So Esme ran. She ran towards Calcott, she ran towards death and final vengeance.

The dogs barked and strained at their leads, the officers kept up. There was a tense silence in the woods except for the dogs.

'Over here!'

Several officers with torches ran over to the tree. They found the discarded rucksack. 'She's headed up towards the house,' one of them said. 'Radio in and tell them that she's headed that way.'

He stood back a pace, anxious not to touch what might be evidence and ran his torch over the ground. It was then that he saw the little white sock.

Will ran up through the garden. He ran past the front

of the house and down along the side of it, past the kitchen windows. Anna saw him and she too ran out of the back door and onto the wet grass which soaked her bare feet.

'Esme?' he shouted, running towards the dovecote. 'Esme! Please Esme, don't do anything stupid. Esme, please . . . !'

Kicking the door of the dovecote open, Will could hear Maya's cries and Anna's voice right behind him. He saw the baby, lying on a rug, crying and flailing her legs and arms wildly in the air. He saw Anna go to her, take her and fold her into her body, weeping uncontrollably. He sank to the ground. 'Thank God for that,' he murmured. 'She's safe.' And he covered his face with his hands.

Chapter Twenty-six

It was late, 1.00 am, everyone was exhausted, but still DS Taylor couldn't let it go. 'It just doesn't make any sense!' she said for the third time. 'How can someone just disappear into thin air? One minute she was there and the next she's gone.'

'Unless of course it wasn't her,' Superintendent White replied. 'The infra-red cameras are good, but there's no way of knowing if it was a male or female down there, they might have been tracking Will Turner for all we know. He was out there looking for her.'

DS Taylor digested this information and took a sip of her coffee. 'You don't think we should have . . .'

White shook his head. 'No, I don't. Annie, I couldn't carry on an expensive, man-intensive ground search once the baby had been found. It wouldn't have been viable.' He stood up. Everyone had gone home for some rest, they were alone in the incident room and it had been a bloody long day. White was done in. They had a result, but as far as he was concerned the case was far from closed. 'Look, what if the fire had nothing to do with Esme Turner? It could have been anyone's. All we know is whoever took the baby went through the woods to the house with her – hence the sock – but there's nothing to link the abduction to the fire, that was Turner's idea. Esme Turner might be nowhere near the area for all we know. Yes we had confirmation from Broxwood that she'd been released into the community, but they said London and who knows, she might still be there. Has there been any sighting of her in the village or surrounding area at all?'

DS Taylor shook her head.

'No, exactly.' He sighed. 'I don't know, I've looked at her file and the previous crime and I'm really not sure that she's a suspect for this case. It doesn't really fit.'

DS Taylor finished her coffee and said, 'So who was it then? And what do we do now? Do we release Pritchard and Slater?' White shrugged. 'I don't see what else we can do, for the moment.'

'Surveillance?'

White thought about it for a moment. 'What would you do, Annie? Surveillance is expensive, the baby was unharmed, it was very probably a one-off crime. Should I spend the money?'

DS Taylor stood up. 'On Slater, definitely. He had motive and opportunity. We'll check his alibi with this Dr Mitchem in the morning, but it still doesn't clear him. He had enough time to take the baby and deposit her in the dovecote before taking off for London.'

'Motive?'

'Jealousy, spite, to teach his wife a lesson?'

White picked up the phone. 'OK, I'll put someone onto Slater and release both suspects. Is Turner definitely out of the frame, d'you think?'

'I'd say so. He made a hell of an effort to try and find the baby, or at least to get involved, at his own personal risk.'

'Hmmm . . .'

'You're not convinced?'

White shrugged. 'That tells me that Turner is either very stupid or very clever.'

'Or very much in love.'

White smiled. 'Perhaps.' He dialled and spoke on the phone for a few minutes. DS Taylor listened, then bristled. As soon as he hung up, she said, 'So you don't trust my judgement? Turner is under surveillance as well?'

White stood up and stretched. He reached for his coat. 'Until we catch the culprit, Annie, no one is ever out of the frame.' He looked at her. 'Remember that. The game isn't over till the ref blows the whistle.'

DS Taylor smiled. 'I never thought of you as a sporting man, sir.'

White shook his head. 'I'm not,' he replied.

Darren unlocked the passenger side of the car he'd borrowed, but didn't open the door for Debbie. He walked round to the driver's door, opened it and climbed in. He started the engine.

'Where d'you want to go?' he asked as she got in beside him.

'To Calcott please. I need to collect my things and I'll find my own way back to London in the morning.'

'Suit yourself,' Darren said. He indicated and pulled off. They drove the seven miles to Calcott from Chichester in silence.

Outside the house, Darren stopped the car and turned the engine off. He dropped his hands in his lap and turned to Debbie. 'Are you going to tell me then?' he said.

She shrugged. She had an inner strength and he could sense it, but she was wary too. She wasn't about to say anything until she had put some physical distance between them. She opened the door and climbed out, leaning in towards him, just out of reach.

'When you turned up this morning,' she said, 'I was in the garden. I was trying to think what to do. You see, the first time I was pregnant you hit me, you called me a slut, or a bitch – I can't remember what exactly – and I was so distressed that I got rid of it . . .' She swallowed hard. Does the pain, she wondered briefly, ever lessen? Darren sat and stared straight ahead; he had been expecting something like this. He moved his hands up to the steering wheel and gripped it. That was the only outward sign of his anger.

'I'm pregnant again,' Debbie said. 'I did a test this morning and I had it in my hand when you turned up. I kept looking at it, at the little blue dot in the window, and I kept thinking that I don't care, I don't care about you, or what you say or your family, or what you want. Being pregnant is all I care about, me and my baby. And this is *my* baby. I'm going to make the decisions for it and . . .' She stopped, momentarily breathless. Yes, it was an inner strength, it was a sure courage that being pregnant gave her. 'I'm going to keep it.' Her face was flushed with the effort of such defiance. 'But when I saw you I got scared, like I always am with you. You're a bully, and even though I love you I can't live with that. So I ran. I had the test in my hand and I didn't want you to see it. But you ran after me and once that happened I couldn't stop.' She dug in her handbag and took out the white plastic pregnancy test. She dropped it on the seat. 'But not any more. I'm not frightened any more, not of you, or of anything. I can't afford to be, I've got a baby to think about.' She smiled. 'So here,' she said, 'have it. Have the test.' She stood straight and took a deep breath.

'Because it's all you're getting!' And slamming the car door, she walked away, up the steps and into the house.

Max came out of the police station and stood for a few moments in the dark, swamped with relief. He had called a taxi earlier to take him to Gatwick Airport and it was waiting for him in the car park. He crossed to it, knocked on the window, identified himself and climbed in.

'The Gatwick Hilton,' he instructed. It was the only place he knew he could get a room at this hour and he was buggered if he was going back to London with Anna and his baby – no matter how supposedly safe – still in Sussex. He leant his head back against the seat for a few moments and closed his eyes as the cab pulled away. But it was *only* a few moments. There was something in his head, one stray thought, and it kept bugging him, it kept going round and round his brain. It was: What really happened? Just now, or before, way back then; what really went on?

A short while later, he opened his eyes and took his phone out of his pocket. He dialled, waited – quite some time – and the line was finally answered.

'Hello Chrissy? It's Max! Yes, I'm sorry, I know it's one am, but it's important, Chrissy, I'm in trouble and I need your help. Yes I know, but . . .' He stared out of the window. Why the hell had he thought that she would help? He must have been mad, deluded. 'What, sorry?' He let out a sigh. 'Well, for old times' sake and because I really do need some help and I can't think of anyone else to ring and . . .' He stopped. There was a moment's silence, then he said, 'Thanks Chrissy, I really appreciate this . . .' He smiled. 'All right, I won't go on. Yup, sure, I'll hold.' He continued to stare out of the window at the lack of traffic on the A27 as he waited for Chrissy to come back on the line. 'Hi, yes, thanks Chrissy. Look, can you get onto the internet for me now and find some information, press reports, anything at all about a manslaughter case last year. You might have to go through the whole year, I don't know exactly when it was, but it shouldn't be too difficult to spot, it involved a woman named Esme Turner who shook her baby to death. Yes it was gruesome I believe. No I can't, I'm in a cab on my way to Gatwick. Can you call me as soon as you have anything? Hopefully there'll be a fax at the hotel. Thanks Chrissy, it's really good of you, I don't know what I'd do without . . . Yes, OK, I'll shut the fuck up!' He smiled again. 'Thanks, I mean, sorry, yes, OK. Bye.' He ended the call.

Anna couldn't sleep. She had heard Debbie come in, heard her exchange words on the stairs with Will, but she didn't leave her bedroom. She couldn't bear to see anyone – particularly not Will. He had convinced her that it was safer here than anywhere else, that she couldn't possibly go back to London alone in the middle of the night. He had insisted, taken charge, and stupidly she had allowed him to do so. Only now she resented that fact and she was frightened. Not of anything tangible – no, that would have been easier in a way, to have something concrete she could fear. Now she was frightened of everything; she was full of dread. She kept telling herself that it wasn't too bad, that she just had to get through the night, but it hardly helped. She sat in a chair still dressed, with a single lamp on, and stared out of the window at the darkness beyond. Maya slept in the cot beside her, breathing gently, unharmed, but Anna would not close her own eyes, not even for one moment.

There was a knock on the door and she started.

'Hello Anna? Anna, it's me. Let me in, will you?' Will stood outside in the corridor with his face pressed close to the door.

Anna stayed still. Perhaps he would think she was asleep.

'Anna, are you awake? I can see the light still on and I wanted to talk to you, to explain . . .'

Anna wrapped her arms around herself. For some reason, just the sound of his voice unnerved her, maybe it was a reaction to the shock today, maybe it was just fatigue.

'Anna? Please open the door.'

Anna sighed. She stood up and glanced at Maya again before crossing to the door. She unlocked it and opened it.

Will went to step towards her but read her body language and stopped himself. 'Are you all right?' he asked.

'No.'

'Can I do anything?'

He was always there, always pushing, even just the smallest bit, pushing to get closer. Was it really help? Or was it something entirely different? Anna shook her head and stared at the ground. 'No,' she said. 'There's nothing.' She couldn't even look at his face.

'Anna, please talk to me.' He reached for her hand but she moved it away and dug it in the pocket of her jeans.

'Anna, please don't shut me out like this.'

'I'm not, I just need . . .' She stopped as her phone rang. 'It's my phone, I'd better answer it.'

'OK.' Will went to move off, but glanced over his shoulder as he did so. 'Try and get some sleep, Anna,' he said. 'You'll feel better in the morning.'

Anna nodded, then she closed the door. She moved across to the bed, picked up her mobile and sat down, pressing the connect button.

'Hello?'

In the twenty-four-hour business centre in the hotel, Max paced the floor. He felt a surge of relief when Anna answered the phone and made a conscious effort to keep his voice calm, or at least much calmer than he felt. 'Hello Anna,' he said. 'It's me, Max. Anna, look, I don't want you to panic but I've got a strong feeling that things aren't right with Will Turner.'

Anna bit her nail. 'What do you mean, aren't right? What the hell is that supposed to mean, Max?'

'I'm just not sure that Turner is telling the truth.'

Anna felt the sudden rise of anger. 'And you always have, have you, Max? What would you know about Will Turner and the truth?'

Max kept his patience. More, he wanted to say, than you'd think. But he let it go, Anna didn't need his angst on top of her own. 'Look Anna, this isn't axe-grinding, I promise. I just want to warn you, that's all, to let you know that things might not be what they seem. I'm waiting for a fax now on the trial last year and I—'

'Max, please,' Anna interrupted. 'Let it go. It's been the most terrible day and I've got enough to deal with. Please, stop all this nonsense and . . .' She was tearful. 'Just leave it alone.' There was a silence and Max was diverted by Chrissy's fax, which had started to come through.

'Hello? Anna, hello?' He looked at his phone. Anna had rung off. 'Fuck!' He glanced at the girl on the desk and murmured, 'Oh God, sorry . . .' Then he ripped his fax off the machine.

'Bugger!' he snapped. Then, 'Can you order me a taxi at this hour?'

The girl on the desk nodded. 'Of course. I'll do it now. Where to?'

Max was reading the fax with a stony expression on his face. 'Sorry?'

'Where to?'

He was dialling Anna's number again. 'Oh, sorry, to Widbry, West Sussex. It's near Arundel. As quick as you can.' The line connected, rang and he got the answer service. 'Oh Anna,' he muttered, 'turn your bloody phone on . . .'

Anna sat for a few moments after ending Max's call and looked at her phone, then she made up her mind and switched it off. She needed some space, some peace. She needed time to think. Crossing to the door, she put her ear up against it and listened. There was no sound on the other side, so silently she turned the key in the lock. She needed some distance, some time alone. She went back to the chair and sat down.

Where had Esme gone? she asked herself. If it really had been her, then where had she gone? One minute the whole area was surrounded with police and the next it was deserted. Esme had vanished, seemingly just disappeared. But what if it wasn't her? Who had suggested that it might be and what did they have to gain by that?

Anna bit her fingernail. If it wasn't Esme, then who would want to harm her and her baby? Or perhaps not harm, but just frighten? Who would want to exert their power, show their strength? Who was able to lie to Anna, who had lied to Anna, and who could she trust? Anna thought and thought, but the more she tried to sort things out in her mind, the more confused she became. She had a growing sense of unease, a vague but persistent awareness of danger, and again, for some reason, she was frightened.

DS Taylor was in bed when she got the call. She had been asleep but it wasn't an easy sleep, it was more as if her body was resting while her brain continued to work. She rolled over, opened her eyes and felt the heavy soreness in them that comes with lack of sleep. She eased herself onto her elbow and reached out for the phone.

'Hello?'

The call was from the station. DS Taylor sat up. 'What time is it?' she asked, trying to focus on her watch. It was 3.00 am. 'OK, yes, keep tracking him and I'll come straight in. Does the Super know?' DS Taylor climbed out of bed, still holding the phone in the crook of her shoulder. 'Well ring him and tell him that Slater is on his way to Widbry . . .' She began unbuttoning her pyjamas. 'And get some back-up. I don't want anyone to move until I'm there. What?' She glanced at her watch again and slipped her pyjama top off. 'I'll be about twenty minutes, half an hour at the most.' She hung up. 'Even less if I leave the slap off,' she said to herself and went into the bathroom to wash.

At about three thirty, Anna got out of the chair. She had made up her mind. Picking up her mobile, she made two calls – one to directory enquiries, the next to a local taxi firm – then switched the phone off again. She couldn't afford for it to ring and wake anyone. Next, she went across to the cot, checked that Maya was asleep, and touched her face very gently with a fingertip. 'Won't be long now, angel,' she whispered, pulling the covers up. She was going to leave, now, in the middle of the night. Silently and secretly. She was afraid – of what she didn't really know, but the fear was strong enough to incite action. She had to get away. Immediately.

Picking up one of her bags, already packed, she crossed to the bedroom door, unlocked it and carefully eased it open. She looked out, saw the rest of the doors on that floor were shut, so stepped into the corridor, locked the door behind her and made her way down the stairs. She went into the hall, left the bag by the front door and made her way past the kitchen in the darkness to the boot room for the pushchair. She found it, folded it and carried it back to the hall, feeling her way along the wall, walking slowly, for fear of knocking into something in the dark. That done, she stood and checked her watch, then unlocked the front door. She had twenty minutes to bring down one more bag, wake and dress Maya and take everything outside onto the steps of the house. It was enough time. Actually, it was a little bit too much time. She made her way back to the stairs, started walking up, and stopped dead. Somewhere in the house, probably the study, the phone rang.

Max sat forward in the taxi and prompted the driver to go faster. He held the phone and willed her to answer it. 'Come on, Anna,' he muttered. 'Please be there, please answer the phone . . .' He held his breath, the line rang on and he found himself shaking. 'Please Anna, answer the phone,' he murmured. 'Please find it and pick it up.'

Anna heard a floorboard creak above her and felt a split second of sheer panic. But it was only a split second. She was a quick thinker and made an instant decision. She hurried down off the stairs, ran across the hall to the study, opened the door, found the light switch, closed it again behind her and grabbed the phone.

'Hello?' Her voice was just above a whisper.

Max breathed a sigh of relief when he heard her voice. 'Anna, it's me, Max.' He had no time to waste. 'Look, Anna, this is important, please listen, OK?'

Anna's anxiety had escalated. 'OK,' she said.

'Tell me something, Anna. Didn't you say that Will told you he was out when his sister killed her baby?'

'Yes. He told me that he wasn't here when it happened, that he came home to find the baby already damaged . . .' She stopped and strained to listen for any noises in the house. The radiator behind her creaked and she jumped. 'Why?'

'Because he wasn't, he was there, it says so in the press reports, I've just looked them up. Look, Anna, this whole thing isn't right, it makes me very nervous, you being there with him. Anna, I want you to leave, now, I . . .' Max stopped and shook his phone. 'Anna, are you still there?' He pressed re-dial. The number logged on, but the line was engaged. 'Oh fuck!' he snapped. Then he dialled 999 and asked to be put through to Chichester CID.

Anna had replaced the receiver the moment she heard the distinctive click of another phone on the line, then she'd taken it off the hook. She stood for a few moments, the fear pulsing through her body, then unable to stop herself, she went round to the other side of Will's desk and frantically began to rifle through the drawers. She pulled out file after file, opened them, scattered the papers, scanning everything she saw. Her hands shook and her fear curdled with anger making her feel sick. She moved on to the filing cabinet, pulling open the drawers, taking out files and throwing them on the floor as she identified them as irrelevant. She was looking for something; she knew it was here. Suddenly and without doubt, she knew it was here.

Then she found it.

She held the file and looked at the label. It read: Esme's Trust Fund. She opened it, saw the last letter with its recent date and read it. It was from Myer & Myer, solicitors, informing Mr Turner of Esme Turner's request for funds from her trust. Anna closed her eyes. He knew. He knew that Esme had been released, he knew in Portugal, he knew when he brought Anna here, he knew all the time that Maya was missing. Anna felt faint. She sank to the floor and knelt there for a few minutes, breathing deeply, trying to get her head round the enormity of what she had just learnt. He knew and she had to get away from him. Now.

With trembling hands, she dropped the letter and file onto the floor and stood up. Her legs were weak and she had to hold onto the desk for support. She took a deep breath and walked to the door. She opened it, checked she was still alone, switched the lights off in the study, and holding on tight to the banister, climbed back up to her room.

Once inside, she locked herself in. Then she sat down on the bed and tried to control the terrible shaking that convulsed her body. She had to get moving, she had to wake Maya, dress her, get out of there, but fear disabled her. She sat, wrapped her arms around her body and stared at nothing, numb with shock.

Moments later, she heard a knock on the door.

'Anna? Are you all right?' It was Will. She held her breath. The door handle rattled. 'Anna?' She kept quiet, too frightened to answer. 'Anna, if you don't answer me I shall have to get a screwdriver and open the lock! I'll think something has happened to you.' But still she didn't answer. 'Anna?' She clenched her jaw and stayed motionless. 'Right, if you won't open up then I'll have to come in and get you. This is stupid, Anna! I'm going to get something to open the door.' There were footsteps, they receded and Anna stood up. Her mind spun in panic and she did the first thing that came into her head.

She opened the window, threw down one of Maya's blankets, then a pair of her shoes, picked Maya up out of the cot and ran across to the wardrobe. If he came in he would think she had climbed out.

The wardrobe was a door in the wall, a huge walk-in cupboard – like many in the house – and opening that door, she took the key out of the lock, stepped into it and locked herself and Maya in. She backed right to the very edge of it, as far away from the door as she could get, and squatting down, leant against the wall, breathless in the darkness.

Something moved.

Anna jerked forward in fright, Maya let out a small cry and she cradled her close to her breast. Moments later, when her courage returned, Anna felt behind her. There was a crack in the wall, she could feel it. She ran her fingers along its edge. It was a door – she was certain of it – but it was pitch black in the cupboard and she had no way of seeing where it went to. Maya began to stir, she made small mewing noises and Anna panicked. Turning round, she held Maya tight and edged through the door. Terrified, she closed it behind her and sat in the pitch black, her whole body throbbing with the pulse of fear.

Then she saw the beam of light and, knowing there was no way back, she moved forward towards it, half-walking, half-crawling. She could hear a noise, a rustling, animal sound, and she was so afraid that she began to cry. Her foot slipped and she let out a stifled sob.

'Who's there?'

Anna stopped. She held Maya tightly and braced herself. A torch beam shone towards her. It stopped on her face and its light was so sudden that she was momentarily blinded by it.

'It's all right,' a voice said. 'I won't hurt you or the baby.' Anna stuffed her hand in her mouth to try and stop her sobs. 'Please, don't be frightened, please . . .' The torch beam moved, off her face and slowly down along the ground. It rested on a face, opposite her, a small, pale face. 'I'm Esme,' the face said.

'I know,' Anna answered.

Esme shuffled back and put the torch on the floor between them. 'You're frightened,' she said, 'of him.'

Anna looked at her. The torchlight threw her face into relief but it didn't disguise the fact that she was beautiful.

'I've been frightened too, for years.' She looked at Anna. 'He killed my baby, shook her to death.' She kept looking at Anna, but Anna realised that she no longer saw her. 'He told them it was me and I was so hysterical that they believed him. He told them I was unbalanced, but I'm not. I'm more sane than anyone I know.' She shook her head. 'Not surprising, after a year in a mental hospital.'

Anna shrank back and Esme lifted the torch off the ground. 'Come on, you want to get out of here. This is a priest hole, there are steps, down to the cellars and from there a passage that runs underground to the woods.'

'That's where you went to,' Anna said. Her voice was frail and she had to clear her throat. 'You were there, in the woods.'

Esme shone the torch on Anna's face again. 'I didn't take your baby,' she said, 'but I saw *him* do it. He ran with it, past me in the woods, past where I was hiding, to the dovecote. He runs fast and he keeps an old Land Rover, at the edge of the estate, with the keys under the bumper. He drove half and ran half. He's very fit, he always has been. I saw him, like I saw him last time.' She moved the torch beam. 'And he knows it. Come on.' She held the torch in front of her and started to move off. Anna followed, scraping her arms on the rough stone walls.

'Steps, down. There's a rope to help you.'

Esme went down, then guided Anna down with the torch. She didn't offer to take the baby, she knew Anna would never relinquish her. At ground level the roof of the passage was higher and Anna stood up.

'Keep close,' Esme said. 'It's about a mile.'

Anna did as she was asked. She held Maya with one hand and felt the wall with the other, keeping close on the heels of Esme. It was the longest and slowest mile of her life.

At the end of the passage Esme stopped. Anna was sweating and out of breath and her arms ached with Maya's weight. Esme shone her torch up and said, 'There. There's a trap door, up to the woods. It'll bring you out near the edge of the estate. You can get to the road north from there.'

She kept the torchlight on the steps and Anna couldn't

see her face. 'What will you do?' she asked, placing her foot on the first step.

'Wait for him,' Esme said.

Anna held Maya and climbed up. She pushed the door over her head with all her force and it creaked open, then swung back. Night air rushed in and she stepped higher, emerging into the wood.

'You don't need to wait for me, Esme,' Will said. He stood over Anna, with his shotgun loaded and aimed. 'I'm already here.'

Max's taxi pulled into the gates of Calcott Manor, and Max shouted at the driver to stop. He jumped out, stood on the road and listened hard. He'd heard something, it sounded like a gun shot. He called to the driver to turn the engine off and tensed his body, straining to hear. It came again.

'Christ!' He looked to the right, certain it came from that direction, and started to run. 'Call the police,' he shouted over his shoulder. 'And get them here quick!'

Anna stood between Will and Esme and tried to pacify the screaming baby. She was terrified.

'You see how easy it is?' Will aimed the shotgun and fired again. There was a soft thud and Anna saw a dead rabbit. 'I could shoot you both just as easily, as easily as I shot your beloved doves, Esme.'

Anna put her head down to Maya and rocked her gently back and forth to try and stem the howling.

'I can extinguish life when I want to.' He lowered the gun and looked at Anna. 'I trusted you, Anna,' he said. 'I loved you, but you wanted to leave, just like Esme wanted to leave me, for him, for that thug!'

Esme stood completely still. 'Is that why you took her baby? To frighten her? To make her stay?'

'I didn't take Maya, I found her.'

'Yes you did!' Esme cried. 'I saw you. You took her and hid her in the dovecote, I saw you. Just like I saw you kill my baby, just like I saw you—'

'Yes I took her!' Will suddenly shouted. 'I took her and I gave her back. It was to keep Anna, it was so that she'd know how much I cared for her. I did it all, all of it, because I loved her, just like I loved you.'

Esme stared at him. 'You knew,' she said. 'You knew that I'd been released, didn't you? And you told him where I lived. It was because of you that he hounded me. You wanted him to, didn't you?' It wasn't a question, it was a statement of fact. Will made no reply. 'What happened to that social worker, Will? She never came back. What happened to her?'

'I got rid of her, Esme. And I wiped all record of you off their system. I read her report, you see – it was garbage! She said you were rational, reasonable, sensible. Christ, you've never been rational in your life! If you had you'd have stayed with *me*. *I* was the one who loved you. You should never have been let out. You should be locked up, out of harm's way. I had to do it. You're mad, Esme, you seem to have forgotten that.' He looked at Anna. 'I was trying to protect you, Anna, I was—'

'No you weren't!' Esme's face was creased with pain. 'You were trying to protect yourself. You're the one who's mad Will, not me. You were obsessed with me, with me and Sophia, you wouldn't let me have a normal life, never! You were jealous of me, insanely jealous. You're the one who's mad.'

'I loved you Esme and you should have loved *me*!'

Esme's voice rose. 'You didn't love me' she cried. 'How could you have loved me if you did that to me? Killed my baby? Had me locked up? How is that love?' She started to cry and Anna trembled with fear, clutching Maya, who had begun to howl even louder.

Suddenly Will turned. 'Shut that fucking baby up!' he shouted. 'Shut her up!'

Max took a flying tackle. He wasn't a fit man, nor strong, and he was two inches smaller than Will, but he had the advantage of surprise and he knocked Will to the ground from behind. Will lost hold of the gun and Esme sprang forward, lunging for it before Max had even got it in his sight. She held it up, aimed and fired at Will. Anna closed her eyes. There was a second of complete silence, then Maya let out a scream and Max felt the warm wetness of blood.

He moved.

He put out a hand and reached for Anna. He touched her leg, she opened her eyes and saw him. Weeping, she staggered towards him and fell to her knees beside him. 'Are you . . .' She touched his face, and as she did so, Max opened his arms and pulled her in to his body. All around them there was sudden blinding light, voices, engines, sirens. He cradled his wife and his child and at that moment, he was more certain than he had ever been in his life before that nothing else mattered.